D1047693

no more heroes

ALSO BY LOREN RHOADS

In the Wake of the Templars
The Dangerous Type
Kill By Numbers

NO MORE HEROES

IN THE WAKE OF THE TEMPLARS   BOOK THREE

LOREN RHOADS

NIGHT SHADE BOOKS
NEW YORK

Copyright © 2015 by Loren Rhoads

All Rights Reserved. No part of this book may be reproduced in any manner without the express written consent of the publisher, except in the case of brief excerpts in critical reviews or articles. All inquiries should be addressed to Night Shade Books, 307 West 36th Street, 11th Floor, New York, NY 10018.

Night Shade books may be purchased in bulk at special discounts for sales promotion, corporate gifts, fund-raising, or educational purposes. Special editions can also be created to specifications. For details, contact the Special Sales Department, Night Shade Books, 307 West 36th Street, 11th Floor, New York, NY 10018 or info@ skyhorsepublishing.com.

Night Shade Books™ is a trademark of Skyhorse Publishing, Inc. ®, a Delaware corporation.

Visit our website at www.nightshadebooks.com.

10 9 8 7 6 5 4 3 2 1

Library of Congress Cataloging-in-Publication Data is available on file.

Cover illustration and design by Cody Tilson

Print ISBN: 978-1-59780-830-9
Ebook ISBN 978-1-59780-849-1
Printed in the United States of America

This book is dedicated to Jeremy Lassen, my hero.

CHAPTER 1

The air on Lautan hung breathlessly still, so thick with moisture that all edges looked softened. All colors were smudged. Unhappy in the humidity, Raena Zacari wasn't paying attention where the crew of the *Veracity* led her. Among her high-spirited crewmates, there was much shoving, teasing, consultation of the handhelds, and starting off in new directions. She was too old for that nonsense. She just wanted a drink.

Much more interesting to Raena were the people roaming around the old district of Lautan's tourist city. The scattered visitors crossed the spectrum between somewhat avian to insectile to reptilian, but Raena saw far fewer furred people than she'd gotten used to. Other than Mykah Chen, the *Veracity*'s captain, and Raena herself, she didn't see another human face.

She wasn't sure if that could be blamed on the planet's climate. The ambient temperature made her feel sticky. She wondered if the city—whatever it was called—had an ocean and whether it was swimmable. That might justify dragging around in conditions like these.

"Finally." Vezali's translator used a high-pitched, girlish voice. The Dagat's tentacles had gone greener than usual, as her body turned a sunset pink. "I'm starving."

Raena looked up to see a highly stylized logo that read "New Bar" in Galactic Standard. How new could it be, she wondered, to be worth the epic hike through the humidity it had taken them to reach it?

Inside the darkened bar, the air was comfortably cool. Oversized screens, flickering with sporting events or weddings or tragedies, provided the only light.

"Xyshin?" Coni asked her. The blue-furred Haru girl wore a sleeveless sundress patterned with large orange carnivorous flowers. They clashed with her coloring.

"Sure," Raena agreed abstractedly, transfixed by the images flashing all around her. It was disorienting to see through all these windows into the galaxy at once.

"Come sit down," Haoun suggested. The big lizard led her through the tables to a corner, where she could get her back against the wall. Once she only had to deal with the screen in front of her, Raena felt better. She frowned, trying to puzzle out what was happening in the video. It seemed to be some form of wrestling match.

Mykah excused himself to chat with a waitress. She switched the channel on the screen that faced them to the news.

Vezali arrived with a large bowl full of swimming ribbons. Raena turned away as her friend reached a tentacle in to catch one. Raena was pretty sure she didn't want to watch Vezali slurp down anything while it was still wriggling.

For the most part, her shipmates turned a blind eye to each other's gastronomic quirks. Although the *Veracity* provided plenty of physical space for the five of them, they still lived more or less on top of each other. The only sure way to put up with each other's eccentricities was to ignore them.

Coni arrived with an oversized bottle of xyshin and a carafe of fizzing water on a tray full of glasses. Xyshin was one of the few types of liquor that the crew agreed on. Raena liked its syrupy sweet flavor, because the sweetness forced her to stop drinking long before she became very impaired.

Raena was entertained that the crew chose to stick together, now that they finally had space to spread apart. All five of them wedged in around the table as the music for Mellix's show came on. "Is this what we're here to see?" Raena wondered aloud.

Mykah grinned. Today he'd braided the hair on the sides of his head so that his skull looked taller and narrower. He was still clean-shaven, a look he'd experimented with and seemed prepared to stick to for the moment. That left only his hair to play with.

Raena accepted the glass of xyshin Coni handed to her and settled back.

The screen filled with low-light footage of Outrider facing them in the dusty warehouse on Verwoest. Raena had had no idea that Mellix had been close enough to record that. She'd had her hands full at the time.

The video showed the firefight with the three Outrider androids. Mykah got shot in the first exchange. He dragged himself behind some crates and put down covering fire for Raena, who launched herself at the androids with a pair of stone knives. The blades worked surprisingly well for dismantling the weird mechanicals.

"Such a badass," Haoun whispered. Raena ignored him, unsure whether he meant to mock her.

In the video, Tarik Kavanaugh, the old war buddy who'd backed her up during the fight, held the androids off enough that Raena had time to disassemble one after another.

The video ended with Raena rolling the last Outrider head up in black Viridian slave cloth. The camera's focus had been on the thing in her hands, tentacles writhing out of the stump of its neck. There could be no doubt it was Templar tech.

Once Raena had the head wrapped up tightly, it went quiescent. Then the camera pulled back to look at her.

Her image filled the screen. There she stood, spiky black hair like a corona around her face, black eyes alight with energy left over from the fight.

Raena felt sick. She'd trusted Mellix to keep her out of the story. Now she kicked herself for being so gullible. She'd known he was an investigative journalist when the *Veracity* took him in.

The documentary moved on, exploring the history of the Messiah drug and its recent reappearance. Raena couldn't concentrate to follow the story. Her thoughts were hijacked by the knowledge that she'd been revealed to the galaxy. In fact, now that she looked around the New Bar, most of its screens had been switched to the same station. Everyone watched Mellix's show.

Raena's first inclination was to run. But where could she hide that would be beyond the reach of the galactic media?

Mykah turned to her, aglow with pride. As soon as he saw her face, his good mood evaporated. "I'm sorry," he said immediately. "I wanted to cut sooner, but Mellix insisted on giving you credit for taking down the Outriders. He said it was important to humanize the fight."

Raena saw the sense of that, vaguely. She wished they'd chosen Tarik Kavanaugh to be the human face of the fight against the Messiah drug. Kavanaugh would have been honored by the attention. Instead, Raena regretted stepping up to mount the attack. She should have trusted it to Mykah and Kavanaugh, although it might have gotten them killed. She should have turned the whole thing over to the authorities. Would have, in fact, if she'd thought there was any way in hell she could have gotten them to believe her. She should have left the Messiah drug to trickle out into the galaxy, do its damage, and destroy humanity. She should have washed her hands and kept her anonymity. Now, she didn't know how or when or why, she was doomed.

"Let me out," she told Haoun.

He got up to give her room to get off the bench and around the table.

"Where are you going?" Coni asked. She stood in front of Raena and laid a warm paw on her bare arm.

"I don't know." Her body wanted desperately to run, anywhere, immediately.

"There's no one left to look for you," Coni promised. "They're all dead. You're safe now."

Raena appreciated the blue-furred girl's assurances, but adrenaline sang in her blood. "I've got to get out of here," she insisted. "I won't leave the city. I just need to get outside. Into the light."

"I'll come with you," Haoun said. "The rest of you should celebrate. Congratulations, Mykah. This is excellent work."

* * *

Coni took Mykah's hand in hers and squeezed. "I'm sorry."

He shook his head. "I knew she'd be upset. But I thought it would be better for her to see how brief the closeup was, so she would know it wasn't much to worry about. We didn't even identify her by name."

Coni rubbed her head on his shoulder, scenting him. He pulled her back down to the bench and picked up his glass of xyshin.

Coni changed the subject. "What's up with Haoun and Raena?"

"Is something up?" Vezali asked, surprised.

"He seems to be finding lots of excuses to be in her company," Mykah observed. "He used to date 'warm girls' on Kai."

Coni and Vezali stared at him. Mykah laughed. "His words, not mine."

"You think he's dating Raena?" Vezali asked.

Mykah turned to his girlfriend. "You're the expert on all things Raena. What do you think?"

"I'm not sure," Coni said slowly. "There's a distinct possibility. I just wondered if I was the only one to notice anything."

"If it's true, that's going to change the dynamic on the *Veracity*," Mykah warned.

"Hope she doesn't hurt him," Vezali remarked.

"Hope he doesn't hurt her," Mykah countered. "Haoun's kind of a playboy. Love 'em and leave 'em," he clarified, in case Vezali's translator didn't know what to make of the phrase. "Haoun doesn't want to tie himself down because he's still in love with his kids, back home."

* * *

Raena paused in the shadowy doorway to check the street outside the New Bar. Nothing looked out of place. People still strolled calmly through the humidity, chatting and shopping and carrying drinks.

She took a deep breath, stepped out, and adjusted her pace to the flow of traffic. She struggled to keep herself from resting her hand on the grip of the Stinger holstered on her thigh.

Haoun kept close by. He stood high enough that he could see over almost everyone's heads. If she'd trained him, he might have been an asset. She tried to keep herself from viewing him as a distraction now.

"Wanna talk?" he asked.

Mostly, she wanted to keep moving, but the streets were narrow and winding and the air was so opaque that keeping watch on all of it overwhelmed her. "Do you think we can find the water?" she asked.

"It's this way."

He led her there like he'd been on Lautan before. The buildings opened up to reveal a charcoal gray ocean stretching off to the horizon. Round green stones the size of her palm covered a wide, mostly empty beach. Raena took another deep breath. This was what she wanted: to be able to see things coming.

Unfortunately, the beach stones radiated the day's warmth back up at her. Haoun pointed out a small copse of frilly trees. It looked shady beneath them. When they got there, the tree bark smelled pleasantly spicy, like nutmeg. Raena put her back against a tree and tried to relax.

"So?" Haoun prompted.

"When I left the *Arbiter*," she said, "I was on the run for a little over two Earth years. During that time, I got captured eleven times. I fought off more bounty hunters than I can count. All I wanted was to be invisible, beneath notice, but the bounty was too high. Hunting me was just too tempting."

She trailed off, staring out at the steely ocean. "I know Coni's right. I know there's no one after me any more. But running . . . that's all I knew for so long. I'm safer when no one knows I exist."

"You need a distraction," Haoun pronounced. "You need something that will allow you to burn off some energy."

"What did you have in mind?"

"There's an arcade—"

The laughter that burst out of her vaporized some of the worry in her chest.

✶ ✶ ✶

Vezali retrieved a glass with one tentacle. The xyshin didn't have much flavor, but its temperature felt very pleasant in this bar. Although they'd controlled the ambient temperature and brought it down a dozen degrees, the place still felt uncomfortably warm. Vezali's plans for the afternoon included a long soak in a bath.

Vezali settled back onto the bench with Mykah and Coni to watch the rest of the newscast.

The Messiah drug story was Mellix's first work since he broke the news of the flaw in the tesseract drive a galactic month ago. That story put an end to casual space travel. Bit by bit, ships across the galaxy were being refurbished with older technologies, but many of the larger shipping companies and interstellar cruise lines—unable to afford to replace the engines on their entire fleets—had chosen to go out of business. They were angry because tesseract travel remained safe the majority of times, except on the occasions when a ship entered tesseract space and didn't come out. Unfortunately, insurance to pay the families of long-distance haulers was too exorbitant to absorb—and casual travelers no longer wanted to take the risk.

It made places like Lautan, where the *Veracity* had landed this morning, so desperate for visitors that they dropped prices on everything from accommodations to alcohol. That made the pleasure planet affordable to working class people like the *Veracity*'s crew. And they deserved a vacation after their work revealing the resurgence of the Messiah drug to the galaxy. Raena Zacari deserved time off most of all.

Vezali fished another eel out of the bowl and slurped it down. These were a treat, even if they were farmed rather than wild-caught.

On the screen, chestnut-furred Mellix mapped out the known spread of the Messiah drug. When the crew of the *Veracity* had discovered it was loose in the galaxy again, they knew they were looking for two crates, each filled with as many as fifty pouches of the drug. Forty of those pouches had already been accounted for and destroyed, but the rest had disappeared. The tracers attached to each individual pouch had gone silent.

Vezali still struggled to understand how exactly the Messiah drug worked. It was a Templar drug, but with the Templar extinct, only humans could use it. During the Human-Templar War, human addicts had destabilized some of the border governments by attacking heads of state in their dreams. For the Dagat, Vezali's people, dreams and memory were the same thing. They couldn't use the Messiah drug and believed they were immune to its attacks.

However, Raena had been the victim of a Messiah user named Gavin Sloane. One of his attacks on Raena had added a memory to Vezali's mind. That meant the Dagat was aware that time had been changed: only once, but that was enough. The experience felt like a violation. Vezali kept probing the altered memory, wondering how to make it go away.

In the newscast, Mellix left it to Mykah to sum up how to recognize a Messiah user's attack and whom to contact for help.

Vezali wouldn't have recognized Mykah, if the screen hadn't help-fully labeled him as the captain of the *Veracity*. He had tied his hair back, shaved his face clean, and dressed up for his big moment. Still, humans with their changeless coloration were difficult to tell apart.

When the broadcast ended, Coni filled everyone's glass with more xyshin so they could have a toast.

"I'm sorry Raena didn't see the whole thing," Mykah said.

"Maybe she will watch the rest of it with you later," Coni soothed, "when she's less upset."

* * *

At the end of the newscast, Ariel Shaad and Eilif Thallian sat back on the sofa as one, each lost in her own thoughts.

Ariel put her feet up on the coffee table. She had known Gavin Sloane died from abusing the Messiah drug. Raena had shown her images of his shriveled corpse, so she could grieve. At the time, Ariel had been angry, had hated Sloane for chasing something impossible when he could have had the love Ariel wanted to give him. Now, see-ing he'd released the drug back into the galaxy rather than destroying it before it could do any more damage, she hated him all over again.

She lit a spice stick and stared at the smoke, wondering what was wrong with her that she'd ever loved that man.

Eventually, Eilif said, "Raena had her scar removed."

Ariel laughed, glad to be pulled out of her thoughts. "Raena said the scar tied her to the person she used to be. Watching her dismem-ber those androids, though . . . The old Raena is clearly still in there."

"She looks more like me now," Eilif mused.

Like Eilif used to look, Ariel realized, when she'd been young. Eilif was a clone of someone who looked a lot like Raena. Somewhere in the cloning process, something had gone wrong with her. She aged faster than normal. Although she was barely twenty, her hair had already gone entirely white. Conversely, Raena's long imprisonment in a Templar tomb had frozen her appearance at around twenty. In actual age, she was closer to forty-five. She could have been Eilif's mother.

Ariel said, "I'm surprised Raena allowed her image to go out on an intragalactic broadcast. She never wanted anyone to see her before."

Eilif poured some more tea for Ariel, then filled her own cup and sipped from it before Ariel had a chance to raise hers. The behavior was a relic from Eilif's life with the Thallians, where she'd served as their chief food taster.

As far as Ariel knew, no one ever died of poison among the Thallians until Eilif drugged her husband herself. Still, Ariel wished the woman's compulsion to taste Ariel's food wouldn't keep reminding them both of what they'd escaped.

Still, if Raena could change and step out into the light where the galaxy could see her, then survival—recovery—was possible for them all.

*　*　*

It wasn't just any arcade. Trust Haoun, who'd learned to pilot the *Veracity* on flight simulators, to know Lautan had a massive entertainment palace.

Entertainment machines from around the galaxy stuffed the building. Some rudimentary machines pitted operator reflexes against weights or gravity. Others required players to climb inside or atop them. Raena had learned to play handheld games at Haoun's elbow on the *Veracity*, but she couldn't beat the precision of his fine motor skills. Here, she was attracted to games that required big physical movements, but her body was too small to make most of these games work.

She stopped in front of the jet scooter race, but didn't mount the machine. Foot pedals controlled acceleration and the handlebars held weapons controls, but she couldn't figure out how to stretch to reach both at the same time.

Haoun loomed over her, bending low so she could hear him over the racket in the arcade. "It's built for a bigger thing than you."

"Show me how it's played?" Raena asked.

"I'm not any good at it," he argued. "I can steer, but I can't shoot at the same time. You need mammal reflexes for this one."

Raena smiled at that, not offended.

"Maybe we could play it together," he offered.

She looked up at his face, but the lizard seemed as expressionless as ever.

"Give you a boost up?"

Now she knew he was teasing her. "Sure, big guy. Help me up."

Haoun's oversized hands were gentle as they fit around her waist. Raena straddled the machine and Haoun stepped up behind her. He pointed out the safety restraints and the firing mechanisms, then hunched over her so he could reach the handlebars to steer.

Raena leaned up against him. "Get comfortable," she suggested. "I'm not shy."

He laughed, knowing that was true, and fidgeted closer.

"Ready?" she asked.

"Let's begin."

He coasted them forward smoothly. They took their place at the starting gate with the other players. The jet scooter's motor made a steady thrum between Raena's knees. Haoun's chest grew warmer against her back.

Raena smiled to herself. She used to be able to disassociate what was happening to her flesh from the objective she pursued. That ability helped her to endure the fights she got into as Ariel's bodyguard, but also to survive her Imperial training and Thallian's beatings. What her body did and felt was separate from who she was and what she wanted.

The boundaries seemed to be melting. She felt extremely conscious of Haoun's long thighs outside hers. She felt his muscles bunch and twitch as he kicked the scooter faster and faster. And there was the smell of him, alien and strange and fascinating and complex. With effort, she focused on the game—but her attention kept drifting.

She'd never been this close to anyone nonhuman before. Oh, she'd fought them, tortured them occasionally aboard the *Arbiter*, but never had such prolonged physical contact. Even when she'd been transported aboard the slave ship, the Viridians had left her alone to preserve her value. Well, they left her alone, as long as she would eat.

One of the other scooters pulled ahead in the game. Haoun growled deep in his chest. Raena felt the vibration against her back. Her blood responded to it.

"Can I fire on the other players?" she shouted.

"Only if we collect the talisman." He nodded toward a green thing glowing far ahead.

"We'd better get there first," she said.

Haoun barked out a laugh and kicked the bike down one more notch. It shot forward, rocking Raena back more firmly against the big lizard.

She got the sense he enjoyed the contact as much as she did.

✳ ✳ ✳

The boy born Jimi Thallian scanned backward through the recording of the Messiah documentary so he could watch the firefight with the androids again. The aggressor, he was certain, was Raena Zacari, the woman who had rescued him. He'd seen her in person only once, briefly, when she helped him get the hopper flight-ready so he could run away from home. Even then, Jim had taken a teenage boy's pleasure in the way her catsuit strained and stretched over her small, slim body, and especially in the fluid way she moved, as if her slightest gesture was part of a dance. It didn't hurt that she was also utterly terrifying.

Watching her twist and roll, fire and dodge, and ultimately dismantle the Outrider androids with a pair of stone knives made him uncomfortably aroused.

Jim stifled that by thinking: I understand exactly what my father saw in her. The chill that followed the thought stopped his breath.

During the War, Raena Zacari had served Jim's father aboard his Imperial destroyer, a nominally diplomatic ship called the *Arbiter*. When Raena deserted from Imperial service, Jonan Thallian lost the last bulwark that kept him sane. In short order, he acquiesced to the Emperor's directive to spread the plague that wiped out the Templars. That genocide led to the destruction of the Empire.

The moment the galaxy turned against humanity, Jonan Thallian fled home like a rabid wolf. He dragged his family and the crew of the *Arbiter* down into his homeworld's ocean, where they waited out the execution of the planet above.

Five years after the War finally ended, after the surface of their homeworld was poisoned and dead, Jimi was born. The only survivor of his crop of clones, he'd grown up ostracized from his cloned brothers, both older and younger. Despite their identical appearance, not one of the others recognized their father's crimes as atrocities.

When Jim finally sought help to escape his homeworld, he betrayed his family and led Raena to them. He remembered sitting in the hopper, ready to run at last, and telling her to kill them all.

And she'd done it. He didn't know how; the news stories weren't as specific as he would have liked. There had been a fire in the castle where his family lived. The domes of the undersea city cracked. Everything he'd ever known had been washed away, exactly as he'd wished.

Raena never came forward to claim the vengeance she'd rained down on his family. Still, Jim knew she was responsible. He would have liked to thank her personally, but Raena had warned him that if he ever so much as thought about coming after her, she would kill him in his sleep.

No wonder his father had adored her.

The comm chirped at him. Even though it had no camera, the boy switched off the news and came to attention beside his bed. "Yes, sir?"

The shipyard master asked, "Jim, are you up already?"

"Yes, sir."

"There's no hurry, son, but there's another racer coming in. Could you pull its tesseract drive before lunch?"

"Glad to, sir." He'd already dressed, made his bed, and stowed his few belongings. Now he scraped his black hair back into a ponytail, then slid his feet into his brand-new work boots.

As he turned to lock up, Jim looked around his little room. True, it was not much bigger than the bed, but it was his alone. For the first time in his life, Jim had his own place, with a door he could lock. He had a job that he loved: fitting outdated drives back into ships that had foolishly upgraded to tesseract drives. He even got paid for the work, collecting a paycheck for the first time in his life.

Jim never saw the surface of his homeworld before the galaxy poisoned it. He'd never seen the surface of any planet, until Raena Zacari helped him leave home. He'd never held a job, or used money, or seen an alien, or talked to a girl his own age.

So many things that he owed to Raena Zacari. The only thing he could do to thank her was to adopt her last name as his own.

*　*　*

As they sped through the finishers' gate, Raena's face felt flushed from the wind of their passage as much as from the proximity of Haoun at her back. Disappointed that the game was over and they'd have to part, Raena blushed still more.

Haoun's clever hands unclipped her from the restraints. He squeezed her back against him in a hug. Raena laughed in pure pleasure.

"Did you enjoy that as much as I did?" his translator said against the top of her head. His voice, whispering against her hair, sounded guttural and rough, but the translator made him sound overeducated and posh.

"Oh, yes." Raena twisted to look up into his yellow eyes. "Maybe more than I should have."

He hugged her again. She wished she could read his expressions and know if he was smiling, but the slit of his mouth didn't change.

"Where should we go to celebrate?"

Raena wished he hadn't left it up to her. If she said the wrong thing, it would screw up everything. The balance on the *Veracity* would be irrevocably changed, no matter what.

Luckily, he could read her better than she could read him. He rescued her by saying, "Your bunk's too small for me."

"That's what I was thinking," Raena said. "There's no privacy on the ship, anyway. Let's splurge."

* * *

Ariel pulled her goggles into place, nodded at Kavanaugh, and stepped onto the firing range. She breathed out, long and slow, and dropped each target in turn as it popped up around her.

She wondered why Kavanaugh wasn't hitting anything, then realized she hadn't given him a chance. She eased off and let Tarik step up.

Working through the range with someone else always made her think of Raena. Raena was content to hang back, let Ariel do the bulk of the shooting. Raena liked to look long-range and see what was coming up, but she preferred to fight up close. She said she liked to hear the sound of something's breath when she killed it. Ariel had taken that as juvenile dramatics, until it proved to be true.

No matter how much they practiced, Raena had never gotten to be the sharpshooter Ariel was, but she could lay someone out with a single punch. Ariel didn't like to let people get that close. They'd worked well as a pair.

Kavanaugh fell somewhere in the middle. He'd grown up on a medical ship during the Human-Templar War, so he knew a little medicine, could shoot like veteran, and was an asset in a hand-to-hand fight. His head had been no match for Raena's fist, though.

Ariel watched Tarik advance through the range, steady and unhurried. It might take him a shot or two to knock down a target, but he didn't skip any.

They finished out the target series by taking turns.

Ariel grinned as she pulled off her goggles. "What do you think of the new Stinger?"

Tarik turned the pistol over, pulled the charge pack out of its butt, weighed it in his glove. "It's lighter. Ought to make it real popular."

"You don't like it?" she wondered.

"Made me worry the charge was draining too fast. Did you see me keep checking the levels? That might cause problems in a fight."

"You'll get used to it," she predicted.

"You don't need to give me one of these," he argued. "My old gun is good enough."

"Not gonna force one on you." Ariel knew how old soldiers were with their sidearms. "I thought I might send a handful of these to Raena. I saw you two taking out those androids on the news. Looked like she was armed with an antique."

"She is." Tarik stripped off his gauntlets and chest shield, setting them back in the cubbyholes in the range's lobby. "She and the kid use guns the Thallians left behind on the *Veracity*. All their equipment dates to before the end of the War."

Ariel clicked her tongue. "Can't have my sister running around the galaxy with twenty-year-old guns."

Tarik laughed. "You don't get them free any more."

"It's not like stealing them from my dad's shop, sure," she agreed, "but part of the deal when I sold his business was that I still get a steep discount on the new models. Besides, Raena's worth it. It's not like she'll stay out of trouble. I can't do anything else to keep her safe."

"Suppose that's true," he agreed.

Ariel pulled off her shield and put it away beside Tarik's. "You want to stay for dinner?"

"Your mom gonna try to set us up again?" he teased.

"Probably."

He grinned. "Maybe you'll listen to her, this time."

Ariel felt her smile freeze for a second, saw that Kavanaugh caught it. She waved her hand between them, blinking back tears. "I know it's stupid. I know Gavin was . . ." Her voice quavered, but she pushed herself to go on. "It was never going to work. He was such an idiot. But I'm not over him yet."

Tarik opened his arms enough to offer a hug in a way that she could ignore it.

Ariel hated herself for crying over Gavin Sloane. Seeing his body on the news haunted her. She put her head down on Tarik's shoulder and clutched him close. He rubbed her back and said, "I miss him, too."

Ariel wondered briefly—bitterly—if Raena ever cried over the man who'd killed himself for her.

* * *

Haoun led Raena up the steep hill in the center of town. Buildings sprouted from it haphazardly. There weren't actual streets between them as much as tracks of varying widths. The neighborhood drowsed quietly at this time of the late afternoon. Up here on the hill, the faintest breeze licked sweat from Raena's forehead.

"Have you got a destination in mind?" she asked.

"Not really. The cheapest places tend to be at the bottoms of hills. You deserve better than that."

"How you talk," she teased. "The places at the bottom of the hill are for people eager to get out of this humidity."

He laughed. The sound was a sharp bark that his translator didn't try to explain. "All right. I won't make you climb the entire hill. How's this place look?"

He indicated a featureless black cube. Raena couldn't figure out where its door was. "That one's scary," she told him honestly.

They rounded the cube to find a spire modeled on a Templar tower, an organic form that looked half-melted in the heat.

"Definitely not," they agreed.

Nearby rose a step pyramid, each of its levels crowned with a garden that trailed languid vines down the building's face.

"What about that one?" Raena asked.

"Let's see what kind of rooms they have." Haoun led her into the heavily air-conditioned lobby. One of its walls held a grid of lighted images: rooms with beds, rooms with tubs, rooms furnished with rocks or trees or tanks of various liquids. One room offered what looked like a nest of pillows and cushions that reminded her of Haoun's bed on the *Veracity*. "How's this?" Raena asked.

"Stellar." He pressed the image, which vanished to be replaced by the price. He pressed the chit on the chain around his neck against the screen. A little slot opened to reveal the key.

Some things were just easier to manage in you had blunt fingertips rather than claws. Raena retrieved the key and turned to look for the elevator.

* * *

On the fourth moon of Staub, a bored Varan pharma tech glanced over the manifest coded to the large crate in front of him. It contained some kind of robot pharmacist and the chemical it ran on.

The tech circled the crate, activating its pressurized locks. Normal security on robots wasn't as tight as this, but no matter. The sooner he finished, the sooner he could take his spice break.

Once the lid slid open, he saw the damned robot lay in individually wrapped pieces inside. The Varan grumbled to himself as he searched for the package knife. The damn knife was always wandering off.

Might as well take his break, he decided.

After his return, he located the head in the crate. He sliced the black wrapping away to reveal a pasty face with scraggly red hair and an oddly shaped nose. Why did it need to be humanoid, he wondered, as he set the head none too gently on the floor. Next, he uncovered a hand, part of a leg, one foot, the torso.

The android's eyes flicked open. Fat, wormlike tentacles extruded from the base of its neck, stretching toward the shoulders. The android assembled itself while the tech's back was turned.

It rose to its feet, took a step forward, and pulled the package knife from the shocked tech's hand.

CHAPTER 2

Raena and Haoun undressed in the late afternoon light that streamed through the hotel room's windows. She was startled to discover that their anatomies weren't compatible.

"It's okay," Haoun whispered. "Just show me what you like."

Raena would have been so much more comfortable acting upon him, but without guidance, she didn't have any idea where to start.

"I've never been with anyone who wasn't human before," she confessed.

"Not to worry. I like human girls. But I know you all have different favorites. Show me yours and let me honor them."

Raena crawled into the sleeping nest. She appreciated that Haoun didn't remark on her scars.

She lifted one of his hands, its extraordinarily long fingers tipped with black talons. "Touch me with your claws," she suggested.

"How hard?" he asked.

"Let's see."

* * *

Dinner with the Shaad family was often like theater, Kavanaugh had decided. You never knew how many of Ariel's adopted kids would be around, passing through on their ways to one humanitarian adventure or another. Some of them worked for the family foundation, identifying human kids who needed to be bought out of slavery or rescued from group homes or plucked from the street. Several worked in medical services. Others did fundraising or public relations. Kavanaugh couldn't keep the kids straight. He wasn't really sure how many there were altogether, but they tended to all talk at once, at a high volume. It wasn't uncommon for food to fly from one end of the table to the other, so you had to watch your head.

Madame Shaad, Ariel's mother, doted on her grandchildren. She had wanted nothing more in life than to spoil the next generation. The only thing that could have made her happier was if some of them had been blood relations. Ariel never settled down long enough to commit to carrying a child. Soon it wouldn't matter any more. Madame Shaad was growing desperate enough that even Kavanaugh seemed like son-in-law material these days.

Still, the food at the villa was excellent, the wine was plentiful, and Kavanaugh found amusement in the whole circus.

Three of the girls were arguing. Kavanaugh didn't pay attention until one of them leaned across the table toward him. She dressed like her mother in a button-down blouse without enough buttons.

"Settle a bet?" she asked. Where Ariel was honey blonde and golden, this girl was sloe-eyed and ivory pale.

"Sure," Kavanaugh said, "if I can."

"I say you are that guy from Mellix's show," she said. "Did you hunt down the Messiah drug?"

"Yeah." Kavanaugh was pleased to be recognized. He'd held off the Outrider androids, sure, but Raena had been the one who took them apart.

"So you know Raena Zacari," the girl said.

Kavanaugh laughed. "Your mom knows her, too."

"She's amazing," one of the other girls gushed. "The way she moves! And in heels, too."

"Who's that?" Madame Shaad inquired.

"Raena Zacari, Mamaw."

"Worst slave we ever had," the old woman proclaimed. "She left your mother alone and unprotected on Nyx . . ."

"Who are you talking about, Mother?" Ariel asked.

"Raena Zacari," one of the girls gushed. "You know her?"

"Yes," Ariel said. "She's one of the first girls I adopted."

Conversation fell silent down the length of the table.

"You adopted that damned slave?" her mother quavered.

"No, Mother. You're thinking of the Raena who died during the War. This is her daughter."

Kavanaugh watched Ariel lie. He knew Raena wanted to build a new life, separate from the crimes she'd committed before her imprisonment, but it surprised him that Ariel kept the fiction up at home.

Ariel avoided his eyes as she told the kids, "You know, Tarik fought alongside her."

"We were talking about the newscast from the other night," another of the girls said. "Raena was brilliant. She could move so fast, and she was so flexible and strong . . ."

One of the boys cut her off. "I want a coat like that! Do you know where she got that military coat, Mr. Kavanaugh?"

"Army surplus," Kavanaugh said. "It dates back to the War." Which was true, if not exactly how Raena had inherited it.

"Did you see that old Stinger she was using?" one of the girls asked. "I'm amazed any of that old Imperial tech still works."

"Just because Mom updates our sidearms every year doesn't mean everyone can afford it," one of the boys pointed out. The argument spun off into a new direction.

Madame Shaad came over to link her arm through Kavanaugh's. She wore a gown spangled with more gemstones than Kavanaugh's ship was worth. "When are you going to marry our Ariel?"

"Whenever she'll have me," he answered, half joking. He didn't believe Ariel would ever tie herself down. She'd settled into the villa and working on her humanitarian foundation, but that was likely to be as tame as Ariel ever allowed herself to get. She was still a gunrunner at heart.

To be honest, Kavanaugh would rather see her happy than married. Maybe, now that Sloane was dead, Ariel could finally find happiness.

* * *

When Raena woke, Haoun lay stretched out at her side, the tip of his tail curled loosely around one of her ankles. His breath whistled across the top of her hair, making it ruffle.

Haoun's scales were cool and smooth along her back, pulling the warmth from her body. She snuggled against him, breathing his complex scent. It reminded her of some kind of metal. Raena pulled up the blanket and tucked it around her.

She thought back over her life from growing up in the Humans First! collective to her Imperial service to running with Ariel and Gavin. Nothing in her past hinted that she'd end up in bed with a lizard. She was so ignorant she didn't even know what Haoun's people called themselves or where they came from or if they commonly took up with warm-blooded girls.

All the same, she felt . . . like someone else, she decided. Sated. Comfortable. At peace.

She smiled at herself. It was tempting to rush into calling this contentment affection, but she didn't really know Haoun. She didn't even know if he wanted a relationship beyond being shipmates. Maybe this was just a fetish for him, a momentary dalliance with someone new. If she tried to make it anything more, she could destroy it.

So, she decided, she'd call what she felt gratitude. For the first time in her life, someone had gone out of his way to make her happy. Even if it never happened again, it was enough to know that it could.

Haoun pulled her closer, burying his snout in the nape of her neck. "Don't leave," he muttered. "Back to sleep."

"Okay." Raena rolled over to rest her cheek against the scales of his chest, breathing him in.

✳ ✳ ✳

On Kolar, the gang of human kids walked into the meeting with a swagger. An Outrider android sat in the middle of an abandoned warehouse at a folding table. It was the only thing in the room cleared of dust.

"Thank you for meeting us," Decker said.

"Always a pleasure to help young idealists," the pusher said. "I'm assuming you saw my ad on Mellix's newscast."

"That's why we're here," Decker said. "Can the Messiah drug really do what Mellix promised?"

"Can and already has. But the government of this planet is Shtrell, not human," Outrider pointed out. "That doesn't make it impossible to take them down, but it will complicate things."

"We're not interested in attacking the government," Decker snarled. "We want to take down the Doranje Corporation."

"I am glad to help you out," Outrider promised. "Did you bring the parts I told you you'd need?"

One of the girls stepped forward to open a case of miscellaneous copper pipes, gaskets, and tubing.

"Perfect," Outrider said. "We have only to discuss payment and you can begin."

✳ ✳ ✳

When Raena opened her eyes, Haoun was watching her. "Hungry?" he asked hopefully.

Raena nodded. Generally, she ate to thrive—as Ariel's dad had drilled into her, back when she served as their slave. Food was a necessary evil. This morning she actually felt ravenous. "Have you got a destination in mind?"

"There's a commuter market," Haoun said. "We can pick up something as we walk."

Haoun stepped into his tunic as Raena slithered into her catsuit. In moments, they were out the door. Only after it closed behind her was Raena tempted to have taken a souvenir, something to symbolize how happy she'd been in the night.

"Have you been here before?" Raena asked. "On Lautan?"

"I stopped off here on my way to Kai, when I was looking for work."

"Where did you come here from?" Raena asked.

He looked at her as if weighing whether to answer.

"Didn't mean to pry," she said quickly. "I just feel like everyone knows everything about my life, but I don't know any of you very well. I've been too wrapped up in my own drama."

"Well, your drama has been pretty epic in scale," he teased. "Mine is much more quotidian."

Raena wondered what he'd really said that his translator would put it that way. "I'm ready for things to be much less epic," she said.

Before they'd walked far, they found the commuter market he'd promised. Raena followed her nose past the pastries and noodle bowls to a spit skewering blackened meat. "Sorry," she said to Haoun, "but that is the best thing I've ever smelled."

"Do you know what it is?"

"Does it matter?"

"I suppose not." He waved the stall owner over and ordered two.

"Let me pay this time," Raena said. "You got the room last night."

* * *

They ended up with two large sandwiches of chipped meat wrapped in some savory flatbread. Raena's hands looked too small to get around hers, but her eyes lit up with anticipation.

They found a tree whose shade seemed inviting. Raena began at the top of her sandwich and worked her way down, turning it every so often to keep the filling from falling out.

Haoun found everything she did entertaining. Unlike the other human girls he'd been with, Raena was the first who seemed truly unselfconscious. Everything she did—eating, drinking, cavorting with him—she did wholeheartedly.

A smile flashed across her face. "Why are you watching me?"

"Trying to figure you out."

"Got a question?"

"What are you doing with us?"

"The *Veracity*, you mean?"

Haoun nodded and took another bite of his sandwich.

"At first, I was just using you to get to Thallian," Raena admitted. "But then Mykah did such a stellar job breaking the news about him to the galaxy and I didn't have anywhere else to go . . . I was kind of just along for the ride, after that. I thought you'd put me out at Capital City and I'd be wandering again, but then Mellix needed my help . . ." Her voice trailed off. "What are you doing with us?"

"Running away." That wasn't the whole truth. "My mate asked me to leave." Mykah knew this, and by extension, Coni probably did, too. "Serese kept our home, our kids, and I went to Kai."

"Why did you come with Mykah when we left?"

"It seemed like a grand adventure, becoming a pirate. I had no idea what ugly stuff we would get involved in."

She gazed at him, waiting for him to finish that thought.

"This has been the best time of my life," he confessed. "For the first time, I feel like I'm actually doing something important. Something that will change the galaxy for the better."

Raena grinned at him.

Haoun reached out his hand. She wove her fingers between his.

"The funny thing is," she said, "I feel the same. I am so lucky to have found all of you."

She snuggled against him. The smell of her skin was electric, straight to his brain. She looked soft, fragile, but beneath her thin skin, her muscles were surprisingly strong. He'd never known anyone like her.

Things might be complicated once they all got back on the *Veracity*. Haoun hoped he hadn't broken anything that he would regret later, but for now, he was glad of her company.

"What do you want to do today?" she asked.

"I need to pick up some souvenirs for my kids," Haoun said.

"How many kids do you have?"

"Two boys and a girl."

"What are they like?"

"The boys are just boys. They like sports. We play a ball game on my homeworld that they're really good at. Jexxie, the youngest, is really smart. She will rule the world some day."

"Is it hard to be away from them?"

"It would be harder to be there."

Raena didn't argue. "What do you want to buy for them?"

"I thought I'd start on the toy street, see what they have to offer."

"I'll come with you, if you'll help me find a swimsuit afterward. I haven't been swimming since I left Kai."

"Me, either," Haoun realized.

She looked down at the remains of her sandwich. "This defeated me," she admitted.

"Never eat anything bigger than your head," Haoun advised. "It's one of the first things we teach our young."

Raena laughed. "I will keep that in mind."

Haoun heaved himself to his feet and reached a hand down to her. As they walked, he asked, "Did you ever want kids?"

Raena shook her head. "Can't have them, at least not the natural way. Thallian had me sterilized."

"What?" Haoun jerked to a halt, stunned by the casual way she said it.

Raena linked her hands around his arm. "No one knows this, unless they've run a medical scan on me. On the *Arbiter*, before I ran, Thallian had my ovaries removed. He was a clone, you know, and all his family were clones. I'm not sure if he was planning ahead to after the War, when we'd retire to his planet and clone ourselves some offspring, or if he was simply trying to control me. It doesn't matter now."

"Weren't you angry about it?"

"The galaxy was different back then." She was people-watching now, her head tracking from side to side. She didn't appear emotionally invested in something that seemed so enormous to Haoun. He tried to remember that it had happened to her a long time ago. Still, it was difficult to believe she had accepted being mutilated by the madman like that.

Raena changed the subject. "Jain Thallian was probably as close to a child as I'll ever have. And really, he was more like a brother to me than a son."

Jain was the Thallian clone who had traveled on the *Veracity*, although he had been a prisoner rather than a guest. Haoun had never spoken to the boy, but—alongside Mykah and Coni—Haoun had watched Raena telling her life story to the kid. Jain had been barely more than a child, but he'd committed at least one vicious murder before Raena caught him.

Not at all sure he wanted to know, Haoun asked, "What happened to Jain after you took him home?"

"He died." Anger made her voice tight.

"You didn't—?"

"No, I didn't kill him. His family put a noose around his neck and left him standing on a parapet. Jain hung himself."

Raena stared into the distance, seeing it again. "I thought about letting him go," she confessed, "but I couldn't figure out how he could survive. Thallian broke Jain—broke all his sons, for that matter—the way he'd broken me. But I got twenty years locked away from him in which to heal. I wasn't about to subject anyone else to that kind of a sentence. Loose in the galaxy, Jain was going to become a serial killer like his father. He wasn't old enough or smart enough to restrain himself. At the very least, if I'd let Jain go, he would have spent the rest of his life hunting me down for what I did to his family."

Haoun didn't know the details of what had happened on the Thallian homeworld, other than the Thallians died and Raena did not. When they finally turned onto the street of toy shops, he was relieved to change the subject.

* * *

Jim toed out of his boots and aligned them precisely beside the door. It had been a long day, climbing and crawling inside an expensive new spaceship, replacing its barely used tesseract drive with a secondhand, refurbished drive. Although his muscles ached, Jim was satisfied with the day's work, happily exhausted.

He switched on the screen to keep him company as he assembled a frugal dinner. When the computer spoke to him, it had a voice similar to Raena Zacari's, low and musical. It read out the messages his mother had sent today. She'd been easy to find, once he looked for her: staying with the family who had owned Raena when she'd been enslaved before the War. Eilif didn't seem to be a slave. Instead, she worked for a charity that bought human children out of slavery and found them homes. Eilif seemed content there. Jim was glad.

"News from Drusingyi," the computer said. Jim dropped the knife in his hand. Luckily, it missed his stockinged foot when it landed point-down in the floor.

"The secondary dome has been cleared of water. Emergency power is restored."

Trembling, Jim played the message again. Once more the computer said, "The secondary dome has been cleared of water. Emergency power is restored."

Nothing more.

"Show me." Jim's voice squeaked up into a higher register. He swallowed hard and repeated himself.

One of the family's surveillance cameras came online. This one looked from the barracks where the crew of the *Arbiter* had lived under the sea. The camera pointed toward the blackened hulk of the castle. Its breached dome yawned open. On the extreme edge of the field of view, an unhealthy greenish glow lit the hospital dome. Inside that dome, the family's cloning lab once stood.

Jim typed in the command to swivel the camera as far as it would go. From what he could see, the cloning lab's dome did seem to have been repaired. Shadows moved inside it, impossible to identify.

"Maybe it's nothing," he whispered. Maybe they were thrill seekers, gawkers who'd come to gloat over the relics of the Thallians. Maybe they were looters or salvagers. But if they wanted to steal his family's belongings, wouldn't they concentrate on the castle? Why would the cloning facility interest them at all? Why would they trouble to repair the dome?

Despite his attempts at logic, it felt like ice clogged his heart. What if Raena hadn't destroyed the family's elderly medical robot? Dr. Poe had cloned generations of Thallians. If he survived, if he could have found any viable DNA, he might have begun the process of bringing the Thallians back from the dead.

It was too soon for clones to have become old enough to cast the shadows Jim could see inside the dome.

Still, someone prowled around his homeworld. Whatever they wanted, it couldn't be good.

Jim finished making his sandwich. Then he sank onto his bed to choke his dinner down. What was he going to do? He had sworn that he would never, ever go back home. He was out, he was gone, and he didn't want anyone to ever connect him with the Thallians again.

If he could get a message to Raena Zacari, she would want to investigate. He kept her warning in mind, though. For the first time in his life, Jim loved his situation. He did not want to die.

Someone, he thought. He had to tell someone. Who could he warn without confiding why he monitored the mass murderer's home? How could he tell anyone without revealing himself as the lunatic's son?

*   *   *

Outfitted with smoked goggles that cast everything into artificial shades of blue, Raena felt much more comfortable. After all the years she'd spent imprisoned in darkness, her eyes were still sensitive to bright light.

She'd changed into the new swimsuit she'd purchased, then left her clothes and gun in a public locker. When she returned to the beachside table where Haoun ate little crabs by the handful, Mykah and Coni had joined him.

"Do you swim?" Raena asked Coni.

"No, but I drink by the ocean," the blue-furred girl joked. "When I get wet, I have to keep moving or I sink. Drinking is much less exhausting."

"That's often true," Raena agreed.

Vezali slid toward them. She deftly slipped her tentacles between the stools and other tourists, pulling herself along as smoothly as gliding. "I wouldn't have recognized you," she confided to Raena, "without your entourage." She lifted a tentacle to indicate the goggles.

Raena guessed that was fair enough. Of the whole Dagat people, Raena had only ever seen Vezali, who changed in color from a deep blackish green to fiery orange as emotion took her. Raena couldn't guess how Vezali's people told each other apart.

"Mykah, would you keep my translator for me?" Vezali asked.

"Coni will. I'm going in the water, too."

"You swim?" Raena asked.

"No, I wade. And look at shiny rocks. I never learned to swim."

Vezali unbuckled the braided gold belt she wore around her midriff and set it on the table amidst the glasses. Raena realized she'd never seen Vezali without it before. She'd also never heard the squid creature's natural voice. Unlike Haoun's voice, which spoke a second ahead of his translator, Vezali's translator provided the only sound Raena had ever heard her make.

Haoun nudged a glass toward Raena.

"What is it?"

"The bartender said it's a kind of cider."

"Earther cider?" she asked.

"Be adventurous," he teased.

"Careful what you wish for," she told him.

Coni and Mykah traded a glance. Raena almost choked on her first sip. Clearly, the gossip had already started. She should have known there would be no secrets amongst the *Veracity*'s crew.

* * *

Mykah let the waves play against his ankles as he gazed out at the horizon. It felt good to be on a planet again, even if the gravity of Lautan was slightly heavier than he preferred and its steamy air less pleasant than Kai's desert heat. The air smelled alive here. Birds sang in the jungle that surrounded the city. A winged lizard skimmed above the water, fishing.

He felt as if something in his chest unhitched. He'd been wrapped up in producing the Messiah newscast with Mellix for the last month, holed up in a secret studio in the Tohatchi asteroid belt. The pressures had been enormous: to get everything right, to keep Mellix hidden as they researched, to represent humanity as the victims in the Messiah puzzle.

And to heal. Mykah had been shot by the Outrider androids. Luckily, the torso shield Raena insisted he wear caught most of the bolt, or he would most surely be dead. As it was, he hadn't sealed the shield exactly right and some of the energy seeped through the seam. He'd broken his pelvis and gotten a really impressive scar.

The bone hadn't been bad to heal. Kavanaugh had gotten him immobilized and packed off to the hospital immediately after Raena put the androids out of commission. Mykah chose to keep the scar, though. It branched across his stomach and onto his chest, white against his dark skin. Its surface was still ultra-sensitive. In fact, he could feel the sun's heat on it now. Belong long, he'd need to join Coni under an umbrella.

He looked out over the steely water for Raena. Her small head with its cap of completely black hair bobbed a hundred meters out, where she was playing with Vezali and Haoun. Vezali picked Raena up with one tentacle, lifted her from the water, and Raena somersaulted back down. He couldn't hear her laughter from this distance, but he could see it.

He turned back to the horizon. Unless one of the *Veracity*'s crew won big at gambling while on Lautan, Mykah figured they could afford a week on the ground. After that, they would need to look for work.

He wasn't sure what should be next for the *Veracity*. Mellix had encouraged him to follow up Raena's interest in the Viridian slave trade, but that problem was so huge, so diffuse, that Mykah couldn't imagine where to start.

Behind him, someone called, "Hey! Aren't you the guy on the news yesterday?"

Pleased to be recognized, Mykah turned, only to find himself partly surrounded by a half-dozen or so large Walosi. The toad-mouthed people did not look like fans.

"You a friend of Mellix's?" one of them demanded.

Mykah wasn't going to lie about that. "Yes."

He saw the first punch coming and dodged, but they had formed a semicircle around him and he couldn't get back to the beach. Raena would go over the top of them, probably with some kind of crazy scissor kick, but the stones under Mykah's feet shifted uncertainly. He backed up a step into the water.

"Come on, human," one of them taunted. "Isn't your kind always up for a fight?"

Mykah didn't answer. You would think in twenty-four years of being harassed for being human he would have come up with something to say at times like these, but every clever thing he'd ever said had only made his attackers more determined. It never defused the violence.

"Mellix," another muttered. "We ought to make him tell us where the goddamned rodent is hiding. We could sell that information. I got kids to feed."

"Yeah, you said," another growled, shoving the angry dad forward. Mykah danced back even farther. The water lapped up over his hips.

The others advanced. They didn't even have to hit him, Mykah realized. They just had to back him up into deep enough water. He had no chance to swim away from them.

One of the thugs dropped with a splash. He lay unmoving on his back in the water. Another screamed and clutched his face.

Something grabbed Mykah's thigh and yanked his legs out from under him. He fell forward onto his face. Before he could panic, a number of tentacles hauled him away from the fight. One tentacle encircled his forehead and pulled his head above the water.

Vezali blinked at him. Mykah spluttered, "Thank you," but knew she couldn't understand him. Her translator was back at the table with Coni.

Raena walked out of the water with a handful of stones. One of the thugs dared to laugh at her. She whipped a stone sideways and it struck him in the throat, shutting off his laughter with a yelp.

The remaining four rushed her. Raena flung the handful of stones into the first one's face, then vaulted over him as he fell. She avoided the whole slippery footing issue by not letting her feet touch the ground. She stood on the fallen to kick the attackers, leapt over the falling to move on to the ones hanging back.

A camera drone buzzed overhead, recording the fight.

After Raena had dealt with the Walosi, she scooped up another handful of rocks. Mykah saw her taking aim at the drones. "No!" he shouted, just in time.

Raena twisted toward him, puzzled.

Vezali propelled him closer with such a smooth motion that it felt like flying through the water. "Don't take the cameras down," he panted. "So far we haven't broken any laws, but if we damage property belonging to Planetary Security . . ."

Raena dropped the rocks. She skipped toward him through the surf. "You okay?"

"Thanks to Vezali."

At the sound of her name, the Dagat rose from the water behind him, striding forward on her tentacles.

"Where's Haoun?" Mykah asked.

"I sent him to get help." Raena nodded toward the beach, where Security had corralled the one Walosi who'd gotten away. Haoun stood beside Coni. Vezali's golden translator glinted in her hand.

Raena grabbed hold of two of the fallen Walosi and started dragging them back to shore. Vezali grabbed three more. That left one for Mykah to manage.

"I can't believe you took them out barefoot and in a swimsuit," Mykah said.

"The footing had them off balance," she said. "And I was armed."

"With rocks," he pointed out.

"They didn't expect it."

As soon as Mykah's feet cleared the water, Coni clutched him in a hug so emotional it nearly knocked him over. "I was so worried," she said.

Mykah laughed and hugged her back. "I was worried, too, but I shouldn't have been."

He extricated himself from her arms and went to speak to the Planetary Security detail. The smoked face-shields of their helmets turned his way as he came nearer. "I'm Mykah Chen, captain of the *Veracity*," he said. "These are my crew. Are we in trouble?"

"We're reviewing the security video, Captain Chen. Please stand by."

The pause went on long enough that Mykah began to be concerned. He looked back at his crewmates. Coni talked to Vezali, who'd put her translator back around her midriff. Raena leaned against Haoun, who had curled up to drowse in the sun.

Mykah noticed that Raena's swimsuit looked like an opaque violet leotard. It covered her completely from the base of her throat to her muscular thighs. The worst of her scars were all hidden.

She had her arms folded around her waist, the picture of nonchalance. As she watched the Security agents, her face remained impassive behind the gargoyle shades. If you ignored the way muscles corded her arms—and you hadn't just seen her take down six guys twice her size with a handful of beach stones—she looked like someone's kid sister.

"Captain Chen, we've reviewed the security recordings. You were clearly not the aggressor. You are free to go."

"And my crew as well?"

"Yes, sir."

"Thank you."

Raena nudged Haoun as she got to her feet. He opened one eye, then heaved himself up onto all fours. "What was that all about?" he asked, when Mykah got near enough.

"The Walosi recognized me from the newscast," Mykah said. "I'm guessing that they're out of work because of the tesseract flaw. They blame Mellix. And they didn't seem to care for humans very much."

"Even humans have rights," Raena muttered, the punchline to a joke that had been circulating—and mutating—since the War.

"Exactly," Mykah said. "Thanks for coming to my rescue."

"Any time." Raena nodded back toward town. "I saw a nabe place down the beach. Anyone else hungry?"

"I'm going to sleep through dinner," Haoun warned. "There's too much excitement for me here."

CHAPTER 3

A riel heard someone crying in her office. The sound was awful, shredding a human voice almost past enduring. Unable to recognize who could be making those noises, Ariel leaned into a sprint.

The last thing she expected to see was Eilif sitting at her desk, bent double with sobbing.

Ariel knelt in front of the little woman and tried to pull her hands away from her face. Eilif shook her head and wouldn't let go.

"What's wrong?" Ariel asked gently. In many ways, Eilif remained half-feral, too traumatized to interact with the ugliness in the galaxy.

"He's alive," Eilif whispered. Terror made her voice unfamiliar.

Ariel's core temperature plummeted. She also had been tortured by Eilif's husband. No matter what she did to blot out the memory, her body would never forget.

Ariel forced the words past her numb lips: "He can't be. You saw his body burn."

More than that, Raena had *promised* her. Raena said that she and Eilif stood shoulder to shoulder and set Thallian on fire. Raena said she had pulverized his bones and scattered his ashes and burned the castle down around his ghost.

Eilif pulled one hand from her face long enough to wave vaguely at the screen beside her. Dreading what she might see, Ariel leaned around Eilif and opened the message there.

The boy on the screen was no more than thirteen. He held himself ramrod straight, like Raena or Eilif. He wore his glossy blue-black hair tied back at his nape. Black brows arched over eyes so much like his father's that Ariel felt she'd been punched in the chest. Those silver eyes marked him as a Thallian.

However, this Thallian was still a child, whatever that meant in a universe where monsters like Thallian would clone themselves sons.

Despite the boy's youth, Ariel could only see the face of her rapist when she looked at him. She set the message to play and stared at the floor.

"Mother, I'm sorry to have tracked you down like this. I didn't know where else to turn. I need you to pass an urgent message to Raena Zacari, who saved me from our family. She must have saved you as well. I'm hoping you will know how to reach her. I hacked into the cameras in the city beneath the sea. Someone has patched the hospital dome and restored power. I saw someone moving in there. It may be nothing. It may be looters. I . . . I want it to be looters. I don't want to think that Dr. Poe would try to bring him back."

Ariel glanced up. The boy's eyes shone with unshed tears. He looked just as frightened as they were.

"Raena forbade me to contact her. She said she would kill me and I believe her. But I . . . She needs to know this. As soon as you can tell her."

Ariel demanded, "Which son is that?"

"Jimi," Eilif said with certainty. "Raena told me she'd let him go."

"Do you trust him?"

"Yes." Eilif didn't dissemble or explain.

"Shift," Ariel ordered. Eilif abandoned her chair without complaint. After Ariel took it, she marked the message Extremely Urgent and forwarded it to the *Veracity*.

And that was all she could do for now. If Raena had a comm code like a normal person, she hadn't given it to Ariel. Since her escape from prison, they'd never had an emergency that necessitated anything beyond leaving a message on the Shaad family priority channel for Raena to pick up at her leisure. Now Ariel didn't dare wait around for Raena to check in. As far as Ariel knew, Raena never went far from the ship.

To calm Eilif, Ariel echoed what the boy said: "Maybe it's nothing." But like the young Thallian clone, she feared it was something awful.

Ariel hit the silent alarm that would lock down the villa. She didn't know if Jonan Thallian would come looking for Raena or to reclaim Eilif, but Ariel didn't want to give the madman an opportunity to hurt any of them ever again.

She didn't generally walk around armed in the house, but she kept a pistol tucked in her desk. She retrieved it and brought it back to Eilif.

"It's past time for you to learn how to defend yourself," Ariel told her. "Come down to the range and I'll show you how this works."

✳ ✳ ✳

Although the nabe restaurant was mostly empty at this time of the afternoon, the staff still squeezed the five of them around a low square table toward the back. Haoun stretched out along the wall, put his chin down on his arms, and went to sleep.

No one said anything about Raena keeping him up too late, for which she was grateful.

Raena ordered soup for the crew. The slender lizard waitress delivered a big iron kettle full of broth and set it on the burner in the center of the table to boil. She brought out two large platters, one heaped with vegetables, the other with shellfish and mystery slices of meat. Chankonabe used to be one of Ariel's favorite foods. Raena hadn't tasted it since before her imprisonment. Nabe restaurants used to be easier to find, she thought, but maybe that was a function of where she used to find herself.

While the crew watched her stirring the vegetables, Mykah poured sake for everyone.

"Do we need to be drinking again?" Coni asked.

He laughed. "I need to be drinking. Here's to surviving the morning."

Before they put their cups down, Mykah told Raena, "At the risk of freaking you out again, I wanted to apologize for the documentary yesterday."

She sipped her sake. "I don't blame you," she said at last. "I knew Mellix had a camera. I should have covered my face. I am an idiot for trusting a journalist to understand how much I loathe having my image broadcast across the galaxy."

"But you're a new person now," Vezali pointed out.

"This new person is still paranoid," Raena answered. "None of you know what it's like to be hunted, never sure when or where you can sleep. The Empire had agents everywhere I went. Of all the things that have happened in my life, being on the run was about the worst."

They digested that in silence, then Coni reminded, "There's no one after you now."

"No one that I know of," Raena argued.

"I'm still sorry," Mykah said. "Mellix might not have known, but I knew how you felt about it. I should have argued more strongly against including that close-up. I'm sure Mellix would apologize, too."

"I doubt it," Raena countered. "He's enough of a showman to recognize a good story when he sees one."

There was a pause in which she could see that they wanted to refute that, but couldn't.

"He owes you his life," Vezali said at last.

"And I can believe that revealing me to the galaxy was his way of thanking me. Doesn't every celebrity believe that fame is the greatest gift they can share? But whoever attacked Mellix on Capital City is still out there. If they can't find him, will they come after me?"

No one answered. Raena stirred her chopsticks around the cauldron. "I think it's ready. Hold your bowls out and I'll serve."

* * *

After they'd polished off a second kettle of soup, Coni and Vezali went to use the facilities. Haoun went to settle the check and order himself some takeout. Mykah leaned over to talk to Raena. He knew he was drunk, but this might be the only time he had the courage for this conversation.

"Can I ask you about the fight today?" He heard himself slurring and swallowed hard, trying to regain control of his tongue.

Raena nodded, her face closed off like usual.

"What should I have done? They had me surrounded before I knew they were there. I knew you would have leaped at them, but the rocks underfoot seemed slippery. I knew if they got me face down in the water—hell, if they got me on my back in the water—I was dead."

She took his hand and held it in both of her little ones. Beyond the differences in size and skin tone, hers was much more scarred. "Look, Mykah, you did exactly the right thing. You survived. You're unhurt. Don't second-guess that."

"But what if you hadn't been there?"

"Don't be afraid to make some noise and call for help."

"Will people help us? Since we're human?"

"You won't know unless you ask. If you're shouting, you're going to attract the lifeguard's attention on the beach, the bouncer's attention at the bar, Security's attention on the street. People will help because they don't want to be seen shirking their jobs. Cameras will come. That always helps, if you're anywhere civilized."

"If I'm alone?"

"If you'd had a gun, you should have kneecapped the leader. But you didn't—and often you won't. Use whatever you can reach. The beach stones. The sake bottle. Anything. All you want is to make the ringleader hesitate enough that you can run away."

"That's not very dignified."

"Fuck dignity." She snarled it so angrily that it sobered him. "It took years to get my dignity beaten out of me. Dignity will get you hurt. You do whatever you have to do to survive."

That wasn't what he wanted to hear. "I thought you'd have a no-fail attack," he said sadly.

"I do." She took another sip of sake. "Everyone underestimates me because I'm small. That means any attack I make is a surprise. That means I always start the game a move ahead. And since I don't have any dignity left and I can make anything into a weapon, I'm hard to beat." She clinked her cup against his. "As usual, Mykah, you don't want to do what I've done to get into my position."

"No lie," Mykah agreed. Still, he envied her ability to take care of herself. "Thank you for coming to my rescue today."

"My pleasure."

He sensed it really was.

Before the silence could turn awkward, Raena said, "I have a question for you."

"Anything."

The conversation didn't go in the direction he expected. "What's it like to date someone who isn't human?" she asked.

"Up until I started working on Kai, I never dated anyone who *was* human," Mykah said. "Human girls . . . well, they were hoarded for a while."

"You mean like harems?"

"Not really. So many humans died in the War that there was a big 'save the species' push. Women were valued for their ability to save us, so they got the best educations, protected jobs, plenty to eat, safe places to live, as long as they pledged to help repopulate."

"Eugenics?"

"Yeah. Eugenics."

"Cloning would have been easier."

"The galaxy would have wiped us out," he corrected. "There had been a cloning war out here before humans left Earth. The technology is still forbidden."

"That's why you didn't spread the news about the Thallians all being clones," she realized.

"Actually, we debated it. I was all for full disclosure, but Coni pointed out that the cloning revelation would just make humans look that much more depraved. We didn't need to do any more damage."

He realized that none of that really answered her question. "It's great to date anyone," Mykah said. "In my not-vast experience, love is love. Some people don't have strong affinities for one species over another. Others do. I've never cared where my girlfriends came from, only how they treated me."

"Thank you," Raena said. "I've never concerned myself with gender before, but this is my first time with someone as cold-blooded as Haoun."

He saw she meant it as a joke. Mykah wondered hazily if he should warn Raena about Haoun. Probably that ship had left the spaceport.

He didn't know a lot about Raena's romantic history, beyond Thallian and Sloane, but Haoun was so much less of a psychopath than either of them. Mykah wasn't sure how things would play out, but he doubted that Raena would feel compelled to kill Haoun at the end of their relationship. That thought actually made Mykah laugh.

Raena looked at him quizzically. "I'm cutting you off, Captain. You're not going to make it home safely if you're chuckling to yourself."

"My big, strong girlfriend will take care of me," he assured her.

"No doubt."

* * *

Raena thought the end of the meal might be uncomfortable, but Coni wanted to hustle Mykah off to sober up and Vezali had plans for a spa visit, so Raena and Haoun were left to their own devices.

By unanimous agreement, they tried out another hotel. This one had an enormous tub. Haoun drew the line at a bubble bath, but he made it up to Raena by exploring every inch of her. His overly long fingers were precise as they peeled away her clothing. He followed each article with his long, slightly sticky tongue.

For her part, Raena struggled to relax and enjoy the attention. She was familiar with taking pleasure from the pleasure others took from her. However, now that she was free, to be the recipient of so much attention without being allowed to reciprocate flustered her. She wanted to be an active participant: an equal, not a plaything.

She turned over in the tub so she could look Haoun in the face. Luckily, he wasn't like the pocket-sized lizards she grew up with, who had an eye on either side of their heads. Like a predator, Haoun had binocular vision. She traced his hexagonal scales with her fingertips.

"I love to watch you fight," Haoun told her, trailing his claws lightly down her arm.

Raena wasn't sure if he mocked her. "Why?"

"You look like you're having so much fun. Today, when you came up out of the water to face those guys, you had the scariest grin. You looked like you wanted nothing more than for them to make a move, so you'd know which one to take down first."

Raena smiled. "You could see that?"

"You look like you were born to fight."

"Not born to it, no." She snuggled against him, enjoying his claws skimming the ridges of scars across her back. "Made for it, maybe. Certainly trained for it." For a long time, fighting had been her favorite pastime.

She wondered, "When are you going to show me what your people do together?"

He gave her his barking laugh. "Aren't you tired out?"

"Not yet."

"I don't want to hurt you," he hedged.

"*Please*. You know I'm not going to let a little pain stand in my way."

He buried his snout in the base of her throat, so she couldn't see his eyes. Raena smiled to herself and ran her fingers around the scales around his tympanic membranes. He squirmed. She wondered if she'd made him uncomfortable, but he clutched her closer.

"Come on, Haoun. Be adventurous," she teased.

"You are, without a doubt, the most perverse woman I've ever met."

She took that as the praise it was meant to be. "Stellar."

* * *

Mykah climbed dutifully into the shower to wash the ocean from his skin as Coni settled in to check the news for the galaxy's reaction to the Messiah documentary.

Mykah wanted desperately not to think, but this thing today troubled him. Yesterday he'd noticed that Lautan didn't have a lot of human visitors. Until Raena found the nabe restaurant, he hadn't seen any human food. Raena was too innocent of the modern galaxy to understand what that meant, but Mykah had believed himself to be more aware. Still, he hadn't taken the lack of humans as a warning. He'd allowed himself to relax, to buy into being a tourist. It might have gotten him killed.

He turned the water a notch hotter, hoping to counteract the chill in his blood. He couldn't believe he'd allowed himself to forget. Just because he had a Haru girlfriend and his crewmates were Dagat and Na'ash and he was legal co-owner of a sweet old Imperial ship, it didn't mean he equaled anyone else in the galaxy. Like it or not, he would always be a visible representative of a species that had committed genocide.

Maybe the bullies today had only intended to frighten him, or beat him up a little, but the ocean could have easily taken matters out of their hands, if Raena hadn't been there.

She'd been sparring with him. She'd been teaching him what the *Veracity*'s stock of antique weapons could be used for. Whenever it came down to danger, though, Raena always stepped up and Mykah gratefully hung back, relieved to let her protect him.

The anger buried beneath his fear and shame bubbled to the surface. Mykah promised himself that from this moment on, he would do his share. Unless he started dating her—and not even then— Raena wouldn't always be around to protect him. Until he could defend himself, he would always be afraid.

He hadn't done anything wrong, anyway. The Templar plague spun out while he was a child. His attempts to atone for it seemed to make no difference whatsoever. Mykah was sick of apologizing.

Coni startled him by tapping on the glass wall of the shower. "Are you ever coming out of there?"

Mykah switched the water off. "Yeah," he said, instead of "Sorry."

"Good. I've been missing you." She held out a towel. When he stepped toward her, she began to rub him dry with just enough friction. Mykah felt his anger slink back to its hiding place. Parts of his life really were stellar.

Coni surprised him by asking, "What'd you and Raena talk about at the restaurant?"

"She wanted to know about dating someone who wasn't human."

"Oh? Are they dating?"

"Apparently."

While Coni hung up his towel, she wondered, "Are you jealous?"

Mykah laughed. "You're just asking me now because you think I'll be more honest when I'm drunk."

Coni inclined her head in agreement, but her mouth quirked into a smile. "That's not an answer."

Mykah pulled her into his arms, luxuriating in the softness of Coni's blue fur against his bare skin. "I am not jealous," he said with all honesty. "I hope they can make each other happy. Both of them deserve some peace."

Coni made the trill deep in her throat that meant he was doing something that she liked. Mykah smiled and kept doing it.

✳ ✳ ✳

"What's with the lockdown, Mom?" Gisela asked as Ariel and Eilif joined the breakfast table.

Ariel had been thinking over what to tell her family, how to make the situation seem serious without terrifying the kids. "You know that Eilif came from a really bad situation," she began. None of the kids knew whom Eilif had been married to, only that he was murderously crazy. "We've had some news that implies that she may be in danger again. Even here."

That was exactly the right tack to take, she realized. All her kids had come from varying levels of jeopardy. Without exception, they were grateful to be free of their pasts. They were solicitous and gentle with Eilif, seeing in her what might have happened if they hadn't been rescued as children.

"What do you need us to do?" Gisela asked.

"Stay armed. Stay alert. I know some of you will need to get back to work, so use the protocols when you leave the compound and watch your backs. Once you're out, stay out. I'll give you the all-clear as soon as I'm sure the danger has been neutralized."

Brendon asked, "Eilif, do you need anything?"

She was too shy to look up from the cup of tea she cradled in her hands.

Ariel spoke for her. "If any of you have time, it would be great if you could do some fight training or run through the range with Eilif. It will help her to feel safer if she has some skills with which to protect herself."

The kids exploded in sound, shouting over each other with offers and plans.

Ariel whistled for silence. "One at a time," she reminded. "I appreciate your willingness to help, but be respectful."

Really, though, she couldn't have been more proud. Thallian might have cloned his own bodyguards, but her private army was even more enthusiastic. And not insane. And far better armed.

* * *

Raena's eyes came open in the unfamiliar hotel room. Haoun had curled around her again, his chin resting on the top of her head. His scales had drawn the warmth from her skin. She shivered.

She didn't have any idea what time it was, but sleep had abandoned her for the night. When she flopped over to face Haoun, he didn't even grumble at her to go back to sleep.

She went to fill the tub. Maybe Haoun would wake while she rattled around and be ready to go out after she got herself cleaned up.

This time she did indulge in a bubble bath. She couldn't name the floral scent in the hotel's soap, but it made her think of Ariel's house. Being the wealthy girl's companion had given Raena a taste for expensive things, which Thallian had not allowed her to indulge on the *Arbiter*. Maybe now she could treat herself. The *Veracity* didn't have a tub, but surely Vezali could contrive one for her.

Raena lazed in the water until it grew cold. Still Haoun didn't wake. She decided that it was time to hunt down some breakfast. After she climbed back into the tiny blue dress she'd bought yesterday, she commed Vezali. When she got no response, she tried Coni.

"You're up early," the blue girl noted.

"Hungry," Raena said. "Are you?"

"Sure. Why don't I meet you at the nabe place again and we can find something near there?"

"See you soon," Raena said.

✳ ✳ ✳

Eilif waited anxiously for Jimi to answer her call. When he did, he looked bleary-eyed. Sleep had tangled his long black hair.

"Mother," he said, clearly relieved. "You got my message."

"How did you find me?" she begged to know.

"I traced Raena Zacari's connection to the Shaad Foundation. I was looking for Raena, but found you by accident."

"Then it would be easy for him to find me as well." She heard the quaver in her voice.

"Yes. You need to go back through all your correspondence and execute a global change of your name. There's a way to scramble the change so there's no record of it. That should help you disappear. I'll send you the directions."

Eilif swallowed. "Thank you." She clutched her quivering hands in her lap, below the view of the monitor. "Are you hidden?"

"Yes. I have a couple of layers of mirrors between me and the cameras on Drusingyi. I've changed my name and I'm working on getting papers, so there's no connection to the family."

She nodded sharply. "You look well."

"I have a perfect life, Mother. This has been the best thing that has ever happened to me."

She understood that he meant the destruction of his home and the slaughter of his family. "It's the best thing that ever happened to me, too."

* * *

Coni suggested skewers of unfamiliar vegetables for breakfast, so they bought some from a street vendor and proceeded to window-shop.

"Where's Mykah today?" Raena wondered.

"Back at the ship. He was such a mess last night I saw no point in wasting money on a hotel room."

Coni said it in flawlessly accented Standard, but without any sort of vocal cues that would let Raena decipher how she felt about it.

"I'm sorry," seemed the safest response.

Coni shook her head. "He used to drink a lot more, after he'd been bullied on Kai. This thing yesterday churned up all those emotions again."

Raena nodded. It didn't surprise her to learn that he'd been bullied. She had wondered if Mykah learned free-running for a reason.

She changed the subject. "I think I broke Haoun."

Coni didn't answer, so Raena felt compelled to clarify. "I exaggerate. But he may sleep for the rest of the day."

"I'm glad you two are having fun together," Coni said.

Raena smiled to herself. In point of fact, she was quite fond of Coni's deadpan delivery. Before this, she hadn't considered Standard to be a tonal language.

Coni stopped in front of a window to admire the shoes inside, which puzzled Raena. While feline Coni wore paw covers, they were so simple and unadorned that she made them herself. "Need some new boots?" Coni asked.

Raena came nearer. The window held a forest of boots in every shade and material. One black leather pair had sharp silver heels to match the buckles that climbed their sides. "I may need those boots," Raena agreed.

* * *

Mykah woke after Coni had gone out. His head felt stuffed with dampening filaments, but he forced himself to get up, drink two glasses of water straight down, and consider breakfast.

Not much food remained on the *Veracity*. Before they left Lautan, they'd need to restock. He started a shopping list as he reconstituted some eggs. If he could choke them down, the protein should settle his stomach.

Once he had the eggs scrambled and garnished with some garlic and mushrooms from his garden, he settled in the cockpit to listen to messages.

Coni left a message that she was off for breakfast with Raena. Vezali checked in to see how he was feeling. No word from Haoun, who was probably still asleep. The final message came from Ariel Shaad. She addressed it to Raena, but marked it extremely urgent.

Ms. Shaad had taken the *Veracity* in shortly after they left the Thallian homeworld. Raena had needed a doctor off the grid to look at her shoulder wound and Thallian's wife Eilif needed someone to help her acclimate to the galaxy after her long enslavement. Ariel handled everything without questions.

Now that Raena passed as her own daughter, her relationship with Ariel had grown even more complicated. Ariel seemed to just roll with it. She didn't care if she was Raena's lover or sister or guardian, as long as Raena allowed Ariel to continue to be part of her life.

Mykah would have forwarded the message directly to Raena's comm, but he was curious. And hungover. His impulse control felt extremely tenuous.

Whatever he had expected to see from Ariel Shaad, it wasn't the image of a teenaged boy. The kid looked so much like Jain Thallian, former guest of the *Veracity*, that Mykah had to struggle to see the differences. It was spooky.

He set the message to play. It made him forget all about finishing his eggs.

* * *

Raena paid for her new boots and waited for the humanoid shop girl to hand her a bag with her old boots in it. The clerk's eyes widened suddenly. Before Raena could react, a gun barrel jammed into the base of her skull.

She raised her hands slowly. Whoever stood behind her eased the Stinger from the holster on her thigh.

"Raena Zacari," an unfamiliar voice said, "I am arresting you for charges filed on . . ."

She didn't wait for him to get the rest of the speech out. She kicked back hard with her new sharp silver heel, felt it connect in the most satisfying way. At the same time, she ducked sideways, toward the pistol he was stealing from her.

The stranger's gun put a nice round hole in the artwork behind the register.

Raena turned, raising one hand to catch his gun arm before he could re-aim. She slammed her other elbow hard up into his wizened monkey face.

She snatched her own Stinger back, tossed it to Coni, and said, "Out." The blue-furred girl didn't argue. The two salesgirls minced after her.

Raena got behind the bounty hunter, kicked him in the knee, then jumped onto his back to add her weight to his head as it struck the shoe counter. That took him out. She would have pounded his head down a second time, just to be certain, but the counter didn't look very sturdy. No sense in getting arrested for vandalism.

She plucked his gun from his hand, ejected its charge pack and pocketed it. Then she snatched up her shopping bag with one hand and dragged the unconscious Saimiri bounty hunter out to the street. She dropped him beside the garbage incinerator on the curb. She banged the gun hard against the incinerator to disable it, then flung it down on his chest.

Coni handed Raena's Stinger back. "Who is that?"

"Bounty hunter," Raena said.

"But the charges were dropped on Capital City."

"They never arrested me," Raena pointed out, "only you, Mykah, and Vezali. This is something else."

Raena scanned the street. Other than the people immediately nearby reacting to the unconscious bounty hunter, nothing seemed out of the ordinary.

"What do we do?"

"I need to get back to the ship and get myself armed up. Then we need to figure out who put a bounty on me and if there's a way to settle it. I should've let him tell me what I was charged with, but his gun was too jittery against my head. I thought he'd shoot me before he spit it out."

"What can I do?" Coni asked.

"Comm everyone. Keep them off the ship. If anyone's looking for me on Lautan, they'll loiter around the *Veracity*. I want you all to be safe. Why don't you set us a meeting somewhere for a late lunch, so we can discuss whether we're getting out of here all together or if I'm finding my own way forward."

Raena stuck out her arm so suddenly that Coni jumped. A taxi pulled up in front of them.

Coni followed her into the car. "I'm coming back to the ship with you," she said. "I'd feel better if I got armed up, too."

Raena considered arguing, but Coni was mature enough to understand what she was getting into. She relented. "If I tell you to run, don't look back."

"I trust you," Coni said. Raena hoped that would keep the blue girl safe.

* * *

Haoun wasn't surprised to wake and find Raena gone. He knew she suffered from insomnia. Still, he felt disappointed to be alone. Already he had gotten used to having her warmth pressed up against him.

He crawled out of the nest of blankets and stretched. He had a little shopping left to do, some games he wanted to pick up for the *Veracity*, some snacks he wanted to stock up on. Who knew how long it might be before they made planetfall again? Wouldn't hurt to be prepared.

As he looked for breakfast, he passed a shop that seemed to sell nothing but scarves. A hundred or so fluttered in the breeze blowing off the ocean. Must be a storm coming in, he thought.

He nearly passed the shop by before a scarf caught his eye. It mimicked the green of his scales, shot through with gold thread. The way the semi-sheer fabric flashed and floated on the breeze made him halt.

It was certainly too early in their relationship to be buying Raena gifts. Still, the color seemed so perfect that Haoun couldn't resist.

As he paid the stick creature who owned the shop, a herd of Planetary Security tromped by. Both Haoun and the clerk turned to watch them go.

"Starting early today," the shopkeeper muttered.

"What's that?" Haoun wondered.

"Bullies flexing their muscles." The stick creature folded the scarf into an elaborate bird, which lay flat and weighed almost nothing in Haoun's hand. "Everyone's tense about the lack of visitors, but Planetary Security has decided to stomp around 'keeping order' by intimidating anyone who's left."

Haoun's comm bracelet chirped.

"Sorry," the creature said brightly, changing the subject. "What I mean to say is: Enjoy your visit to Lautan."

Haoun nodded, distracted. "Thanks."

CHAPTER 4

During the course of their taxi ride to the spaceport, Lautan's skies opened up. Rain beat down in sheets, punctuated by great tearing rumbles of thunder. Raena's plan had been to find a way up onto the spaceport's roof and go in over the top, avoiding anyone looking for her on the ground. Thunder put an end to that. She didn't want to be a target for lightning up on the roof. She'd have to walk in at street level like everyone else.

Actually, a good hard rain could be useful. It would drive most creatures under cover to wait it out. There might be more people standing around than usual, but fewer would be moving around out in the wet. That would limit the number of moving pieces she needed to track.

She directed the taxi to pull over at the edge of the spaceport. This would be the worst part, she suspected. Plenty of watchers loitered under awnings or overhangs, but no one seemed immediately suspicious. Raena climbed out of the car, ready for a fight. Nothing materialized.

Coni peered out of the taxi's doorway at the downpour. Raena thought she could read dismay on the blue-furred girl's face. "Go wait somewhere dry," Raena advised. "I'll bring you those supplies from the ship."

Coni shook her head and pushed herself out of the car into the rain.

Lautan's spaceport was arranged like a Mandelbrot set. The docking bays were grouped roughly by size, smaller ships ganged around larger ones. The *Veracity* was parked toward the ocean side of the port.

Raena had to take two strides for each of Coni's, but they moved along at a good clip through the rainstorm.

* * *

As they neared the correct docking slip, Raena turned to Coni. "Hang out here," she said, scarcely louder than the rain. "Let me make sure it's clear."

Coni found a place to shelter from the storm. Her fur had doubled in weight. Heavens, she hated rain.

She was too far away to hear what triggered it, but Raena spun suddenly, crouching low.

Then the loudspeaker over Coni's head boomed, "On the ground now. Face down. Arms out."

Coni stared around, panicked. She didn't know what to do. She wished Mykah was with her.

What seemed like a whole squadron of Planetary Security encircled Raena, rifles trained on her. She looked them over calmly, then knelt, set down her pink shopping bag, and stuck her arms out at shoulder height.

"Face down," the speaker repeated.

From where Coni was standing, she could see that the tarmac had flooded. Raena didn't want to lie down in that.

The woman looked so small that it was hard not to think of her as harmless. Coni wanted to race to her rescue, demand to know the charges, protect Raena—but it made more sense logically to keep from being arrested, to work to get the charges dropped from outside the jail. Coni hated herself for being a coward.

As Coni struggled to decide what to do, she saw Haoun galloping down the commonway toward the *Veracity*. The Security squadron hadn't seen him yet, but he was going to get himself shot down . . . Coni flung herself into his path. "Stop!"

Haoun crashed into her. They skidded on the wet walkway and landed in a heap. "What are you doing?" he growled, shoving her away.

Coni struggled to hold him down. "Don't get yourself killed in front of her," she commanded.

When they looked back, Raena had complied with the soldiers' orders. She lay in the puddle, spread-eagled. Security agents surrounded her with rifles at point-blank range.

Coni expected to see Raena spring up, snatch one of those rifles, and beat the security corps off with it, but she didn't. She lay meekly in the water, let them restrain her and haul her up to her ridiculous boot heels.

Coni scrambled to her feet and pulled Haoun up after her.

"What's happened?" he demanded.

"Raena and I were shopping when a bounty hunter attacked her this morning. We came back here to get some weapons . . . Didn't you get my message to stay away from the ship?"

"Yeah, but Mykah sent another message that we had to get off Lautan right away," Haoun argued.

Coni glanced at her comm bracelet to see it flashing. "What's happened?" she echoed.

"I don't know."

The Security detail marched Raena past them. She didn't turn her head or acknowledge her crewmates at all. The rain had washed her ragged black hair into her face, but with her arms bound, she couldn't wipe it away.

Coni thought: Raena shackled and sodden, surrounded by Security, may be the worst thing I've seen in my life. Then she thought over the things Raena had seen and realized how sheltered her own life had been.

Once Security left, people crept out of the nooks in which they'd hidden. Vezali retrieved Raena's shopping bag as Mykah leaped over the puddles to join Haoun and Coni.

"The *Veracity* has been impounded," Mykah panted. Coni hugged him, desperate for comfort. He kept one arm around her waist and held her close.

"Why?" Haoun demanded.

"It's related to Raena's arrest somehow," he said. "Those same agents locked the docking slip just before you came."

"You're lucky you weren't on the ship," Coni said.

"I was off paying our docking fees so we could get out of here."

"How did you know they were coming?" Vezali asked.

"I didn't. We got a message for Raena from one of the Thallian kids. Someone has apparently started up the cloning machinery on his homeworld again. The kid wanted Raena to go check it out."

Stunned silence greeted that news.

"One of the Thallians invited Raena back to his homeworld," Haoun echoed. "That's why you called us to leave?"

"Yeah, but we can't go now 'til we find out what's going on with Raena and the ship."

"Planetary Security didn't seem to be looking for us," Vezali observed. "Just Raena."

Mykah nodded at the shopping bag in Vezali's tentacle. "Did she steal something again?"

"Not with me," Coni said. "We were doing a little legitimate boot shopping when a bounty hunter jumped her."

"What happened?"

"Exactly what you'd expect when someone jumps Raena."

Mykah's smile flashed past, but he said more seriously, "We need to find out what she's been charged with."

Haoun volunteered, "I'll go to the jail."

"Not yet. If there's a bounty on her, let's find out what it's for. She won't like waiting it out, but they want her alive or the bounty hunter would have shot her instead of engaging her."

"Got a plan?" Coni asked.

"We need to commandeer a public computer so the search can't be traced to us."

"Would the business office at a big hotel do?"

"Perfect. Haoun, can you find us a hotel?"

"On it." He lumbered off.

"What do you want me to do, Captain?" Vezali sketched a salute with one tentacle.

"Get us some walking-around weapons? I didn't have a chance to get anything out of the lockers. I didn't even grab my jacket. My Stinger's still in it."

"Sure. Meet you for lunch?"

"Yeah, let's stick to that plan."

After she left, Mykah turned to Coni. "Did you get a chance to install that kill-switch on the *Veracity*'s brain?"

Rather than answer, Coni pulled the handheld's case out of her shoulder bag and handed it to Mykah. "I'm too wet to do it. Can you sign me in?"

Mykah wiped the handheld case on his T-shirt before he opened it. Once it booted up, he typed in her passwords and brought the *Veracity* online. Coni gave him a string of characters in six different languages. He dutifully typed them in. Coni checked over his shoulder to make sure they were right.

"You're sure about this?" she asked.

"Raena's journal is in there. All your recordings of her. The stories she told the Thallian boy . . . We can't let anyone get those things. They will destroy her."

Coni nodded. She had encrypted some of the early stuff, backed it up in a coded info dump off the *Veracity*. Mellix had other bits of the *Veracity*'s recordings as research about the Messiah drug. But all

Coni's work on understanding humans, her studies of Imperial history, the book she was writing: it made her sick to think so much would be lost. Still, deleting it was the right thing to do. It was her own damn fault for not backing the *Veracity*'s memory up somewhere off the ship.

"Tell it to execute," Coni said. "Then don't turn off the handheld until it's done running."

From this point forward, the *Veracity* would have new memories. They wouldn't include going to Mellix's haven in the asteroid belt. They wouldn't include the days Jain Thallian spent onboard. There wouldn't be anything that connected Raena to the Imperial assassin she used to be. It was for the best, Coni knew.

"Now you need a drink," Mykah said.

"I need to get dry," Coni said. "Stay here."

The rain had given way to a steamy overcast. Coni stepped out into the passage and gave herself a hearty shake. She would be all up in frizz after this, but at least the weight was off of her skin.

Haoun commed Mykah. "Here are the coordinates of the Avah Lodge, at the city edge of the spaceport. You have a reservation for two as Filla Saileish. I'll meet you there with a key."

"Thanks, Haoun." As an afterthought, Mykah added, "She'll be okay."

The Na'ash laughed. "I never thought I'd see her go so tamely."

"She was protecting us," Coni said.

"Which is why we're going to get her out," Mykah promised.

* * *

In the Avah's unoccupied business office, Coni attached the scrambler to her handheld before she cabled it to the hotel monitor. She had been carrying the device around in her bag for weeks, but this was the first time she'd ever found a use for it.

She searched on Raena's name and found a bounty hunters' carousel. A blurry security photo of Raena in a bright blue dress and sunglasses showed her standing outside the *Veracity*. She seemed in the process of shooting out the camera as it captured her image.

"Sloppy," Mykah said. "She must have been in a hurry."

Coni noticed the date. "That was the day we left Kai. Raena was waiting for us to come take control of the *Veracity*."

The next photo down showed Raena at the beach yesterday, dragging the Walosi out of the surf after the fight.

"That's how the bounty hunter knew she was here." Coni didn't know what to make of the price on Raena's head. It wasn't as high as she expected. Wanted alive, the poster said.

"What's she charged with?" Mykah asked.

Coni opened the poster up. "Kidnapping. Theft of an Imperial-era diplomatic transport called the *Raptor*."

Mykah rocked back in the uncomfortable business office chair. The seat was too deep for him to get his feet on the floor. He imagined how Raena felt, with her short legs, in a galaxy where everything had been made for bigger creatures.

"We forgot to pay the docking fees on Kai," he said. "I'll bet they don't really care that we stole the ship; they just care that we didn't pay up before we left."

"So her arrest is our fault," Coni said.

Mykah didn't deny it. They had been so giddy about their good fortune when Raena offered them the chance to become pirates. She'd been focused on preparing for her showdown with Thallian, which she hadn't expected to survive. The rest of them had been exploring the parameters of their new ship. Nobody thought about the open account they left behind.

"Maybe we can settle the *Raptor*'s docking fees from here without admitting it's the same ship," he said.

"I'll check."

"Do they plan to take her back to Kai?"

"At least to stand trial for the kidnapping."

"I don't know if you and I can go back to Kai, after we disrupted the jetpack race," Mykah said. "Are they likely to charge us for that, too?"

"I don't know," Coni said. "I'll find out."

* * *

When the jailers processed her into the local hoosegow, they took her Stinger and its holster without comment, but her stone knives puzzled them. That kind of low-tech weaponry was apparently a new thing on this pleasure planet. Raena had to surrender her brand-new boots, too.

After that, they ran all the standard identification tests. Raena hadn't been arrested since the Imperial days, but she had faith her new identity would hold up, since it had gotten her in and out of Capital City. Once they ran the medical scanners and found out her body was only twenty, no one would believe that she really was the Imperial assassin who shared her name.

Security in Lautan's planetary jail was adequate, if you weren't used to busting out of Imperial prisons. Raena played with the idea, but her new ID was clear so far. She decided to wait to see what she'd be charged with. Had they reconsidered her defense of Mykah on the beach yesterday? Had one of the attackers died? Or was she being charged with beating up the bounty hunter? That used to be considered self-defense.

Jail guards escorted her to a holding cell. It seemed surprisingly full. Maybe Lautan was having a crime wave as things got tough— or maybe the government had decided to raise funds by increasing arrests. As much as she'd been enjoying her vacation, Raena wondered if it had been worth getting off the ship.

While she looked over her cellmates, she entertained herself by assigning crimes to them: shoplifting, grifting, brawling. She had the big simian girl down for belligerency, if that was a crime here. Poor thing had a seriously pouty expression.

Raena walked over to the three Chameleon girls sprawled on the lone sleeping bench. "Shift," she told them nicely.

They appraised her with narrowed eyes.

Raena smiled. "Ladies, they took my boots because I sent a bounty hunter to the hospital this morning with them." Not entirely cause and effect, but both parts of the sentence were true. "I don't want to stand around barefoot. Shift."

They turned pointedly away.

Raena snatched hold of the closest girl, flung her to the floor, and held her down with one dirty bare foot across her neck.

The other two launched themselves off the bench together.

Careful not to injure the girl beneath her foot, Raena struck out hard enough that the skull of one girl cracked into the skull of the other. They collapsed to the less than sanitary floor in a tangle of limbs.

Raena let the third girl up, but the fight had gone out of her now that her sisters were down. The confrontation ended so quickly that the jailers didn't notice. Raena smiled again.

She climbed up onto the bench and folded her legs under her. When she looked up, the one she'd labeled belligerent stood over her.

"Want a seat?" Raena asked. "There's plenty of room."

The simian girl sat down. "What happened to you?"

"They made me lay in a puddle in the spaceport." Raena rubbed her hand over her head, but her hair was still too damp to stand up. "How about you?"

"They locked me up for not paying my hotel bill. I thought my boyfriend had gotten it. Instead, he got my sister and left me behind."

Raena shook her head in sympathy. "How long have you been waiting to get out?"

"Three days. The consulate was supposed to have contacted my parents to bail me out."

"Three days?" Raena echoed.

"Yeah. We may be in here for a while."

"Good thing we've got a place to sit."

✳ ✳ ✳

Haoun sat under an umbrella on the beach, gazing out at the steely waves. The temperature was more pleasant now that the storm had passed. He wished Raena was with him, then laughed. She probably wished it, too, wherever they were holding her.

He remembered the first time she came out of her cabin on the *Veracity*, six months ago. She'd worn a short, bright blue dress that revealed her thighs. The human girls he'd dated before had been curvier, softer, and certainly taller. He'd been put off by her size and configuration.

For a while, Raena seemed to avoid him, preferring to spend her time with Jain Thallian and Mykah. Once Haoun learned more about her, about how long she had been imprisoned alone, her aloofness seemed more like shyness. It wasn't that Raena disliked nonhumans; she'd had so little interaction with them that she was afraid of misreading them, of offending them. Most of all, of frightening them.

Only after he'd seen her working to befriend Coni did Haoun realize that Raena was as hungry for companionship as he was himself. While she struggled to unravel Sloane's attack on her with the Messiah drug, Haoun went out of his way to keep her company.

She made him feel protective. He'd thought at first that was because of her size. Now that he really thought about it, he realized it was because she tried so hard to protect all of them. She had been willing to die to protect Mellix, simply because he was Mykah's friend. She asked to have herself imprisoned on the *Veracity* because she worried the Messiah drug might make her a danger to the crew. And she'd gone into the meeting with Outrider in an attempt to protect the galaxy from the Messiah drug. Raena might not recognize it, but to Haoun, she seemed like a hero.

Haoun hoped she was okay now, wherever she was being held. He hoped the other prisoners wouldn't pick on her, that she wouldn't be drawn into anything she couldn't fight her way out of. She'd been imprisoned so often that she probably had strategies aplenty to survive one more day. Still, it seemed intolerable that she should ever spend another hour in captivity. The galaxy owed her some freedom.

Haoun promised to go and see her in the morning, Mykah's paranoia be damned.

* * *

Their late lunch was a fairly somber affair. Since the *Veracity*'s crew didn't know if they were in trouble, no one wanted to use their credit and identify themselves. They pooled their cash before they placed the order.

Haoun picked the restaurant. Every dish had insects of one form or another in it, whether fat juicy larvae or crunchy beetles. It wouldn't have been Mykah's preference, but he felt hungry enough now to eat anything. The grasshopper stir-fry had a nutty flavor that actually wasn't too bad.

Coni picked the bugs out of her food and set them aside. Haoun scraped them into his own dish. "What's this about the Thallians?" he asked quietly.

"You know Raena's Imperial boss was a clone," Mykah said. "The guy who captained the *Raptor* was one of his brothers—also a clone. The kid we transported was as well. So one of the son-clones has a message for Raena. He hacked into his home planet's security cameras and saw someone moving around in the cloning lab under the sea."

"First," Haoun said, "I didn't know Raena left any of the Thallians alive, other than Eilif."

"Second?" Mykah asked.

"Why are we trusting a clone of Thallian's not to lead us straight into a trap?"

"Raena would know if we could trust him," Mykah said confidently.

Vezali headed off an argument by asking, "How did the message come through?"

"Via Arial Shaad, that old friend of Raena's who helped us get her new identity legalized."

"Have you told Ariel that Raena was arrested?" Vezali asked.

"Not yet. I messaged all of you, then went off to settle with the dockmaster. When I got back, Security was locking us out. Since then, we've been more concerned about the ship." Mykah reported what they'd discovered about the *Veracity*'s docking fees.

"How did everything fall apart?" Haoun demanded. "Yesterday morning, this was just a vacation."

"Raena would say it was because she appeared in Mellix's documentary," Vezali pointed out.

"I don't see how they could be connected," Mykah argued.

"Actually," Coni said, "it's connected to the Walosis attacking Mykah yesterday. Once Raena caught the notice of Lautan's Planetary Security, that connected to Kai's warrant for her. Apparently, the fight made the planetary news last night, so every bounty hunter on Lautan knew she was here."

Mykah would have apologized for starting the trouble, but he hadn't started it. Instead, he suggested, "Why doesn't everyone come back to our hotel room for the night? We'll bail Raena out in the morning."

"Why wait?" Haoun wanted to know.

"Because the bounty hunters can't get her in jail," Mykah said. "She's safe for now."

He turned to Vezali. "Did you have any luck finding us some guns?"

"The pawnshop's sidearms weren't too pricy, but they'd marked the power packs up to an outrageous degree." Vezali opened the bag at her side with two tentacles, then reached in with three more and pulled out several guns at once. "You'll have to choose your targets carefully."

"Hopefully, we won't need weapons at all," Mykah said. "Give me the bill and we'll cover it out of the ship's fund."

"Thank you. Otherwise, this spree zeroed out my gambling winnings from last night." Vezali offered a Stinger in one tentacle to Mykah. "It's a couple of generations younger than the one you've been using, but I thought you'd be more familiar with its range and limitations than something newer."

She gave Coni a pistol large enough for the Haru girl's hands. "This should fit into your shoulder bag."

Haoun got a long-barreled Shtrell weapon. "No trigger guard," Vezali pointed out, "so your claws won't catch."

As they looked their secondhand weapons over, Vezali said, "I need to modify them so they can all run on the same kind of power pack. I'll do it tonight in the hotel room, so don't start any fights until I get things adapted."

"What did you get for yourself?" Mykah asked.

She laughed. "It's basically a zip gun. It fires darts, instead of energy. It's light enough that I can strap it to a tentacle and not feel fettered."

"What's its range?" Mykah wondered.

"Let's just say it will take down anything that the rest of you miss."

* * *

The hotel room at the Avah was so cold it practically felt refrigerated inside. Coni walked straight over to the window to let some warm air in while Haoun fiddled with the atmospheric controls.

When she turned away from the window, Coni bumped into Mykah. The room would be cramped for the four of them. Haoun stretched out along the inside wall. Vezali sat on the floor to begin altering the new weapons. Mykah sprawled on the bed and turned on the news.

A handful of human kids had been arrested on Kolar, complete with a packet of the Messiah drug. They were so new to using the drug that they hadn't aged very much at all.

"They must have been betrayed," Haoun observed.

"It's hard to believe that Planetary Security could act so quickly otherwise," Mykah agreed.

The news segment finished with a clip from Mellix's documentary to thank him for alerting the galaxy to the renewed menace of Messiah. The segment they chose to show, of course, was Raena wrapping the Outrider android's head in the Viridian cloth.

"Raena's not going to be happy about that," Vezali noted.

Coni excused herself and went down to research some more in the business office. She needed to check if Kai wanted her and Mykah for pranking the jetpack race.

Once she got everything cabled together, Coni called up the coverage of the jetpack race. Mostly it focused on the crowd favorites, racers that gamblers were likely to follow. She found a featurette about Raena soaring on her makeshift wings between the skyscrapers, turning somersaults and going into swan dives for the pure thrill of flying. Coni had been there to see it happen live, but she watched the footage again with a smile. Raena looked like the embodiment of fun.

Although Mykah and Coni also appeared in that video, none of the three of them were named. Several athletic gear companies were looking to identify Raena, in order to offer her spokesmodel contracts. That in itself was remarkable, because humans rarely featured in such visible roles in advertising. Coni and Mykah, though, were dismissed as tourists on Kai who'd gotten caught in the middle of the race without knowing better.

The commentator mentioned that prizes had gone missing from some of the buildings along the scavenger hunt, but not enough had been stolen to change the foregone conclusion of the race. He shrugged it off as a clerical error.

Fortunately, there were no warrants for any of them for their adventure that night. While Coni felt relieved, she knew Mykah would be disappointed.

Coni glanced around the business office, but she was still the only person using it. She turned the puzzle of Raena's arrest over in her mind. Kai wanted Raena for kidnapping Jain Thallian and stealing the Thallians' Imperial-era diplomatic transport: both things Raena was actually guilty of. She had captured Jain, although not to ransom him. Instead, she held him prisoner on the *Raptor* and took him home to his family. She hadn't even asked for a ransom before returning the boy. Was there an opposite of kidnapping?

In terms of stealing the *Raptor* itself, Raena had commandeered the ship, true. However, the Thallians and their soldiers had no further use for it after she fought them off. Either they were dead or imprisoned on Kai for instigating violence on the weapons-free world. Was it theft if you simply appropriated something left lying around? Apparently so, if you didn't pay the docking fees before you left with it.

Maybe, Coni thought, if she poked around a bit, she could find something that would help in Raena's defense without connecting her to the assassination of the Thallians.

As it turned out, the Kai Security records were fairly easy to open. Coni accessed the video recordings of the day they'd left Kai. It took some looking around, but she finally located video of the *Raptor* landing at Kai's spaceport.

When they came off the ship, the *Raptor*'s crew looked like soldiers, rather than tourists. All human males of approximately middle age, they wore matching black uniforms completely inappropriate for the desert heat of Kai. Their pockets sagged. Although Kai was designated a weapons-free world, Coni suspected the soldiers hadn't simply packed sandwiches.

The last two people to step off the *Raptor* were the Thallian clones. Jain she recognized. While Coni had never actually spoken to him, she'd watched Raena bonding with the boy as the *Veracity* took him home.

At first, Coni had pitied the child locked in his small cell all day. Then she confirmed what Raena already suspected: Jain was responsible for the torture and murder of at least one of the men who had rescued Raena from her tomb. Jain looked like a child, but he was not innocent by a long stretch.

The final person in the security video was the ship's captain, Revan Thallian. He had been Jonan Thallian's older brother. Coni didn't know Revan's part in the creation or dissemination of the Templar plague, but she did know Revan hid his younger brother after the Human-Templar War ended and the human tribunals began, then did his brother's bidding in the galaxy afterward.

Coni wondered how Kai could connect the *Raptor* to the *Veracity* without realizing that the Thallian murderers had roamed their capital city at will.

After the Thallians left the *Raptor*, it stood quietly for hours. Coni sped through the recording until Jain returned alone to the docking slip. He hastily parked his jet bike on the tarmac and rushed toward the *Raptor*'s hatch, fumbling his glove off as he went.

As if she'd fallen out of the sky, Raena landed atop the ship carrying a stun staff. Coni searched her memory. Raena said she'd followed the boy on a jet bike of her own. She ditched it in midair and let it crash into the next docking slip over. Coni remembered how Mykah had used the smoke as a beacon to lead him to the *Raptor*. Coni had thought her part in sneaking onto the ship had been exciting, but it paled in comparison to Raena's original commandeering of it.

In the recording, Raena lay on the upper hull of the *Raptor*, then flipped gracefully over its edge, stun staff at the ready. From the way she held the staff, it appeared that she used the business end on Jain in the *Raptor*'s hatchway. Thanks to the angle of the camera, nothing questionable was actually visible. An argument could be made that Raena merely brandished the stun staff at him, without actually striking him with it.

After a brief time, Raena walked out of the *Raptor* alone. She looked around and aimed a Stinger at the camera. The video ended.

Coni set her handheld on the desk and rubbed her eyes.

That was it? That was Kai's whole case? Raena landed atop the ship, she walked into the ship with a stun staff, and she walked off it with a pistol. There was no real evidence she had hurt—to say nothing of kidnapped—the boy. There wasn't even any evidence she'd flown away in the *Raptor*. Without footage of her intentionally crashing the jet bike, the only illegal thing she'd done in the recording was to vandalize the camera.

Coni searched for other cameras around that section of the spaceport to see if she could find anything more damning.

How desperate was Kai that they would issue a bounty on such flimsy evidence? Were they simply hoping to extort money from Raena in order to have the charges dropped?

Yawning, Coni wondered if the crew of the *Veracity* had enough money between them to get everything paid off in the morning. The stress of the day was catching up with her. She hoped the hotel bed was big enough for her and Mykah.

CHAPTER 5

Raena never imagined the crew would abandon her. Coni and Haoun had watched her get arrested. After the Messiah revelation, the ship had plenty of money. It should have been easy for them to come bail her out. When hours passed and no one came—and no charges were pressed—she began to feel anxious.

She would have thought twice about submitting so meekly in the spaceport, if she'd known she would have to sit in a holding cell for any length of time. She hoped she hadn't inspired the kids to be so paranoid that they just ran away without her. The other creatures in the cell stayed out of her way as she paced.

Eventually a squad of ten Planetary Security agents came to retrieve her. Raena looked her escort over. That strength of numbers seemed entirely unnecessary for delivering her to a hearing. It looked surprisingly like a firing squad.

"What's going on, Commander?" she asked.

"You're being extradited."

"I haven't been charged yet," she protested.

"Doesn't matter to me."

His agents took their places around the edges of the forcefield's aperture, guns drawn. Raena looked them over, picking the one to take down first, planning angles of attack. The dispirited creatures in the cell huddled together, as far from her as they could get. Once the firing started, it would be a slaughter.

She couldn't do it. These were innocents in the holding cell, pickpockets and grifters at worst. In the past, she wouldn't have cared if they died during her escape attempt. In the past, she would have been running from Thallian. Now, she realized with a shock, she didn't want their deaths on her conscience.

As soon as Raena stepped past the barrier, the smallest agent raised the manacles. "Please turn around," she said.

Raena couldn't see the person's face behind the smoked faceplate, even to judge her species, but the agent sounded like little more than a kid. With a sigh, Raena complied and clasped her hands behind her back.

She noted that the Chameleon girls had taken control of the bench again.

"I haven't seen the consul either," Raena complained as the manacles locked into place.

"There isn't any human consul on Lautan," the squad commander said.

Someone nudged her with the butt of a gun. As they marched her out of the cellblock, Raena kept her head up, face forward, but her eyes scanned relentlessly. Too many jail guards lounged around for her to try anything, even to test the slack in the restraints, which—like everything else on Lautan—had been made for a larger creature than her. Without knowing where she was headed or what charge she had to face, it was stupid to consider any escape that might get her killed.

Oh, but she wanted to run. Adrenaline flooded her blood. Raena struggled to remember that, wherever they were taking her, it was not back to Thallian.

* * *

Ariel jolted awake, her heart hammering in her chest. She listened, but her room remained entirely silent. The lockdown telltales flashed from the monitor, but none of the alarms had been tripped. Everyone was still safe.

She crawled across her oversized bed to check messages. No word from Raena, not even an acknowledgement from the *Veracity*. The message had been opened, but no one had bothered to respond.

That meant trouble.

The sweat that slicked Ariel's body turned icy. Raena would understand what Ariel was going through here. Even if she decided that Ariel was a big girl who could take care of herself, Raena would want to protect Eilif. If Raena hadn't answered, it was because she couldn't.

Ariel threw off her covers and went to shower.

Raena had to be okay. Ariel wouldn't trust anyone else to spy on the Thallian world and survive.

* * *

The Planetary Security detail hustled Raena down a hallway and straight into the back of a patrol wagon. The truck had lights inset into its ceiling behind a heavy-duty screen. Built-in benches lined its walls. Raena didn't see any sort of crash webbing, so this was a simple planetary vehicle. Hopefully, she'd get her chance to run on the other end, before they rushed her onto a ship.

The security corps didn't remove the restraints that pinned her wrists, which made it uncomfortable to sit on the bench against the truck's cab. Raena braced her bare feet against the agents' boots to keep from being bounced around.

The agents regarded her through their smoked faceplates, but didn't move their feet out of her reach. They also didn't holster their sidearms. Someone must have studied the recording of her defense of Mykah on the beach. They weren't taking any chances that she'd attempt to escape.

She remained confident in the identity that Coni built for her, but she wished she knew where they were going. She couldn't think of anything illegal she'd done recently that deserved this level of security.

Since her escape from the tomb, Raena had been to Brunzell with Sloane, where she never stepped outside after the night he'd taken her to dinner. From there, they'd gone to Kai to meet Ariel. She'd joined Mykah and Coni disrupting the jetpack race, but since those two hadn't been arrested alongside her, she doubted that was what this was about. She'd never been linked to the bombing of Mellix's apartment on Capitol City. He'd gotten her cleared of the fire on Verwoest. What could this possibly be about?

Something exploded softly in front of the truck. The whole vehicle shuddered as its engine made a weird stutter. The patrol wagon drifted to the left and continued around at a speed that felt ill advised.

The commander shouted, "Jhen, what are you doing up there?" He got no response.

As the truck toppled over, Raena scrambled to brace her bare feet against something more solid than the Security agents. A pistol barely missed striking her in the head. It lay there, just centimeters from her face, taunting her.

The soldiers hadn't been fastened down either. The writhing mass of them ended up in a pile against the lowest wall of the truck.

The vehicle slid, grinding and bouncing, over the roadway. It finally crashed to a halt. The lights went out.

Raena sat up. The restraints on her arms were loose enough that she could easily slip her legs through and get her arms around in front of her. There was plenty of groaning and cursing in the darkened truck as the agents picked themselves up. Even disoriented and injured, they remained between Raena and the still-locked door. She decided to bide her time. She curled up as small as she could, trying to look harmless.

One of the Security agents folded open the lower door. As the agents duckwalked out of the truck, someone outside shot them down in the street.

Raena hoped that the *Veracity*'s crew hadn't mounted a rescue attempt. If they were identified fighting Planetary Security, that would put an end to their ability to travel freely around the galaxy right quick.

Whoever was outside, though, was too efficient for her crew. The street filled with fallen Security agents, but Raena hadn't even glimpsed the attackers yet. She also didn't see any bolts. Whatever the attackers were using, they weren't energy weapons. Who would risk killing Security forces?

The Security agent left to guard her yelled into his comm, "No, I need backup now! The prisoner is still restrained. Don't worry about her. Everyone else is down. I need help!"

She could help. Raena waited until he'd turned the comm off and took his stance with his rifle before she went into action. She swept his legs out from under him and somersaulted backward, getting her arms in front of her body finally. As he flopped on his back, struggling to aim the rifle at her—she was too close, he would have done better to drop it—Raena sprang to her feet. She kicked him hard in the chest and snatched up his rifle.

While he was trying to gasp in a breath, Raena braced her back against the truck's wall, balanced the rifle on her hip. Whenever the attackers came through the door, she was ready.

They didn't make her wait long.

As they flung the topmost door back upward, the streetlights finally revealed them. They wore the same featureless gray uniforms as the soldiers who had attacked Mellix's apartment on Capital City.

Raena was small and it was dark inside the truck, but she had no sort of cover. Her only hope was to shoot enough of the gray attackers to block the doorway with their bodies.

She didn't bother shooting to stun. Whoever these guys were, they hadn't come to her rescue.

"Drop!" someone ordered. Raena flung herself down on her face. Only then did she realize that the voice had spoken Imperial Standard.

The grays split in half. Some pivoted to deal with the threat outside. The others started toward Raena.

She recognized an EMP grenade as it spun into the truck. Someone outside was trying to disable the grays' combat helmets.

The grenade had been pitched to strike the upper wall. Everyone standing caught the blast wave in the head. They collapsed like unstrung marionettes.

That was unexpected. The EMP should have just messed up their displays. The gray soldiers didn't even seem to be breathing.

"Come on out, Raena," the voice outside called.

"I'm afraid to," she answered. She looked down at her stolen rifle, but the EMP had disabled it, too. She dropped it and crept forward to grab one of the gray soldiers' sidearms. It was a surprising weapon, sinuous and bulbous. She'd never seen anything like it, couldn't imagine what it was supposed to do. It didn't even seem to have a trigger.

"You want us to come in and get you?" His voice held a hint of threat.

"No, I'm coming," Raena promised. "Tell me you want me alive."

The person outside laughed. "If we wanted you dead, that truck would be full of corpses right now. The bounty's only good if you're alive."

Ah. Bounty hunters. That was familiar territory. Raena put the unusual weapon gently back on the bottom wall of the truck. She stepped over the fallen bodies, alert for one of them to grab her. No one moved.

The bounty hunters stood outside in the street, no doubt in full view of any security cameras. One was a grizzled human man with long, wild hair. The second male was something large and humanoid with mechanical arms. The last was a twitchy white-furred creature with a black face. All of them trained weapons on her.

"You all right?" the man asked.

"Not shot," Raena said.

"That's good. Let's get out of here before these gray ghosts get reinforced. Those boys are nothing but trouble."

Raena kept coming toward the bounty hunters, trying to work out the angles. The three of them were staggered, far enough apart that there was no taking out two of them before the third brought her down. If she'd had time to get out of the manacles or if she'd had a working rifle or if she had boots or if the nighttime air wasn't like breathing through a wet blanket . . .

The man slung his rifle and came to loop a cable through her restraints. "We'll get those off you once we're underway. All right?"

Raena nodded. The other two took positions to flank her.

"Just a hop, a skip, and a jump," he promised.

Since he seemed in a chatty mood, Raena asked, "Who put the bounty on me?"

"Kai's Business Council. I love these mercantile gigs."

Raena couldn't puzzle that out. What could Kai be charging her with? Her end of the fight against the Thallians had clearly been self-defense. Kai couldn't be charging her with that, could they?

The bounty hunters' car waited in the next street over. Raena climbed in docilely, to be sandwiched knee to knee with the man and his giant friend. The monkey creature drove. The car took them through town and right up onto their ship. She never had another chance to run.

* * *

Kavanaugh found Eilif sitting by herself in the farthest corner of the garden. She jumped guiltily when he stopped in front of her.

"How are you?" he asked gently.

She bit her lip as she glanced up at him, then immediately dropped her gaze. "It's all too much," she whispered. "I know they want to help, but there are so many of them. And they're loud. And . . ." She started to cry.

"And it's scary to defend yourself," Kavanaugh guessed. "He hurt you every time you protested."

She shivered like a frightened mouse.

Kavanaugh went down on one knee to make himself smaller. "I've seen Raena's scars," he said. "I don't know if you knew that we were friends when she was running from him. I saw what he'd done to her when she was young."

"He trained her to fight," Eilif said, "so he could beat her when she fought him. He trained our sons to fight, then he broke their bodies. He . . ." She faltered, unable to name the things that Thallian did to her.

"It's all right," Kavanaugh promised. "Ariel didn't ask if you wanted to learn to fight, but you don't need to. There are other ways to escape." He didn't list them, because surely she understood. "Just know," he said, "that all of the Shaads, Ariel included, will put themselves between danger and you."

"How is she so brave?" Eilif asked hopelessly.

Kavanaugh had his own theories on that, but he said, "Some people fight for the love of it. Some because they have to. Ariel has come a long way, but she's still an arms dealer at heart. She still wants to die with a gun in her hand. Raena is a warrior. She wants to die on her feet, fighting a worthy enemy." He put his hand on the small, broken woman's. "How do you want to die, Eilif?"

She stared at Kavanaugh, but her tears had stopped. He could practically see the thoughts spinning through her head.

"I don't want to be afraid," she said at last.

"What would give you courage?"

"Knowing that he can't hurt me any more."

"He's dead," Kavanaugh reminded. "You watched him burn."

"Yes."

That wasn't enough, he saw. He tried another argument. "All the clones were different, weren't they? Some were cruel and some were cunning and some were . . ."

"Clever," she said. "Gentle. Wise."

"Even though they were genetically similar, none of them grew up to be exactly like your husband. Even if the robot is cloning more Thallians somehow, none of them will be him."

She nodded, thinking hard. "Even with Jonan to train them, none of the boys was as vicious as he was."

"How long did it take, from beginning the cloning process until they were born? How long until they were grown? Until they would be dangerous?"

"It would take years," she said.

He could see that he had given her some comfort finally.

She surprised him by asking, "How do you want to die, Mr. Kavanaugh?"

"In my bed, in my sleep, after a long and satisfying life."

She smiled at him. For a moment, he saw Raena echoed in her face. His blood chilled. Then her green eyes caught the sunlight behind him and the illusion dissolved.

Kavanaugh smiled back at her. He wasn't sure how old Eilif was, except that she had been born after the War ended. She could not be more than twenty, but worry lined her face and her hair had gone entirely white. Ariel believed that Eilif had been artificially matured, so she could serve as Thallian's wife and the mother of his children. Worst of all, Eilif didn't even know she was a clone. But even if her growth had been accelerated, they were not in imminent danger of a Thallian attack. It would still take time to get new Thallians up to speed.

* * *

The cabin the bounty hunters put Raena in was only slightly more spartan than her own cabin on the *Veracity*. Smaller, and likely the comm was disabled, but she wouldn't be uncomfortable there.

The guy with the mechanical arms came in, followed by the grizzled human. He asked, "You want the restraints off?"

"Yes, please."

"Here's how we're gonna do it: Chale is gonna hold you still for me while I do the cutting. You're gonna relax and pretend you're at the spa. Anything happens to me or Chale or you make a grab for the cutting torch, Skip is going to gas the lot of us and you'll wake up in the crash web. Got it?"

"I don't want trouble," Raena said. "You don't have wandering hands, do you?"

"Chale is the jealous type," he promised. "So don't get all wily on me."

"Stellar."

They settled on the bunk. Chale wrapped one mechanical arm across Raena's shoulders and pulled her back against his chest. She didn't give him any reason to tighten his hold.

The man sparked the torch and began to cut the left restraint.

"Why'd you speak Imperial Standard to me?" she asked.

"Because I knew your mother." He didn't look up from his cutting.

"Did you serve together?"

He laughed. "No, I was a hunter during the War. Ran with a crew that chased her. Money was too good to resist. I'm the only one who survived it."

Raena didn't remember him at all. Into the silence, she had to say something. "What was she like?"

"Your mother was crazy," he said decisively. "We thought she had a death wish, that she would be easy pickings. It wasn't a death wish so much as she didn't care what happened to her, as long as she didn't go back to him."

"Thallian?"

"Yeah. Between the two of them, my crew never stood a chance."

"I'm sorry," Raena said. "I've heard those were bad times."

He glanced up at her, then went back to work. "It's amazing how much you look like her."

"I've been told that." Raena wondered if he would know who Ariel was, if he'd care that she might be able to match any bounty offered by Kai. She didn't suppose you lasted twenty-five years as a bounty hunter if you sold your captives to the highest bidder.

"How long am I going to be your guest?" she asked.

"That depends. You hear about the problems with the tesseract drives?"

"Yeah."

"We haven't been able to afford to replace ours yet. Still paying off its installation, in fact. So as long as we don't have any statistical hiccups, this'll be a fast trip."

Otherwise, Raena understood, they were going to vanish into tesseract space and never been seen again. She shivered.

Chale chuckled behind her. "C'mon, Bihn. No need to frighten her. She's being a model prisoner, so far."

Raena changed the subject. "Thank you for getting me away from those guys in gray."

"You run into them before?"

"Yeah. They seem like soldiers, not hunters. Pretty risky, taking down the Lautan Planetary Security like that."

"Yeah. PS was supposed to deliver you to us at the spaceport, but once we saw the ghosts creeping around, we thought we'd better come make sure we got you onboard safely."

"Why do you call them ghosts?"

"No insignia," he said. "Never see them without their helmets. Never see them, actually, unless they're on a mission. Then it's best to make sure they don't see you."

"Have you been seeing them a lot?"

"More and more. Where'd you see them?"

"Capital City."

"I didn't hear about that one. The news is keeping their existence really quiet."

"Are they government?"

"Don't think so. Private militia, which limits who they could belong to. Who'd you piss off?"

"Other than businesses on Kai? I've got no idea."

He finally got the second restraint cuff off her arm and switched the cutting torch off. "Thank you for being sensible about all of this."

Sensible, Raena wondered, or overly cautious? In the past, she would've made her move hours ago. Now she kept finding reasons not to risk her life. Was that a change for the better, if it garnered her thanks from bounty hunters?

* * *

Haoun got down to the jailhouse early in the morning, to try to beat the heat of the day. Unfortunately, everyone else had the same brilliant idea. The thick air had already heated up when the line advanced enough that he could get into the building.

After he cleared the security checkpoint, he lined up again with the other visitors. An officious little Pityuka came by with a handheld, asking each visitor the name of the prisoner they wanted to see.

"Raena Zacari is no longer in custody," she told Haoun.

"When was she released?"

"She was remanded to transporters for extradition to Kai during the night."

"What?" He hadn't meant the question to come out so loud. The poor little Pityuka quivered, ruffling her yellow feathers.

"I'm sorry," Haoun said, although he wasn't, really. "She just got arrested yesterday."

"Yes, well, Kai seems eager to have her back." The Pityuka consulted her handheld again. "Looks like her effects were unclaimed. You can retrieve those from Property."

So he wandered off in search of that office. He would have liked to comm Mykah and arrange transportation to Kai, but the jailhouse was dampened so that his comm wouldn't connect.

It took Haoun a while to locate the Property office. Of course, once he found it, he didn't have any ID to connect himself to Raena. Haoun sighed. Mykah would have to come back with the crew manifest.

* * *

Mykah checked his handheld against the number on the docking slip. The *Veracity* really was gone.

Anger overrode his paranoia. He marched down to the dockmaster's office.

"Where's my ship?" he demanded.

"According to Planetary Security, it wasn't yours," the clerk said, after consulting the computer. "They said it was the *Raptor*, stolen on Kai six months ago. It's in the process of being towed back to Kai, where it will be auctioned off to pay back fees. If you hurry, you can probably get there in time to buy it back."

Mykah noticed the dock's security team moving into place behind him. Raena was nowhere around to get him out of this fight. Besides, even she wouldn't take on Planetary Security face to face. He sucked in a shaky breath. "Did you even look at the *Veracity* before you let them take it? Did anyone compare the ID numbers?"

The clerk did that for herself. "Hm."

"Yeah," Mykah said. "Hm. Somebody was in a hurry to steal my ship and you just let it go."

"I wasn't on duty when it was—"

Mykah cut her off. He kept his voice low, calmer than he felt. "I want the name of the clerk on duty at the time the ship was released.

I want a copy of the records, complete with signatures. I want to know who took the bribe that bought my ship. Then I'm going to calculate lost revenue as well as travel expenses. I will bill Lautan for not preventing the theft of my ship from their spaceport."

And he was tempted to call Mellix. This incident was so much smaller in scale than the journalist usually looked into, but maybe it indicated a larger issue, if Kai—or pleasure planets as a rule—were impounding and selling independent spaceships at will on any sort of trumped-up charges. Because of the tesseract flaw, big cruise liners were already not traveling to the pleasure planets. If the pleasure planets tried to make up the revenue on the back of independent travelers, they would put themselves straight out of business.

Maybe he didn't even need Mellix's name behind this exposé. He just needed to find out if the *Veracity* was the only ship to be stolen like this. Was it targeted—or was this a trend?

* * *

The bounty hunters were as good as their word. They left her alone.

Raena spent her time searching every crevice of the room. She wasn't sure why they didn't come in to stop her. Perhaps the room didn't have a working surveillance system. She considered doing something lewd to see if they were paying attention, but decided it wasn't worth the fallout.

Maybe they were all asleep. Or maybe Chale and the human had something better to do than watch a girl. It didn't matter to Raena. After she discovered a jagged wedge of metal jammed in the top of the doorframe, she was ready to take the room apart.

Her stomach grumbled. She'd lost track of time, but she couldn't remember eating anything since breakfast with Coni on Lautan. She missed Mykah's cooking. That boy could turn the blandest vegetable protein into a feast.

The lights in her cabin went out. Raena wasn't sure if she'd tripped something or if her captors simply decided it was time for her to sleep. The sounds of the engine did not change, so she got to work reconfiguring the ventilation system. She was almost more comfortable in the dark than in the daylight—and she didn't want them to be able to gas her when they made planetfall on Kai.

* * *

Haoun discovered there wasn't any human consul on Lautan. He went to the Shtrell Embassy instead. In general, the Shtrell were fussy enough that bureaucracy suited them. They were also nosy enough that it should be easy to enlist their aid, if he piqued their curiosity.

As he'd hoped, the ambassador had time to see him, now that travel had fallen off on the planet. Haoun brought a bribe. He set a bag of mixed dry roasted insects on the desk as he sat in front of it. The ambassador hooted, pleased. "How can I help you?" she asked.

"My girlfriend got arrested yesterday," Haoun said. "Before she'd even been charged with anything, she was transported to Kai in the night. I'd like to get a message to her, make sure she's all right, but the jail wasn't any help. And since there's no human embassy here—"

The Shtrell clicked her beak. "Your girlfriend is human."

Even though their translators both spoke Galactic Standard, Haoun's still decoded the words for him. It didn't give any context for the emotion behind the Shtrell's words, but Haoun didn't entirely like the bureaucrat's tone.

"Yes," Haoun said. "Could you help me find her? You know how humans are mistreated in the galaxy. I'm worried about her."

The Shtrell ruffled her feathers, but merely asked, "What is her name?"

After Haoun told her, the ambassador poked around on the computer. She fluffed and resettled her feathers again.

"She was taken from a holding cell around midnight," the Shtrell said. "By Planetary Security."

"That seems a strange time to transfer someone who hadn't even had a hearing yet," Haoun said.

"It gets stranger. On the way to the spaceport, the truck crashed. Apparently, the entire contingent of Planetary Security agents were injured in the wreck. Your friend was removed from the wreckage by a trio of bounty hunters."

"What?" Haoun leaned forward. "How bad was the crash? Was Raena hurt?"

"There's a video." The Shtrell turned the monitor so that Haoun could see. The truck lay on its side, but didn't look particularly damaged. Raena walked out of it with her hands fettered in front of her. One of the bounty hunters—a human—clipped a lead to her restraints and led her away from the camera.

Raena appeared unharmed. She walked upright, straight and proud as ever, despite being barefoot. Haoun could see no obvious bruises or blood on her—even though fallen Planetary Security agents lay all over the street. It didn't look like a vehicular accident so much as the site of an attack. While Haoun had never seen an attack in real life, he had played enough games to recognize one.

"Who are those guys?" he wondered aloud. "How did three of them take out a truck full of Planetary Security?"

"They haven't been identified officially," the ambassador said.

"Is there any indication where they might take her?"

The Shtrell pecked at the keys, then sat back and cocked an eye at her screen. "There's a bounty put on her by the Business Council of Kai."

"Nothing else?"

The Shtrell stared at Haoun, unhappy that Haoun already knew about Kai's bounty. "I don't see anything else."

By tesseract drive, Kai was only a day's flight away. Since the bounty hunters were likely to have a slower ship, no telling how long the trip would take. The only way Haoun would know if she got to Kai would be if the bounty was claimed. Otherwise, Raena was lost in the galaxy.

It wasn't the Shtrell's fault. Haoun struggled to remember that. He flexed his hands, wanting desperately to shred something. "Thanks for your help," he ground out as he got up to leave.

* * *

Haoun met his crewmates on the beach for lunch. Coni had never seen him angry before, but the way the muscles bunched alongside his jaw was ominous. She knew that whatever he was about to say would be bad news.

"Raena was extradited to Kai last night," he announced. "As local Planetary Security escorted her to the spaceport, their transport truck was attacked. In the end, a crew of bounty hunters took her off Lautan."

"Is she all right?" Vezali asked.

"Lautan does not seem to care. Apparently, their responsibility for visitors to their planet ends when anyone else accuses those visitors of a crime. I mean, she's only human. Who's going to protest if she's hurt?"

Coni was surprised to see just how much Haoun cared for Raena.

Haoun continued, "If they could blame her kidnapping on her—or on us—they would. They're just relieved that she's gone."

"Strangely enough," Mykah said, "they feel the same about the *Veracity*. It was also kidnapped in the night."

Coni watched the others react to the news that their home had been stolen away. She knew the fury and bewilderment they felt.

"Is this happening because we stole the *Veracity* from the Thallians?" Vezali asked.

"The *Raptor* was never reported stolen," Coni answered. "Anyone who might claim it is dead. It's registered in Mykah's name. The loan was refinanced and paid off. We own the ship free and clear. Even the ID numbers don't correspond to the *Raptor*'s. The only connection between the ships is that they are both Imperial diplomatic transports and both were on Kai."

"Can you make them believe that?" Haoun asked.

"There's no evidence to contradict it," Coni said. "Kai's dockmaster obviously confused the two ships. Everything else follows that mistake."

"Stellar," Vezali cheered.

"What do we do about the charge for kidnapping the Thallian boy?" Haoun asked.

"Again, no one reported Jain missing," Coni said. "All Kai has is the video of Raena following him onto the *Veracity*. Once she gets to trial, it should be easy to refute."

"What can we do now?" Vezali asked.

"Some of us are going to have to go to Kai to get the *Veracity* back," Mykah said. "It would be cheapest to find a working passage, if there's a delivery ship going from here to Kai. But that might take a while to arrange."

"Or we could all get on the first transport out," Haoun insisted.

"It's too costly," Coni protested. "We'll need to save enough money that we can afford a place to stay when we get there."

"And pay the docking fees to get the ship back," Mykah said.

"And whatever Raena's fine is going to be," Coni added.

"She has some money of her own," Haoun pointed out. "Didn't her friend Ariel set her up with a trust fund?"

"It won't do us any good," Coni said. "We can't access it for her."

"Have you told Ariel that Raena was arrested yet?" Vezali asked. "Maybe she can arrange to pay Raena's fine from Callixtos."

"*If* Raena's been taken to Kai," Haoun pointed out. "Since the bounty hunters captured her, they could be taking her anywhere."

"All the more reason to get the *Veracity* back first," Mykah argued. "Once we have the ship, we can go after her."

"Call Ariel," Coni soothed. "She deserves to know what's going on."

★ ★ ★

Ariel expected a call back from Raena, but she wasn't expecting to hear from the former waiter from Kai. "Captain Chen," she acknowledged. He looked like he was calling her from a bar.

"Hi, Ms. Shaad. We got the message you forwarded to us, but there's a problem."

Before he could tell her what the delay might be, Ariel asked, "Is Raena all right?"

"She was arrested on Lautan yesterday."

"On what charges?"

"Kidnapping the Thallian boy and stealing an Imperial transport on Kai."

The *Veracity*, Ariel understood. Ariel had told her sister that prank would bite her in the ass. Anger prickled over Ariel's skin. She couldn't believe Raena had been stupid enough not to obscure the ship's origins.

Mykah interrupted her thoughts. "The officials on Lautan mistook the *Veracity* for the *Raptor* and impounded it. An honest mistake," he said, rolling his eyes, "since they're the same class of ship, but if they'd just compared the ID numbers . . ."

Ariel drew a deep breath, relieved the kids had that taken care of. "Sounds as if you ought to sue for wrongful seizure."

"We're trying to figure out how to get to Kai to file now."

"What do you mean, trying?" Ariel stared at him, but Mykah wouldn't meet her eyes. "Is it a matter of money?"

"Well, there are four of us and we can't all afford to go anywhere until we get our ship back . . ."

Ariel cut him off. "Captain Chen, you know I consider Raena family. If you need to get to Kai to bail her out and get her chosen home out of hock, then arrange it and let me know how much it's going to cost. Don't waste time being too proud to take a handout. I would do anything to help Raena."

"Thank you," he said, awed. "We're pretty confident we can get the ship back. But there's still the kidnapping charge . . ."

Ariel suspected that particular Thallian clone was dead. She would have to ask Eilif. In the meantime, she said, "I'll have the Foundation investigate. Since Raena's one of my wards—and it was my idea to take her to Kai in the first place—I am responsible for her. Can you send me a copy of the charges?"

The boy looked to someone offscreen, then nodded. "They're on the way to you."

"We'll get this handled," Ariel promised. "I have an advocate on retainer to protect my family in court. But the shadows on Drusingyi . . . Don't go without Raena. I met him—" she paused, unwilling to say Thallian's name. "I was his prisoner during the War. If we can't get Raena to explore this, I will turn it over to the galaxy to handle. I want them all erased."

Mykah nodded. A string of numbers came across her screen. "This is my comm code. Let us know if there's anything we can do to help with Raena's defense."

"Thanks." But as Ariel signed out, she was tempted to go to Kai herself and straighten everything our firsthand. The sooner this was cleared up for Raena, the sooner Ariel would know what was going on in the Thallians' undersea city.

CHAPTER 6

When Raena got the ventilation to her cabin blocked up, she returned the grate to its place and tightened it back down. Whenever the lights came up again, the bounty hunters shouldn't be able to tell she'd been tinkering.

She climbed down onto the floor and rested with her back against the bunk. If she slept, her body would use less oxygen. It would be stupid to die because she'd cut off her own air supply.

How many hours had she been awake, anyway? The day began with a bubble bath in Haoun's hotel room, she remembered. That seemed so long ago.

She rested her head on her arms and thought about what she'd like to be doing with Haoun right now.

✳ ✳ ✳

Ariel watched the news from Lautan, but didn't see anything about bounty hunters capturing a small human tourist. Only after she delved deeper into the public Planetary Security records did she find what she was looking for. Raena Zacari, ward of the Shaad Family Foundation, had been arrested on a warrant from Kai.

Interesting that they should designate Raena as one of the Shaad Foundation wards. Ariel had run into the Security system on Kai twice before, after Raena went chasing off after Thallian. The first time, Ariel and Gavin Sloane had been picked up by Planetary Security and held in the local jail until Ariel's mother paid their bail. They'd used false names then, but when Sloane returned to Kai later to beat up the Thallian soldiers left behind, he'd been subjected to a truth drug and blown their cover. Once Kai knew their real names, they'd called Ariel to pay Sloane's bail. And she'd refused, because he'd burned his last bridge with her. Kai seemed to drop the matter.

Now, months later—when times for pleasure planets were hard—Kai remembered that Ariel had money. Apparently, they had decided to help themselves to some of it.

Ariel returned to the computer search to see what else she could find.

During Raena's transfer to Lautan Spaceport for extradition, the truck she was riding in had been attacked. The entire PS detail had been taken out of commission. Raena had been seized by three bounty hunters.

That drew Ariel's attention. How had three hunters taken out a truck full of Security? Why would they risk it, if they were only transporting Raena to Kai—where they would presumably turn her over to Kai's Planetary Security? Ariel poked around some more, expecting to find warrants for the hunters, but there was nothing. It looked as if they'd gotten away with poaching a prisoner from Planetary Security. How was that even possible?

Planetary Security was a relatively new organization, created during the chaotic years after the Templar Plague. Security agents all trained on a planet out in the Guida system, then were hired as independent contractors by each planetary government according to that planet's security needs. On duty, they usually wore helmets that didn't reveal their species. That was supposed to protect their identities and keep them from being subject to bribery. Since they were planet-bound, Ariel suspected that corruption crept in to the organization anyway—and the helmets only made it more difficult to assign blame. She generally tried to avoid their notice. It wasn't that any particular Security agent was dangerous, but there were always plenty of them. Like wasps, they didn't take kindly to having one of their own attacked.

Ariel turned up a video that showed Raena leaving the Security truck. The public recording was only a snippet, which—interestingly enough—didn't show the bounty hunters' assault on the PS crew. The recording had been edited down to Raena walking out of the truck, onto a street littered with fallen Security agents.

Ariel froze the image to study it. Among the security detail lay a couple of figures in gray uniforms. Their mirrored helmets made them as anonymous as Planetary Security, but something about them caught Ariel's attention. Which side had they been on during the confrontation?

They didn't match up with the scruffy hunters, one of whom was Chale. Ariel recognized the metal-armed giant from the Coalition days. Chale was reasonably honorable, as bounty hunters went. He didn't mistreat his prisoners—at least, he didn't used to. And he wasn't interested in girls, so he and Raena shouldn't get into a confrontation over that.

Ariel put out some feelers. Maybe she could reach Chale, make an offer to buy Raena back.

The Shaad Family Foundation would still have to face the charges on Kai, but if Raena could go into the trial as a free woman, she'd be a whole lot happier.

Besides, Ariel thought with a grim smile, Kai had picked this fight. Ariel had every intention of ending it.

* * *

Raena jerked awake. The sound of the bounty hunters' engine had changed. No longer a basso drone, it had shifted to a higher pitch. She'd never flown on a tesseract-powered ship before, so she didn't know if the change meant they were coming out of tesseract space or getting stranded in it.

Not much she could do about either one, locked in her cabin. She decided to hope it meant they were nearing Kai. If that was the case, the bounty hunters would gas her soon. She would know, because they'd turn on her lights so they could watch her pass out.

She crawled up onto the bunk, stretched out on her back, and crossed her ankles demurely. She had whiled away much of her imprisonment in the Templar tomb lying that way. It was also the best position from which to greet the hunters when they finally unlocked her door.

The lights came on in her cabin. Raena lay still, breathed shallowly, and kept her eyes shut.

* * *

Ariel found Eilif down in the range with Kavanaugh. He'd gotten a pistol into her hands again, but the little woman still just held it, arms extended in front of her, elbows locked. The target advanced toward her, but she didn't fire. Ariel suspected Eilif's eyes were closed.

"Let's start her with bull's-eyes," Ariel suggested. "Once she gets used to firing the gun, we can worry about targeting her shots."

Eilif lowered the gun abruptly. When she turned toward Ariel's voice, Ariel drew, aimed, fired, and re-holstered her pistol in a single breath. The holographic man on the range froze in place, pierced through the forehead with a small black hole.

"Now you're showing off," Kavanaugh said.

"Yes."

Ariel came down into the range as Kavanaugh took the pistol back from Eilif.

"I don't know if I can kill anyone," Eilif said softly.

"You don't have to," Kavanaugh reminded.

"You might just want to slow someone down," Ariel said. "Sometimes, seeing someone holding a gun, even if that gun is shaking in her hands, will make a person think twice."

Kavanaugh caught Ariel's eye, but he held his tongue. No shaking gun would slow a Thallian down.

"Raena's been arrested," Ariel said. "She was taken off Lautan by some bounty hunters last night."

"She okay?" Kavanaugh asked.

"Don't know. She's charged with kidnapping one of the Thallian boys on Kai."

Eilif would have stumbled, except that Kavanaugh caught her elbow. "She captured Jain on Kai," Eilif said. "She brought him home to die with the others."

Ariel nodded. "Are you angry at her for that?"

Eilif's eyes flickered up to meet Ariel's, but no, of all the complicated emotions in Eilif's face, Ariel did not see anger there. "He chose to die at home," Eilif said. "Jain was Jonan's favorite son. He was Raena's favorite, too."

Ariel changed the subject abruptly. "How did Jimi find you?"

"Through my messages to potential adoptive families, he said. The boys spent a lot of time on the grid, searching for Raena. Jimi must know searches I can't imagine."

"Tell me about him."

"Jimi was never like the others," Eilif said immediately. "He wasn't a warrior. Revan told me that when the family still lived on the planet's surface, when there were many of the clones, some were scientists and some were engineers. Some were artists. But after the Templar plague, after the galaxy attacked and the family fled to the ocean floor, all that survived were warriors. Jonan had a special antipathy for Jimi. He saw him as a throwback. Jonan would have killed him, except that the cloning process was breaking down and fewer and fewer children survived to be born. Jonan's brothers argued to keep Jimi alive. He was precious to the family, even if Jonan loathed him."

It was a longer speech than Ariel had heard Eilif make before.

Kavanaugh busied himself picking up the range and putting things away, shutting the holographs down. Ariel was glad he hadn't found an excuse to leave. She planned to draw him back into the conversation before long.

First, though, she had to ask: "What did you think of the boy?"

"Jimi could have been a poet," Eilif said unexpectedly. "His mind was different from the others'. Since he wasn't allowed to express his soul in words, he did it in machinery. He understood how things worked. He could fix anything."

Ariel wanted to ask if Eilif had loved him. How could she ask that of a woman who understood her role had been to die for her keepers if someone tried to poison them? She had been cast as the boys' mother, but they weren't her flesh. She'd had no choice but to nurture them. Thallian would have killed her if she'd done anything less.

Ariel fell back on asking again, "Do you trust him? Jimi betrayed his whole family."

"I would have done it," Eilif argued softly, "if I'd had any idea how."

"But you might have been killed when Raena came," Ariel argued. "She could have killed you with the others."

Eilif's smile was complex. "I think Raena saw herself reflected in me."

"I wouldn't have counted on that for protection," Ariel answered, "and I've known her a long time." When they were teenagers, Raena's self-loathing had sometimes sunk to frightening depths. Ariel found it easy to imagine that Raena might have thought killing Eilif would be a mercy, as killing her own clones had seemed.

"I was ready to die with the rest," Eilif said. "I couldn't envision any other life. My purpose was over. Raena wouldn't allow me to give up."

Somehow they'd gotten off the subject. Ariel shook her head. Trying to imagine herself in Eilif's place was just too painful.

"I have an idea for Raena's defense," Ariel said. "It hinges on Jimi. Can we rely on him?"

"He is as indebted to her as I am," Eilif said. "He will be honored if you ask him."

"Perfect. Let's take a little vacation." Ariel turned to Kavanaugh. "Tarik, I need to hire a ship to get to Kai. Are you interested in the job?"

* * *

There was a whole lot of cursing outside her cabin. Raena didn't understand the words, but the tone was clear.

She kept her face blank, in case anyone wanted to peek in on her. It sounded like blocking up the ventilation to her cabin had had consequences elsewhere on the ship. Oops. She hoped she hadn't knocked out the one hunter who knew how to land the ship.

The door unlocked and a plasma rifle poked through the gap. Raena lay still, eyes slitted, until the white-furred bounty hunter stood over her. Then she exploded upward, knocking the rifle's muzzle away from her body.

Skip was too professional to fire on her or release his hold on the gun, but now she was too close for the weapon to serve as anything other than a club. That, she could work with.

He was wiry and strong, with prehensile big toes, so fighting him was a whole lot more fun than she had expected. Raena couldn't remember the last time she'd fought someone for real, someone just as well trained and serious as she was.

Eventually, he lost his temper and gave her an opening. He leapt up to use the wall to change directions and launched the crown of his head straight into her fist. He hit her so hard that she felt it all the way to her shoulder.

He dropped at her feet.

Shaking her hand to get the feeling back, Raena snatched up his rifle with her free hand and slung it across her back. When she peeled off his gas mask, he was breathing, but his pupils were uneven. At least, he hadn't cracked his own skull open, silly thing. She dragged him over to the crash web and got him secured.

When she tried to get out of the cabin, she found the door still sealed. The lock didn't need a combination, just an electronic key. Raena went back to search the furry hunter. The key must be on one of the chain bracelets around his wrists. She removed all of them and brought them back to the door, trying each until one keyed open the lock.

The air in the corridor stung her eyes. She pulled the bounty hunter's breather over her face and switched it on. It smelled funky inside. She hoped he preferred a concentration of oxygen similar to humans. If she got giddy, this would be the shortest escape attempt ever.

She found Chale snoring in the pilot's chair. Raena dragged him over into the copilot's seat and locked him into the crash web. She braced the plasma rifle against the console and rigged the trigger so that if one of Chale's metal arms moved, the gun would fire over his head. The plasma rifle probably wouldn't do the bulkhead any harm, but the sound would alert her when he woke up.

She checked the nav comp: yes, they were coming up fast on Kai. That much of the console readouts she could understand. Unfortunately, the controls were completely unfamiliar, not at all similar to human tech. Clearly, she should have played a whole lot more piloting games with Haoun. She couldn't land this ship without help.

Time to pick up the pace. She found extra breathers stashed by the main hatch. She looped one over her elbow, but the air looked less murky now. She hoped that meant that whatever they'd tried to dose her with was finished pumping into the air system.

Also near the hatch she found their gun locker. Luckily, one of the keys she'd already stolen opened it. She made herself a knapsack full of weapons and left it in the locker where the breathers lived. Then she tossed the key to the gun locker in with the rest of the weapons and closed its door. Likely it wasn't the only gun locker key on board, but not having it would slow at least one of the hunters down.

She kept opening hatches until she found Bihn's cabin. He sprawled face down on the deck. She grabbed some clothes out of his cupboard and swam into a shirt that hung practically to her knees. That was better than the damn dress she'd been wearing for the last several days. She wadded the dress into the breast pocket. Then she dragged Bihn up to the cockpit.

Once she got him settled in the pilot's seat, she slipped a breather over his face and switched it on. She retrieved the plasma rifle and arranged herself on the other side of Chale.

The breather helped counteract the gas. Bihn roused with a groan. When he opened his eyes, he actually jumped at the sight of Kai filling up the view screen.

Raena peeled off her mask so she could talk to him. "You do know how to land us, right?"

"Fuck." He drew the word out until it was several syllables long. "You are your mother's daughter, ain't you?"

"Nobody's dead yet," Raena pointed out.

He leaned forward and started slapping the controls into place. She got the feeling he put on a show for her, that he really did have things more under control than it appeared.

Kai's Flight Control hailed them.

"On the speaker," Raena directed. Bihn complied.

"Repeat: *Khangho*, we have been expecting you. Do you have the Business Council's prisoner onboard?"

Bihn was smart enough to look to her to answer. "Yes," Raena said. "She's still onboard. We will be ready to collect our bounty when we turn her over to you."

Bihn glared at her, but Raena made the slightest motion of the plasma rifle toward Chale's head. The bounty hunter settled back.

"Standing by for the landing coordinates," Raena said.

She gave Flight Control time to send them through, then switched off the speaker and smiled at Bihn. "You know that's not where you're letting me off, right?"

"Look," he said, completely exasperated, "I'm a businessman. I'm just trying to do a job . . ."

"And pay off your ship. Right. I get that," Raena said. "I'm in your debt, since you rescued me from those creeps in the gray uniforms, but I don't appreciate being kidnapped. So you're gonna drop me off, out in the desert. You're gonna leave me a transmitter, so I can contact my ship. And I'm gonna let you go your own way."

"How do I know you haven't booby-trapped the ship while we were all conked out?"

"You don't. Except that I'm not my mom and I've got no reason to kill you, until you give me one."

"You gonna strap yourself down before we hit atmo?" he snarled at her.

"Wasn't planning on it." She climbed into Chale's lap and wound her free hand in his crash web, resting the barrel of the rifle up under his chin. "Fly careful, okay?"

"When Kai's done with you, I am so going to kill you."

"Thanks for the warning."

* * *

Mykah took the records from the dockmaster and his handheld down to the jailhouse, where he managed to claim Raena's things. In addition to the Stinger, its holster, and a couple of spare power packs, all of which he expected—he got back three knives that he hadn't known she carried. One looked like an antique that had been sharpened many times. The other two were some kind of chipped stone. He wondered if she could carry them through metal detectors. Also in the lot were her brand-new gargoyle shades, her barely worn boots—one of which had blood on its shiny silver heel—and her wallet. Other than some odds and ends of local currency, it was empty.

The last thing to be returned was Raena's comm bracelet. Mykah wrapped it around his wrist, but found it too small to clasp. He ended up hooking it around a tool loop on his pants.

Raena didn't carry a handheld and didn't wear jewelry, so her life boiled down to weapons. Mykah hesitated to think how much junk he wore stuffed into the pockets of his cargo pants or hidden inside his jacket. When he wore a jacket, that is. At the moment, his jacket was being towed across the galaxy aboard the *Veracity*.

Somehow Raena survived with only the clothes on her back and what she could tuck into her boot-tops or carry around in her head. It made him sad.

He packed everything of Raena's into a single disposable shopping bag. When he returned to the street, Coni handed him the Stinger Vezali had bought him.

"Haoun called," Coni reported. "He's found a Na'ash passenger ship bound for Kai."

"When do they leave?"

"As soon as we get there."

"Let's go."

＊ ＊ ＊

When the *Khangho* diverted from the flight plan, the comm screeched at them. Raena switched it off again.

"You don't know nothing about Kai, do you?" Bihn accused. "The whole planet is desert, except for Kai City. It's a rock, nothing but abandoned Templar ghost towns. Soon as you contact your ship, Planetary Security will know exactly where you are."

"Then I better do it now." She signed into her online scrambler. Once the computer had connected, she keyed in the *Veracity*'s comm code and said simply, "I'm on Kai. Come and get me."

No one answered right away, but she would have been startled if they'd been on the ship, waiting for her call. They were probably still on Lautan, trying to figure out where she'd gone.

While she was at it, she put in Ariel's code, too. "Hey, I'm never going to forgive you for dragging me to Kai."

Then she signed out of the scrambler and shut the comm off again.

"Somebody's following us," Bihn said.

"Planetary Security?"

Bihn gave her a look that expressed his contempt for Kai's Planetary Security.

"You think it's the guys in gray?"

"Watch Chale's head," he ordered, before banking the ship sharply starboard. Raena clutched the crash webbing and hoped she wouldn't be thrown to the deck.

"What'd you do to piss these guys off?" Bihn demanded.

"I honestly do not know. They attacked Mellix on Capital City and I kneecapped five or six of them."

"Should've killed them," he grumbled.

"You don't think that would have pissed the rest off more?"

He didn't answer and she didn't push it. She'd seen people flying for their lives before.

The comm screeched again. Raena leaned forward to slap the channel open. "We are under attack," she said through gritted teeth. "If you want your prisoner, you're going to have to come to our aid."

Bihn went into a steep climb that pressed Raena away from the comm.

"You have escape pods?" she asked.

"Yeah."

"All right, I'm outta here. They should let you go after that, right?"

"Who knows?" he answered. "At least it will split their fire."

"Good enough." She pitched the plasma rifle down the hall. Since they were climbing almost straight up, Raena wasn't sure where it would end up, other than a long way from Bihn's reach. She struggled up out of Chale's lap to the arm of the copilot's chair, crossed her arms over her chest, and jumped, plummeting down through the ship, bare feet first, knees slightly bent to absorb the shock of whatever was going to stop her fall.

✳ ✳ ✳

The Na'ash ship was a large yacht apparently hauled out of mothballs to make the pleasure planet circuit. Although the captain and her crew were Na'ash like Haoun, the twelve passengers ran a gamut.

Mykah sent Coni off to their cabin with Raena's shopping bags, which were practically all the luggage they had. He hoped that when they saw the prices on Kai, they wouldn't wish they'd done more shopping on Lautan. He and Coni, at least, would need clothes for attending the trial. Vezali never wore much, because she didn't like anything to impede her tentacles, and Haoun wasn't picky about what he wore, as long as it was baggy enough.

In the meantime, Mykah consulted the schedule the captain had posted for the guests: welcome drinks, dinner, nightcaps, first breakfast, late breakfast, midday meal. At least the trip would go quickly, with all the eating. Mykah looked forward to getting back on a regular meal schedule.

* * *

Raena missed her grab at her cache of weapons as she rocketed past the main hatch. Bihn twisted the ship into a corkscrew that knocked her into every surface in the hallway. She would have thought he was punishing her on purpose, but one of the attackers' shots landed. The lights went out and the whole ship juddered, before he got it back under control.

"Are you to the pods yet?" he yelled back to her.

"Starboard or port?"

"Port."

She caught a railing and hung on, winding her legs around it, too. She could see the airlock from here. "Give me a hard left."

He cranked the ship hard to port and she let go her hold. She caught the handle outside the airlock.

"I'm back to the pods," she called.

"Get the hell off my ship," he ordered.

"Yes, sir." She wished she'd been able to take any of his weapons. She wished the plasma rifle hadn't vanished. She wished she had food or water or any way to survive in the desert. She wished she hadn't been dragged back to Kai.

Climbing hand over hand, she got to the first of the escape pods and pounded its escape sequence in. Then she climbed over to the next and sent it to follow the first, and so on, until she crawled into the next to last pod. She'd leave him one, in case he and his crew needed to bail out, too. "I'm in!" she shouted at Bihn.

The pod's hatch slammed shut, barely missing her head. Teeth clenched in a grin, Raena flung herself onto the bench and pulled the crash web over her as the jets engaged.

Glad to be rid of her, it seemed.

* * *

As soon as she noticed the message light flashing, Ariel listened to the snippet from Raena: "I'm never going to forgive you for dragging me to Kai." Ariel heard the amused fatalism behind Raena's words. The old joke harkened back to their adolescence together. Hungover, Ariel would groan it in the morning, after Raena had gotten them home safely from yet another ill-considered adventure that Ariel had proposed the night before.

Ariel tried to respond to the message, but got back "unrecognized communications code" in answer. Raena had used a scrambler to call. Not unexpected.

Ariel's next call was to Tomur Corvas, the Varan attorney who had been her friend since he and his son had adopted one of her orphans. Corvas would know how to defend Raena.

* * *

The *Khangho*'s escape pod plummeted straight down. The pod was really bare bones, just the crash web and a small locker beneath the bench. It didn't have any kind of viewport or controls, not even a comm console. Raena hoped the pod had enough shielding that when she slammed into the ground, it wouldn't disintegrate on impact.

Some days it just wasn't worth having walked out of her tomb.

She hoped that the attackers, whoever they were, weren't about to blow her out of the sky. If the boys in gray were pursuing her, either they wanted to capture her or witness her death, or else they would have simply blown up the truck back on Lautan. She hoped she could escape them a third time.

While she was dropping, Raena twisted around to try the bounty hunters' keys against the locker. One of them popped the door. Inside she found a rucksack jammed with water pouches, nutrition bars, and other survival supplies. It was the first thing that had gone right in days.

She bit the tab off a pouch of water and sucked its contents down, then a second, then a third. That ought to lighten the pack a little.

She pawed around inside the pack, looking for any kind of weapon. The best she found was a multi-blade survival tool that could be used as a knife. Better than nothing.

The escape pod jerked suddenly upward. After that, its descent became much more gradual. It must have some kind of parachute. That ought to alert her pursuers right where she was landing.

Raena wished she knew how much farther she had to fall. She unclipped herself from the crash web and crouched over to the hatch. The release was a simple red handle. Would it blow the door open explosively and should she save it as her best weapon? Or would it merely glide the door open and politely invite her pursuers in?

She decided it didn't matter. She was in a mood to run. She pulled the rucksack onto her back and tried to psych herself up to be ready to jump as soon as the ground came close enough.

*　*　*

After they finished dinner on the Na'ash yacht, the *Veracity*'s crew retreated to their suite of rooms to watch the news. There had been another gang of humans arrested with a packet of Messiah, this time on Shtrell.

The news showed the footage of Raena with the Outrider head again.

"It would be awesome to see the androids knit themselves back together," Vezali said, as she opened a bottle of xyshin with a pair of tentacles. "I didn't know the Templars had tech that could do that."

"It was terrifying to watch at the time." Mykah held out his glass to her. "Raena would take the androids apart, but they'd just reassemble themselves when her back was turned."

"And they looked completely human?" Vezali poured for Coni and Haoun and passed their glasses to them.

"Yeah," Mykah said. "They could breathe, sweat, bleed. Absolutely eerie."

"I don't understand why tech like that would be wasted to deal in drugs. That's so specific," Coni said, "so trivial."

"I don't get why, if you had tech like that, you would only make androids that looked like Outrider," Haoun said. "Why wouldn't you also make robots that looked like any other species in the galaxy? Is it more possible that the Templar androids only mimic humans— or that there are other camouflaged robots at work in the galaxy even now, doing who knows what?"

That question put an end to the conversation.

Mykah changed the subject. "Are you sure Raena's identity has held up?"

Coni hugged him. "Absolutely certain. It was tested when we went to Capital City. She will be fine."

"I hope so. In so many ways, she's just a babe in the galaxy," he said. "It's changed so much and she's spent so little time in it . . ."

"You're tired," Coni diagnosed. "Have you seen Raena? She always lands on her feet."

CHAPTER 7

Raena pulled the red lever that blew the door off the escape pod. The wind outside tugged at her, but she kept a good hold on the pod as she looked out. The ground was still a surprisingly long way down. It seemed to be mostly rock, broken by rivers of sand. She wondered if this desert had once been the bed of an ancient ocean. How long had the Templars lived on Kai? Had they known the planet when this desert had been lush as the jungles on Lautan?

Now that she could see out of the pod, she discovered it was almost sunset on Kai. Perfect. Darkness would give her more shadows in which to hide.

She was still up high enough that there would be plenty of time to put the pod's homing beacon out of commission before she jumped. Raena hauled herself up onto the roof of the escape pod, but the beacon wasn't up there. Hm. Maybe she couldn't smash it until she landed.

The parachute snapped and fluttered above her head, yellow against the crimson sky. She could see where the other pods had landed behind her, their parachutes bright as flowers against the dark brown ground. Turbo skiffs had already stopped to check out two of the other pods. A third skiff still chased the *Khangho*, barely a glint at the horizon's edge, heading back into space. Excellent. One less thing to worry about.

Raena crouched at the base of the cables connecting the parachute to the pod. She wished she had some gloves. Then she opened up her survival tool and used the blade to saw at one of the three cables. It nearly took her eye out as it twanged past her head.

Gonna have to be more careful, she told herself, or she'd had that scar back again. Maybe this time it really would cost her an eye.

She pulled the spool of survival cord from inside the rucksack and wove herself a sling between the remaining two cables. Once she had herself tied in, she bent and used another tool to pry the cable anchor loose from the top of the escape pod.

The parachute yanked her suddenly upward as the escape pod plunged away beneath her. Raena concentrated on relaxing, letting the wind bear her away. The pursuers would be after her soon enough. They'd be moving faster than windspeed or gravity.

The escape pod clanged down the rock behind her. Only then did she realize how quiet the desert was. The only other sound she heard was the rush of wind in her ears.

Ahead of her rose a mountainous stone mesa cut by a maze of narrow fissures. Raena steered the parachute by shifting her weight. She aimed herself toward the uplands. There might be wildlife there, but she would have more cover than on the bare rock below.

Twilight drew on faster now. No lights glowed anywhere below her, but off in the distance behind her, she could see Kai City reflected against the clouds. It was a hundred kilometers or more distant, too far to hope for help.

One of the skiffs rose from the escape pod it had been investigating.

Raena stopped lying stiff and flat, facing into the wind. She forced her body downward, spread-eagled to catch as much wind as possible. It slowed her somewhat, so that when the updraft rose from the base of the mesa, she steered herself over the mesa top. Then she clenched her teeth, grabbed the cradle of rope, and sawed the survival tool through it.

The wind tore the parachute away. It grew smaller as it flapped off.

And a helmet, she thought. Wish I had gloves and a helmet.

Raena tucked into the fall, but the pack on her back made landing awkward. She lost a layer of skin on one leg. At least she managed not to break anything.

Before she could uncurl herself, a turbo skiff whizzed beyond her, chasing the parachute.

She hadn't much time. Growling at herself to move, Raena got to her feet. She limped over to the nearest crevasse and slipped over its edge, feeling for toeholds as she went.

The sky grew darker by the moment. Dark was good. She could work in the darkness.

Raena struggled to keep her mind focused on the climb, wedging her fingers into the rock, keeping her body relaxed, evening out her breathing.

She hadn't gone far before her mind wandered again. The rock face was still hot from the daytime. It didn't burn her, but it hinted at how warm the desert would get, come morning.

Not only did she lack shoes, but she'd left her gargoyle goggles on Lautan. She remembered how bright the light had been last time she'd been on Kai. Crossing the desert in daylight was likely to burn her eyes right out of her head.

Focus, she ordered herself. She'd lost track of how far down the canyon face she'd come. It jolted her when she put her foot down on a boulder just above the canyon floor.

Searchlights caressed the top of the mesa overhead. One or more of the skiffs had come to look for her.

Raena hopped down off the boulder to the canyon's floor. Then she darted into the darkness.

A channel ran straight down the middle of the serpentine canyon, clearly engineered rather than natural. Raena wondered if there used to be irrigation ditches on the surface of Kai. Maybe she could still find water. That would become important in a day or two, when she finished the water in her pack.

Without warning, the crevasse spat her out into a courtyard barely visible in the twilight. The ornate facades of a handful of buildings faced the courtyard. Bihn told her there were Templar ghost towns on Kai. It seemed that she had discovered one.

Raena ducked into the middle doorway. The building was pitch black inside. She forced herself farther in, wondering if Kai had critters who would seek shelter inside the abandoned houses. She had an emergency lantern in her survival pack, but if her pursuers saw it flashing around in the darkness, they'd know exactly where to look for her.

She stopped to listen. The old house held its breath. Raena couldn't hear anything beyond the rush of blood in her ears, just like being in her tomb. Remembered terror shivered over her.

Raena forced herself to sit on the stone floor, to breathe in the darkness. She was safe for now. She had a little water and some food. They didn't know where she'd gone.

She pulled one of the nutritional bars from her pack and unwrapped it, careful to put the wrapping back in the pack so it couldn't betray her later. She nibbled the bar, trying to eat it slowly rather than gobble it down as her body wanted to do. It tasted of sweetness, but felt like some kind of small nuts or seeds. Not a bad flavor, if unfamiliar. She hoped eating it would still the tremor in her hands.

If her pursuers had infrared, they would find her. If there were enough of them and they searched long enough, they would find her. While she was curious what they wanted from her, she wasn't interested in dying to find out.

If what Bihn told her was true and Kai City held the only civilization on the planet, then it offered her only hope of getting back into space.

Raena knew where the tourist spaceport was, but at the moment, barely armed and still barefoot, she had little to trade for passage off-world. Not enough for anyone to risk anything, if they knew Planetary Security wanted her.

She could lurk around the spaceport until she found a human ship to commandeer. One thing she'd learned as Ariel's bodyguard, though, was that you didn't steal from rich people. Working people might let a slight go, because they couldn't afford to fight you and what else were they going to do, but the rich wouldn't let it drop. They would hunt you down—or pay someone else to do it.

That meant she would have to find the secondary spaceport, the one for deliveries and workers. Kai had more human employees than Lautan did, but she would still be individual enough to be noticeable. She'd have to be extra cautious until she hijacked a ship. She would also have to wait until she found one capable of being flown by a woman whose knowledge of piloting was twenty years out-of-date.

As much as she loathed the idea, planetary custody offered advantages. It meant she would be fed, kept out of the sun, and sheltered from the gray militia. Maybe the only thing that made sense was to turn herself in to Planetary Security and wait for the cavalry to come get her.

Once the night settled in for real, Raena could not have moved if she'd wanted to. No telling if the floor of the old house was solid or how far back it went. The stone where she sat felt so smooth that she wondered if it had been swept. Had someone else set up housekeeping here?

She would have been happier with her back against something, anything, but without turning on her light, she wasn't about to crawl off in search of a good solid wall.

To pass the time, she thought over what she knew about the Templars. She wasn't certain of very much. They were an old species, maybe the first to travel the stars. No one knew where they o iginated. By the time other people crept off their homeworlds, tl e Templars had already colonized planets strewn across the galaxy. T..ey were ready to trade, but to trade with the Templars, new worlds had to give up their interplanetary weaponry. Those who could not abide by the Templars' rules were annihilated.

Mostly the Templars traded their technology for food. The translation devices Vezali and Haoun wore were Templar tech. Even the comm system the *Veracity* used to connect to the galaxy in real time was based on Templar tech, stolen and adapted by the Empire. The machines that made most colonized planets' air breathable and water drinkable had come from the Templars. The galaxy relied on Templar-made fabrics and construction materials and miscellaneous electronics.

The galactic peace might have endured forever, if humanity had not run up against Templar space. The Empire wanted to expand—and they didn't want to give up their weapons to trade by the Templars' rules.

Between the Empire and the Templars stood the border worlds. These managed to form a Coalition between their nonhuman governments and the human refugees fleeing the Empire. If any of them had had weapons of war, the border worlds might have joined the conflict on the Templars' side. Unfortunately, the masters of the galaxy had destroyed all the weapons they'd confiscated before the War. The only way the Coalition governments could arm themselves was by hijacking Imperial convoys or by scavenging Imperial ships. They were late to the party.

The galaxy at large merely looked on in horror, unable to offer aid or even defend themselves.

The War had been going on for years by the time Raena ran from it. She'd never seen a living Templar, nor had most humans. If an

Imperial craft came across a Templar ship, they destroyed it. The same happened if the Templars saw an Imperial ship first. The initial aggressor always won the exchange, at the price of total obliteration of the enemy.

Things seemed fairly evenly balanced when Raena was imprisoned on the Templar cemetery world. Wiping the Templars out must have struck the Emperor as the only gambit to level the playing field.

He hadn't counted on humanity's aversion to genocide. Everyone who had an opportunity to do so switched sides, choosing to live in the galaxy rather than assist the Empire's plans to take it over.

Raena didn't know what the Templars would have done if they'd succeeded in overpowering the Empire. Would they have wiped humanity out or seen its people enslaved? She was fairly certain the rest of the galaxy wouldn't have censured them over it. Everyone was too reliant on Templar-derived tech—the tesseract drive as case in point—to be thrilled when they had to reinvent or reverse-engineer the things they relied upon every day.

Raena suspected that the failure of the tesseract drive was just a harbinger of things to come. Other tech would start winding down before much longer. If nothing else, without the understanding to manufacture translators that could add new languages, there would be no way to easily communicate with new peoples. Misunderstanding would escalate.

Without the Templars to enforce galactic peace, Raena expected that many governments were already experimenting with interplanetary weaponry. At first the weapons would be justified as self-defense, but eventually someone would claim offense. Then there would be war again.

There was nothing she could do about it here. The silence of the dead village worked on her. Normally sleep was difficult for Raena to find, but now, in the blackness, it stole over her and she couldn't resist.

* * *

When Raena opened her eyes, a faint green light glowed in the back of the house. She watched it, but it came no closer. The silence stopped up her ears.

Her body had stiffened up. Climbing painfully to her feet, she crept cautiously toward the light. It burned with an even emerald glow that was easy on her eyes. When she reached the room where it shone, she marveled at the size of the place. There was nothing cozy or inviting about the empty stone room. It had clearly been fashioned out of the rock for the huge Templars.

A faint mist floated ankle-high above the floor. Raena told herself it was a trap. She should be planning how to cross the desert and get herself back to Kai City. How could she overpower her pursuers? How could she be certain she'd be able to fly a skiff, if she stole one? How was she going to muffle its engine so the sound of it didn't alert the others to follow her?

Instead, she stepped into the room. As she crossed the threshold, the ankle-high mist gathered itself into a sleeping couch.

Twenty years after its masters were erased from the galaxy, the faithful house still remembered the Templars, still worked to offer them comfort.

Desperately lonely, Raena sat on the couch. The mist moved around her gently, conforming to her body, supporting her aching and abraded limbs. Ariel had told her that human chemistry shared startling similarities to the Templars. Apparently, they were alike enough to trigger the furniture's nurturing response.

It was so pleasant just to rest. Raena leaned back into the misty couch and closed her eyes.

* * *

When Raena woke again, she heard a pattering sound, like water. She stood up. The wonderful couch that had supported her dissolved back into mist and evaporated.

Following the sound of rain, she discovered another room lit by a pale green glow. Gentle droplets filled the air inside. She tested the spray with her left hand, but it was only water. She stepped into the shower and let it wash the sweat and worry from her face and hair. Later, perhaps, she would regret getting her clothing wet, but now she took the dress from the breast pocket of Bihn's shirt and rinsed it out, too.

The couch had healed her while she slept. All her aches had been eased. The scabs washed from her abraded leg to reveal new skin beneath. She felt better than she had in days.

Rather than drain into plumbing and vanish, the shower water collected into a stream that ran down into the mountain.

Raena pulled the emergency lantern from her knapsack and followed the stream. It led down a winding stairway into the mountain. Eventually, the water trickled into an underground river that flowed farther than her light could reach.

She settled down on the shore of the river. The stone had been worked into a series of rises, smooth and flat, that would provide safe footing and a place to draw out boats. Mooring posts still protruded from the rock. She shined her lantern overhead, examining the ceiling of the cavern. Normally, Templar stone was rough-surfaced, covered in jagged nubbins, but this stone had been polished until it was softly reflective. She hoped that meant the river had been used as a highway.

She set the light aside so she could see as she pulled everything out of her pack. When she'd checked the pack in the escape pod, she'd noticed the inflatable raft. At the time, she had been tempted to leave the raft behind to spare herself the weight, but decided it might provide shelter in the desert, if she could find nothing else.

The pack didn't contain anything she could use as a paddle, but it didn't matter. The river seemed to have a good current. She hoped it was flowing to the ocean and not a waterfall, but she would soon find out.

✷ ✷ ✷

Once she got the raft into the water, Raena scrambled to climb aboard. The river rushed with gathering speed away from the lonely house. Its course seemed to have been cleared of obstacles, so that Raena never encountered rapids or whirlpools. She stretched out in the bottom of the raft so that her head would not strike the ceiling, if ever it dipped toward her. In her cozy nest, she ate another bar and drank more water from her pack. After what seemed like hours, she slept again.

She woke when light caressed her face. The cave grew brighter as she neared its mouth. It did not seem to be daylight quite yet, but dawn was coming.

The scent of the air changed, as the water grew brackish.

The river spat her out into the ocean. Raena could see Kai City up on the cliffs a couple of kilometers down the coast, but the current was bearing her away, out to sea. She quickly collected her trash from the bottom of the raft, stuffed it into her pack, and then dove over the raft's edge. She swam parallel to the beach for a while, long enough to get out of the current.

When she broke free of the outflow, she set out toward shore. The pack made swimming slightly awkward, but she wasn't ready to abandon it yet.

✳ ✳ ✳

Although the hour was not long past dawn, Raena watched for signs of pursuit, whether her friends in the gray uniforms or more bounty hunters. Instead, she seemed to have the beach to herself for as far as the eye could see.

She sat in the sand to eat the last of the nutrition bars. She had become fond of their flavor, whatever it was. She considered saving a wrapper for Mykah, so he could stock some on the *Veracity*, but that future seemed so far away that she didn't give in to the temptation. Now that she knew they existed, maybe she would encounter them again.

She changed back into the dress she'd been wearing on Lautan. It was still slightly damp from being rinsed out in the Templar shower, but she figured wearing it made her look more like a tourist than Bihn's oversized shirt.

She pulled the survival tool out of the pack. Even though she knew weapons were outlawed on Kai, she wasn't prepared to give it up yet. She left the pack on the beach for someone else to find and started walking.

The isolation made it difficult for her to appreciate the morning's beauty. Rosy light stole across the empty beach. The total solitude was eerie enough that Raena began to hope that Kai City had not been evacuated. It would be miserable to find herself altogether alone on the planet. The way her luck had been going, that was a possibility.

Eventually she walked past a familiar trio of stone arches offshore. Not far beyond that, she found the boardwalk where she and Ariel had jogged on their first morning together on Kai. She wondered if Ariel ever felt nostalgic for that beautiful dawn.

That, she remembered now, was the morning she'd met Mykah. Funny how she'd felt so fond of Kai after that trip.

As Raena crossed the outskirts into Kai City, things seemed to be coming alive. She stopped to ask directions, but eventually she found a resident who could direct her to the Planetary Security station. She threw the survival tool in the incinerator outside.

Raena ran her fingers through her hair to comb the tangles out. After that, there really wasn't anything more she could do to fix herself up. She climbed the steps into the Central Security Station, took a seat in the anteroom, and waited her turn most politely.

They gave her a lot of time to rethink her decision. Stealing a ship, running away, would be so much more satisfying than simply sitting here. Once she ran, though, she would always be running. Kai already had hunters after her. No doubt Lautan could find something to blame her for, too. She could hide in Ariel's villa, never to go out again. She could alter her face and body so she wouldn't recognize herself. Or she could grow up and try to live according to the galaxy's rules.

Finally, the clerk called her number. The black-feathered bird creature at the window tipped its head to regard her with a shiny button eye.

"My name is Raena Zacari," she said. "The Business Council of Kai put a bounty on me. I'm here to turn myself in."

The Shtrell seemed bored by the whole process until it looked Raena up in its computer. "Oh, good heavens," it squeaked. "Really? You are turning yourself in?"

"Yes," Raena said, not showing the amusement she felt. "I escaped the hunters who'd captured me. Do I get to claim my own bounty?"

The bird must have triggered a silent alarm. An entire squad of Planetary Security agents poured into the waiting room. Raena turned slowly to face them, hands held straight out from her shoulders. As she knelt, she checked where the cameras were in the room. She gave them her best smile, hoping they were recording how docilely she gave herself up. Maybe her defender could show the recording to the jury on the first day of her trial.

She'd forgotten that Security on Kai didn't carry weapons, other than stun staves. No one seemed particularly like he wanted to stun her now. They just surrounded her, confused by the little barefoot human girl waiting calmly for their orders like she'd done this all before. Eventually, the commander ordered her up onto her feet and they marched her into custody.

Raena kept her face composed. She could have taken the whole gang of them down several times over. Security on Kai was even softer than she remembered—and the last time she'd been here, she'd stolen a staff from one of them in order to subdue Jain Thallian. She was pretty sure that stun staff was still riding around on the *Veracity*, wherever Mykah had squirreled it away.

None of these agents held their staves right. As she watched, one juggled and nearly dropped his. They left too big a margin around her and bunched up so close to each other that they would have been stunning each other if she'd made any threatening moves. Clearly they'd never captured an actual criminal.

Planetary Security turned her over to the city jail, whose guards didn't even have the benefit of helmets or armor. They ran the identity tests and got her booked. This crew also didn't carry weapons other than sleep grenades and more stun staves. Maybe they were hand-to-hand artistes, but Raena doubted it.

From what she'd seen so far, Kai was not going to provide her any protection if a couple of hardcore bounty hunters showed up to take her out of here. The gray militia could probably level the place with a dozen soldiers.

Oh, well. She'd already bought the ticket. Hopefully, she'd be allowed to talk to Ariel before long.

First, though, they delivered her to a cell somewhere in one of the jail's towers. Raena walked around the cell with one hand on the wall and her eyes closed, trying to get a sense of its size. It was smaller than her tomb had been, of course, but larger than her cabin on the *Veracity*. She supposed that counted as a blessing.

The cell even had a window. It was higher than her head, so she couldn't see out, but it opened to the air. Raena stood on the dry stone bench beneath the window and studied the wall behind it.

The cell's wall was rough black Templar-extruded stone. She thought she could see enough protrusions to form a climbable face. Anyone larger or heavier than Raena probably couldn't find enough to dig its toes into, but she felt disappointed. She had expected escape to seem challenging enough that planning for it would entertain her a while. Knowing that she could just waltz out of here any time she took a mind to made the prospect much less enticing.

Besides, where would she go? She'd already done the math about leaving Kai. For now, she would have to relax and just see what luck came her way.

* * *

Raena spent most of the day cursing the solitude of her cell before another creature was shoved inside with her. It was some form of living rock. It took one look at Raena and started pounding on the door.

"Oh, no, you don't!" it shouted. "You're not locking me up with a human. This is cruel! Let me out."

Raena remained seated on the sleeping bench, watching the show.

The creature kept glancing over its shoulder at her, making sure she didn't sneak up on it. It kept up its racket for a remarkably long time, considering it got no response at all from the guards outside.

Eventually, after what seemed like hours, it gave up. Whimpering to itself, it crept over to the far wall, where it squatted down and stared at Raena.

"Don't like humans?" Raena asked mildly.

"Don't talk to me!" it shouted. "Don't even look at me. I'll squash you like a bug."

"Okay," Raena said. She kept gazing at the creature without moving from her bench.

"I mean it. Don't look at me. I know what your kind is like."

"Really?" Raena asked. "I'm not even sure what kind you are."

"That's good. It means you can't manufacture some disease to wipe us out."

Not in here, Raena thought. She had the sense not to say that aloud.

* * *

Raena found herself dreaming of her imprisonment in the Templar tomb, shifting images of darkness and hunger and despair. She remembered the days when she sang every advertising jingle she had ever heard, the hours when she remembered the face of every person she had killed. She would work through the crewmembers of the *Arbiter*, recalling everything she knew about each one. She would remember every meal she'd ever eaten and every drug she'd ever sampled and every sip of anything she'd ever tasted. And still her imprisonment dragged on.

The darkness became more oppressive, almost solid, weighing down on her, crushing the breath from her.

Raena wrenched herself awake. Her roommate lay atop her in the cell on Kai, crushing Raena to the sleeping bench with the weight of its stone body.

Raena thrashed around, trying to dislodge the lumbering creature from atop her. Pain flared suddenly sharp and bright in her chest.

"Why don't you die, human?" the creature screeched at her. "I'm going to kill you. Hold still!"

Raena succeeded in wriggling out from beneath the creature. She bumped the creature off balance and knocked it to the dirt floor. It flailed on its back, screaming abuse.

It would have been funny, if she hadn't hurt so much. Pain shot through her with every breath. At least one rib was broken. Raena didn't even want to touch her torso to probe how many fractures she had.

She scuttled away from her cellmate, but nothing in the cell could qualify as a weapon, certainly nothing she could use against something clad in rock.

Raena huddled as far away in the cell as she could get. Maybe she could still climb up to the window, but it would mean dodging her cellmate's grasping arms, then scaling the wall. She wasn't sure she could put any weight on her right arm, to say nothing of crawling through the little window. And she didn't know where she was in the building or how far she might have to climb down on the outside.

So this was how it was going to end: dying in a jail cell on Kai, killed by a cellmate who attacked her in her sleep.

Raena laughed at herself, but that led to a wet cough that felt like she was being stabbed in the chest.

"Die!" her cellmate screamed. "Just die already!"

The other creatures in the cellblock started shouting for her cellmate to shut it, people were trying to sleep. The cacophony grew worse until Raena felt herself blacking out. She wedged herself against the wall, afraid that if she fell down, she would puncture a lung.

Anger made her shake. She didn't want to die. She wanted to see Ariel again, and Haoun, and Vezali, and Coni, and Mykah. She wanted to walk on the outside of the *Veracity*'s hull and look at the stars. She wanted to eat more of Mykah's inventive cooking. She wanted to swim in every ocean and buy every pair of black boots she saw and she wanted to fly on makeshift wings among the skyscrapers again. Dying was stupid. And this was a stupid way to die.

The guards finally burst into the cell, stun staves at the ready.

"Raise your hands," one of the guards ordered.

"Can't," Raena wheezed.

Her cellmate gloated, "Did I hurt you, little human? Did I break you? So fragile!"

One of the guards held out a hand to Raena. That was the last thing she saw as her knees buckled.

* * *

Raena woke in an infirmary ward. Cuffs pinned her limbs to a table. The pain in her chest had been replaced by a warmth that lingered on the edge of burning. That was better.

An orange-furred nurse noticed she was awake and came over to offer Raena a drink through a straw. The water was icy cold. Raena drank gratefully.

"How do you feel?"

"Better." Her voice sounded familiar again. "Did you reinflate my lung?"

"Yes. We're mending your bones now. You need to lie still to let the machine work. If you don't think you can do that, I will sedate you."

"I can do it," Raena promised.

"Would you like some entertainment? I can put the remote in your free hand."

"Actually, I'd like to call my sister."

"I'll connect it for you."

The nurse typed in the comm code Raena gave her. Raena was certain that everything would be recorded for use against her, but she was tired of fighting alone.

Eilif answered the call. The nurse looked from the image on the screen to Raena and smiled gently at the similarities. "I'll leave you two to chat."

Raena didn't correct her.

"Have you been injured?" Eilif asked.

"Attacked by my cellmate. They're mending me now."

"Shall I wake Ariel for you?"

"Please."

When Eilif went off on her errand, she left the channel open. Raena tried to puzzle out where Eilif and Ariel were. It wasn't Ariel's office on Callixtos, or onboard Ariel's racer. Definitely a ship, though. It looked old-fashioned, human-made, but not as antique as the *Veracity*.

Before she puzzled it out, Ariel appeared on screen. Her cheeks were flushed and her hair was coming loose from her braid.

Raena recognized what that meant. "Didn't mean to tear you away from anything important," she said by way of apology.

"Kavanaugh says hi," Ariel answered.

Raena laughed cautiously, so she wouldn't wiggle.

"Where are you?" Ariel asked.

"An infirmary on Kai."

"I heard you got arrested," Ariel said sympathetically.

"Oh?"

"Yeah. Small galaxy." Ariel's eyes probed Raena's face. "You all right?"

"Better. My cellmate attacked me in my sleep. Luckily, the guards stopped it from killing me."

Ariel made a note on a handheld. "Have you talked to a defender yet?"

"They haven't even arraigned me yet. Do you know what the charges are?"

"I know what was on your wanted poster. I'll look into seeing how long they can hold you without charges. And I'll get you transferred to a solitary cell, if that's okay."

"Might be safer. I get the feeling that someone somewhere doesn't want me to survive to be tried." Raena realized how paranoid that sounded, but didn't retract it.

"All right. Since you're one of the Foundation's wards, I should be able to negotiate better treatment for you."

Their eyes met and Raena got the feeling that Ariel understood everything Raena didn't say.

"Thanks, Ari. Tell Kavanaugh I say hi, too."

Ariel smiled and signed off.

Raena tried to call the *Veracity* next, but the comm code had been disabled. She hoped the kids were all right.

CHAPTER 8

U nder the bone growth accelerator, Raena drifted off again. For a change, her sleep was untroubled by dreams. When she woke at last, the burning in her ribcage had simmered down to a nice toasty warmth. She remembered not to stretch just in time.

She opened her eyes to find an unfamiliar man about to touch her shoulder. He wore a crisp cream-colored shirt beneath a brick-red jacket. His sandy hair had been trimmed close to this head and his eyes were an unremarkable brown in an unimpressive face. He swallowed audibly. "Are you really awake?"

She nodded. "Have you come from the consulate?"

"I'm the Deputy Consul on Kai."

"Did Ariel send you?"

He looked down at his manicured hands. "Ms. Shaad is well known for her work on humanity's behalf," he said. "You're the first of her wards that it's been my honor to meet."

Raena smiled, thinking that he was not the first diplomat she'd met. Instead, she said, "So far, I haven't been officially charged with anything. I haven't seen a defender. I haven't been able to contact my shipmates. And I've been hauled from one pleasure planet to another without any explanation. How will the consulate help me straighten this out?"

"Apparently, your arraignment was scheduled for this morning. I got it postponed, since you are unable to attend."

"Thank you," Raena said.

"There does seem to be an added level of drama to your case, Ms. Zacari. And the legal system on Kai is often full of drama."

"That doesn't bode well."

For the first time, the Deputy Consul smiled. "I will petition the court to reschedule your arraignment as soon as possible. You can't begin to prepare a defense until you know what you're being charged with."

"Thank you."

"Ms. Shaad's Foundation is arranging a defender for you. I'm not sure where he's traveling from, so I'm not sure when he will arrive. Therefore, I will accompany you to the arraignment, if he is unable to attend."

Raena wondered what that was costing Ariel. Clearly this all required some extra special making up to her sister, once things were settled.

"I've also spoken to the jail commandant. When you are transferred back to the jail, you will be placed in a solitary cell. He has been made to understand that your safety is his personal responsibility."

"I appreciate all you've done for me."

"The Shaad Family Foundation is a powerful ally," he said.

Raena nodded. She had clearly underestimated her sister when she thought of Ariel as simply insanely wealthy. She hadn't realized Ariel had any political power, but that came, no doubt, of heading up a humanitarian cause that no one could argue with—and having a hot temper and the money to see your will done.

"One last thing," the Deputy Consul said. "Kai doesn't have much of a broadcast entertainment industry, since most of the populace are transient visitors. Because of that, they record their legal proceedings for galactic broadcast."

"What?" That was an unexpected twist.

"You have the right to say no, but they would like to broadcast your trial."

"I don't want to become a spectacle."

"Understood. They will record the arraignment, but we can block its broadcast. Recording is not optional."

"I see. Thank you for warning me."

A different nurse came in. This one was a delicate lizard with limbs as thin as a bird's. She checked the readout on the bone accelerator. "I think you'll be out of here soon," she said cheerily.

"Then I'll take my leave," the Deputy Consul said. "Keep your head down and we'll try to get your case settled as quickly as possible."

"Thank you, sir."

The nurse leaned over Raena. "I need you to take the deepest breath you can."

Hesitantly, Raena breathed in, waiting for the pain to resume. It didn't.

"Good as new," the nurse chirped. "I'll go start the process to get you released back to the jail."

* * *

Her new cell was smaller than the first, but if that meant that it was hers alone, Raena decided not to mind. She stretched gently, making sure that everything inside her was really as good as new. From stretching, she progressed to a handstand, then to climbing the walls. This cell also had a high window. This time, she decided to find the path up to it in advance, in case she needed it again at a moment's notice.

Once she'd accomplished every time-killer she could think of, that left empty hours ahead of her. It was hard not to dwell on the last time she stood trial.

When the Imperial guards removed her from Thallian's torture device aboard the *Arbiter*, she had believed the end was nearly upon her. She hadn't eaten or slept in days; how many days, she wasn't sure. She could no longer stand on her own, so the guards carried her.

Treatment in the Emperor's private prison was much better. The prison guards fed her by hand until she could feed herself. They allowed her to shower. She could dress, finally. And best of all, Thallian could not touch her. She began to feel less like a scarecrow of herself. It didn't make sense to her that they treated her so well when all that stood ahead of her was a firing squad, but she savored every slight pleasure she had left. She so looked forward to escaping her life.

They brought her uniform to her at last. She dressed with care, polishing her boots and brushing her long straight hair. She knew this would be the last time Jonan ever got to see her, so she fixed herself up for him. She prayed he would be tortured by her memory.

The Imperial guards returned to escort her. She assumed they would take her to the prison square for summary execution. Instead she was marched into an auditorium and put on display as an example of what happened to those who flouted the will of the Empire.

The list of charges against her took most of the morning to present. Some of those things she regretted now: she wished she'd found some way to evacuate the prisoners from the mining prison, rather than leaving them to die when she vented their air into space. Of course, the Empire wasn't accusing her of the prisoners' deaths, only of destroying the prison. Despite her remorse over her mining prison escape, she didn't regret scuttling the quasar-class *Avalanche*. Those butchers deserved to die for what they'd done on Zaja IV. If any of them survived Raena's demolition of their ship, they would have found themselves on the wrong side of the tribunals after the Templar Plague. One way or another, they were all dead now.

During her show trial, Raena was relieved no one had calculated the civilian casualties for which she must certainly be responsible. Most likely, the Empire didn't care about them. They had enough evidence to kill her several times over, without worrying about all the collateral damage.

She claimed full responsibility for her crimes. Execution should have been inevitable. Her chief hope was that Thallian would be required to watch it.

It surprised her, then, that Thallian went so far out on a limb to plead for her life. He kept trying to present mitigating circumstances, to blame others as her instigators or accomplices. He argued that she was too young to understand what she had done, that she was too damaged to be truly responsible. Every word led him farther into the trap they'd set for him.

Raena didn't understand until much later, after the slab had closed on her tomb, that she had only been the bait. Her trial had never been about her guilt—only about Thallian's.

It was paranoid to think the same might be true now on Kai. Even so, Raena could not honestly think of any crime she'd committed since she'd walked out of the tomb that would require this level of multi-planetary collusion. No innocents had been hurt, either by her actions or inaction, since she left her tomb. She had damaged no property, except the Thallians'. As far as she knew, she hadn't even broken any laws, other than forging her new identity. If anyone was ever going to try her for war crimes committed in the service of the Empire, it wouldn't be a pleasure planet like Kai.

Despite that, Kai wanted her in jail badly enough to put a price on her head. The guys in gray had now chased her across three worlds. Given her history, Raena could not help but think those things were merely theater, distractions from whatever was really going on in the galaxy. She wondered how long she would have to wait to see the curtain pulled back.

That day and the next day passed in a haze of boredom, broken only by the arrival of meals. As prison chow went, the food here surpassed any she'd had before. Something could be said for being locked up in rich people's prisons, she thought.

* * *

Coni and the crew of the *Veracity* gathered with the other passengers in the yacht's lounge to look at Kai before they landed. The planet burned in shades of ember and coal against the blackness of space. As the ship came around, Kai City shimmered like a gaudy spill of jewels at the edge of the ocean.

Coni had liked Kai all right when she lived there. Her job as a social worker, checking on the humans employed in the service areas of the tourist city, had been interesting. She felt she had really been able to help people with the contradictory regulations and bigotry they encountered.

When Mykah suggested she run away with him, she hesitated. Who would help the clients she was leaving behind? But Mykah made it sound so tempting: to apply what she knew to helping more people on a grander scale, to change the galaxy, to become a pirate for good. It would be an adventure.

And it had been. She was proud to have had a hand in revealing the Thallians' hideout to the galaxy. She was relieved to have helped expose the Messiah conspiracy before it destroyed any more governments. She hadn't been able to do much social work aboard the *Veracity*, but she had helped Raena settle in to her new life. She was proud to call the reformed assassin her friend.

She understood why Mykah had come back to Kai, even though he'd said he never would. He was offended that they'd stolen his ship. He was outraged that they'd picked on Raena, who had done so much good for the galaxy, even if her credit for it wasn't widely known. Haoun was here because he'd become infatuated with Raena. He was more concerned about her as a person than as a symbol. Coni saw nobility in that. Vezali might have only come along for the ride. Sometimes it was difficult for Coni to understand why she did things.

Coni hoped this experience would cement them more together as a team. It could just as easily blow up and scatter them all farther apart.

At least, if their time on the *Veracity* had ended, she would be back on Kai, where she knew she had work to do. The trick would be persuading Mykah to stay with her there.

* * *

After Raena showered on her fourth day in jail on Kai, a quartet of guards showed up to escort her down to the court. She spent the walk counting cells along the hallway, the floors down in the elevator. Then she calculated how many prisoners the jail could hold if it was full.

She couldn't imagine that there was much serious crime on Kai. It wasn't like you could fly in, knock over a casino, and leave without Planetary Security getting in your way at some point. With only one city, it wasn't like you could land elsewhere on the planet without them knowing about it. Whether you went through one of Kai City's spaceports or not, they would have a record of you.

So who were all the other people locked up here? Was Kai arresting people on trumped-up charges, simply because they'd look good on camera? What was to stop the Business Council from jailing anyone they took a fancy to?

She didn't bother to ask the guards, none of whom were human. They were simply doing a job. To them, more prisoners meant steady paychecks.

The guards escorted her into a holding area near the courtrooms. They led her to a chair where she could wait. After she settled, they activated a forcefield around her. It spat and sparked, on the verge of shutting itself off. If she stumbled into it, she could probably short it out. Instead, she tried to look meek, a model prisoner.

She wondered if the Deputy Consul would come to her arraignment as he'd promised or if she'd be left to defend herself.

An hour or so passed. Other prisoners were taken in to their hearings. Raena watched them go, trying to assign crimes to them. None of them looked like hardened criminals. She saw no other humans.

The Deputy Consul breezed in at last, greeting her with a wave. Today he wore a burnished copper suit. "Nice to see you up and around."

"Thank you," Raena said. "I'm feeling much better now that I have a cell of my own."

"Good to hear it." He stared toward the courtroom door, as if he could hear something she could not over the forcefield. Raena noticed he had a line down his jaw where the shade of his makeup didn't match the color of his throat.

"Were you able to prevent them from broadcasting this hearing?" she asked.

He nodded unhappily. "As I told you, it's your choice about whether to broadcast or not. Sometimes they will offer you a bribe to reconsider."

They hadn't. Maybe that should surprise her more, but she was merely relieved.

She realized that the Deputy Consul might not get many chances to have his image broadcast across the galaxy. He'd dressed up for his big moment, just in case. She consoled him by saying, "Maybe they're waiting to see if I give them a good enough show today."

A bribe wouldn't change her mind, but he didn't need to know that.

Finally the bailiff summoned them into the courtroom. The guards seated her in a defendant's chair surrounded on three sides by a low wooden box to hold it separate from the rest of the courtroom. It faced a single magistrate in a shining white robe. The creature was an Eske, a little curry-colored rodent with big membranous ears. Raena had run across a shipful of them before, when the *Veracity* transported food to Capital City. Those Eskes hadn't liked humans very much.

"Raena Zacari," the black-feathered court clerk read, "you were welcomed as a visitor to Kai City six standard months ago, correct?"

The Deputy Consul looked to her to answer, so Raena said, "Yes."

"You were traveling with two other humans, Ariel Shaad of the Shaad Family Foundation and Gavin Sloane of Sloane Incorporated, a dealer in Templar artifacts."

They had been staying on Kai under aliases, but clearly someone had blown their cover. Raena considered briefly whether to deny it, but the Deputy Consul already knew about Ariel. As long as she needed his help, she wouldn't get him into trouble. "Yes," she admitted.

She expected the avian clerk to bring up the fight with Thallian's merry band of kidnappers, but instead it skipped straight ahead to, "When you left Kai City Spaceport, you kidnapped a young human and stole the Imperial-era transport on which he had been traveling."

"No," Raena said emphatically. It was a lie, but she committed to it wholeheartedly.

The magistrate came alert in his chair. "You deny the charges?" he squeaked over his translator.

"I do," Raena said.

"Consul?" the magistrate prompted.

The Deputy Consul stood up. The camera zoomed over to him. He posed to show off his good side. "Ms. Zacari, you understand that if this case goes to trial, your friends may be subpoenaed to testify."

Ariel was counting on that, Raena suspected. She always liked a good fight.

The consul added, "They may be subjected to charges of their own."

"Sloane is already dead," Raena said. "His corpse was broadcast around the galaxy on Mellix's last documentary."

At the mention of Mellix's name, the magistrate jumped back into the conversation. "If you plead guilty now, the fine is very reasonable. If we proceed to trial, the fine increases exponentially every day you are in court."

So this was all about money. "What happens if we go to trial and the Business Council can't prove their case against me?" she asked.

"They pay you," the Deputy Consul explained. "They reimburse you for the time you've been inconvenienced."

"Does that include the time I was locked up on Lautan, hauled across space by bounty hunters hired by Kai's Business Council, and traveling alone through Kai's desert?"

The Consul had a slight twinkle in his eye, but he turned to face the court clerk.

It said, "Yes. If the Business Council is found to have brought frivolous charges, you will be reimbursed for the sum of your inconveniences."

She was guilty as hell, but Raena finally understood what Ariel wanted her to do. "I demand a trial," she said.

"Very well," the magistrate said. "I'll leave it to the clerk to put it on the schedule. Next case."

✳ ✳ ✳

Haoun had never been inside a jail before. He assumed that Raena would be brought down to meet him in some common area, but instead, after he was passed through a screening machine, guards escorted him up to her cell.

The bare black stone room had nothing to brighten it except the small black-haired woman in her short blue dress. Haoun rushed over to take her in his arms. Raena grinned as if genuinely relieved to see him. He buried his nose in her throat. She smelled of sweat and worry, absolutely intoxicating.

She twisted to slip her tongue between his lips. He shuddered happily and clutched her closer.

"I missed you," she whispered.

"Are you okay?" He set her feet back on the floor. "Are they treating you all right?"

"Yes," Raena said. "It's a constant party in here."

She led him over to the stone bench that protruded from the wall. Once they'd settled, he noticed she was barefoot.

"No boots allowed?" he wondered.

"They confiscated them on Lautan and no one's bothered to find me a replacement."

"Shameful," Haoun said. "I'll get on that." He took one of her little feet into his hands and massaged it. It was filthy with black dust and cold to his touch.

His hand wandered up her thigh.

Raena dropped her hand on his and nodded toward the camera above the door. "I'm not opposed to an audience," she said, "but they have a creepy desire to broadcast the things they record. You have a family to think about."

He stared at the camera. "Have they been watching you all the time?"

"As far as I know."

"Even when you shower?"

She shrugged, not particularly upset by it. Maybe it was one of those things she had gotten used to, having spent so much time imprisoned.

"I'm so sorry this happened to you," he told her.

"Thank you. At least I finally got arraigned today."

"Finally?"

"They haven't seemed in any great hurry to start my trial. Do you have any idea when I'm getting out of here?"

"No. Ariel's supposed to arrive tonight. She says she'll take care of everything. Oh, and while I'm thinking of it, Mykah says you must insist on having your trial broadcast."

"No."

"It's imperative, he says. And it's your right."

"I don't want my life on the intragalactic news," Raena insisted. "That's what got me into this mess in the first place."

"What got you into this is a pleasure planet's greed," Haoun argued. "Kai has been looking to shake someone down to make up for the downturn in tourism. They could find you. They couldn't find Mellix."

"Mellix's documentary is what led them to me."

"Mellix's documentary isn't connected in any way to your arrest. It's just a coincidence."

"I wonder." She offered Haoun a little smile and slipped her other foot into his lap. He rubbed it as well.

"How did Kai know where to look for me?" she asked. "We hadn't been on Lautan for long."

"Apparently your defense of Mykah at the beach triggered Planetary Security to find your warrant from Kai. It just took them a little while to negotiate the price of your extradition. And it led to them seizing the *Veracity*. They seem to have mistaken it for some other ship." His eyes darted meaningfully at the camera. "We got here as quickly as we could."

Raena sighed. "No good deed goes unpunished."

Haoun changed the subject. "Have you been able to sleep in here?"

She nodded. "The dreams have been bad, but nothing unusual has happened in them."

"That's a relief, isn't it?" Haoun asked.

"Yes. If I have to be locked up, at least I'm not under attack."

A guard tapped on the door.

Haoun sighed. "I wish I could stay longer."

"No, go," Raena said. "Plan my defense. I want to get out of here in the worst way."

* * *

"We're on Kai finally," Ariel commed. "Come to Kavanaugh's docking slip. We need to talk."

So Mykah and the rest of the *Veracity*'s crew traced the coordinates she gave them to the battered retro-futurist Earth-made hauler. Kavanaugh's *Sundog* looked, as always, as if it had seen better days.

"I thought Kavanaugh always did his business in a bar," Coni said.

Mykah shrugged. "Guess they don't want to discuss the trial in public."

Kavanaugh waited for them at the hatch. He shook everyone's hand—even Vezali's tentacle—and ushered them onto his ship. He drew Mykah aside at the back of the group to ask, "How did you heal up?"

"Good as new, thanks to you. I kept the scar, though."

"Thought you might." Kavanaugh looked past Mykah after the *Veracity*'s crew. "How are the kids holding up?"

"It's been hard for everyone to have all our stuff stolen out from under us."

"How'd they get onto your ship?"

"The dockmaster on Lautan let them in. Never occurred to me to booby-trap it."

"I can show you how to set a password on the external lock," Kavanaugh offered.

"I'd appreciate it."

Once again, Kavanaugh's manner impressed Mykah. Tarik offered his expertise without making Mykah feel self-conscious or stupid. He hoped to grow up to be as cool as Tarik someday.

In the *Sundog*'s lounge, Ariel was holding court at the card table, glasses of green poured for everyone. It always startled Mykah that Ariel's skin was the shade of sunlight on the water, a lovely gold that looked like leisure, like money. Until you compared her with Eilif, Ariel looked perfect. Eilif, though, was so symmetrical she had obviously been engineered.

"Nice to see you again," he said gently.

Eilif dropped her gaze, rather than meet Mykah's eyes. "And you as well, Captain Chen."

"Sit down and have a drink, Mykah," Ariel ordered. "I want to hear what you know about the charges Raena is facing."

✳ ✳ ✳

When Mykah finished telling her everything the *Veracity* crew had learned so far, Ariel asked, "So you're sure we can refute the theft charge?"

Mykah looked to Coni, who nodded. "The *Veracity*'s provenance is seamless."

"Good. Then it's just a matter of making the court think that the dockmaster's office scrambled the recordings of two very similar Imperial transports. Can you do that?"

"Already have," Coni said.

Relieved, Ariel sipped her green. She wasn't sure how Raena had befriended these kids, but she'd done well for herself. They were first-class.

"What about the kidnapping charge?" Haoun asked.

"Since no one reported the boy missing," Ariel said, "Kai is simply hoping to make that charge stick. On Kai, Raena will be considered guilty until she demonstrates she's not, so it's all on her to prove she didn't capture the boy. Luckily, I have the solution to that," she promised.

"Are you going to defend her?" Vezali asked.

"No. One of my attorneys should arrive tomorrow. Corvas is on retainer to the Foundation to protect our kids when needed. Since

Raena's new identity kicked in, she's under the Foundation's aegis. Corvas is scary smart. He'll know how to game Kai's legal system." Ariel topped off their glasses of green and said, "The only thing that worries me is the murder charge."

"When did they charge her with murder?" Haoun asked.

"They haven't yet, but they will." Ariel sipped her drink. "Have you ever watched the courtroom show from Kai?"

Only Mykah had.

"I've been studying up," Ariel said. "The Business Council broadcasts their trials, as a way to shame anyone who acts up on Kai. If they bring charges that can be proven to be unfounded—and the judges rule against them—the Business Council pays out to the defendant. So once they get you in the system, they keep throwing charges at you until you can't rebut something. They can prove Raena killed Revan Thallian and some of his guards the day you all lit off in the *Veracity*."

"We've seen the fight," Coni said. "It was broadcast everywhere afterward. All that talk about how weapons-free worlds didn't keep people safe made Raena laugh."

"But you and Sloane," Mykah argued, "clearly you were attacked. Raena simply defended you."

"If she'd merely gotten us out of the fight," Ariel answered, "Kai might not be able to make the charge stick. But she moved on from the guys who grabbed us to subdue the whole party of Thallian's soldiers."

The *Veracity* crew protested, all voices raised at once. Ariel smiled. The ruckus reminded her of home.

"You're right," she said over them. "There wasn't anything else she could have done. If we'd run, the Thallians would have followed. They weren't going to let her go just because she cracked a couple of skulls. I know that—and you know that—because we know whom those soldiers belonged to. Kai still hasn't officially identified them."

Silence followed that announcement.

"If we name Revan," Mykah asked, "are we going to have to explain why he was after Raena?"

"Raena's daughter," Ariel reminded. "Since Raena's posing as her own daughter, we'll have to explain why the Thallians wanted my sister's daughter."

"They'd tracked Raena and Sloane to Brunzell," Coni said. "Raena left a dress behind in Sloane's apartment there. The Thallians found it and brought it onboard the *Raptor*. Raena found it in Revan's closet."

"There are probably Security recordings of the Thallians on Brunzell, then," Ariel said. "With those, we could prove they were hunting her before they came to Kai."

"I'll find them," Coni promised.

Mykah asked, "Are you going to connect Jain with murdering the guy who helped get Raena out of her tomb?"

Kavanaugh interrupted quietly, "His name was Tom Zhao Lim."

Mykah had forgotten Kavanaugh had been the boss of the grave-robbing crew. "I'm sorry," he said quickly. "I never knew his name."

Ariel shook her head. "I'm sorry, too, Tarik. As much as I would like to solve Lim's murder for the galaxy, I don't think we need to bring it up in this court at this time. The galaxy hasn't connected the murder to the Thallians or to humanity at all. I don't want to add any fuel to the 'humans are violent and dangerous' debate. Jain was punished for his crime."

Haoun interrupted. "Raena said he hung himself."

"That is true," Eilif said quietly.

Ariel touched Eilif's hand in sympathy. "We should keep Jain's crimes separate from Raena's. If she'd killed him on camera, we might need to justify her, but since she only took him home—where his father meted out the punishment—that's beyond the scope of Kai's justice."

Mykah slid a surreptitious look at Eilif. What would it be like, he wondered, to know someone you considered your son was a savage murderer? To watch him die, condemned by your husband—whose crimes were even more monstrous and extensive? Eilif was so guarded that the depth of her pain might never be known.

"All right," Ariel said. "Kai allows one visitor per prisoner per day to their jail."

"I'll go back," Haoun said. "I want to make sure she's okay."

"You've seen her already?"

"I went this afternoon. She looked better than I expected. The sun comes in her cell, so it's warm in there, but they're feeding her well. She's sleeping and able to exercise. She's still wearing the dress she had on when she was arrested, though. And she's barefoot. They confiscated her boots on Lautan and she hasn't gotten anything to replace them."

"I don't think Kai has jail uniforms," Ariel said. "I'll get her some clothing, so you can deliver it tomorrow morning. Where are you staying?"

"There's a boarding house near the delivery docks," Mykah said. He pulled the coordinates up on his handheld and sent them to Ariel's comm bracelet. "Haoun and I have stayed there before."

"Is it rough?" Ariel asked.

Mykah met her eyes. "Not if we're together."

She nodded, understanding what exactly he meant by that: humans were tolerated in mixed company. "I would be glad to put you up someplace more centrally located," Ariel said.

"Let us talk it over," Mykah said. "We're okay where we are, but if the trial drags on . . ."

"I'll do what I can to get things expedited," Ariel promised, "but not until Corvas gets here."

* * *

The advantage of being confined alone was that she had her own shower. Kai rationed water, so Raena couldn't stand in it all day long, but she treated herself to killing time under the water as often as she could.

Today the shower cut off before she was done luxuriating in it. "You have a visitor coming up," a guard said over the comm.

Raena rubbed her head dry and wrapped the towel around her body. The blue dress she'd been wearing when she was arrested on Lautan was getting threadbare from being worn so often, but she shouldered into it anyway.

When Haoun strode across her threshold, Raena melted gratefully into his arms. "How long can you stay?"

"I'm just making a delivery," he said. "They're going to call you for your trial today, but Ariel wanted you to have something decent to wear."

He handed her a clear plastic shopping bag. It held a shimmering metallic blue dress. Raena tugged off her old dress to slip into the new one. Haoun stood back out of her way, but watched her avidly.

The dress wrapped around her in such a way that it implied more curves than Raena actually possessed. The loose skirt fell past her knees. She spun around to make it swirl. Ariel always did have nice taste in clothes.

"No boots?" Raena asked.

"Apparently, boots are proscribed. Or maybe only for you, I'm not clear. It feels like they change the rules whenever they choose to." He handed her a pair of soft black slippers.

Can't kill anyone with these, Raena thought, but didn't say anything aloud. She looked up to see Haoun was probably thinking the same thing. He laughed at her.

"Brush your hair?" he asked. "Or is it meant to look like that?"

"Don't you like it?" she teased, petting it upward.

"I like it, but you're not dressing for me."

"Pity."

✳ ✳ ✳

After she'd groomed herself, Raena came to sit in his lap. Haoun petted her back gently, careful not to snag his claws in the fabric of her new dress. "Nervous?" he asked.

"Not really," she said, but he felt the flutter of her heart beneath her thin, soft skin. He wished he could do something to make the waiting easier.

"Have you ever been in jail?" Raena asked.

Haoun was surprised they hadn't had this conversation before. "Never."

"Never been caught?" she teased.

"You know how cautious I am." Caution had cost him his mate and children, but he hadn't really thought caution was a bad thing. He'd always been cautious, up until he asked Raena if she'd play the jet scooter game with him on Lautan.

She rested her head against his chest. "Regretting anything?"

"Only that I should've taken up with you sooner."

"My bunk's too small," she pointed out.

"Vezali could fix it." After the words left his translator, he wished he could call them back. What if she didn't want to be with him on the *Veracity*? What if this didn't mean anything to her, if she was only glad of his company because she'd been trapped in solitary confinement and she was lonely, bored, and frightened?

"I'd rather come sleep in your nest," she said. "Much more comfortable."

"Really?" he asked hopefully.

Raena said decisively, "Really."

He wove his long fingers between her short ones. "No regrets," he promised.

Their moment was ruined by a voice announcing over the comm, "Prisoner Zacari, the court is preparing for you now."

Raena stood up and shimmied the dress down into place. "Do I look scary?"

"You look nice," Haoun said. "Good luck today."

"Thank you. Will you be there?"

"Coni is saving me a seat in the courtroom."

"I haven't met my defender yet," she said abruptly.

"Ariel said he is on Kai," Haoun soothed. "He'll be there for you today."

"What if he is attacked by those soldiers in gray? What if someone prevents him from getting to me on time? What if—"

He cut her off. "You aren't alone. Ariel is here. If the defender gets held up, we will think of something. We are all in this."

Raena's breathing grew choppy. Haoun thought back over the time he'd known her. Before she went alone down to the Thallian home-world to wipe them out, before she'd gone to Capital City to protect Mellix, before she led the assault on the Outrider androids: before any of the attacks, she had been calm, relaxed, in her element. Only when she'd fled the New Bar after seeing herself in Mellix's documen-tary had she seemed anxious. This was even worse.

"This will be over soon," he promised. "Then I owe you a bubble bath."

A voice said over the comm, "Prisoner Zacari, stand away from the door."

Raena snatched up Haoun's wrist and pulled him with her to the opposite side of the cell. She turned around to face the wall and put her hands up on it at shoulder height.

"Do I need to turn around, too?" he asked, as nervous as she had been.

"No, you're fine." She seemed calmer suddenly. "Just keep your hands where they can see them, step out of their way politely, and don't make any twitchy moves."

Four guards came into the cell. Three carried stun staves. One of them moved to cover Haoun as another advanced on Raena with an old-fashioned set of shackles. She submitted docilely as he bound her wrists and ankles, then attached the leads that prevented her from taking a long step or raising her hands above her waist—or would have done, if she hadn't been so tiny.

Raena kept her face blank, as if she hadn't noticed she was barely hobbled. Where nerves had made her fluttery before, now she looked very, very still.

It made Haoun think of a yaska, a fuzzy little prey animal from his home world that froze when it became aware you were hunting it. It let you think it was frightened, before it leapt up to bite at your eyes. They could burrow into your brain and kill you in the space of a breath.

The guards formed up around her and marched her out the door. Haoun followed, but one directed him back to the visitors' elevator. He hoped Raena wouldn't kill the guards on the way to the courtroom.

*　*　*

Once Haoun had lumbered out of earshot, one of the guards—a twiggy tree creature—asked, "Who's that?"

"My boyfriend."

The guards burst into laughter. Raena just smiled to herself.

"I think she's serious," the canine guard pointed out. He reminded her of Skyler, who had traveled on the *Panacea* with Kavanaugh, when they were young.

"That's just sick," the frog-faced guard said. "You humans will throw yourselves on anything, won't you?"

Raena didn't bother to point out that she hadn't made the first move. She also didn't point out that the galaxy had done a pretty thorough job of spreading humans thin across space. No matter what she said, people like these would find a way to be disgusted.

She just hoped that whatever magic Ariel was preparing, they could all get out of here soon.

CHAPTER 9

The jailers escorted Raena back down to the holding cell at the courthouse. She sat on the same rickety chair and again had to concentrate on not overloading the forcefield by accident. She worried whether her defender would arrive in time, or if someone would contrive an accident for him. If he wasn't able to defend her, would the Deputy Consul step up again? Or Ariel? Her sister didn't have any official legal training that Raena knew of, but Ariel learned her way around a binding contract at an early age.

A bipedal lizard dressed in a flamboyant yellow and orange robe scurried over to her. He was slim and chisel-faced, with eyes that moved independently as if on turrets. He wore a translator on his chest like a flashy medallion. "I am Tomur Corvas. Ariel Shaad hired me to defend you in this matter. It's my pleasure to meet you, Ms. Zacari, although I wish it had been under better circumstances."

His voice sounded like a series of hisses and sighs, but the translator changed it to a musical tenor.

"Thank you for taking my case."

He waved that away with hands that had no fingers, only two opposable sides so that he could grasp things. "This area is not recorded for broadcast, but it is probably monitored, nonetheless. Let's proceed as if everything we say here is on the record."

"Understood," Raena said.

"Ms. Shaad filled me in on your case. I have spoken to most of your crewmates from the *Veracity*. The information they've given me will form the basis of your defense. You are not required to address the court yourself, but you are welcome to, if you like. Also, we should talk about whether your trial will be allowed to be broadcast."

"I prefer not to make a galactic spectacle of my life."

"You are already a celebrity after the Messiah documentary."

"It was not my wish to appear in that."

He nodded, but said smoothly, "Captain Chen points out that the case before us references business practices that may have wide-ranging implications. He encourages you to reconsider."

That sounded like something Mykah would say. Raena asked, "What does Ariel suggest?"

"I would prefer not to quote her, but she agrees with Captain Chen."

That didn't surprise Raena, either. If there was a fight to be had, Ariel would be all for having it in public. "All right," Raena said at last. "If it's your recommendation that I allow it to be broadcast, I will."

Afterward, she would reconsider her stance against having her appearance permanently altered.

Corvas pulled a handheld from his satchel and made a swipe across it, sending a message he had already loaded. "Yes," he said, when he looked up again, "I would definitely recommend it. You're much more likely to get a fair hearing if Kai feels that the galaxy is watching."

That was the first time anyone had offered a context she understood. Raena already appreciated having the lizard on her side.

"I don't know how the judicial system on Kai works," she admitted.

"The Business Council is the planetary government of Kai. For the most part, all serious cases are brought by the Business Council against tourists, although tourists, tour operators, and shopkeepers may sue each other as well. Broadcasting the Business Council's trials started as an advertising ploy to demonstrate how colorful—and safe—Kai was. It has morphed into a moneymaking venture, particularly since the tesseract flaw's impact on tourism. To generate more income, the Business Council also sells tickets to audience seats in the courtroom."

Raena nodded for him to continue.

"Three judges will preside over your case. They will be drawn by lot to represent a variety of people. They will have to reach a consensus. Otherwise, they'll declare a mistrial and we will have to go through this whole process again, presenting new evidence each time. The judges may be hostile to you, because that makes for better theater and draws more viewers."

"What are the odds of getting a human judge?"

"Zero. There are no human judges on Kai."

Raena would have been surprised if there had been. "What are the odds of having a mistrial declared and needing to go through this ordeal again?"

The lizard made a gargling sound that Raena realized was a chuckle. "Most trials on Kai do end in a mistrial the first time. Several have been dragging out for planetary years. That's more lucrative for the players involved. However, I will do my best to see that you receive a definitive judgment the first time through."

"Thank you."

He inclined his head. "I've been on retainer for the Shaad Family Foundation for a decade. I know Ms. Shaad has no patience for wasting time."

To put it graciously, Raena thought.

"So the judges will be introduced. The court clerk will read the charges. We can choose to deal with the charges in any order that we like. We ask to see the evidence they have against you, then we are required to prove your innocence. As you've noticed, you are presumed to be guilty and the burden is on us to demonstrate that you are not. It's quite likely that additional charges will be brought during the course of the trial. We will deal with those as they arise."

"What outcome is Kai hoping for?" Raena asked.

"This is all about money. Kai does not have a prison for long-term incarceration, so prisoners who cannot defend themselves against the charges are heavily fined. If they cannot pay the fines, they are transported to Farrington Prison at their own expense and incarcerated until their fines can be met."

Raena didn't know that prison by name, but as she was not going back to any prison ever, it didn't really matter. She would kill herself first.

"Kai has very little in the way of violent crime—the lack of weapons and the general wealth of the visitor population limits the sorts of trouble that occur here."

"What about the workers?"

Both the lizard's eyes rotated to look at her.

"When Captain Chen worked on Kai," Raena said, "he was harassed by anti-human bullies. Did he have any recourse?"

"No. In cases where violence is discovered amongst the workers, both parties are fined and exiled from Kai. Since they've allowed Captain Chen to return, it's likely he never pressed charges."

No wonder Mykah had been so eager to get out of here when Raena initially offered him command of the *Veracity*.

The courtroom guards marched toward Raena's chair. "Ah, good," Corvas said. "Time to get started."

Both his eyes rotated back toward Raena. "Trust me," he said. "I'll get you out of this."

* * *

The guards frogmarched Raena into the courtroom. This time they locked her shackles to the legs of the defendant's chair so that she could stand when addressed by the judges, but she couldn't roam.

The courtroom Mistress of Ceremonies was a feline creature with overdeveloped feminine attributes that threatened to spill from her tiny tightly-laced dress. She introduced Raena as the former bodyguard of a Melisizei "businessman" and a ward of the humanitarian

Shaad Family Foundation. The cameras buzzed over to close in on Ariel, who smiled at them and waved.

The court clerk was a shiny black bird, maybe the same who'd attended the arraignment hearing. It read over the charges being brought by the Business Council and noted that Raena had requested a trial, as was her right.

Two cameras buzzed over to get a close-up of Raena's face. She ignored them, looking instead at her judges. As Corvas promised, there were three of them: a gray-skinned female with oversized blue eyes, a twiggy insect creature, and a rock creature similar to the one that attacked her in her cell. That couldn't be good. For all that Raena could tell them apart, it might be the same rock creature. All three judges wore matching white robes that flowed to the ground. They sat on thrones facing the courtroom.

"We can begin as soon as the defense is ready," the gray female said.

Corvas looked to Raena, who nodded.

"The first of the charges against my client that we would like to challenge is that she stole an Imperial-era diplomatic transport." The defender pressed a key on his desk to show the image of Raena's wanted poster.

The audience in the courtroom reacted to the sight of the little woman in a short parrot-blue sheath dress, her knee-high leather boots, and the Stinger pistol in her hand. Raena heard grumblings about the violent nature of humans, about making yourself feel bigger with a gun in your hand.

"In the image, is your client carrying a weapon on Kai?" the rock judge asked.

The defender turned to Raena, who spoke up: "Yes, sir, I was."

Corvas said smoothly, "She hasn't been charged with that, your Honor."

"I'm sure the Business Council will rectify that," the insect judge rasped.

The defender glanced down at Raena, who shrugged. Corvas said, "We will not contest the charge."

Raena wondered how much the fine would be. Was there any chance it would equal time served without charges being filed?

"Where are you in this image?" the rock judge demanded.

"A docking slip at Kai City Spaceport," Raena said.

"What's the designation of the ship visible behind you in the image?"

"I'm not sure of its designation," she answered. "The ship is called the *Veracity*. It's been my honor to serve on it since I left Kai."

"The dockmaster of Kai City Spaceport claims this ship is in fact the *Raptor*."

Corvas asked, "The *Raptor* is also an Imperial-era diplomatic transport?"

"Apparently."

"I'm not familiar with the *Raptor*, your Honors," Raena said.

"It landed on Kai the same day as you left."

Raena looked to her defender, unsure how to respond to that. Corvas said, "I have not been able to find any evidence linking my client to the *Raptor*. Will the court show us the basis of the theft charge?"

The clerk played the recording of an Imperial-era ship landing in a docking slip. After the engines had cooled, the Thallian crew disembarked. Raena got her first unguarded look at Revan Thallian, older brother of her nemesis.

Oh, she'd seen Revan's video log aboard the *Veracity*, after Coni had broken its encryption. In those recordings, made privately and intended to be viewed only by his younger brother, Revan had spoken as if to his commander. The video recorded on Kai left no doubt he could rise to command when needed.

Revan was clean-shaven, where Jonan wore a spade-shaped beard. Revan held himself like a prince as he dealt with the dockmaster and ordered his hit squad around, but he didn't have the air of complete disdain that his psychotic little brother used to affect. Raena wondered if she would have liked Revan if they'd ever had a chance to talk.

The recording cut, then resumed when Jain Thallian raced into the docking slip on a jet bike. He parked his bike, hopped off of it, and scurried up the ramp to the ship's lock.

A moment later, Raena leapt down atop the hull of the ship. She appreciated her own three-point landing, with the stun staff held behind her at a precise angle. "Such a badass," she heard Haoun say, somewhere in the gallery to her left. Raena kept her face blank, but she agreed with him.

In the recording, she slipped over the edge of the ship's hull and went after Jain. The camera was in the wrong place to see her stun him and drag him onto the ship.

Not much time passed before she came back off the ship and shot out the surveillance camera in the docking slip. The screen filled with snow. The clerk turned the recording off.

"Looks like the Business Council needs to charge you with carrying a stun stick, too," the gray judge said.

"We will not contest it," Corvas said. Raena was glad. If he had wanted to challenge that charge, she would have to explain where the stun stick had come from—and she didn't want to admit she'd taken it from a member of Planetary Security when she stole his jet bike to follow the boy. Better to defuse the whole explosion.

Corvas seemed just as eager to get the trial back on track. "To clarify," he said, "we have a recording of the *Raptor* landing on Kai. Has the court identified the men who stepped off of it?"

The clerk consulted the dockmaster's records and read a list of names. Before Raena could say anything, the defender spoke up for her. "Your Honors, my client would like to correctly identify the leader of this group." He turned to Raena.

"The man issuing the orders is Revan Thallian," she said.

Corvas swiped his crabbed hand across his handheld and put Jonan's old War-era wanted poster up on the screen. "The court no doubt recognizes Jonan Thallian, architect of the genetic plague that annihilated the Templars." He ignored the angry outbursts from the courtroom audience. Beside Jonan's photo Corvas put up a still taken from the footage of Revan Thallian on the Templar tombworld. Finally, he added a still image of Revan taken from the recording they'd just watched. "This is Revan Thallian, as identified by my client and the documentaries about the looting of the Templar tombs. You can see the obvious resemblance to his infamous brother."

The insect judge said, "You're telling us that one of the Thallians came to Kai."

Over the racket behind her, Raena said clearly, "Yes, your Honor. In fact, if his body has not been destroyed, it is lying unclaimed in Kai City's morgue right now."

A roar of outrage greeted that remark.

The judges exchanged a glance, then stood as one. The gray female said, "This court will adjourn for the rest of the morning or until we can establish the truth of this allegation."

The defender leaned over to tell Raena, "Nicely done." Then he stepped back so that the bailiff could unlock the shackles that held Raena's legs to her chair. The bailiff and a guard with a stun staff marched her out of the courtroom.

* * *

When the court came back in session after a lunch that rivaled one of Mykah's pasta creations, Kai City's coroner was called to the stand. He had run a hasty genetic scan of the unidentified human corpses in his freezer. To his horror, he found that one directly matched Jonan Thallian, the notorious mass murderer. He apologized profusely for not identifying Revan Thallian sooner. Shuddering with disgust, he asked permission to destroy the body.

The court granted it.

Corvas came to speak with Raena while the bailiff tried to calm the enraged audience in the courtroom.

"Why did they keep his body all this time?" Raena asked quietly.

"Kai hoped that his family would identify and claim the corpse, at which point they would have been charged for six standard months' cold storage. Now that Kai knows who he was, they are in a hurry to prevent any more Thallians from coming to the planet."

"They know all the Thallians are dead, right?" Raena asked.

"Not all of them," Corvas said enigmatically. Raena shivered.

* * *

Eilif stared at the video screen in Kavanaugh's lounge, where they had been watching the broadcast of Raena's trial. Eilif blinked, startled to find her eyes so dry. She had known Revan died on Kai. She had known that Raena killed him. Jain reported those things when he'd returned home. But to discover that Revan's body still lingered, anonymous and unclaimed after all this time, was as painful as being stabbed.

Eilif didn't know what she had expected to have happened to Revan's body: some kind of release from this world, at least. She'd vaguely supposed that he must have been unceremoniously dumped into a pauper's grave or cremated and scattered to Kai's desert winds—anything, other than trapped in this ignominious state of waiting.

She wanted to claim him now. Unfortunately, even in the unlikely event that they let her have his body, she couldn't take him home to lie with his brothers. Raena had obliterated the Thallians and burned the castle down. She hadn't wanted to leave anything left to clone.

Eilif's eyes no longer registered the courtroom drama on the screen. The grief she had not allowed herself to feel before submerged her. Of all the Thallians, Revan had behaved gently with her. He laughed with her sometimes, told her stories. He treated her like a friend, rather than a family possession. Secretly in her heart, Eilif had loved him.

She believed Revan had died without knowing that. Jonan would have killed her if he'd ever had any indication she was unfaithful, even in her thoughts. She wasn't sure what Jonan would have done to his beloved older brother. To protect Revan even more than herself, Eilif had never breathed a word.

She excused herself and retreated to the tiny cabin Captain Kavanaugh set aside for her, where she could mourn privately.

*　*　*

Following the coroner, the court called Kai's dockmaster to the witness stand. He faced a lot of questions from the judges about how he could allow a Thallian onto the weapons-free planet without confirming his identity. Raena didn't pay much attention, because she could see where the case was headed now. Once the dockmaster had been discredited over his failure to recognize and detain a man sentenced to death by the galaxy, it would be easy to prove he couldn't tell the difference between two very similar Imperial-era diplomatic transports.

Raena felt mildly sorry for the dockmaster. No doubt he was just doing his job, as decreed by the Business Council. The spaceport probably paid exorbitant taxes, which would be more difficult to meet now that tourist travel had tapered off. The spaceport might even have a quota of ships to impound and auction off. Raena wondered if this was a new scam, or one Kai had worked flawlessly before. Maybe all the pleasure planets did it.

Raena glanced around the courtroom. Ariel sat in the gallery on the left side of the room, where the VIPs were separated from the rabble. The *Veracity*'s crew sat beside her. The Deputy Consul sat nearby. He nodded when he noticed her looking at him.

Ariel wore her standard uniform: a pair of soft, tight dove gray trousers above some complicated woven wire sandals that did not look at all comfortable. Today she'd buttoned her white blouse enough to seem fairly chaste. She unconsciously twirled an unlit spice stick in her fingers.

It felt like ages since Raena had taken a real, long, appraising look at her former mistress. Ariel's honey blond hair had grayed at the temples. Time had whittled the softness of her body to leanness. Although she had the resources to hold it at bay, she had chosen to let life mark her face. She looked strong and compassionate.

More than being a spoiled heiress now, Ariel had become a grand dame. She was just as passionate and faithful as ever, and she still loved Raena like a sister. Kai might have won this case, if they'd targeted anyone else. Instead, they'd underestimated Ariel's ferocity. Now that they'd gone and made Ariel Shaad angry, she would see this fight to the end, until everyone who'd attacked Raena had been destroyed.

Corvas put an image on the screen of the *Raptor* taken from the Kai City Spaceport recording, alongside a similar image of the *Veracity* from Lautan. He quizzed the dockmaster on the finer points of telling one ship from another. The poor stuttering toad creature seemed on the verge of tears.

Now that the trial had hit its stride, Raena started to think beyond it. For a change, she had a debt that she wanted to repay. She wondered what she could do for Ariel to thank her for organizing her defense. What could you give a woman who could purchase anything?

Raena considered what Ariel might want. She had wanted Sloane, the one man whose loyalty she had been unable to buy, but Sloane was dead. Family was important to Ariel. She still lived with her mother in the compound where she'd grown up. She'd raised her adopted orphans there. And she'd never married, because that would have limited her freedom.

Raena wished she could have been the companion Ariel deserved. Ariel needed someone who understood the essential goodness of her nature, someone who could ignore the flash of Ariel's temper and would support her do-gooding crusades. Someone who could co-parent the strays she continued to take in. Someone like Tarik Kavanaugh. Raena wondered if there was anything she could do to encourage Ariel in that direction.

Really, living in Ariel's shadow had been the best part of Raena's life, up until she set foot on the *Veracity*. Even so, she never wanted to be planet-bound again. Only in space, only in motion, did Raena feel safe.

It was an illusion, she knew, but every bounty hunter that had ever captured her had taken her on a planet. The Thallians had attacked her on a planet. She'd spent decades imprisoned on a planet. The *Veracity*, while traveling: that felt like home.

And there was Haoun to consider now. Raena enjoyed his company because the pilot didn't put any limits on her. She understood that he loved his kids and held out hope of someday coming home to them. He didn't want to settle down with Raena. He simply took pleasure in touching her, savoring her warmth and flavor, in making her happy.

The relationship was perfect, as far as Raena could tell. They both enjoyed it, didn't ask too much from it, and got what they needed out of it. Someday it would dissolve naturally, but for now, Raena looked forward to resuming it when Kai finally let her go.

She looked up out of her thoughts to find Mykah had taken the stand.

"My crew and I," he said, "we're working people. We saved our money, pooled it together, and bought the *Veracity*. Vezali has worked hard to refurbish the ship and make it a home for us. Then to have Kai issue an impound order for it without

allowing us to settle the fees first—without so much as presenting us a bill—one has to assume that it is far more lucrative for
Kai City Spaceport to steal small independent ships and auction
them off, rather than collect what is legitimately owed to them in
docking fees."

The twiggy judge asked, "But you don't dispute that the *Veracity*
left Kai without paying its docking fees?"

"No, sir. My first officer looked for the receipt for those fees and we
haven't been able to find it. Of course, we haven't been allowed back
onto our ship to look for it in the *Veracity*'s memory, so we've had to
do everything at a distance. However, it's possible, with the confu-
sion between the *Raptor* and the *Veracity* at Kai City Spaceport, that
the wrong ship was billed for our docking fees. That's for the court to
decide. We, however, are ready to pay the fee for the hours that the
Veracity was on Kai before we took possession and left in it."

"We'll see if we can get that calculated for you," the rock judge
said.

"Thank you. I would like to be able to compare the amount we
owe against the money we've lost by having our home stolen away
from us on Lautan, the expenses we've accrued to travel back to
Kai, and the wages we've lost while trying to resolve this matter. As
you know, accommodations on Kai are not cheap. None of us can
work until we get our equipment back. Luckily for us, the crew of
the *Veracity* has collected some significant rewards for revealing the
whereabouts of the *Arbiter* survivors, the Thallian tampering with
the Templar tombs, and the resurgence of the Messiah drug into the
galaxy, so we have been able to afford to come get our ship back. But
another crew who had not been so lucky and well-compensated as we
have been—say, a crew delivering tourists to Kai or bringing in food
or liquor—would simply have lost everything they owned because of
an accounting mistake."

He paused to check he had the camera's attention. "I would like the court's assurances that this wanton theft of an independent, cooperatively owned ship, without warning or recourse beyond traveling to the planet of the thieves, is not common practice on Kai. I want to know this was a one-time error—and not an ongoing pattern of abuse."

The gray judge collected herself enough to say, "That's a grave accusation, Captain Chen. The court will explore whether Kai City Spaceport is impounding other ships, or if yours was singled out. Thank you for bringing the matter to our attention."

"I appreciate your assistance, your Honors. And I look forward to resuming possession of our ship."

* * *

When the court adjourned for the day, Ariel invited the crew of the *Veracity* to come by the *Sundog* after dinner.

Coni decided they should bring a gift this time, instead of just showing up to drink Ariel's expensive liquor. Mykah tracked down a box of chocolates. He knew the clerk at Chocolatier Rouge from his days of waiting tables on Kai. She cut him a deal.

This time Ariel met them at the *Sundog*'s hatch. She took one more drag off her spice stick, then threw it down to the tarmac and ground it out with the sole of her sandal. "Thanks for coming."

"What's happened?" Mykah asked.

"This isn't regarding Raena," she said. "Come in before you ask any more."

* * *

A young woman met them just inside the hatch. She had deep blue eyes and skin so pale it looked like ivory. She was dressed like Ariel in tight trousers and a blouse with not enough buttons. She also carried a very large sidearm.

"This is my daughter Gisela," Ariel said.

Gisela said, "I'm so honored to meet the crew of the *Veracity*."

Mykah laughed as if he thought she was teasing, but as Gisela shook their hands, Coni could tell that the girl was serious. She was starstruck.

"Come on back," Ariel directed. "There's someone else you need to meet."

Kavanaugh and Corvas sat in the lounge with Eilif and someone that Coni didn't recognize. This human's black hair hung loose like a veil, shielding the face. Coni heard Mykah's sharp intake of breath as soon as he saw the figure, but she didn't understand why—until the boy looked up. His eyes glowed a vivid gray. Except for the length of his hair, he looked exactly like Jain Thallian.

"This is Jim Zacari," Ariel said.

"You took her name?" Haoun asked. The translator did not do justice to the growl in his voice.

"I didn't know how else to honor her," the boy protested.

"This is your defense to the kidnapping charge?" Vezali guessed.

"Yes," Eilif said quietly. "Jimi will pass for Jain."

"Does anyone have a problem with that?" Ariel asked. "Jim is taking an enormous risk to break his anonymity. We need to be united in supporting him, because we know how shaky Security on Kai really is. Either I feel that Jim will be safe, or I won't put him in that courtroom."

"We need to hear his story first," Mykah said. "All we know about the boys was learned by watching Jain."

"Raena didn't tell you about me?" The boy's voice held the same quiet tone as his mother's.

Mykah was the only one to answer. "I didn't know any of the clones survived, until I saw the message Ariel forwarded to Raena."

"Did she ever get a chance to see that?" Ariel asked.

"No one saw it but me," Mykah answered. "I went straight off to pay our docking fees so we could leave Lautan, but the ship was impounded before I got back. Then Raena got arrested right in front of us. We destroyed the message when we overwrote the *Veracity*'s memory."

"Any of you mentioned it to her yet?"

"No," Haoun said. "We agreed not to say anything, until she could do something about it."

"We were afraid she'd bust out of jail," Mykah said. "Then things would be worse."

"Things might be getting better," Ariel promised, "but you need to drink first, before we tell you how."

Kavanaugh passed around bottles of ale. No one wanted to sit beside the Thallian boy, so Ariel sat on one side of him and Eilif took the other. The crew of the *Veracity* stood around awkwardly.

"Peace offering." Mykah set the box of chocolates on the table.

Ariel grinned. "This is a treat, Mykah. Thank you." She pulled the lid off the box and peeled back the wrapping paper inside. "Jim, you've probably never had these before." She picked one out with her manicured nails.

The boy held his hand out flat, then lifted the chocolate to examine it. "What is it?"

"Chocolate-dipped orange peel," Mykah said.

They watched the boy discover chocolate. It was heartbreaking to see how much surprise and pleasure he took from something so small.

Ariel pushed the box of chocolates toward the *Veracity*'s crew. Coni stepped forward to take one, as did Mykah and Vezali. Haoun wouldn't come any closer to the boy. "What's the matter?" Coni asked.

"They want Raena to go back to their planet," he said. "She got shot the last time. Don't you remember? She lost so much blood . . ."

"I remember," Coni said gently. "Eilif helped us save her life."

Ariel spoke up. "I wouldn't put Raena in danger. Hell, I would do anything to keep her out of danger, but we know that's not going to work. Look at the new recording Jim made, before you make any decisions."

Kavanaugh switched on the screen in the lounge and Jim typed in a command that activated a camera in the city under the sea. Most of the shattered domes were shadowy, filled with twisted and broken buildings blacker than the shifting ocean. Only one dome looked whole, lit from within by a weird green glow that flickered with movement.

"Where have you seen that color before?" Ariel asked.

"It looks like Templar fire," Haoun said. He was the only one of the *Veracity*'s crew old enough to remember it.

"That's what I thought," Ariel agreed.

"What was in that dome?" Mykah asked.

"That's where the cloning laboratories were," Eilif said. "Raena poisoned all the clones in process there. My husband believed they were contaminated to the point that none of their DNA would be salvageable. There were clones of her, too. Jonan had been very excited at the idea of presenting her with children when she came back to him."

Coni watched her crewmates all take a hefty drink at the thought of Raena executing her own clones.

"She burned the bodies of all of Jonan's brothers, all our sons, so there would be nothing left to clone ever again. But someone has repaired the dome," Eilif said. "Someone is working in the cloning lab."

"I wish we were drinking something stronger," Mykah said.

Ariel laughed. "For Jim's sake, I wanted to opt for less drunk, rather than more."

"Why are we trusting him?" Haoun demanded. "We don't know when this recording was made. We don't know if it's real or animated or otherwise tampered with. He's a Thallian. Look at him."

Instead, everyone looked at Haoun.

"I thought you would be the last one to be prejudiced," Ariel said icily. "Thallian raped me. He's done so much worse to Raena. I absolutely would not send her back to his planet if I thought there was any way he could have survived. But Eilif and Raena burned his body."

"To ashes," Eilif confirmed.

"Someone is messing about in the Thallians' cloning lab. It may be the family's medical robot, which might have escaped destruction when Eilif blew up the city's domes. But it looks like Templars—and if they can be cloned back into the galaxy . . ." Ariel's voice trailed off.

"All that is theoretical," Haoun said angrily. "Why are we trusting that boy?"

Jim stood up. With a flourish, he pulled off his black work shirt, flung it down on the table. His torso was a map of burns, a web of scars. His skin revealed him as kindred to Raena.

"My father hated me." Jim's low voice was hoarse. "Father could sense that I recognized him as a monster. He thought that the more he beat me, the more I would learn to respect him. Raena offered to help me find a shipping lane near my homeworld, so that a passing ship would find my hopper before I died alone in space. I told her my point of origin. I'm the reason you knew which planet my family was hiding on."

Ariel put her hand on Jim's wrist. He snatched his hand away, struggling with whether to say more. Eventually he subsided and put his shirt back on.

"Jimi has as much reason to hate his family as any of us," Eilif said. "He has as much reason to be grateful to Raena."

"I've struggled with the knowledge that something is happening on the Thallian homeworld," Ariel said. "If I tell the galaxy, will they muster up an avenging force to swoop into the ocean and pull every brick apart? Would they crack the planet's core?

What if it is Templar cloning going on there, rather than anything related to the Thallians? I thought Raena would want to know what was happening, that she would want to investigate for herself. But the more time passes, the more I worry what damage is being done . . ."

"I'll go," Vezali said.

The others stared at her.

"It's an ocean," she said. "I'm the only one who can explore it without a craft."

"The city is two kilometers deep," Jim said.

"I'll have to take it in stages," Vezali said. "I can manage."

"There are leviathans," Eilif said. "You will want to go armed with something to scare them away from you."

"I can help you with that," Ariel promised.

"I can take you to the planet," Kavanaugh said, "but we'll have to hire a ship. Eilif and Jim are staying here."

"Kavanaugh and Gisela are serving as their bodyguards," Ariel argued. "That's not going to work."

"I'm not going to volunteer," Haoun said. "Going to the Thallian world, no matter what's creeping around on it, is suicide."

"Stay with Raena," Vezali said calmly. "She needs you here."

"I can help guard Eilif and Jim," Mykah said. "I won't be as much protection as Kavanaugh would be, but I'm probably better than nothing."

"I go where he goes," Coni said. Besides, she was curious to get to know the Thallian survivors better.

* * *

The crew walked back to the boarding house where they were staying. Each had sunken into his or her own thoughts.

Mykah's comm buzzed. "The *Veracity* has been released!" he read aloud. "We owe back docking fees, but they are willing to waive them if we drop our suit for travel damages."

"That's a relief," Coni said. "Are you going to drop the suit?"

Mykah turned to face them all. "The *Veracity* is a democracy," he reminded. "What do we want to do?"

"I won't be here to help you with the lawsuit," Vezali said.

"I want to concentrate on getting Raena out of jail," Haoun said.

"Ask Ariel for her advice," Coni suggested. "She's the one who paid our travel bills. She'll also have a better sense of what our chances of winning might be if we proceed."

"Let's get off the street first," Haoun urged, heading toward the closest bar. "I need to drink something stronger than ale."

While the others procured liquid sustenance, Mykah settled into a quiet table at the back of the cantina. He commed Ariel and told her about the message from the new dockmaster. "What do I do?"

"If it were me," she said, "I'd pursue the suit and damn the cost. But you have a chance to get your home back. It won't cost you another credit and you won't have to stay in the boarding house any longer. Which way do you find yourself leaning? I'll support whichever choice you make."

"I want the *Veracity* back."

"Then take her back. Have they put any conditions on you?"

"Like what?"

"A gag order? Are they forbidding you to discuss the impoundment?"

"They haven't mentioned it."

"They know—or they should know—that you're a journalist, Mykah. They will try to silence you. Tell them you've already been in discussions with Mellix about this matter."

"I have been," he said, surprised that she would guess that.

"Perfect. If the torpedo's already in the tube, so much the better. Let them know that anything they say to you is on the record. If they try to gag you, tell them their threats are being recorded and you will proceed with your suit."

Haoun handed Mykah a glass of xyshin and sat down beside him.

Mykah nodded his thanks, then asked Ariel, "You think they'll cave?"

"They'll cave," she promised. "They're already regretting that they started this debacle. Now they just want us out of here as soon as possible, so they can begin the damage control."

"Thanks, Ariel. I appreciate your advice."

She laughed. "Always glad to help."

The first round of drinks was the most celebratory by far of their homecoming on Kai.

CHAPTER 10

Once the night got good and dark, Eilif and Jim transferred to the *Veracity*. They settled into the spare cabins. Gisela came too, to continue to guard them. Haoun decided he'd stay at the boarding house, rather than live so close to the Thallians. Ariel planned to continue on in her hotel near the Hall of Justice, but she came to say goodbye to Kavanaugh and Vezali.

While Mykah pulled out a range of weapons, Vezali looked the *Veracity* over to make sure it hadn't been tampered with, that it was still space-worthy. Mykah was sorry to see her go, but admired her bravery for volunteering to explore Drusingyi with Kavanaugh.

The Thallians had been used to fishing and fending off predators in their home ocean, so they had a number of weapons designed or modified to fire underwater. Mykah spread them out in the lounge for Ariel's inspection. She seemed impressed by the variety of antique weaponry.

"They had all this onboard when you took over the ship?" she asked.

"And more," Mykah said. "Raena's been teaching me what it all can do."

"It looks like everything is in excellent shape."

"We only had what Father brought with him on the *Arbiter*," Jim said. "We had to take care of things, because nothing could be replaced."

No one had an answer for that, so Ariel changed the subject. "If we were dreaming here, I'd send Vezali with the new 728 pulse rifle. That would stop a leviathan dead, guaranteed."

"No place on Kai to buy one," Kavanaugh pointed out.

"I could order one for you to pick up en route."

"No," Kavanaugh said. "Let's just get this done. There's plenty here to choose from."

Ariel nodded. She picked out a couple of guns and had Vezali hold them, get the feel of them. "It's a shame you can't actually test-fire anything," Ariel said. "That would give you a sense of how hard it's going to kick. You can't tell much about a gun just by picking it up."

"I don't want to carry much," Vezali said. "It will be awkward to swim if I'm weighted down."

"How many tentacles do you need for swimming?"

"I'm used to using them all, but I can adapt. I'm concerned about the drag as I swim with something in my arms."

"I should be able to rig up a carrying case," Jim offered, "something smooth-sided enough to be hydrodynamic."

Vezali nodded her eyestalk. "That would be great, Jim. Thank you."

*　*　*

Kavanaugh insisted that he and Vezali walk Ariel back to her hotel. "I'd feel better if you'd stay on the *Veracity* with the kids," he confided.

"I'll be okay," she promised. "Now that we've seen the Templar fire, I'm much less worried about things coming off of Drusingyi after me."

"I'm worried about things on Kai coming after you," Kavanaugh argued. "If you were armed, I wouldn't worry at all, but how many days of trial is it going to take before they decide that Raena isn't the only threat to them?"

Ariel smiled. "They won't give me that much credit."

"They've got to know who's paying Corvas."

She shrugged. "That's obvious, I suppose. But they didn't put much thought into this mess before they stirred it up. Otherwise, they wouldn't have chosen the *Veracity*. I mean, come on. The faintest bit of research would uncover all the mysteries the *Veracity* has revealed to the galaxy. Why would you attack someone who is going to expose you?"

Kavanaugh didn't have an answer for that, but Ariel figured it out on her own. "This goes deeper than the Business Council of Kai," she said.

"Somebody put them up to this, that's for damn sure," Kavanaugh agreed. "The question is: is this only about keeping Raena off the street? Or are they distracting you from something?"

Ariel stopped in front of her hotel and looked around. The travel ban had obviously affected Kai badly. Six months ago, when she and Sloane had hidden Raena here, the city had bustled with life at all hours. Now there was almost no one on the street, even though it wasn't much past midnight.

She shook that thought away. The silence stretched awkwardly, then Kavanaugh stepped over to kiss her goodbye. Ariel wrapped her arms around his shoulders and held him close.

"Be careful," she ordered.

"We will," Vezali promised.

✳ ✳ ✳

The following morning, Raena had an unexpected visitor. Ariel looked nervously inward before she stepped into the cell.

"I'm surprised to see you here, Ms. Shaad." Raena got off her bench to give Ariel a deep, hard kiss. "I can't offer you much hospitality, but come sit down."

"Thanks," Ariel said shakily. "They only let one of us come each day and Haoun has been pretty determined he'd be that one."

Raena smiled. "He's really a pussycat."

"You just like it when he growls," Ariel teased.

"Among other things."

Ariel grinned.

"It's good to see you," Raena said. "Been a while since you've been in jail?"

"Actually, I was in this one last time we were on Kai—right after you left. Planetary Security gassed everyone who didn't run from the souk and dragged the survivors here. One of Thallian's men is still here."

"Oh? Corvas said Kai didn't hold prisoners long-term."

"This guy is a special case. They're hoping he'll become sane enough for trial. No prison will take him until he's been found guilty in court—and no one is offering to transport him to a psychiatric hospital on charity. Kai won't pay to get rid of him, so here he sits."

"Does Corvas know about him?"

"Yes. Kai is going to press more charges today, so our friend may become involved in your defense."

"Keep away from him," Raena ordered. "Seeing me is going to spark his conditioning. Everyone in the courtroom will be in danger."

"You think he's been brainwashed?"

"Of course. Jonan would never have let him off the planet unless he was absolutely confident in his loyalty."

"There's more good news," Ariel threatened. "If the Business Council decides to blame you for bringing the Thallians to Kai, Corvas wants to get into why they were after you. He wants to trace it back to your 'mother.' Kai knows some of the story already, since Gavin used RespirAll on our friend, but of course the story got all garbled. Anyway, the first Raena may come up in court today. I wanted you to know in advance."

Raena took a deep breath, understanding exactly what Ariel meant by that. Corvas wanted to connect Raena Zacari, the Imperial assassin, to the Thallians. There was no 'first Raena,' only Raena herself, pretending to be her own daughter. She hoped like hell the identity Coni had created for her would stand up in court.

Ariel offered her hand and Raena clasped it, her fingers naturally finding their places between Ariel's. They sat silently, shoulder to shoulder. Eventually, Raena said, "Thank you for warning me."

"Not something I wanted sprung on you in public." Then Ariel collected herself and handed Raena another transparent shopping bag. "I brought your costume for the day."

Raena turned the bag upside down. Out tumbled a silver catsuit, supple and reflective as mercury. She smiled, truly pleased. "The crew got the ship back."

"Last night."

Raena peeled off her dress and skinned into the catsuit. "This makes me feel more like myself than I have in weeks," she said. "Thank you, Ariel."

"I know what you like, little sister."

Raena grinned at her. "You do, don't you?"

✳ ✳ ✳

As everyone settled into the courtroom for the second day of Raena's trial, Mykah watched the Mistress of Ceremonies preparing to face the cameras. Her dress was even tighter today, her heels even higher, as if her appearance had to compete with the subject matter of the trial.

The Mistress of Ceremonies spoke into camera number one. "Yesterday was an explosive day of testimony, wasn't it? We learned that one of the terrifying Thallian clan had been killed on Kai. You'll be relieved to know that the dockmaster who allowed Revan Thallian onto the planet has been arrested by the Business Council. I'll bet his replacement does a much more thorough job of screening visitors to Kai."

"Meanwhile," she continued, turning to the second camera, "the Imperial-era *Veracity*—impounded by Kai City Spaceport on our sister pleasure planet Lautan—has been released from custody. Apparently, there is no evidence to prove it was the same ship as the *Raptor*, which has now been linked to the Thallians. The *Raptor* itself seems to have completely disappeared. Let's hope the new dockmaster can whip the spaceport into shape.

"The *Veracity* has been returned to Captain Mykah Chen and his crew, who were the first to pick up the distress call from the survivors of the *Arbiter* on the Thallian homeworld. Let's chat with him now. Captain Chen, do you have a moment?"

"Of course," Mykah said. He smiled at the feline MC, seeing echoes of Coni in her face.

"Yesterday," she said, "you asked the court if Kai was in the habit of impounding ships. Do you have any reason to think the *Veracity* was singled out?"

"There's no reason—that I know of—that it should have been." Mykah stared into the camera, thinking, "Even humans have rights."

The MC prodded a little more. "Do you have any evidence that other ships have been impounded unjustly?"

"The judges said yesterday in court that they would look into it. That satisfies me for now."

And really, that was all he was prepared to say on the subject, until Raena was out of Kai's clutches. Both Ariel and Corvas had cautioned him not to put her into any more danger. He intended to be careful.

* * *

Haoun didn't actually hate Kai as much as Mykah did. His own job here had been fairly cushy. He'd shuttled tourists out into the desert to explore the Templar ghost towns. Mostly Haoun waited in the temperature-controlled buses, playing video games, while the tourists exhausted themselves in the heat. If the tourist parties featured any human females, he invited them for revivifying drinks afterward. He'd met a lot of people, collected a satisfying amount of tips, and dated some very nice warm girls.

He hadn't realized he was bored until Mykah offered him a job piloting the *Veracity*.

Haoun looked down at Raena, who was once again chained to the defendant's chair. Today she wore a skin-tight outfit that shimmered in the bright courtroom lights. The reflective catsuit wouldn't leave any of her body to the imagination, except that you couldn't look straight at her with the glare it gave off. He wondered how it registered to the cameras.

He also wondered if anyone else understood the social critique she offered without saying a word.

The three judges took their places in the courtroom.

The Shtrell court reporter said, "The prisoner here before us has been charged by the Business Council of Kai with kidnapping a young human male who has not yet been identified. Raena Zacari has requested that the charge go to trial."

The court recorder replayed the video of Jain Thallian jumping off his jet bike and running toward the lock on the ship now recognized as the *Veracity*. Haoun had to admit, he was impressed with the job Coni and Mykah had done altering the metadata on the recording to make it appear that this was a different docking bay than the *Raptor* had landed in. He didn't know how they'd managed to change the record under Kai's nose. It was scary that they had that kind of power. He hoped that would continue to use it for good.

* * *

When the video of Jain's capture finished, Raena looked up at Corvas. He smoothed an invisible wrinkle out of his blue and aquamarine caftan and said, "I call the next witness."

Preceded by an oversized blue-furred Haru bailiff, a slim boy came out of the waiting room. He wore an expensive sleeveless green brocade pullover with a high silk collar. It looked to Raena as if it hid body armor. Muscles striped his bare arms. His posture was perfectly straight, shoulders back, chin up, and yet he didn't look haughty as much as frightened. He held himself too taut, as if he might crumble.

He had the bluish black hair, the silver eyes, the long straight nose and pointed chin, but this was not Jain Thallian. Raena had respected Jain, even felt comradeship for him, damaged as he was. She'd known Jain was just as proud as she was of what they'd survived at his father's hands. She guessed this must be Jimi, Jain's younger brother, the sole surviving Thallian clone.

The boy's eyes flicked to Raena's face. She gave him a nod that didn't begin to encompass her gratitude. Raena hadn't known Jimi well enough to feel any affection for him, but she understood exactly what it cost him to appear in public.

"State your name for the court," Corvas said.

"I traveled to Kai under the name Jim Zacari," Jimi said, "but my given name is Jain Thallian. My father was Jonan Thallian, the man who carried out the Templar genocide."

The audience in the courtroom exploded. Jimi flinched away from the furor. The Haru bailiff came to stand protectively over him, arms crossed on his too-broad chest. The boy shrank from him as well, uncertain if the blue-furred guard was for his protection or not.

The judges howled for silence, but the crowd struggled toward the half wall that separated them from the courtroom set. The cameras turned toward the mob, recording their anger in all its spectrum of details.

Shackled as she was, Raena remained seated in the defendant's box. She scanned the area around her, but saw nothing that could be used as a weapon. If anyone came over the railing within her reach, she would have to kill them barehanded, before they could touch Jimi. Undoubtedly, that would play well around the galaxy: the ultimate proof that humans were violent and dangerous. Raena wondered if she had been set up.

A forcefield shimmered into place just inside the half wall, isolating the courtroom from the audience. The forcefield flickered several times until the old circuitry stabilized.

"It's been a while since we needed that," the gray judge said.

"Glad it still works," the insect answered. "I thought we were going to have a full-scale riot."

"We may yet." The rock judge nodded toward the audience, who still shouted and gesticulated behind the wall of silence. To the bailiff, he said, "Will you pass along an order to clear the galleries and close the court? We'll proceed without all that foolishness."

Corvas came over to talk to the Thallian boy. "You all right, son?"

"Yes, sir. That's the reason I work and travel under an assumed name."

"Very understandable."

The judges looked past Raena to check on the audience, but the evacuation seemed to be underway at last.

"When can we resume?" the stick insect asked.

"Whenever the court is ready," Corvas said.

"Let's give them another moment," the gray judge suggested.

Raena spent the time breathing deeply, gazing at the floor between her feet. She felt sick, amazed at herself, ready to die to protect a Thallian.

"All right," the female judge said at last. "They've gone."

"Jim," Corvas said, "tell us your story."

So the boy spun out a tale of how he and his uncle Revan and a handful of soldiers from the *Arbiter* had come to Kai to capture Raena Zacari. How they had trailed her to the souk in Kai City and how they attacked her party there.

"Did you know Raena Zacari before the attack?" Corvas asked.

"Yes," the boy said. "I had been in contact with her over the grid."

"Why?"

"I needed help to escape my family."

"Why was that?"

A camera zoomed closer to get a tight shot of the boy's face. He glanced at it, glanced back to Ariel seated calmly in the gallery, then focused on Raena. "Because my father was a murderer of epic scale," the boy said. "My brothers and I were prisoners on Drusingyi, because of the crimes our elders committed before we were born. My father's generation weren't the glorious heroes they wanted to believe they were. What they'd done disgusted me."

It had been one thing for Jimi to tell Raena how he felt on the cusp of his escape, right before she wiped his family out. Now, with the galaxy listening in, he revealed the depths of his loathing. It was obvious from the fury trembling in his voice that he did not lie when he proclaimed how much he hated his family.

"How did Raena help your escape?"

"She made sure that Uncle Revan couldn't follow me."

"By killing him?" one of the judges asked.

"Yes, sir."

"Then what happened?"

"She followed me back to Captain Chen's ship and we left Kai together."

"Captain Chen's ship is the *Veracity*?"

"Yes, sir."

"And where did you go?"

"I took them through the satellite defenses to Drusingyi."

The levels of dishonesty in Jimi's account made Raena's head swim. Reality bore so little resemblance to what he said on the witness stand that she was amazed the judges couldn't taste falsehood in the air.

In reality, Jimi had never been to Kai before. He'd never been off of his homeworld, until Raena told him how to reconfigure a hopper and offered a distraction to cover his escape. Yes, Jimi had given her enough information that she could bring the *Veracity* to Drusingyi, but he'd done it inadvertently.

Or so she had believed. She gazed at the boy now, calculating. He lied to his family for years about his feelings for them. More than that, he'd lied to his father, an Imperial torturer who once lived to root out dishonesty. The boy must be craftier than she'd thought. Jimi was, after all, one of Thallian's sons.

"What happened after you reached Drusingyi?" the rock judge asked.

"The *Veracity* picked up the distress call from the men from the *Arbiter*. A malfunction had destroyed the city's air filtration system. The men were stranded on the planet's surface, without any kind of supplies or survival equipment."

"None of this is related to the trial here before us," Corvas pointed out.

"True," the twiggy judge agreed. "It's fascinating nonetheless."

The defender inclined his head. One of his eyes slid sidelong to look at Raena. Then he faced the judges again. "Since Jain Thallian clearly was not kidnapped, I ask that the charge of kidnapping be dropped against Raena Zacari."

"We will withdraw to chambers to discuss," the head judge said. "Court is dismissed for the rest of the morning. We will meet back here this afternoon."

* * *

Again the lunch they brought Raena was impressive, a green salad flecked with nuts, seeds, and dried berries. The accommodations might be dusty and the showers rationed, but the food could not be beat.

The jail guards escorted her back into the courtroom afterward and chained her once more in the defendant's box. Jimi had gone back to hiding in protective custody. The audience seats seemed even fuller than they had been in the morning, but with a noticeable increase in the number of Planetary Security agents stationed around them.

"Raena Zacari," the court recorder said, "the Planetary Business Council of Kai has agreed to drop the charge of kidnapping. Instead, it charges you with being a party to violence on a weapons-free world, violence that ended in the murder of four men. How do you answer these charges?"

"If I killed anyone on Kai, it was in self-defense."

"Kai does not recognize self-defense as justification for violence," the rock judge said. "How do you plead?"

Corvas pre-empted her response. "We insist on our right to trial. Please show us your evidence for the charge."

A security cam, meant for catching shoplifters, provided grainy low-res video of seven men and Jain attacking a small party of tourists in the souk on Kai. One minute Ariel Shaad, Gavin Sloane, and Raena Zacari were sampling exotic fruits under a silver-shot canopy. The next, a soldier dressed in nondescript black livery had grasped Ariel's arm and tried dragging her away. She fumbled for the gun no longer hanging at her thigh.

Gavin Sloane turned right into another assailant's fist. Sloane staggered into a wall and slid to the dirt.

Raena Zacari spun into her own attacker's grip on her arm and brought the heel of her free hand up hard under his chin. Still turning, she pulled him off balance and used his body to take the blow aimed at her by his accomplice. Then she dropped the man with the busted jaw and leapt onto the next man. In a movement as economical as poetry, she had broken his arm, several of his ribs, and vaulted over him as he dropped so she could come to Sloane's aid.

Sloane's attacker didn't even know Raena was coming. Jumping onto his back, she twisted his head sharply enough to snap his spine, then turned to deal with the man dragging Ariel away. Less than a minute had passed, and already three attackers were down. One was dead.

Raena moved from one man to the next efficiently, dropping one with a scorpion kick, the next with a roundhouse punch. Her small stature made her tricky for the larger men to grab. The high-heeled boots she wore proved lethal. Most unnerving of all, she laughed through the whole attack, as if it was the most fun she'd had in years.

Then her gaze locked on Jain Thallian in the shadows.

A smoking canister dropped at her feet. Others rained down around her. Jain pulled his mask up from under his chin. Raena leaned into a sprint toward him, but Revan Thallian bulled after her. They came at Jain so fast he couldn't do anything more than raise the shock net he carried.

Raena wound her fists in the sparking net and yanked hard. She hauled it out of Jain's grasp and whirled, catching Revan upside the head with it. Then she tugged on the edge of the net and sent Revan to the dirt.

She turned a cartwheel after him and brought the toe of her boot down hard on Revan's throat. He wilted, obviously dead. Raena snatched the mask off his face and held it over her own nose. For the first time in the fight, she seemed to be breathing hard.

Bending down, she scooped up a sleep canister with her spare hand. When her head came up, her insectile sunglasses fixed on Jain. Both of them ran out of frame.

The broadcast video usually cut at that moment, but this version continued long enough to show seven bodies in black uniforms strewn across the cramped market street, with barely a splash of visible blood.

The recording ended with a rain of sleep grenades. Pale blue smoke shrouded the scene.

Over the stunned silence in the courtroom, Corvas said, "I call Ariel Shaad to witness."

*　*　*

Ariel strode out of the gallery to sit in the witness box. Mykah noticed she'd dressed up during the lunch break: ropes of gemstones shimmered on her chest and both wrists sported gem-studded bracelets. She'd traded her usual uniform of white blouses and gray trousers for a warm green dress that played up the flawless gold of her skin. Only the braid remained, but even it was more complicated than usual.

Now she looked less like a veteran and more like the upper-class clientele of Kai. When Corvas introduced her as the head of the Shaad Family Foundation, she looked the part. It was hard to picture her as the heir and one-time owner of the Shaad Arms Company.

Ariel told about her first visit to Kai, soon after the War ended. She and her mother had come to gamble, to be pampered, to relax. In a galaxy where humans—even those who fought with the Coalition— seemed more in danger all the time, they'd had a wonderful time and felt very safe on Kai.

Because of those fond memories, Ariel's mother had come back to Kai several times since, bringing all her wealthy friends. Ariel never worried about the older ladies on Kai because she'd known that Planetary Security was so good.

So when it came time to choose a place to bring Raena, Ariel's only choice had been Kai. Ariel expected that Kai's weapons-free status would keep Raena safe.

And they had enjoyed a marvelous stay on Kai. Ariel name-checked the restaurants, the amusements, the casinos they'd frequented. It was as good a commercial for the pleasure planet as anyone could wish. Mykah expected an advertising flack somewhere was even now figuring out how to illustrate the list so that a human woman wasn't seen to be the spokesperson gushing about how great Kai was.

"But when we needed Kai to protect us," Ariel said, "they failed utterly. They didn't arrest the Thallians at the spaceport. They allowed Revan Thallian and his kill squad to roam around Kai City, armed with a shock net and sleep grenades, if not additional weapons that they didn't get a chance to use against us. When the Thallians attacked my party, Kai Planetary Security didn't arrive until well after the fight had broken up. We are extremely lucky that Revan Thallian didn't plan to kill Raena until after he'd taken her hostage, because if he'd wanted to kill her on Kai, Planetary Security provided no defense at all."

Corvas set the video of the assault in the souk to play once more. This time, it had a counter embedded in it, clicking off the time parts before the Planetary Security team finally arrived.

It was long enough for Raena to incapacitate three soldiers and kill the rest.

"Where were you?" Ariel asked. Anger choked her voice. "I trusted Kai to protect us. Not only did no one come when we needed help, now you are prosecuting Raena for not going docilely to her death. You're blaming her for bringing violence to a weapons-free world, when you did absolutely nothing to prevent that violence from happening here. I'm sure she is not the last person to visit Kai who expects your protection."

She almost said more, but Corvas gestured and drew her attention. Ariel took a deep breath and leaned back into her chair.

"Raena Zacari was orphaned by the War. I took her under my Foundation's protection. Her safety is personally important to me. I'm disappointed that it wasn't as important to Kai."

"Thank you, Ms. Shaad," Corvas said. "I'd like to call prisoner #1823 to the stand."

*   *   *

The man was marched in and shackled to the witness box. He looked calm for the moment, if not particularly clear. The jailers hadn't made much of an attempt to clean him up. He wore an ill-fitting jumpsuit that hung on him. His hair had been washed, if not combed. His bleary gaze fixed on nothing.

Raena wasn't exactly sure what her role in this bit of theater was going to be, but she inched toward the edge of her chair in readiness.

Her ankles were chained to the base of the chair. The chair was bolted to the floor. The tether that connected the restraints around her wrists to her hobble allowed her to raise her arms about shoulder high. Her wrists could reach about a half-meter apart.

The judges questioned the man about who he was, why he'd come to Kai. He muttered, "Can't tell. Can't reveal the family."

Raena watched the three judges exchange a look.

Corvas stepped forward, moving quickly enough that he caught the prisoner's attention. Suddenly the man came alert, eyes clear and focused.

Corvas asked, "Son, do you know who this is?" He stepped aside to reveal Raena sitting behind him.

The soldier launched himself forward. The attack was all the more frightening for being entirely silent. He was hobbled, just as Raena was, but the chain that attached him to the witness stand tore the wood apart. He bounded forward like a beast.

He slapped Corvas to the floor as he plunged toward Raena. She stood to meet him.

The first punch came toward her head. She sidestepped it easily. The second one aimed down toward her heart. She raised her manacled hands, tangled the cable between them around his arm. A quick circle of her foot wound her hobble around his calf. She yanked hard, falling backward into her chair as she shoved his shoulders away from her.

He lost his balance and fell. His head hit the floor with a thud.

Raena clutched the seat of the chair and managed to prevent herself from falling atop him. She disentangled her leg from his, wrapped her feet in the tether running down his body, and yanked him over onto his stomach. Then she pressed his head to the floor with her foot.

He flailed beneath her, trying to flop himself over. Raena got her other foot atop his shoulders and pushed down as hard as she could. If the chair hadn't been bolted to the floor, she would have fallen. For once, the restraints worked in her favor.

The bailiff had moved into place to protect the judges. Only now that Raena had the soldier pinned did the guards finally move into action.

She knew they were going to stun her before anyone else had figured it out. They really couldn't stun the soldier without hitting her, too, and they weren't going to get close enough to grapple with him until he was unconscious. She would have done the same thing.

She was glad when the cameras zoomed in close. They would show how defenseless she was as the stun staff put her down.

Damn, she hated the feeling of current running over her skin, co-opting her muscles. She clenched her teeth to keep from biting her tongue.

*   *   *

Haoun exploded to his feet to go to Raena's rescue. Ariel had been expecting that, so she grabbed his forearm. Belatedly, Mykah took hold of him too. Luckily, Haoun hesitated before doing something foolish.

"She's okay," Ariel said quietly. "Settle, before you catch the cameras' attention."

Haoun sank back to the bench, shaking. "What was that all about?" he whispered angrily.

"Proof that Kai couldn't protect her," Mykah guessed. "Did you see how fast she is?"

"But how does that help her?" Coni asked. "Kai doesn't recognize self-defense as an appropriate response."

"She didn't fight him," Mykah explained. "She stopped him. Kai couldn't stop him, now or when he attacked her before." He turned to Ariel. "Do you think they'll drop the charges?"

"No. They'll still try to fine her. That's why we'll have to prove he came from the *Arbiter* and they should never have let him onto the planet in the first place."

The bailiff helped Corvas to his feet. He limped over to speak to the judges, cradling one of his arms awkwardly across his body.

"Oh, Corvas is hurt," Coni said.

"He's lucky it wasn't worse," Ariel said fondly. "I warned him. He was supposed to get out of the way."

"You knew this was going to happen," Haoun accused.

"Yes," Ariel admitted.

"Did Raena?"

"As soon as she saw him, don't you think?" Ariel offered him a tight smile, not liking his tone. "I told her this morning that Corvas planned to call for him."

Raena was being unshackled from her chair now. She wasn't unconscious, but she looked pretty out of it. One of the guards heaved her across his shoulder. Her limbs hung down, swinging like a doll's.

Three other guards picked up the soldier.

"Court is adjourned," the bailiff announced.

"'Bout time," Ariel said. "I need a drink. Anyone else?"

"Is she going to be all right?" Haoun asked. "She looks terrible."

"You know she's had worse, right?" Ariel asked. Then, relenting, she said, "I'm the last person to be unsympathetic to Raena, but I also know how much she's endured. Stun is uncomfortable, but it doesn't cause lasting effects unless you get hit repeatedly in a short amount of time. Even then, it won't leave a mark."

They all understood she was referring to the scars striping Raena's back.

"She won't like it," Ariel summed up, "but it won't damage her."

"I'm going to see if they'll let me up to sit with her," Haoun said.

"She's only allowed one visitor a day," Coni reminded.

"Every legal system has its price," Ariel told Haoun as she stood up to give the big lizard room to get past her. "Take her some food. The stun will make her hungry when she wakes up."

"You've been stunned before?" Coni asked.

"In my misspent youth." And that was all Ariel wanted to say with the cameras still buzzing around. She smiled at Coni and Mykah. "I'm serious about getting a drink. Please come keep me company."

* * *

The guard placed Raena back on the bench in her cell, making sure her head went down softly, then left her alone. Raena couldn't even turn over yet, but the stun was wearing off. She felt as if medium-sized insects crawled all over her skin, biting out mouthfuls of flesh.

Stars and sky, she hated to be stunned.

She wasn't sure where the trial would go next, but Kai would have to respond to the accusation that they couldn't protect the wealthy people who came to enjoy their hospitality. She had to admire Ariel for attacking the pleasure planet's most vulnerable point. If the Business Council wasn't careful, Ariel could end tourism to the planet.

Raena realized this might be a dangerous time for her, alone in her prison cell with no one to watch her back. Too bad the Business Council had already tried the deranged roommate gambit to settle the case before the trial started.

At the very least, they would hold Raena responsible for drawing the Thallians to Kai. She wondered what kind of blame-the-victim crime they would label that.

She hoped that Corvas was okay. He'd hit the floor hard enough to snap something. Raena knew the bone repair technology on Kai was state of the art. She just wished they weren't so often in need of it.

* * *

The kids let Ariel pick the bar, so she chose a funky little place lit with strings of multicolored lights. Ariel summoned the serving robot and paid before anyone could object.

The kids were fond of Raena, which was enough of a point in common for Ariel. Crusading Mykah reminded her of her own kids. Coni's sense of humor made her think of Heddryn, a Fossa she'd been friends with back in the War. Heddryn had been dead more than a decade, but it felt good to honor her memory now.

Once everyone had tasted their drinks, Ariel asked, "What's going on between Haoun and Raena?"

"It started on Lautan," Mykah said.

"No, it started on the ship," Coni corrected. "It might have been all on his part then, but he was always sitting beside her, trying to get her to notice him."

"Raena can be kind of oblivious," Ariel said fondly. "He knows her story?"

"She's been open with us about it," Coni said.

"She's Haoun's type," Mykah added, "meaning human. He used to romance the human ladies when he was working here on Kai."

"It's different with travelers passing through," Ariel pointed out.

"We worried about that at first, too," Coni said. "This seems more serious."

Ariel raised her glass and wished, "May they find happiness."

The others hurried to join the toast.

* * *

Despite the discomfort of the stun wearing off, Raena must have drifted off to sleep. When she jerked awake, Haoun had placed her head on his thigh. He stroked her hair.

"Hey," he said softly. "Are you with me again?"

"Yeah." She pushed herself into sitting up and wiped the back of her hand across her mouth. "I wasn't drooling, was I?"

"Were you? I didn't notice." He handed her a foil-wrapped tube still toasty warm to the touch. "Ariel said you would be hungry. It's human food. A tikka burrito."

Suddenly, she'd never wanted to eat anything as much as she wanted this. She tore the foil away and bit off a huge mouthful of tortilla stuffed with saffron rice and some kind of poultry. Once she got that swallowed, she asked, "What'd you get for yourself?"

"Apparently, I got it for the guards," Haoun said. "They told me I could bring you food, but I couldn't bring a picnic."

"Want a bite?" she asked with her mouth full.

"Eat what you want first."

She was so ravenous that she couldn't stop to make conversation. Haoun didn't seem to mind. He watched the patch of sunlight traveling across the opposite wall. Raena watched him. He sat twisted sideways on the bench, so that his tail could trail off onto the floor, which meant he couldn't put his back flat against the wall. For the first time, she realized that, just as things in the galaxy weren't made for her because of her size, things were also not made if you had to watch your tail. She stopped feeling quite so singled out.

She made herself offer the burrito to him again. "Please help me eat this."

"I'll just have a taste." His bite was as big as three of hers.

"Thank you for this," she said, when he handed the burrito back. "I'd forgotten what it was like to come out of stun."

"You're welcome. Are you starting to feel normal?"

"As normal as ever." She leaned her head against his shoulder. "How long can you stay?"

"'Til morning."

"Don't tease me," Raena said seriously.

"I'm not. I bribed the guards."

"You didn't really," she accused.

"Ariel said all legal systems have their price. Luckily, your guards had a price I could afford."

She set the remains of the burrito aside and wrapped her arms around him. "Did you really?" she asked again.

"I was worried about you. I know I'm not a lot of protection, but I couldn't stand the thought of you in here alone tonight. I may not be able to stay awake in court tomorrow, but I will watch over you while you sleep tonight."

She snuggled against him, thinking, *this is the best boyfriend I've ever had*. Judging from the last two, her taste must be improving.

"I don't think anything will happen." She yawned. "They have me under surveillance." She nodded toward the camera she knew about, the one in the corner above the door. There were undoubtedly others she didn't know about.

"They had you under surveillance the night you were attacked by your cellmate, too," Haoun pointed out. "Coni got a hold of the recording for Corvas."

"Ariel made my safety the personal responsibility of the commandant after that."

Haoun looked at her with a tilt of his head that she read as skepticism.

"Not that it matters," she said. "I would rather have your company."

"Go ahead and snuggle down," he said. "I've got you."

Raena got up to wash her face and hands. Her stomach felt almost too stuffed now. Should have shared more of the burrito, she thought. Now, though, she should sleep well.

CHAPTER 11

The bedroom was entirely dark, which was exactly how Raena wanted it. She stood in the darkness, shoulder to shoulder with Eilif, as they waited for Jonan to wake. When he did, he thrashed around on the bed, testing the strength of the restraints Raena had repurposed to hold him. She hadn't left much give. After the metal cuffs broke his skin, she smelled his blood on the recirculated air. She refused to lick her lips.

Instead, Raena thumbed open the lighting fluid and flicked it out across his body, drenching his pajamas.

"Eilif?" Jonan asked hopefully. Raena hadn't ever heard that tone in his voice before.

Eilif took Raena's hand, squeezed it hard. "Yes, my lord. I'm here."

"What's happened?"

Raena handed her the accelerant.

"I poisoned you," Eilif said matter-of-factly, as if it was something she did every day.

That made no sense to him, so he ignored it. "Where's Raena?"

"I'm here, too." She struck her thumbnail hard against a match.

Thallian leered at her, shifting his hips to draw her attention. She didn't bother to look.

"Goodbye, Jonan." Raena flicked the burning match at him. It tumbled through the air, arcing slowly above his sodden clothing. The fumes ignited with a whump that crushed him down against the bed.

Nothing in her life had given her as much joy as that moment when the flames took hold.

* * *

Into the middle of her dream, Haoun said, "Wake up, Raena. I smell smoke."

Raena sat up, still half asleep, and rubbed her hands through her hair. "I don't smell anything."

"You will," he promised.

She walked over to touch the door with her left elbow. The metal seemed the same temperature as the ambient air, but now that she stood close to it, she could smell . . . something out of place. Voices shouted in the distance.

Fire dropped from the ceiling of her room. It fluttered downward toward Haoun, who grabbed the thin mattress and dragged it out of the way before the flames could catch. Raena sprinted for the shower, soaked her towel, and beat the flames out before they took hold of anything. She didn't have much in the room that could burn, other than the bedding. If she'd been asleep . . .

"What's going on?" Haoun demanded.

Someone in the cell next-door started screaming. The brutal sound was terrible to hear. Apparently, that prisoner had not been lucky enough to be out of bed when the fire rained down.

Raena tugged the mattress into the shower and soaked it.

"What's going on?" Haoun repeated. He came to rinse the soot off her towel.

"We're under attack. If it's aimed at me, they don't know where I am. So they're setting all the cells on this level on fire."

She dragged the sodden mattress across the cell and tipped it up on one end to block the cell door. Haoun helped her to get it into place.

"Where are the guards?"

Raena looked at him, unable to answer.

He nodded. "What do we do?"

"I am small enough that I could get through the window, but I won't leave you here." She was thinking on her feet now. "Did they let you keep your comm bracelet?"

"They said it wouldn't work in here."

"It won't. I'm going to take it outside and see if I can get us some help. Who's it keyed for?"

"Mykah." Haoun unwound the bracelet and handed it to her. "What should I do?"

"Get the towel. Wave it around in front of the camera. Shout for help. I don't know who is supposed to be monitoring us, but maybe you can get their attention."

She waited until he was in place, then scrambled up the wall. She stuck one hand out the window first, waved it around, but no one shot at her. She confirmed her grasp on the wall inside the cell, then cautiously poked her head out. Again, no one shot at her.

She could see the fire in the cell next to hers. The creature, whatever he was, still screamed, but the sound had grown weaker, sorrowful and ready for the pain to be over. Fires burned in other cells. Other voices shouted or shrieked or prayed. Even with all Raena had seen and done, this random violence shocked her.

She got her arms out of the window and switched on the comm bracelet. Mykah didn't answer immediately. Raena hoped that he and Coni weren't being so intimate that they were undistractable. She hoped they weren't out in some loud casino, where he'd never notice the call.

"'Lo?" Mykah asked sleepily.

"It's me," Raena said. "Fiana." She hoped he was awake enough to remember her code name. "The jailhouse is under attack. The guards aren't coming. We need help."

"Oh my god," Mykah said. "I can see the fire."

She didn't ask where he was. "Sound an alarm. Grab a camera. Get some attention somehow. People are dying in here."

"I'm on it. Coni, get up." Then to Raena again, he asked, "Are you safe?"

"At the moment. I think the structure is Templar stone and won't burn. But the smoke—"

"Do what you can to stay safe. We're coming."

As Raena got ready to climb back down into her cell, distant lights caught her eye. Ten or a dozen figures blasted off from the exterior of the jailhouse. Their jetpacks lifted them so quickly that they were difficult to see through the smoke and the flickering firelight. Raena was certain they wore mirrored helmets and unmarked gray uniforms.

Smoke gathered against the high ceiling of the cell. She gasped in a last clear breath, then scrambled down the wall.

Haoun sat on the floor of her cell with the singed towel pressed to his face. Raena duckwalked over to him, tugged on his arm, and nodded toward the shower. "I don't know how long the water will hold out, but we should wet ourselves down."

"Is it bad out there?"

She nodded.

"Go," he said. "It's stupid for us both to die."

"We're not going to die," Raena promised. "I've been in much worse danger than this."

"I never have been."

He wasn't too stubborn to move, she realized. He was too frightened. She tugged on his arm again. He was too big for her to carry. She wondered if she could drag him. "Come on, Haoun. Focus on what you can do right now. Don't worry about what might happen.

Trust me. If I have to crawl out of here, attack the guards, and steal us some breathers, I will. But right now, we're in a room that's not burning. No one is shooting at us. Neither of us is injured. The situation is scary, but we're okay."

He swallowed hard, then crawled after her into the shower. "How do you live like this?"

It was a tight fit for them both under the showerhead, but the rush of the water blocked out the shouting outside in the cellblock.

"I don't live like this," she told him. "I live with you and Mykah and the others on the *Veracity*. Life there is pretty calm. The food is great. Someone's always having an interesting conversation about media manipulation or computer games or the latest sporting contests. I wouldn't trade it for anything."

He pulled her close and buried his snout in her neck. "Tell me we'll be okay," he begged.

Raena pulled his head up so he could meet her gaze. "We'll be fine," she promised. "Help is on its way. Mykah will go into journalist mode. This will make the galactic news, whether my trial has or not. Kai will pay us to leave, before long."

He laughed grimly. "I can't believe you can joke at a time like this."

She smiled. "What makes you think I'm joking? I'm not afraid at all."

Actually, with the guys in gray on the loose outside, she preferred to be holed up in here, where she didn't attract their notice.

* * *

Mykah cabled the camera to his handheld, checked to make sure everything was charged, and scrambled into his clothing.

Coni tried to reach Corvas on her comm. "There's a fire at the jail," she said when he didn't pick up. "Raena's alive. We're going to find help."

Gisela met them in the *Veracity*'s corridor with her gun in her hands. "What's going on?"

"Don't know," Mykah said. "Stay here. I'm gonna lock you in." Thank goodness Kavanaugh had shown him how to do it.

"Call your mother," Coni suggested. "Make sure she's okay."

"Why wouldn't she be?" Gisela followed them to the hatch.

"Because this is a distraction from something else," Mykah said. "I don't know what's going on, but all eyes will be on this fire." He kissed Coni's cheek. "You sure you don't want to stay here?"

"I go where you go," she reminded.

"Let me cover you," Gisela said. She moved into position at the edge of the hatch. Coni keyed it open. Luckily, the docking bay remained empty outside. Mykah ducked out first, then raised the cover on the exterior palm lock. He attached the scrambler Kavanaugh had recommended, told the screen the new passcode, then closed everything up. The hatch slid shut, locking Gisela inside with Eilif and Jim.

"Let's go." Mykah took Coni's hand in his and they ran.

* * *

The loudspeaker said, "Prisoner Zacari, remove your barricade from the door. The guards are outside to assist you."

"Do you trust them?" Haoun asked.

Raena stood up and turned off the shower. She handed Haoun the sodden towel to hold over his face. "We've got three choices. We can stay here and hope the building can withstand the fire. We can fight our way out, unarmed and unarmored, against the guards, whatever prisoners are free, and the fire suppression team. Or we can trust that they have really come to help us get out of here."

She grabbed hold of the mattress and pushed it away from the door. "Choosing one of those doesn't necessarily negate the other two choices." But, she thought, if the soldiers in gray stood outside her door, they'd just called her by name. They knew where she was.

She moved to the far side of the cell to watch the guards come in. This time there were only two, both wearing breathers, dressed in the standard jailer uniform. Only one had a stun stick, which he held casually. She could have plucked it from his hands. Would have, probably, if Haoun hadn't been with her. She wasn't sure how far the lizard could run in the murky air.

"Prisoners are being assembled in the courtrooms downstairs," a guard said.

No shackles, Raena noted. She waited for them to stun her as she walked toward the door, but they let her go. She offered her hand to Haoun. "Keep your head down and the towel over your face," she said. "I'll get you out of here."

* * *

Ariel joined the mob in the street outside the Hall of Justice. Kai might not have ever seen so much chaos. People milled around, shouting and crying. Scuffles kept flaring up, but Planetary Security moved quickly to break things up.

Overhead the desert wind spread flaming debris from the jail to buildings nearby. Seemingly every firefighter on the planet zipped around overhead, attacking the new fires before they could grow.

Ariel missed her guns more than ever now. Not that she felt physically endangered by the blazes or the panicking crowd, but being armed would have given her a measure of comfort. Now she simply felt small and vulnerable amongst the creatures of the galaxy, most of whom were larger than she was. She didn't even have the benefit of Raena's high-heeled boots.

Ariel caught a glimpse of Mykah and Coni with a pair of cameras, interviewing people on the street. Thank goodness she didn't see Jim or Eilif, who she hoped were locked safely in the *Veracity*. Gisela was level-headed enough to keep a good watch over them, but she was young and hadn't seen real combat. Ariel hoped her daughter wouldn't be tested tonight.

A voice came over the loudspeaker above the crowd. "Visitors and citizens of Kai, we are attempting to restore order. Return to your homes and hotels. The Business Council has declared a curfew of midnight. Anyone found on the streets after that time will be arrested and fined."

In the silence that greeted the announcement, someone shouted, "What about the prisoners?"

"My husband is in there!" another voice shouted.

"My daughter!"

"My brother!"

The crowd washed toward the steps of the Hall of Justice. Planetary Security advanced on the mob, stunning anyone who got in their way.

Ariel could do the math. Unless they'd been modified, which she doubted, those stun staves held enough charges to stop twenty people max. Once the staves ran down, those Security agents were going to find themselves surrounded by a sea of enraged tourists and armed with clubs. This would be a bloodbath.

She struggled over toward Mykah and Coni. Mykah had shimmied up a streetlight, where his camera had a clear view of the pandemonium.

Coni saw Ariel coming and waded out into the chaos to catch hold of her. "Thanks," Ariel panted. "We've got to get Mykah down. If Security reinforcements show up with sleep grenades, they're going to take out the journalists first." She looked up at him, with his long legs twined around the lamppost so that his hands were free to hold the camera steady. From that height, the fall would kill him.

She put her room key into Coni's hand. "Go up to my hotel room. The balcony has a good view down into the square."

"Where are you going?"

"To check on Raena."

"Don't you want us to come with you?" Coni asked.

Ariel said, "If I get my head bashed in, it will be my own damn fault. I don't want to be responsible for you."

The blue girl's expression was unreadable, but she nodded. "Good luck."

"You, too," Ariel hoped.

* * *

Ariel skirted the edge of the riot, trying to look harmless and lost. She slipped into an empty doorway to comm Corvas. He answered instantly. "Are you safe?" she demanded.

"I'm still in the hospital, getting my forearm mended," he said. "What's going on out there?"

"A huge fire in the jail. Now there's a riot outside the Hall of Justice. The Business Council set a curfew for midnight." She ducked deeper into her doorway as additional Planetary Security rushed toward the fray on jet bikes. "I need to get Raena out of the jail now. Advice?"

"Go around to the back of the building, where it faces onto the alley. Tell the guard you got separated from your party. You're frightened. Cry."

"All right, that gets me in. Then what?"

"Have they evacuated the cells?"

Ariel stared up at the smoke drifting out of the jail tower. "I hope so. The damage looks bad."

He didn't answer her right away. She wondered what he was looking up one-handed. "Disaster protocol says they will assemble prisoners in the courtrooms. You're sure she won't use the distraction to escape on her own?"

"She can't," Ariel said. "Haoun's with her."

"All right. That should get you to her. I'll see if I can negotiate bail for her from here, but they may be too panicked to let anyone go tonight—even you."

"Understood. Thanks, Corvas."

"Be careful."

* * *

"Prisoner Zacari," the bailiff called.

Raena looked up to see the last person she expected standing in the doorway at the back of the courtroom. A pair of Planetary Security agents flanked Ariel. She had been crying, but she looked steely now. Raena clasped Haoun's hand and pulled him after her.

"You're being released on bond," the Haru bailiff told her. "If possible, your trial will resume in the morning. You should present yourself here at 0800 Kai Standard Time. That's 14:20 GST."

Raena launched herself into Ariel's arms. Ariel laughed quietly into her hair. When she set Raena's feet back on the floor, she kept hold of her hand and drew her toward the back of the building.

"Secret exit?" Raena wondered.

"The street outside is a mess. We're going out the back way. Then we'll have to find another way back to my hotel."

"We can do that," Raena assured.

"You sound hoarse," Ariel noted.

"Not enough breathers to go around," Haoun explained.

Ariel nodded. "Do you need oxygen?"

"Just out of here."

* * *

As soon as the back door of the Justice building locked behind them, Raena smelled Doze gas. The night was preternaturally quiet. She stifled a cough in the crook of her elbow. "Define mess," she said.

"Riot," Ariel answered.

"Smells like it's been pacified now."

Ariel checked the time on her comm bracelet. "We need to be off the street before midnight. That gives us forty minutes."

"You take point," Raena said. "Haoun, you're in the middle. I'm gonna see if I can scare up some walking-around weapons."

* * *

"What does she mean by that?" Haoun asked.

"If you have to ask, you don't want to know," Ariel told him. "For now, stick close to me and keep quiet. We don't want to alert Planetary Security that we're out here creeping around."

He scooted close enough to shadow her. Ariel flashed him a reassuring smile, then turned to pay attention to their surroundings. She jogged up to the corner, motioned for Haoun to wait, then peered around it. The cross street was empty, but a block to their left, emergency beacons reflected off the buildings surrounding the square.

Ariel trotted across the intersection. Haoun followed right behind her. Raena was gone already, but Ariel trusted she was somewhere within shouting distance.

They crossed several more deserted intersections before turning back toward the hotel. There weren't many people on the street even here. Most had their heads down, hurrying somewhere, like Ariel and Haoun. Once she saw a quartet of Walosi that she thought might cause trouble, but the creatures turned aside when they decided Haoun really was with her.

She and Haoun were barely half a block away from the hotel when a trio of soldiers in unmarked gray uniforms materialized out of the shadows.

Haoun stiffened in recognition. Before Ariel could say anything, Raena dropped from overhead. She held a stun staff in front of her like a bat. She bashed one of the soldiers to the ground with the height of her fall.

Ariel grabbed Haoun and pulled him around the fight toward the lights of the hotel's entrance.

Raena reversed her hold on the staff and thrust it backward into another soldier. It sparked hard enough to throw him off his feet.

The third attacker pivoted to fire at Ariel. That gave Raena the opening she needed. She flung the stun staff like a javelin. The staff discharged across the back of the gray soldier's armor, lighting him up. He toppled like a tree, all his muscles locked.

One of the assailants' guns had fallen to the street. Raena hooked her foot under it and kicked it up into her hand.

As she advanced on him, Ariel shouted, "Run! It's almost midnight."

Raena sprinted toward them. When she caught up, she handed the weirdly bulbous gun to Haoun. "Please put this in your pack," she said. "Gently."

He unzipped the pack he wore slung across his chest and eased the weird weapon inside.

The hotel's private security stopped the three of them at the door until they confirmed Ariel was a registered guest.

As the three of them strolled into the empty lobby, Raena said, "Haoun, get us another room, please. We're moving Ariel out of hers. An internal room, if they have them. With two big beds."

"In an alias?" he asked softly.

"Yes, please."

Ariel watched him go. "You think that's necessary?"

"Either they knew which hotel was yours, or they're watching all of them."

"Those guys in gray?"

Raena coughed quietly into her elbow.

"Who are they?" Ariel asked.

"Don't know. But they're the ones who started the jailhouse fires. There are at least nine or ten more of them around Kai City somewhere."

"Mykah and Coni are up in my room, filming the riot."

"Comm them. Tell them to grab anything you're going to need tonight. Leave the rest."

Once Ariel had done that, Raena asked, "What happens at midnight?"

"Curfew takes effect," Ariel said. "I didn't want you to be caught violating the terms of your release already."

* * *

As soon as Mykah strode through the door of the new hotel room, he came straight over to hug Raena. Hard. It made her cough.

"You okay?" he asked.

She nodded. "Scared out of my mind, but okay."

The warm buzz of having everyone together chilled.

"Tell us," Ariel said.

"Come sit down." Raena waited until they'd settled on the beds and the floor. "Those soldiers in gray: they're the ones that attacked Mellix's apartment in Capital City. They caused the truck accident on Lautan and would have killed me there, if the bounty hunters hadn't stopped them. They were waiting for us on Kai, so either they can travel faster than a tesseract ship or there are more than the thirteen I've seen at one time. Then tonight, they were dropping fire on every prisoner sleeping on my level in the jail. If Haoun hadn't been guarding me, I would have been burned alive like the poor bastard in the cell next to mine."

"No idea who they are?" Mykah asked.

"None. I thought they were after Mellix on Capital City. That's the logical assumption, right? But Capital City was the first time I'd been off the *Veracity* and used my own name. I think they were looking for me. Bihn, one of the bounty hunters, said he'd seen them several places around the galaxy, always wearing their mirrored helmets, always on a mission. He said that the galactic media was keeping their existence quiet."

"I'll ask Mellix about them," Mykah offered.

"Please do."

"What are you going to do?" Ariel wanted to know.

Raena coughed raggedly. It left her even more hoarse. "What are the odds that court will be in session tomorrow morning?"

"You're not thinking of going back?" Haoun asked.

"I'm out on bail," Raena reminded. "If I leave Kai, they'll destroy Ariel and her Foundation."

Coni agreed. "They'll need to wrap up the trial for the broadcast audience. Leaving the planet now will be spun as evidence that humans aren't trustworthy, that Ariel is finding homes for thugs and criminals."

"Actually, I'm pretty sure they're hoping you'll jump bail," Ariel said. "They stand to make a small fortune. They ought to put my name on the jailhouse when they rebuild it."

"I'm sorry," Raena said. "You shouldn't have let them blackmail you."

"I wanted you out of there tonight," Ariel argued.

Raena leaned over to kiss her. "I want to go back in the morning and clear my name, if we can do it," she said. "In addition to tarring Ariel, if I leave Kai, anyone who travels with me will be considered a criminal. At the moment, they're only charging me with a planetary crime, but if we run, the Business Council could petition the Council of Worlds to take up their case against me. They could make it so the *Veracity* could never visit any civilized world again. None of you could ever go home. I don't want that for you."

No one had any response to that.

Raena's cough rattled her whole body. Mykah got up to bring her a cup of water. Finally, after she got the cough back under control, she rasped, "Are Eilif and Jimi safe?"

"They're on the *Veracity* with Gisela," Mykah said.

Before Raena could ask, Ariel explained, "One of my daughters."

Raena nodded. "Have you checked in with them recently?"

"It's late," Haoun pointed out.

"Eilif will answer," Raena said. No one asked why she knew that.

"I'll comm her," Ariel volunteered. She got up off the end of the bed and walked over to the corner of the room to do it.

"Is Vezali with Kavanaugh?"

The *Veracity*'s crew exchanged a look.

"All right," Raena asked, "what haven't you told me?"

* * *

Mykah told her everything they knew about the activity on Drusingyi, from Jim's initial message to Vezali's plan to swim down into the ocean and take a look.

Raena sighed and laid back on the bed, rubbing her chest. "I'm touched you think I can solve anything," she said hoarsely, "but I'm not sure what you want me to do about this."

"If the robot was cloning him again . . ." Mykah started.

"I didn't leave anything for the robot to clone," she promised. "Jonan had hauled all the boys and his brothers together into the dining hall. I made sure they were all ashed. If there were cloneable cells stored elsewhere, the power was off for who knows how long after the ocean had swallowed everything. Nothing could still be viable. Even if somehow, someone managed to clone a Thallian or two back to life, they wouldn't have Jonan to turn them into monsters."

"We thought you'd be eager to make certain," Coni said.

"Jimi's more of a danger than any hypothetical clone," Raena said. "I don't trust him."

"He got you out of a kidnapping charge," Ariel pointed out as she came back into the conversation.

"And I'm grateful," Raena said. "But he didn't have to lie about being Jain. Kai hadn't identified the Thallian boy I kidnapped. Jimi could have claimed his own name, but instead he lied. Did you see how smooth he was? Practiced. He lied to his family from the time he contacted me until I helped him prep his hopper for escape. He lied to Jonan for years before that." Raena sat up and shook her head. "I spent years watching Jonan work. No one lied to him for long."

"Do you think he sent Vezali and Kavanaugh into a trap?" Mykah asked.

"I don't know. Something doesn't add up." Raena turned her attention to Ariel. "What's the word from Eilif?"

"She didn't answer. It is late, though. Sometimes she takes sleep drops when she's anxious and can't wind down. I left her a message to call as soon as she wakes up."

Raena closed her eyes and nodded.

"What if it is Templars cloning themselves back from the dead?" Mykah asked.

"That sounds hopeful, doesn't it? Having them back would negate humanity's greatest sin. Unless they have a hankering for vengeance."

"You're just full of cheer tonight," Ariel snapped.

Raena worked up a smile for her. "Just because you know I'm paranoid, don't let me do all your worrying."

She turned to Haoun. "Let Ariel take a look at the gun."

He unzipped his pouch and cautiously took it out. Ariel accepted it with both hands.

"Any ideas?" Raena said.

"Never seen one like this before." She held it carefully by the barrel, which she kept pointed at the floor.

"No trigger," Raena told the others.

"Uh-huh." Ariel didn't look up from her examination. "The power system is enclosed, so either it's rechargeable or it's disposable."

"Templar tech?" Raena asked.

"Possibly, but I'm no expert on Templar weapons. And I haven't seen every gun in the galaxy yet." She looked up at Raena. "This what you took off that gray soldier out in the street?"

"Yeah. They had them on Lautan, too, but I was afraid I'd blow my own head off if I tried to use it then."

"Have you seen them fire it?"

"No. They'd drawn and were advancing on me when the bounty hunters took them down on Lautan. Tonight I stunned the last soldier before he could take his shot." Raena watched Ariel set the bulbous gun atop the clothes cupboard.

"We're either going to have to figure out how it works or how to dispose of it come morning," Ariel said. "We can't take it into court and we can't leave it in the room when we check out, or Kai will bust us for possessing another weapon."

Raena nodded. "I don't want to give the Business Council another credit. I'll find a way to get rid of it."

Ariel looked around at the others. Now that the excitement of the evening had worn off, they all looked exhausted. Raena could see it, too.

"Haoun, do you mind taking the floor?" she asked.

"I'd prefer it."

"You sleeping in the bed with me?" Ariel asked her.

Raena grinned at her, but said, "Wasn't planning on it."

Ariel laughed. "Good. I'm too tired for your shenanigans tonight."

Raena found an extra pillow and a blanket in the cupboard, then rolled herself up in it and snuggled her back up against Haoun. He put an arm over her, rested his chin on the top of her head, and was asleep before they'd turned out the lights.

Raena smiled and closed her eyes, but she didn't think she'd get any more sleep tonight. Her thoughts zoomed in too many directions. What she needed was to finish the trial and get off of Kai soon, before she died here. The problem was that now she was responsible for Ariel, the crew of the *Veracity*, the remaining Thallians, and Ariel's daughter. How could she possibly protect them all?

* * *

Raena woke everyone in the morning with her coughing. She sat up, trying to get a grip on it, but the soot in her lungs had decided it was time to get out. She shut herself in the bathroom. The door muffled her coughing only slightly.

Ariel tapped on the door. "If court's not in session this morning, we're going to the hospital."

"All I need is some RespirAll," Raena argued, "but I'm not taking it if we're going to court."

Ariel laughed.

"Have you checked in with the court?" Raena's voice sounded worse than it had the night before.

"I will," Ariel promised.

As she came back into the sleeping room, the others were sitting up and blinking. Both Coni's fur and Mykah's hair stuck upward at weird angles.

"Mykah, will you order us some breakfast? You know what everyone will like. Charge it to the room and I'll pick it up."

"Got it." He bent over to dig around in the pile of clothes beside the bed to find his comm.

"Coni, will you call the court and find out if we need to get down there this morning?"

The blue girl nodded.

"What do you want me to do?" Haoun asked.

"Take care of Raena. She'll accept it better from you."

He crawled up off the floor and headed for the bathroom.

"Get her into the shower," Ariel suggested. "Both of you need to get the soot off your skin."

Ariel settled on the end of the bed to try reaching Gisela or Eilif again.

* * *

Unsurprisingly, court would not be in session this morning. The courthouse staff was still trying to release or rehouse their prisoners, so the courtrooms were unavailable. To Coni's surprise, they didn't even want Raena to present herself until afternoon, if then.

Raena continued to cough in the bathroom. It sounded as if she was having trouble getting her lungs back under control in the humid air of the shower.

"What's RespirAll?" Coni asked Ariel.

"It's a medicine designed to help humans breathe unfamiliar atmospheres," Mykah explained.

"It's also a truth serum," Ariel added, "if you get too much. Dosage is really tricky. If you've used it before, and Raena has, you're more susceptible to the side effects."

"Do you think it would ease her cough?" Coni asked. "I could go see if the hotel can provide some."

Ariel shook her head. "She needs to go to a hospital. RespirAll isn't going to clear the soot from her lungs. She needs to get it suctioned out and get some oxygen, but you know how she feels about medical procedures."

"I'll go with her," Coni volunteered.

"She'll feel better if you would," Ariel said. "Thank you. You could check on Corvas, too, if he's still there."

"Any word from the *Veracity*?" Mykah asked.

"I haven't been able to get through to any of them yet." Ariel's voice shook with worry. "I'm going to try again. Does anyone know if the curfew is lifted yet?"

"I'll check on it," Coni promised.

* * *

Gisela rolled her eyes open, but it took a moment for her to recognize what she was seeing. She lay on the deck of the *Veracity*, looking across a large puddle of blood.

She put one hand to her head tentatively, trying to ascertain if her brain really was in danger of falling out. Her head pounded, but her skull seemed intact.

Eilif lay across her legs. As Gisela's vision cleared, she could tell the little woman was dead. Blood ran from her ears, nose, and mouth.

The sound that woke Gisela repeated. She crawled across the deck, leaving a red smear, to slap at the comm button. Then she leaned against the console to fight off a tidal wave of vertigo.

"Answer me," her mom repeated. "Are you all right?"

"No," Gisela said. "Eilif's dead. I've got a head injury. Don't know where Jim is."

She heard Ariel suck in a deep breath. More calmly than Gisela expected, her mom asked, "Can you stand?"

Gisela used the console to wobble to her feet. "Shaky," she said.

"I'll be there as soon as I can. For now, make sure you are safe. Seal up the ship if you're alone. Are you armed?"

"My gun's gone. I'll get something else."

"Good girl. Call me when you find Jim."

Gisela didn't nod because she was afraid to slosh her brain around.

As soon as she stepped out of the cockpit into the passageway, she felt a hot draft blowing through the ship. The main hatch yawned open. She closed and locked it, but she knew Jim was gone.

The gun lockers by the main hatch stood open. In fact, every cubby where Mykah had hidden weapons was empty. Gisela wasn't sure what that meant, but she knew it was bad.

She searched the ship, dreading to find Jim's body bleeding out like Eilif's, but she didn't. In the process, she'd tracked bloody footprints all over the ship, but she didn't think she could deal with them herself without blacking out again.

Once she was sure she was alone, she went to the galley to make herself an ice pack and a cup of tea and to wait for her mom to come.

CHAPTER 12

Raena came out of the shower finally. Her skin had gone a weird reddish shade, like a sunburn beneath her normal coloring. She'd gotten the coughing somewhat under control, though.

She skinned into one of Ariel's extra dresses, a loose green sundress that hung to her feet. Tricky to fight in, Mykah would have said, although Raena's boot heels would have helped somewhat. They'd have to retrieve her boots from the *Veracity* later. Until she stopped coughing, though, she didn't need to be fighting.

Breakfast came while everyone rotated through the shower. Mykah had ordered a spectrum of food: eggs, pastries, crunchy beetles for Haoun, stir-fried vegetables and rice, something that would pass as miso for Raena. She smiled at him gratefully as she settled down over the thermos to eat.

Glancing at her comm bracelet, Coni said, "Oh, the curfew is over now."

"About time." Ariel took Raena's face in her hands and kissed her good and hard. Then she grabbed some of the pastries and headed out the door. Mykah and Coni stared after her, waiting for Raena to let them know if they should worry. She didn't put her miso down.

"Where's she going?" Haoun asked.

"To check on her daughter," Raena rasped.

"Should we worry?" Mykah asked her.

"If she wanted us to worry, she would have said something."

Mykah shifted, more bothered than Raena appeared to be. It seemed out of character for Ariel not to have told them whether she got through to the *Veracity* or not.

"What should we do about the gray soldiers' gun?" Coni asked at last.

"Maid cart?" Haoun suggested.

"Don't get anyone else in trouble," Raena said. "Is there a trash chute in the hallway? A window to a light well?"

"No, the hotel has concentric circles of rooms," Mykah said. "The outside circle has balconies and windows. The inside rooms, like this one, don't have any connection to the outside."

"Before we dispose of it, we should go clear out Ariel's other room," Raena said.

Coni said, "I could hack into the hotel's security system and see if anyone had been in there."

Raena nodded. "That's a good start. It will help us know if they came through the hotel, but not if they came in from the balcony."

"You think they actually messed with her stuff?" Mykah asked.

"Don't know. I can't figure out what they were doing last night."

* * *

When the security video turned out to be clear, Raena led Mykah and Coni upstairs. They let themselves into Ariel's room, but as far as Coni could tell, it was in the same shape as the night before. Ariel wasn't one to live in military tidiness, the way Raena did. Clothing and jewelry lay scattered all around the room.

Raena checked the balcony door and poked around halfheartedly. After that she helped collect up Ariel's stuff briefly, before lying on the bed while Mykah and Coni finished up. Her breathing had gotten more ragged.

"All right?" Mykah asked.

Raena laughed softly. "I think I broke something with the coughing this morning."

Coni looked at her sharply.

"Kidding," Raena said.

Coni wasn't convinced.

On the way back to the elevator, Raena detoured into the room at the end of the hall that housed the vending machines. When she stooped to collect her bottle of water from a machine, she gently unwrapped her skirt from the bulbous gun, placed the gun on the floor, and nudged it under the machine with her toe. The movement would have been too smooth to see, except that Coni had been watching for it.

"What's the plan for the rest of the day?" Mykah asked.

"Hospital," Raena rasped.

"I'm coming with you," Coni said.

"Good."

They went back down to the other room to drop off Ariel's stuff. Haoun was waiting to let them in.

"Ariel's at the *Veracity*," he said. "Mykah, she wants you to meet her there."

"Will do." He gave Coni a big hug, then slipped out the door ahead of them.

* * *

Raena found the walk through Kai City eerie, like the morning she had walked in from the underground river. Was the stillness a function of the early hour or had people frightened themselves with the previous night's rioting and Planetary Security's enthusiastic response?

In the jail, she'd worried that Haoun, with his head up higher than hers in the smoke, would damage his lungs. Now it hurt to draw a deep breath. The cough didn't seem to want to leave her alone for long.

She was grateful for Coni and Haoun walking on either side of her, but she knew if it came to a fight, they would be less than no help. She'd seen the limits of Haoun's bravery, and Coni . . . Well, she knew Coni could run away. For her own part, Raena decided to simply lie down and take her punishment. Last night, the grays had proven how little they cared about collateral damage—but her own surrender might give the others enough time to escape. At this point, she would rather lie down and take a beating than stand up, doubled over and coughing.

The area around the hospital seemed especially quiet. Raena hoped that meant the doctors had processed everyone who'd come in before curfew took effect, so she'd be able to waltz in and waltz out.

The waiting room gave the lie to that. Raena hadn't known there were so many people on Kai.

Coni gently led the way through the crowd to the intake window. Raena heard her cough echoed throughout the room. The clerk had ceased being sympathetic.

While Coni checked her in, Raena looked over the waiting room. The people looked thoroughly miserable: eyes streaming from smoke, heads aching from Doze gas, completely traumatized by Planetary Security beating them back, compounded by the nightlong wait for treatment. Raena sympathized. She wondered if she could find a little patch of floor to curl up on and pass out.

To placate the people trapped in the waiting room, several screens played news from around the galaxy. One screen showed Raena fighting the Thallians' soldier in court yesterday. Raena watched herself, noting how she could have done the takedown more elegantly. Just like Corvas's video of her fight against the Thallian abduction squad, this video counted the amount of time between when the soldier launched himself from the witness stand at her and when the courtroom guards finally stunned him. It took longer than she expected.

After Coni finished the intake process, she occupied herself by making calls on her comm bracelet. Raena leaned against Haoun for support as much as for comfort. The lack of oxygen made her woozy.

A knot of young humans, followed by their disapproving nonhuman chaperones, came to encircle Raena, Haoun, and Coni. Haoun positioned himself protectively in front of Raena. She smiled up at his back, even though he couldn't see it.

"You're from the *Veracity*, right?" one of the boys asked eagerly.

Haoun nodded skeptically.

"We've been watching the trial."

About the same time as her crewmates, Raena realized that the kids wore "Free Raena Zacari" T-shirts.

"Have they dropped the charges?" one of the girls wanted to know.

Raena shook her head. "Out on bail." Her voice sounded alien to her own ears.

Others in the waiting room began to recognize her. The crowd around them grew denser. People wanted to congratulate her for killing the Thallians or ask where she'd trained. One guy wanted to hire her, either as a bodyguard or as a companion, Raena wasn't clear. Not all the attention was approving, but Raena had trouble tracking it. The kids closest to her all babbled at once, something about role model and standing up to anti-humanists and what an honor. Raena wondered if they were breathing up all her air. Haoun kept a grip on Raena's shoulder, holding her upright.

Then Corvas appeared, wading through the crowd. Even though the slim lizard was much smaller than Haoun, he knew how to command space. He cleared a margin around her. The kids stared at him, starstruck. Security cameras buzzed around, getting a good view of Raena being supported and protected by Haoun, Coni, and Corvas. She wondered if that would make it into the broadcast of her trial.

A human doctor showed up, flanked by a couple of hospital security guards. They cleared a path for Raena into the treatment area.

Raena whispered to Corvas, "What just happened?"

His eyes rotated to regard her. "Exactly what Ariel hoped would happen."

* * *

The doctor asked Raena to sit on an examining table. Luckily, Haoun was there to boost her up. Her skin looked even more sunburned now, the reddish tone brightening under her usual color.

"You need the soot suctioned from your lungs," the doctor said. "It's filling the alveoli and making it hard for you to get enough oxygen. The suctioning process is uncomfortable. You need to hold absolutely still or there's a chance that we could puncture your lungs. Sedation is not optional."

Raena reached out and Coni took her hand. The blue girl said, "Haoun needs to be treated, too, but Corvas will stay with you."

"Where are you going?" Raena rasped.

"Something has happened on the *Veracity*. Mykah wants me to meet him there."

Raena's vision went black around the edges. She felt her body going away.

* * *

"Everyone out," the doctor ordered.

"I'll stay," Corvas said calmly. "You know who she is."

The doctor nodded.

"I'm losing count of the number of attempts on Raena's life on Kai," Corvas said. "I know you will do your best for her, Doctor, but for your safety, she needs a guard. I will be it."

"All right. Everyone else . . ."

Coni took Haoun's arm and tried to nudge him away.

"I'm staying, too," he growled. "She didn't leave me last night. I'm not leaving her now."

"I don't care who stays or goes," the doctor snapped, "but I need to help her now."

Coni led the other two back out of the doctor's way. "The *Veracity* was attacked in the night," she said quietly. "Ariel wants me to pull up the video. I need to go."

"Go," Corvas said. "We'll watch over Raena."

* * *

Coni wasn't sure what she expected as she walked across Kai City, but the strange and frightening silence that filled the morning wasn't it. Most shops remained shuttered. Most tourists seemed to have kept close to their hotels. She was almost the only person loping through town.

She watched for the soldiers in gray, but they didn't seem to be lurking around. She tried to remember if they'd ever attacked Raena in the daylight.

Coni had never particularly worried about her own safety before. On the scale of people in the galaxy, she was average size. Her teeth and claws were sharp enough to make most creatures think twice about getting too close. She'd taken some self-defense classes in school, but now she wished she'd sparred with Raena aboard the *Veracity*. More fight training might have made her feel more confident this morning.

That spun her thoughts off into another direction. She didn't know what to expect aboard the *Veracity*. Mykah had locked Ariel's daughter and the two Thallians aboard last night. Coni hoped that Raena's mistrust of Jim Zacari was unfounded. She kind of liked the boy.

* * *

Unlike the rest of Kai City, the spaceport bustled this morning. The party on Kai seemed to be over. Ship after ship powered up around Coni, taking off in search of a good time elsewhere.

When she reached their docking bay, Coni found the *Veracity* locked. She commed Mykah, who didn't pick up. As she left him a message, he opened the ship from the inside. He glanced over her shoulders before stepping back out of her way.

As soon as she crossed the threshold, Coni smelled blood. Death. "What's happened?"

"Someone got onto the ship last night." Mykah's voice quavered with fury.

"I thought you locked it," Coni said, before she thought better of it. She realized it sounded like an accusation.

"I did. It looks like Jim opened it from the inside. We need you to access the *Veracity*'s recordings to see if you can figure out why."

"Who is dead?" Coni heard a flutter in her own voice. Mykah turned back to take her in his arms, holding her close.

It was comforting, but she couldn't see his face when he said simply, "Eilif."

A little noise escaped her.

"It's bad in the cockpit," he said. "Can you work in our cabin?"

"Is Jim all right? Gisela?"

"I'll tell you everything," Mykah promised. "Let's get to work first. I want to know what happened, too."

As she followed him down the passageway, she caught a glimpse of Ariel on her hands and knees in the cockpit, mopping the floor. Shuddering, Coni closed her eyes and tried to wipe the image away.

"Is Planetary Security on their way?" Coni's voice still had the shrill flutter to it. The sound made her hackles rise.

"We didn't call them." Mykah opened their cabin door. Coni let him usher her in. She collapsed onto the desk chair. Everything looked normal inside. "Ariel says that they have completely failed to protect us at every opportunity so far. If they find out that we were sheltering another Thallian, beyond the one they already knew about, they will spin Eilif's death into more charges against us—or against Raena, since she was out of jail last night. Ariel wants us to find out who killed Eilif, so Raena can avenge her."

Coni's hands trembled as she reached out to wake the screen. She realized he hadn't told her about Jim or Gisela, but she was afraid to ask again.

* * *

Last night's recording from the cockpit's camera showed Gisela, Eilif, and Jim gathered together to stare down at the view screen. It was impossible to see what they were looking at, but the argument was easy to hear.

"You know he's dead, Jimi," Eilif said. "You've seen the video."

"We've seen all kinds of videos," Jim argued. "I know everyone believes Raena killed him. What if it was one more cover-up? What if Kai couldn't admit that they had him? That he was injured, but they patched him up and let him go?"

"At least set a test for him. Ask him something only Revan would know."

Coni sat back from the screen and stared at Mykah. "Revan?" she echoed.

"Can you pull up last night's recording from the exterior cameras?" Mykah asked.

"Do you want the *Veracity*'s cameras or the security cams in the docking bay?"

Mykah hugged her, amused to have been given a choice. "Let's see what they saw in the cockpit first."

Coni typed in the right commands and triggered the playback. On their screen, the docking bay filled with a squadron of soldiers in gray, their heads covered in mirrored helmets. They all looked similar in size and shape. "Human, do you think?" Coni asked.

Mykah shrugged. "We can rule out a whole lot of people they're not."

In the video, one of the soldiers stepped forward and stripped off his glove. He popped open the cover on the *Veracity*'s palm lock and laid his hand on the screen. The *Veracity* chirped as if it recognized him, but the door remained locked, waiting for Mykah's passcode.

The soldier stepped back out of the hatch alcove. He reached up under his helmet, unfastened its strap, and pulled it off. Then he gazed at the *Veracity*, silver eyes stormy with displeasure. It certainly looked like Revan Thallian.

"Are there more of them?" Mykah asked. "More Thallians than we knew about?"

"Gods, I hope not," Coni said. She toggled back to the cockpit's camera.

Jim walked out of frame. Eilif leaned over to Gisela and suggested quietly, "Hide."

Coni pressed pause on everything. "I'm not sure I can watch this."

"I need to see," Mykah said. "Why don't you ask Ariel to come, too?"

Coni was only too happy to get up from the desk chair. Fear swirled around in her blood. She took a couple of steps toward the cockpit, before deciding she didn't really want to see what Ariel was scrubbing up.

"We're watching the video," Coni called down to her, "from the external cameras. Do you want to come see it?"

"I do," Gisela said quietly from inside her cabin. "I can't remember what happened."

Coni was so relieved the girl was still alive that she felt lightheaded.

When Gisela came to her cabin door, her face looked even paler than normal, her dark eyes even darker. Coni offered a hand to steady her. Gisela took it gratefully. "Are you all right?"

"I hit my head last night," the girl said. "I don't remember how. I was out almost all night."

Ariel joined them in the passage. Around the edges, her clothes were damp and stained with pink. Her mouth clenched in a grim line. "You're supposed to rest," she told Gisela.

"I'll rest better when I know what happened."

Ariel didn't argue with that.

They crowded into Coni and Mykah's cabin. Coni stood near the door, so she could duck out if she needed to. Mykah unpaused the video.

In the recording, Gisela slipped inside one of the lockers in the cockpit. Eilif closed its door after her, then stood in front of it, blocking it with her body. Coni was startled to watch the transformation that came over Eilif, once she heard the gray soldiers board the *Veracity*. Her posture shifted. Her head sank so that her gaze focused on the floor. She reverted to being a slave, not the free woman she had become.

The Revan soldier came into the cockpit.

Eilif said quietly, "Raena Zacari found the message you left for me."

"You followed it, of course," Revan snarled.

"Of course," Eilif answered.

"Pause it again," Ariel said. Mykah complied.

"That's not really Revan Thallian," Ariel told them. "Raena found a photograph of Eilif in that military coat of Revan's. It had no message, except as evidence that Revan secretly loved Eilif as much as she secretly loved him. Eilif was testing this guy. She just proved he was an impostor."

"That doesn't help us know who he is," Mykah pointed out.

"It narrows it down. He looked enough like Revan that Eilif wasn't sure and Jim was fooled."

"The ship recognized him," Coni observed.

"Then he's been altered or manufactured in some way to pass for a Thallian," Ariel said.

"Why would anyone do that?" Gisela asked.

"The question is," Mykah corrected, "who would have the technology?"

"Let's see some more," Ariel said. Mykah set the video to play again.

Jim followed his uncle's doppelganger into the cockpit. He glanced around for Gisela, then focused on his mother. Eilif didn't look up from the floor.

Revan rounded on Jim. "Can you fly this ship?"

"Not alone, sir."

"Then we'll scuttle it." Revan turned to his men, waiting in the passage out of view of the camera. He nodded sharply but didn't issue any order aloud. Then he asked Jim, "Do you know where they've hidden their weapons?"

"Yes, sir."

"Help my men confiscate them." He turned on Eilif. "Gather anything you want from this ship."

"Where are we going?" Eilif wondered quietly.

"Home." He glanced up at the *Veracity*'s recorder and smiled. Sharpened teeth filled his smile.

"Pause it again," Ariel said. "I've got to sit down." Rather than get her bloodstained clothes on Mykah and Coni's bedding, she sank to the floor. "It's a trap for Raena."

"We have to watch the rest of it," Gisela argued. "I want to know how Eilif died."

"You can tell me later," Coni said. "I'm going to call Corvas and check on Raena."

✳ ✳ ✳

After Coni had retreated into the lounge, Ariel asked, "Is she okay?"

Mykah nodded. "Coni's visual memory is very sharp. She remembers things from news programs she watched as a child that still trouble her. It's better if she doesn't see this."

He looked to Gisela, leaning against the wall by the door. "Please sit down," he invited.

Moving languidly as if not to rattle her brain around, Gisela settled on the floor. She leaned against Ariel's shoulder. Mykah started the playback again.

Eilif waited until all the gray soldiers were occupied elsewhere. Silently, she eased open the locker where Gisela hid. "You have to get a message to Raena," she whispered. "Tell her the *Veracity* is compromised. Don't tell her where we've gone. It's a trap."

She spun around half a second before Revan strode back into the cockpit. He held a bulbous gun like the one Raena had stolen the night before. "I'm sorry, my dears," he said. "We want the boy. We don't need you."

The second before he fired at them, Eilif flung herself in front of Gisela. The blast caught her squarely. She toppled back into Gisela, who struck her head on the locker door. Revan stood over them, gun ready, but neither of them moved. Eilif was already hemorrhaging onto the deck.

"It's a sonic weapon," Ariel said. "What a horrible way to die. You are lucky you didn't catch any more of the blast."

"She saved me," Gisela said, awed. Ariel put her arm around her daughter's shoulders. Gisela hugged her tightly.

Mykah turned away. He toggled through the other cameras, watching the soldiers empty the gun lockers and place the *Veracity*'s weapons into a crate. He reversed the recordings to watch them a second time.

"What did you see?" Ariel asked.

"They only took the weapons I got out to offer Vezali," he said. "Only the things that Jim had seen me put away. I didn't bother to haul everything out that night, because I knew there would be more than Vezali could carry, more than Kavanaugh would want. So that *really* wasn't Revan. He would have known where things could be stowed on his own ship."

"So we're not completely unarmed," Ariel echoed.

In answer, Mykah got up and pushed in the wall panel above the bunk. It clicked and dropped open. Two Sharpshooter rifles, a matched pair of Stinger pistols, and the weapons Vezali had bought them on Lautan were still hidden there.

"That's a relief," Gisela said with a sniffle.

Mykah handed her a Stinger and gave another to Ariel. Both of them ran through the same sequence of checks as they examined them. Mykah took his own Stinger, checked its power pack, then slipped it through the back of his belt. He wouldn't be able to carry it if he left the ship, but it comforted him now.

Once they were armed, Ariel asked, "Have you seen what they did to sabotage the *Veracity*?"

"Coni will have to search. She knows where all the cameras are stashed on the ship." He shook his head ruefully. "I wish Vezali were here. She's worked over most of the ship already. She would be able to see anything out of place."

Ariel didn't offer advice, which Mykah puzzled over. Then he realized it was a sign of respect, her way of allowing him to make decisions about his own vessel. "Let me talk to Haoun," Mykah said. "He had some other friends that we considered taking on as engineer, if Vezali said no when we left Kai the last time. Maybe one of them is familiar with old Earther ships and can help us get out of here."

"We can't leave right yet anyway," Ariel said. "Not until this stupid trial is settled."

"Let's watch the rest of the video," Gisela said. "I want to see what happened to Jim."

Mykah toggled back to the *Veracity*'s exterior camera. Once Revan replaced his mirrored helmet, he was interchangeable with the other gray soldiers.

Jim came down the *Veracity*'s ramp, followed by more soldiers. "Where's my mother?"

"She's not coming with us." The Revan replica's voice was strangely modulated by his helmet.

"I want to say goodbye," Jim insisted. He started back up the ramp.

"It's too late." The closest soldier jabbed him in the back with something. Jim collapsed with a groan. The grays doubled him up and dumped him into the crate atop the stolen weapons. Then they carried him out of the docking bay.

"So the whole attack on the prison last night was a subterfuge so they could kidnap Jim?" Ariel asked. "How many people are dead, between the fires and the riot, just so the grays could snatch the Thallian boy?"

"You think it wasn't really about killing Raena?" Mykah asked.

"I don't know. That Revan thing was sending her a pretty clear invitation to come after them. We may not know why until she gets back to the Thallian homeworld."

"My head hurts," Gisela said.

"You and I are off to the hospital, my girl," Ariel said. "Mykah, keep Coni out of the cockpit until everything dries. We need to get everyone back up to fighting trim and get the *Veracity* checked out, before anyone goes anywhere else."

* * *

Raena woke to find Corvas standing beside her, poking at his comm bracelet. Raena realized she'd never seen the lizard sitting. She wasn't sure if he could. She also realized he wore the blue and aquamarine caftan he'd had on the previous day in court.

"How's your arm?" Her voice sounded ragged, but it no longer hurt to speak.

His eyes swiveled to her and he flexed his hand. "Good as new."

"You haven't been back to your hotel room yet?"

"The curfew was still in effect when they finished with me last night. Then Coni called to say you were on your way to the hospital, so I stayed to meet you."

"Thank you for all you've done for me, Corvas."

One of his eyes turned toward a camera mounted in the corner of the room. Raena followed his gaze, then looked back at him.

Corvas dug around in the satchel slung over his shoulder. He pulled out his handheld, clicked around silently, then handed it to Raena. The screen showed a video of two teenagers: one human, one whatever Corvas was. "These are my boys," he said. "Ariel helped me adopt Saul when Tarash was an infant. They've grown up together. You've never seen such friends. Anything I do for Ariel, I am really doing for Saul."

Raena typed onto the screen before she passed the handheld back: *Are they safe somewhere?*

"Yes," Corvas said aloud. "Thank you."

"When can I get out of here?"

"Now that you're awake, we're waiting for the doctor to give you your walking papers. Unfortunately, Dr. Fishawk is the only human doctor in the emergency room today, so it may be a while before he can get back to you."

Raena wriggled herself into sitting up. The effort winded her, but nothing seemed painful. "How is Haoun?"

"They're treating him now."

"Is Coni with him?"

Corvas met her eyes. "No."

Raena exhaled hard. Corvas was even more paranoid than she generally was, but she had to believe—after all she'd been through on Kai—that he had his reasons. "What are the odds that I will miss my time in court?" she asked.

"You're right to suspect that being hospitalized is not an acceptable excuse for missing your trial. The court was still closed when

I checked in with them just now. However, since you were injured by the smoke in the jail—which apparently does not have a functioning fire-suppression system and so is not up to minimal galactic safety standards—the Business Council of Kai has agreed to cover the cost of your treatment here. Haoun's treatment, also."

Raena gave him a lopsided smile. "How is he?"

"Apparently, in better shape than you were. They were able to use some less invasive treatment on him, something that would help him to expel the soot. Didn't sound pleasant, but it also didn't require sedation. He's supposed to find his way back to the waiting room and wait for us there."

★ ★ ★

Kavanaugh concentrated on flying through the Thallians' mine-field. Most of the mines had been deactivated when the big rescue ships had come to collect the *Arbiter*'s survivors six months ago. Still, he didn't want to bump up against anything the minesweepers missed.

The planet ahead certainly looked dead. Kavanaugh flew them up on the nightside, where not a single artificial light gleamed in the blackness. It made him think of the Templar tombworld, another ghost world that memorialized a lost people. Both planets were little more than tombstones now. In a way, he supposed, they were book-ends: the victims of genocide and their killers.

"Were you on Drusingyi's surface before?" he asked Vezali.

"Yes. We landed to pick up Raena and Eilif after they'd destroyed the Thallians' city. The planet is pretty much a wasteland. Its surface is freezing cold, covered in poisoned snow. No surface vegetation. Not much surviving native wildlife, either, except in the oceans. The Thallians grew everything they ate inside their domes. Those farms must have gotten contaminated when the seawater crashed in."

If ships hid somewhere on the planet's surface now, their engines were cold and their life support systems shut off. Kavanaugh couldn't read any energy signatures at all. He set the *Sundog* to orbit, just to make sure they didn't miss anything, but it really didn't look as if there was anything to miss.

Vezali got up to fix them something to eat, which meant popping two readymades into the warmer. Still, Kavanaugh appreciated the gesture. He wasn't any sort of cook, especially not compared to Mykah. Generally, he let his passengers fend for themselves. Rarely did they think to feed him while they were at it.

The planet offered no surprises. Like the Templar's tombworld, it was pretty much just a rock, albeit a rock mostly covered with a slightly toxic ocean. "Are you sure you want that water on your skin?" he asked.

"Things pass through my system fairly quickly," Vezali assured. "Maybe I'll treat myself to a spa afterward, to make sure I detox."

They strapped themselves down for the trip through the atmosphere, still turbulent seventeen years after the galaxy bombed the planet into permanent winter. Vezali fastened her comm bracelet around one of her tentacles like a garter. She tested to make sure it linked to the *Sundog*.

Kavanaugh aimed for the coordinates Mykah had given him. No one but Raena and the two surviving Thallians really knew where the city lay under the ocean, but Kavanaugh triangulated between the spot where the *Veracity* picked up Raena and Eilif and the snow caves where the *Arbiter's* survivors had holed up. That narrowed down the range of Vezali's search a little. "Do you want me to let you off on solid ground?"

"No, I might as well just dive in and get it over with," she said. "Can you hover?"

"Sure."

Her skin had turned a cloudy grayish blue. Kavanaugh wondered if she meant that as camouflage or if it signified nerves. Vezali looked very small compared to the planet's big ocean. Kavanaugh hoped that the weapons Ariel had chosen would be enough protection for the tentacled girl.

CHAPTER 13

When Dr. Fishawk returned for Raena, he brought Haoun along with him. Raena reached out for Haoun's hand, held it to her cheek.

"Your color's better," the doctor observed.

"I'm going to live," Raena assured. "Are we good to go?"

"Yes. I've cleared you. The Business Council accepted your bill. I'm going to show you out the back way, rather than have you go out through the ER waiting area."

"Perfect," Corvas said. "We don't want to start any more trouble on Kai."

Raena hopped down from the bed to follow the man and the two lizards out into the corridor. Haoun pulled her close against him and nuzzled her hair.

"Thank you for keeping them from smothering me in the waiting room," she said.

"I've never been around a celebrity before," he teased. "Will you need security everywhere you go now?"

"Could be," the doctor replied. He opened an unmarked door to a stairway. "Your case has been a topic of much discussion on Kai, Ms. Zacari."

"Oh?"

"We think there is a reason you were targeted." He held his tongue while two other medics passed them on the stairs. The Shtrell looked twice at Raena, but neither she nor the furred one stopped.

Fishawk waited until the door banged shut behind them. "The android from your Messiah documentary—"

"Outrider?" Raena asked.

Fishawk nodded. "He was seen in the service district in Kai City before your trial began. People didn't know who he was until Mellix's documentary ran. By then, he was gone."

"Outrider on Kai?" Haoun echoed.

"Yes. He was stirring up trouble among the human workers."

"That explains a lot of things," Raena said. They reached the bottom of the stairs. Raena shook the doctor's hand. "Thank you for all you've done."

"My pleasure." He opened the door, which let out into a loading zone. "Just, please, keep your head down and get off Kai safely. You have come to mean a lot to people here. There will be more trouble, if anything more happens to you."

* * *

Ariel met the three of them at the *Veracity*'s hatch. "Come to Eilif's cabin."

Raena nodded.

Ariel let her past, then stepped in front of Corvas and Haoun. "Just Raena for now, gentlemen."

The lizards exchanged a glance. Haoun asked, "Where's Mykah? We should get stocked and start making ready to get out of here."

"In the galley," Ariel answered. "Corvas, do you mind hanging out for a bit? I'm ready to make a deal with the Business Council. We need to have a plan in place."

"Do you want me to make you an appointment tomorrow?"

"Tomorrow is good. Damn the cost."

"I'll make it happen."

All her errands assigned, Ariel showed Raena to the little cabin where Eilif's body lay. She'd cleaned the clone up and bound her body in a tarp. Only her face remained visible, an unnatural bloodless color beneath her bone white hair.

Raena sat on the edge of the bunk, one hand on Eilif's shoulder. "This is what they were doing last night while Kai was rioting?"

"Yes," Ariel answered. "They came here to get Jim. Eilif and Gisela were extraneous."

Raena looked up at Ariel, but before she could ask, Ariel said, "Gisela's injured, but not badly. She'll survive."

Raena looked back at Eilif's corpse. "She may have been mine," Raena confessed. "I didn't want to say anything to her, because we'll never know for sure. But Thallian had my ovaries removed while I served on the *Arbiter*. She could have been cloned from those eggs."

Ariel sank down beside Raena and took her hand. "I—"

Raena shook her head. "It doesn't matter. It would only make what Thallian did to her seem worse. It couldn't have been any worse. At least she was free of him when she died."

"One of the grays here last night used Revan's likeness to persuade Jim into letting them onto the ship. The *Veracity* recognized him, but Eilif tested him and made sure he wasn't Revan. It's possible he was an android like Outrider. Maybe all the grays are androids."

"Any indication where they took the boy?"

Raena's tightly controlled voice betrayed no anger or emotion at all. Ariel had heard her use that tone years ago, while they were running from Thallian. It was the voice Raena used to deal with Imperial officers, the voice of command she'd learned from her master. Goose flesh shivered over Ariel's skin at the sound of it.

"Home," Ariel answered. "The Revan soldier said they were taking Jim home."

Raena nodded.

"He ordered his men to scuttle the *Veracity*. Mykah has been waiting to talk to Haoun about hiring some engineers to repair it. I don't expect the damage will be too bad, though. This whole thing is a trap for you. They won't want to slow you down too much, just enough that they can get to Drusingyi before you do."

"I want to get out of here as soon as I can," Raena said.

"I know. I set Corvas on the Business Council. As soon as the ship is ready to go, you'll be ready, too."

Raena looked down at Eilif again. "What do we do about her body?"

"Coni's forged a death certificate to look like she was killed in the rioting last night. I am having her cremated here on Kai. I'll take her ashes back to Callixtos."

"I'm sorry for the loss of your friend," Raena said. She opened her arms to Ariel, gathered her close. Ariel finally let her tears fall, knowing Raena would understand them. Raena herself remained too infuriated to cry.

* * *

A short while later, Mykah tapped on the door to Eilif's cabin. "We have a message from Kavanaugh."

Raena stood up as Ariel wiped her face. They moved toward the door together, holding hands.

"In the lounge," Mykah said.

The gathering struck Raena as strange. Coni and Haoun were a minority now, outnumbered by the humans.

Kavanaugh's craggy face filled the screen. "Vezali hasn't come back up yet, but she got some video of the cloning labs." He reached off-screen to set it to play.

The seam on the cloning dome was ugly and brown, compared to the elegant surviving structure of the transparent dome. Many figures swarmed around inside. Several were recognizable as Outriders. Raena saw the antique medical robot that had served as the Thallian family doctor. Towering over them all was an insectile figure with a shiny black carapace and far too many legs.

"Are you seeing that?" Kavanaugh asked.

"Yes," Raena answered. "Looks like a Templar Master."

"Now we know for certain what they're cloning," Kavanaugh said.

"We'll be there in a couple of days," Raena said. "Don't wait for us. As soon as Vezali comes back to you, get off the planet. We'll meet you on Callixtos afterward."

"Understood," Kavanaugh said. "See you there."

The screen went blank and no one spoke. The Master was chief commander of the Templars' military forces. There was only ever one at a time, as far as Raena knew. This one could be cloning himself an army.

Seeing the shocked expressions around the lounge, Raena asked, "Mykah, what have we got to drink on this boat?"

★ ★ ★

The next morning, Kai's Business Council agreed to hear Raena's final plea. Raena dreaded to think what setting up the meeting had cost Ariel: one more thing to be grateful for. She realized that she'd lost count.

The Business Council's chambers were opulent, swathed in rich dark fabrics that played up the austerity of the plain wooden chairs in which Raena sat with Ariel and the remaining crew of the *Veracity*.

Corvas bent close to whisper to Ariel. Raena wasn't sure what their game plan was, but she hoped this was the endgame. She was good and ready to blast off this rock.

"Let's call this meeting to order," one of the councilors said. Her baggy fur was an odd shade of orange, but she wore an elaborate robe covered in dangling copper disks. She had the tallest hat, so Raena supposed she must be the boss.

Corvas said, "My client has been charged with several crimes by the Business Council of Kai. In each case, the charges have been dropped for lack of evidence. She has volunteered to pay fines for minor misdeeds she was not initially charged with. We are asking that she be released from Kai's legal system and that her bail be repaid to Ms. Shaad."

"Your client has been broadcast murdering four people," another councilor said. The profusion of feathers on his hat bobbed as he spoke.

"I'm sure Kai could have claimed the bounty for Revan Thallian, if only the dockmaster had detained him before he attacked my client in your souk. As it is, Ms. Zacari is already being hailed across the galaxy as a hero." Corvas added, "As I am sure you are aware."

Raena wondered if she was due another bounty. Maybe that's what this hearing was about: the Business Council trying to shake her down for some of her reward.

"Yes. Well. The other three soldiers she murdered have not been identified . . ."

Corvas swiped across his handheld and put six photographs up on the council room's screen. The first row of images came from Kai's booking records. The corresponding photographs beneath were Imperial ID photos. "As you can see, we have confirmed the dead men were crewmembers of the *Arbiter*, as identified by Jain Thallian in court. It wouldn't have been difficult to name them, if your coroner had done a basic genetic trace, but we merely compared their booking photos with the *Arbiter's* crew roster." Corvas looked up. "We invite you to press the murder charge—and we will detail your coroner's failure publicly."

"Are you threatening us, Mr. Corvas?" the head councilor asked.

"Stating a fact only. Do you find it threatening?"

"I'm not sure I like your tone," another of the councilors said. This one's blue skin was dotted with orange to match her hair.

Corvas swiveled both his eyes toward her. "It seems to me that Kai lit a fuse without considering where the explosion was going to take place. By leveling trumped-up charges at my client—then broadcasting the depth of Kai's ineptitude across the galaxy—it appears that you've dug yourselves a very deep crater. At this point, the best way out of it might be to hire my client as your new head of Planetary Security, have her fire every incompetent you have toiling on this rock, and then train the rest to be a respectable force capable of protecting the wealthy clientele who come to Kai to escape their fears of extortion and kidnapping."

Stunned silence greeted that proposal.

"Do you *want* a job heading up Kai's Planetary Security?" Haoun asked Raena.

"No."

Ariel leaned forward. "Corvas, if you'll permit me?"

"Please." He made a sweeping gesture and stepped back out of her way.

"I have a theory." Ariel didn't bother to stand up to address the council, merely lounged back in her uncomfortable wooden chair. "I think Kai was presented with a can't-lose money-making strategy. I think the Business Council was aimed at an easy target, one little human who appeared to be a ticking time bomb. It shouldn't have been difficult to provoke her into doing something catastrophic. Her associates were young, but they had pulled in good money from the Council of Worlds. Surely, they would part with some of it, rather than face a court broadcast that would discredit them and end their careers in front of the whole galaxy. But after the match had been struck, the Messiah documentary aired. The kids were linked to Mellix, which was exactly the kind of attention that the Business Council would prefer not to face. Too late to backtrack, though, wasn't it? Whoever had suggested the brilliant scheme in the first place revealed his conditions. It looked less like a can't-fail proposition for Kai and more like blackmail. But by then, Lautan had arrested her. They demanded their cut. The bounty hunters got hold of her and they expected to be paid. Once she disappeared into the desert, you must have breathed easier, but Raena didn't stay lost. The only way out you could see was to have her killed by an unstable human-hating cellmate. Unfortunately, once that cellmate started crowing about the impending murder, you had to either bribe or eliminate everyone on the cellblock. That included some tourists made famous by the court broadcasts. So the jailers rescued Raena at the last minute. Officially, the murder attempt was labeled a bureaucratic error. Cheaper than trying to buy that much silence."

"This is an amazing delusion, Ms. Shaad . . ."

Corvas made another swipe across his handheld and put an image of Outrider up on the screen. He stood in this same council chamber.

"How did you get that?" one of the councilors demanded.

Ariel ignored the question. "Once you saw the Messiah documentary and learned what he was, you had the sense to be afraid of him. But he told you that the drug was already on Kai. He'd already been in contact with Kai's human service workers, some of whom were eager to spend their youth to buy some payback for how they'd been treated here. And Outrider threatened to unleash them on the Business Council, if you didn't do exactly as he told you."

One lone voice asked, "What can we do?"

"You can't stop him," Raena said. "He undoubtedly learned all he needed to know about his targets while you were busy harassing me. He's a sociopath. You are doomed."

The silence that greeted that pronouncement was even grimmer.

Coni looked at Raena. "You've survived a Messiah attack. Help them. Please."

Raena gazed back at her, calculating, then faced the Business Council. "Oh, let me count the reasons I won't risk my life to help you," she said. "First off, if not for dumb luck and sheer incompetence, you would have already sold my corpse back to Ariel. Secondly, I am not magic. Those Messiah addicts could be anywhere in the galaxy by now, although odds are they haven't gone too far. After your government collapses and they are dead, Outrider will want to reveal them, to spread fear to the rest of the galaxy. However, because my friend pleads for you, I'll give you some advice for free. When it becomes clear which of you are under attack, get those council members into restraints or under sedation, where they cannot harm themselves or become a danger to anyone else. The Messiah addicts cannot kill them, but they will do everything they can to drive them mad. There is no bargaining with Outrider and, now that you've given him time to flee Kai, you have nothing that he wants."

"We thought he wanted you dead," one of them told her.

"You're welcome to give that another try," Raena said. "See if my death really does stave off what we all know is coming. Be careful how you do it, though. You wouldn't want to spark another riot. And you might consider this: what if this whole fiasco was only a distraction? Outrider played on your greed and now he's ruined your reputation. Why shouldn't he go ahead and destroy the Business Council altogether? What's to stop him? Where would be the fun in letting you go?"

"But why is he doing this?"

"For the pure love of chaos."

Mykah spoke up. "Here's what you're going to do. You're going to return Ariel's bail money. You're going to pay Raena restitution for dragging her into this debacle. You're going to release an official statement absolving her of guilt. And then you're going to talk to Mellix about how you were played by one of the most dangerous creatures in the galaxy. You'll detail how he contacted you, what he offered you, and what you're afraid of now—so that what has happened on Kai will serve as an object lesson to the rest of the galaxy."

"Absolutely not," the head councilor said.

Mykah smiled. "You don't have any choice about being investigated by Mellix," he pointed out. "He can either tell the story that makes you look gullible and greedy—or the one that makes the Council of Worlds put you on trial."

Raena asked him, "You don't want to stay to do the interviews yourself?"

"We have business on Drusingyi," Mykah answered.

Raena smiled at him. Her first inclination was to argue, to tell Mykah it was too dangerous, to try to protect him. But just as the *Veracity* had not abandoned her to face this trial alone, they would back her up on Drusingyi. Her kids were growing up.

She didn't really care what Kai had to say at this point, but she grudgingly focused her attention back on the sputtering head of the Business Council, who demanded time to consider the *Veracity*'s threats. Raena let her get a good head of steam going, then stood up.

"You'll excuse us, Councilor. We have more pressing things to attend to."

"Where do you think you're going?"

"Your little drama on Kai has been a distraction from the Templar cloning themselves back into the galaxy," she said.

The councilor's mouth closed with an audible clack.

"I am going to meet with the new Templar Master to see if there is anything I can do to prevent him from wiping out humanity. I can think of nothing more terrifying for you to threaten me with. I'll leave it to Ariel and Corvas to work out the particulars of how you're going to clear my name, but you have wasted the last of my time."

When Mykah, Haoun, and Coni joined her on their feet, the Planetary Security guards moved hesitantly to block the exit. Raena darted toward the first of them. As he thrust his stun staff at her, she spun inside his reach and plucked the staff from his hands. She tossed it to Mykah.

He covered her as the next two guards charged to attack. Mykah tangled his staff into one of the attacker's, but it was clear from the lack of spark that the guard had actually forgotten to switch the stun staff on. Mykah swept it from his grasp. Haoun caught it from the air.

Raena was pleased to see the other agent had both switched his staff on and used the lanyard to loop it to his wrist. Still, it didn't seem as if he'd ever sparred against an unarmed opponent intent on fighting back. She yanked his staff over far enough to stun his remaining comrade, then rammed the staff's heavy base back into his chest. He sat down hard.

Raena wiped her hand down across the top of her boot, palmed the knife there, and used it to slice the safety strap.

Coni retrieved the staff from the agent who'd been stunned. Now, each armed with a stun staff, the crew of the *Veracity* turned to face the Business Council of Kai.

"Ms. Shaad," the head councilor squeaked, "can't you control her?"

Ariel laughed. "Raena's in control now, Councilor." When the Business Council had no response to that, Ariel asked, "What would you like, Raena?"

"All this captivity has left me with a whole lot of energy that I'm eager to burn off before we get back into space. However, I would prefer not to fight my way across Kai City, because—despite your best efforts—I am not your enemy. I would like to leave Kai with some shreds of its dignity intact. The choice is up to you, Councilors. Either you can allow me and my crew to walk out of here, or I can show you all the remaining flaws in your Planetary Security. What's your preference?"

"Just go," one of the councilors said. "Don't hurt anyone."

"Thank you."

Raena came over to kiss Ariel goodbye. She wrapped her hand in Ariel's braid and pulled her head back, kissing her long and deeply. Sometimes a kiss has to say everything that words cannot express.

"I will call you as soon as this is over," she promised.

"Be careful."

"As careful as I can be."

"I love you," Ariel said.

Raena smiled at that and let her get the last word. Then she walked up in front of the cringing high hat Councilor and lay the stun staff at her feet. The *Veracity* crew stacked their staves beside Raena's and followed her toward the door.

"Now," Corvas said behind them, "I've prepared an accounting . . ."

* * *

When they got back to the ship, Mykah's crew of engineers met them in the *Veracity*'s lounge. Two were Dagat like Vezali, one was Na'ash like Haoun, and the last was human. Mykah introduced him as Orfeo Wachek.

"It's good as new," Orfeo said. "We repaired everything you noted and tested the fuel lines and power connections. Vezali will want to restock her backup parts—we raided them pretty much down to zero—but you are ready to fly."

"Thank you," Mykah said with a grin. "Coni's authorized the payments to the accounts you gave me. We really appreciate you helping us out at the last moment like this."

"It's been a pleasure," Orfeo said. "This is a sweet old ship."

"It is that," Mykah agreed.

* * *

Raena followed Haoun up to the cockpit. He settled back into his pilot's chair with a sigh and started flipping switches.

"You don't have to come," Raena pointed out. "We can drop you off somewhere safe. You have your kids to think about."

"Not really," he argued, resigned. "You've been thinking about them like a human family: two parents and their offspring, bonded for life. I've let you think that, because that's what I want. But the Na'ash—for most of us—the father leaves as soon as the eggs hatch. The mother raises the young alone. My mate thought it was weird when I stuck around after our boys hatched. When Jexxie was born . . ." Haoun's voice choked up, but he forced himself to continue. "Serese thought it was perverse that I wanted anything to do with our kids. After seeing me in the court broadcasts, she claims she's never going to let me near them again." He swallowed hard. "There is nothing holding me back anymore. The *Veracity* is—look, I like you a lot, Raena, but it's not just you. Coni's been like a sister to me. Mykah's my brother. I feel the same about Vezali. I can't let you all go face the Templars alone. I mean, I'm terrified, and I don't want to die, but I also don't want to survive and know that I let you go to your deaths because I was too much of a coward to stand with you. I couldn't . . . I couldn't live with myself."

Raena perched on the arm of his chair. "I learned a long time ago that courage isn't going into a fight when you're certain you'll win. I have to go to Drusingyi, because I have to try to save what's left of my people. None of the rest of you are obligated to come die at my side. So I respect and honor your courage. I'm grateful to have you as a friend."

"Good. Promise you won't try to erode my fragile bravery by telling me what you expect we're getting into?"

"I promise." Raena slipped down into his lap and hugged him as tightly as she could. "I'll post a sparring schedule once we're underway. I've got three days to whip you three into a fighting team."

Haoun started to protest, but Raena laid a finger across his mouth.

"Mandatory," she said. "I saw how you bobbled that stun staff."

He laughed.

"But I'll make it up to you afterward," Raena promised. She hopped out of his lap. "I'll leave you to the preflight check."

"Send Gisela up, will you?" he asked. "I'm going to train her to copilot."

"Is she coming along with us?"

"She is your biggest fan," Haoun said. "She wouldn't let us leave her behind."

"She goes on the sparring schedule too, then."

* * *

Raena found Gisela lying on the banquette in the lounge. "Which one of Ariel's daughters are you?"

Gisela opened eyes that were a strange blue so dark that it almost looked black. "My uncle sold me after my parents died. I was working as a maid in a brothel on Tacauque when the Shaad Foundation bought me."

"How old were you?"

"Almost eight."

"How old are you now?"

"Sixteen."

"Still living at home?"

Gisela looked at Raena skeptically. "Is this an interview?"

"In a way. I'm trying to figure out how you fit in here."

"You're not the captain," Gisela pointed out.

Raena's smile was tight. "I'm the evil mastermind. That means I outrank Captain Chen."

"My apologies, then." The girl pushed herself into sitting up. "Ariel trained me to be a bodyguard to Madame Shaad."

Raena tossed a Stinger at her. "Field strip that."

The girl took the Stinger apart in seconds, stacking the pieces neatly, then reassembled it in half the time. Clearly, her mother's daughter.

"You a good shot?"

"Not as good as Ariel. Better than everyone else."

"I don't know if we're going to need sharpshooting on this trip. I don't know what we're going to need. What I've got are games players and hackers, but maybe what I need are diplomats. Real diplomats who know how to make peace. And I've never known anyone like that. All I've ever known were soldiers following the orders of crazy people."

Gisela didn't dispute any of that. Instead, she said, "Eilif was the gentlest person I ever met. She mended a bird's wing after the poor creature flew into a window at the villa. She could make anyone feel better. She could tame the most broken child . . . She had a gift. And that *thing* killed her because it didn't need her. She bled to death on the floor of the *Veracity* because I was knocked out and couldn't help her."

"Concussion?" Raena guessed.

"Yeah," Gisela said. She didn't nod. "It's getting better."

"We're not a hospital ship," Raena said. "You're going to have to take care of yourself. If your head gets knocked around again, even if we just have a rough landing, you could be looking at permanent damage."

"I'm used to taking care of myself," Gisela promised.

"Good. I'm not used to taking care of anyone else." After she said it, Raena realized that was a lie. She had taken care of Ariel for years. She relented and said, "Haoun wants you in the cockpit. He says he's going to train you to copilot."

The girl's smile lit her strange-colored eyes. "Thank you, Raena. You won't regret letting me come along."

Raena wondered about that, but she let it pass.

✷ ✷ ✷

The training began as soon as the *Veracity* was back into space. Raena supervised as Mykah and Coni grappled. She noted that they held back, gentle with each other, so she separated the two of them. Her surprise attack on Mykah was full-speed and all-out. He had mass and reach on Raena, but she let him know she wasn't playing this time.

Coni watched, puzzled, waiting for Mykah to complain or ask for help. When she heard Raena break his arm—the groan that escaped him left no doubt—Coni leapt back into the fray.

Raena slapped her hard enough that Coni's head rang. The little woman landed a few more blows on Mykah before Coni succeeded in peeling Raena off of him. She threw Raena back with surprising strength, but the little woman landed on her toes and launched herself back at Coni.

"Are you crazy?" Coni protested. "Stop. Wait. What are you doing?"

Raena backhanded her. As Coni blinked tears away, Raena threw herself into a backflip and went after Mykah, who lay panting on the deck. She kicked him hard enough to roll him over. He doubled up, trying to protect his organs.

Coni sprang after Raena. She pulled the woman off of Mykah, pitched her hard at the deck at an angle so she couldn't pop back up, then pinned her down with one foot.

Her claws were unsheathed and her hand had drawn back, when Mykah grabbed her arm. "Stop, Coni!"

Shaking, Coni stepped back and let him hold her.

Mykah reached his uninjured hand down to Raena. She let him tug her to her feet.

"I'm going to be ill," Coni warned.

Mykah petted her back. "It's just the aftermath of the fight," he said. "Stand up and take a deep breath. It will pass."

Coni looked at him, shaking her head. "I thought she was going to kill you."

"That's what she wanted you to think." He turned to Raena. "Did you see what you wanted?"

She nodded. Blood bloomed on her chest, where Coni's claws had torn her shirt. Raena pressed on the wounds, to slow the bleeding.

"I'm sorry, Coni. I wanted to see what you were capable of. Now I want you to think about whether you can unleash that fury before

Mykah gets hurt. Because if you can't, if you restrain yourself, it may be too late."

Coni sank to the floor, still panting. "I wanted to kill you."

"I know. But we don't have time to be polite about this. I need to know that you can defend yourself, that you will defend all of us. I need to know that you can get angry enough to kill, if you have to—and that you won't freeze up afterward. Because if we get to Drusingyi and there are Outriders there—if there are gray soldiers there—I want to know that you won't go down without a fight."

Raena sat down in front of Coni and reached out to take her hands, before noticing that her own were bloody. "This is going to be hard," Raena promised. "It's going to be awful. If you don't want to come down to the planet, I won't think any less of you and I don't want you to think any less of yourself. You need to decide that if you do come, you will be all in. Otherwise, you or Mykah are going to get killed. If I have to fight alone, I'd rather go alone to do it."

✳ ✳ ✳

Haoun came into the gym hesitantly, unsure what he would find. He'd seen Raena stitching up her chest before she hauled the Thallians' old bone regenerator out to mend Mykah's arm. Coni had retreated to her cabin. Haoun knew Coni and Mykah had been sparring with Raena. Clearly, something drastic had happened.

"I won't bite," Raena promised him.

"I'm not sure a human bone-mender will fix me," he answered.

"Your lesson is different than Mykah or Coni's," Raena said. "I want to see how fast you can move and for how long. We're going to run."

She made him run on the treadmill. And run. And run. Haoun had probably never run so long in his life. He found himself dragging slower and slower. Raena jogged alongside him without getting winded or slackening her pace.

"Jump off," she told him. When he did, she said, "Freeze."

He locked his muscles up so hard that he nearly tipped himself over.

"Good. Very good. If we need to run and then hide, I don't want them to hear you gasping. You're doing great."

He laughed. "What if they hear my heart pounding out of my body?"

"I can't hear it," she said. "Can you ignore it?"

He nodded.

"Okay. Now I want you to attack me."

He'd known it would come to this. He looked down at his claws. He couldn't retract them like Coni could hers. "I don't want to hurt you."

"I know."

"I don't want you to hurt me, either."

"I know."

"I—I don't think I can do this. I'm sorry, Raena. I want to protect you. I want . . ."

She leaned up against him and looked up into his face. "It's all right. I didn't want to set a limit for you. How do you feel about shooting?"

"I'm okay at shooter games. Better at spraying around cover than at sharpshooting."

"Good. I'll train you on the ship's external guns."

He realized, "You're going to leave me behind."

"It's safer for us both," she said. "You are a natural pilot. We need you to get us onto Drusingyi—and we're not getting away unless you survive to fly us out again."

"Why are you going gentle on me after you were so hard on Coni and Mykah?"

"I told you their lessons were different. I wanted to see if Mykah would follow me even when he was in danger. If he would trust I had a plan, even if he got hurt. I'd never gone off-leash on him before.

I wanted to see if he'd panic, if fear or pain would defeat him. He made me very proud."

"Did you mean to break Coni?"

"She isn't broken. She's upset and angry and it may take her time to forgive me. But she stopped to watch when she should have stepped up. It may be just the way her people are, or it may be individual to her, but I've faced those guys in gray four times. They don't freeze. If I ever waited to see what they were going to do next, I would be dead. There isn't time to think in a fight. I can train her to overcome that tendency, but she has to decide if she wants to. If she doesn't, that's fine. I'm not going to beat it into her the way it was beaten into me. Unfortunately, we don't have much time, so I pushed her—both of them—hard."

"You should go tell her that," Haoun said. "She's going to tear herself up over this. She'll feel like she let you both down. She didn't protect Mykah and she disappointed you."

"I'm not disappointed," Raena said. "I will definitely tell her that."

CHAPTER 14

Raena took the last of Coni's moon cakes out of the cooler and carried them back to the Haru girl's cabin. "It's me," Raena said outside the door. "Can I talk to you?"

"It's open."

"I brought a peace offering."

"You didn't need to do that."

Coni didn't get up from her desk. Raena handed the plate of cakes to her and sat on the floor. Coni took a cake and handed the tray down to Raena. They chewed in silence, then Raena said, "You've been a good friend to me. I don't know how much time you put into my defense on Kai, but I know who found the evidence Corvas needed. Thank you."

Coni waved that away, but accepted a second moon cake. "You are family, Raena."

"I feel that way, too. I overstepped today. I am sorry."

"No, I've been thinking about what you said. You're right. I was crazy to think I could fight. I was so scared today, watching you. I couldn't protect Mykah because I was afraid you would hurt me like that. I've been in denial. I thought the fighting would be quick. It would be bloodless, like a game. None of us would be hurt."

"I get hurt all the time," Raena said. "Eilif got killed."

The blue girl nodded. "We're not playing, are we?"

"No, we're not," Raena answered. "I would rather scare you away from combat now, here on the ship, than make you participate and regret it later. We will be safer if we can concentrate on what we're doing and not worry about you."

Coni asked plaintively, "Do you have to take Mykah?"

For once, the emotion in her voice was clear. Raena was pretty sure that Mykah wanted to come, but she told Coni what she wanted to hear. "I can go alone."

"Thank you," Coni said quickly, as if Raena might change her mind. "I . . . He's my life. I don't know what I would do if . . ."

Raena smiled. "You talk him out of coming. I'll abide by his wishes."

*　*　*

Mykah sprawled on the banquette with his arm under the bonemender. He'd pulled off his shirt to deal with the machine's heat. Close to hand, he had a glass of ice water and the remote. He paused the news when Coni came in. "You all right?" he asked, holding out his good hand.

Coni wove her fingers between his and came to scent him with her head. "I'll be all right," she promised. "I talked to Raena just now."

"Did you let her live?" he teased.

She chuckled. "Yes. Raena excused me from going into battle with her." Coni gazed at him with her lavender eyes. "She said you don't have to go, either."

"I know I don't have to," Mykah said. "What made her decide she didn't want me to come?"

Coni looked away from him, at the image frozen on the screen. It was one of Mykah's shots of the rioting on Kai, looking down from the lamppost in front of the Hall of Justice. A Planetary Security agent was in the process of stunning a little Eske.

Coni dragged her gaze away to answer his question. "I don't want you to go."

Mykah pulled her closer, then kissed her so she'd know he really meant it. With the lightest touch, she traced the lightning scar that branched across his stomach and onto his chest. He knew she was thinking of how badly he'd gotten hurt the last time he'd followed Raena into a firefight.

He took a deep breath. The pressure to get this right was enormous. "I am going with her," he said quietly. "Raena can fight us past the gray soldiers. She can take apart the Outriders, if she needs to. But I don't know if she can negotiate with the Templar Master. I don't know if I can either, but I'm afraid to trust the future of humanity to a former assassin."

Coni sat back from him sharply, but he kept hold of her hand and didn't let her get away.

"You know that's what she is," he said. "We can dress it up and call her a warrior, but Raena is a trained killer. I don't want her to charge in there and kill the reborn Templars because she's the only representative humanity's got."

"You don't trust her?" Coni asked.

"I trust her to protect us. I trust her with my life. But the gray soldiers have been taunting her all across the galaxy. I don't trust her temper if they push her too far."

"I don't want you to die," Coni said in Imperial Standard. It was the language Mykah had been born into, the one his parents had spoken to him. Coni used it when she wanted to stress something.

Mykah pulled her back down, so he could feel her fur against his bare skin. "I'll do my best not to die," he promised. He used Haru, Coni's language, so she would understand that he was serious, too.

*　*　*

Back in her cabin, Raena checked messages, curious to hear how things worked out for Ariel and Corvas with the Business Council.

She found several messages from Ariel. One of them was labeled Urgent: Where is Gisela?

Raena marched into the cockpit, where the girl hunched over the controls. She asked Haoun, "Could you give us a moment?"

He looked from one to the other of them and got up without comment.

Once he'd entered the passageway, Raena asked the girl, "You didn't tell your mother you were coming with us?"

"She would have said no," Gisela answered.

"She would have said no because you have a concussion."

"She would have said no because of you," Gisela argued. "She knows if there's danger, you won't back down."

"I don't know what Ariel has told you about me—"

Gisela cut her off. "She hasn't had to tell me much. Eilif told me how you rescued her, how you killed all the Thallians singlehandedly. Haoun showed me the recording of you protecting Mellix outside Capitol City. Kavanaugh told me about watching you disassemble the Outriders. Mykah told me how you saved him from the Walosi on Lautan. I've watched the video of you fighting the death squad on Kai. You step up. You face the dangers. You don't start fights, but you stop them."

"I'm not a hero, Gisela. Heroes are good people who do the right things for the right reasons. That's never been me."

"Who cares what your reasons are, if your actions are heroic? You save people. You protect them. And this thing on Kai, this trial—you showed the galaxy that it's possible to be graceful and calm in the face of enormous bigotry. Like it or not, you're a symbol."

"I never intended that," Raena said. "Pedestals tend to have tiny cross sections and very long drops."

Gisela had no answer to that, for which Raena was grateful. The whole conversation made her vastly uncomfortable. "Call your mother," Raena ordered. "Argue your case to her. If she tells me you can stay, fine. Otherwise, we're putting you out and she can come pick you up."

* * *

It wasn't long before Gisela commed back to Raena's cabin. Ariel wanted to talk. Raena smiled at her sister's image on the screen. "What's your decision, Ari?"

"Gisela can stay, if she stays out of your way. If she's going to irritate you, put her out."

Raena studied her oldest friend. For all Ariel's temper, her heart was tender and fierce. Gisela might not have been hers by birth, but Ariel would believe to the end of her days that the girl was family. Raena wondered if Ariel had ever trusted her with anything as precious.

"Now I'm a damn babysitter," Raena groused.

"Sorry about that. I should have left her on Callixtos, but she is the best shot among my kids and she's been a good bodyguard for my mother. I thought she'd provide the best protection for Eilif and Jim. Going to Kai was meant to be an adventure for her."

"This trip is gonna be an adventure, too," Raena threatened. "Where was she supposed to be when we left Kai?"

"At the hospital, following that nice Dr. Fishawk's orders."

"He was goodlooking," Raena agreed. "So he didn't release her to go charging into battle?"

"No."

"Then I will do what I can to keep her out of one. But you know I really can't promise anything."

"I know, Raena." Ariel took a long drag off of her spice stick. "She's about the age I was when I ran away to join the Coalition. I thought I was so grown-up at the time. Was I really that young?"

Raena laughed. Instead of answering, she asked, "How are things working out on Kai?"

"I had a very nice chat with your friend Mellix. Is his fur really that beautiful color?"

"Yes."

"Lovely. He's sending an assistant to Kai to conduct some interviews in person. In the meantime, you have been publicly cleared of all charges brought by the Business Council of Kai. Even the weapons charges were expunged, considering that you knew there were Thallians prowling around on the planet. It's officially agreed that no one should ever have faced them unarmed. Kai gave you a surprisingly generous apology for dragging you into their troubles, in hopes that you will consult with their new Head of Security. We didn't make them any promises. The bail money has been returned. Corvas's fees have been paid by the Business Council, in addition to lost income and transportation costs and a myriad of other fees that we were able to extract from them. Nothing too outrageous, but I wanted to make sure it hurt. Oh, and you received the bounty for Revan Thallian."

Raena smiled at her. "Now I just need to survive to enjoy it all."

"Yes," Ariel said. "Only that."

"We were on vacation when this started," Raena remembered. "That seems so long ago now."

"Well, I'm not recommending any more pleasure planets to you."

"No blame from me," Raena promised. "I enjoyed Kai when we were there the first time. Shame they got greedy and invited me back the way they did."

Ariel didn't argue with that. "When do you expect to be done with this adventure?"

"Don't know," Raena said. "I really will call you, as soon as I can, afterward."

"Take care then. Tell Gisela to watch her head."

Raena powered down her screen and went to check on Mykah. He still lay in the lounge under the bone-mender. Coni's head rested on his good shoulder.

"How's it feel?" Raena asked.

"Not as hot as it did."

"That's a good sign." She looked over the telltales. "Make a fist for me."

He did.

"No pain?"

"I'm good," he said.

"Good." She initiated the shutdown sequence on the machine. "I'm sorry about that, Mykah."

"No, you made your point. But if you're trying to scare me off of coming with you, you're going to have to do a better job than that."

Raena looked at Coni first, but the blue girl had her eyes closed. "I told Coni I can go alone, if I need to."

"You don't need to," Mykah promised.

*　*　*

The rest of the trip to Drusingyi passed smoothly. Haoun was pleased with Gisela's progress as a pilot. Raena suspected he had ulterior motives for spending so much time with the human girl, but he spent all his spare time with Raena, making up for the days in jail. She even got her bubble bath, as promised. Best of all, though, Haoun consented to play piloting games with her, so Raena could update her skills.

True to her word, Coni forgave her. She seemed resigned to—if not thrilled about—Mykah going into battle. Raena wasn't sure what argument he'd used to persuade his girlfriend, but she didn't question it.

Together she and Mykah went over the weapons on the *Veracity*. They chose their tools, made sure everything was powered up and ready to go, then packed for the trip. Raena got him fitted for a diving suit from the Thallians' stores. And they sparred faster and harder than they had before. He would never be her equal, but he was becoming more of a challenge. For that, she was grateful.

All in all, time passed. Not as quickly as Raena would have liked, but plenty of little things filled her days. Her chief concern was that

Kavanaugh and Vezali had not checked in from Callixtos. They didn't respond to Haoun's attempts to contact them. Raena didn't need to say anything to the others. They knew the silence couldn't be good.

On the final day before they reached the Thallians' system, Raena called everyone into the lounge. They sat on the banquette facing her. Only now that she had them collected up did the differences in her age from theirs strike her. They were all so young. Only Gisela had ever been in a gunfight. None of them had seen real combat.

How had it come to this? Raena had never been a commander. She'd always been a lone gun. The weight of all these lives, dependent on her to figure this out and get it right, was terrifying.

Raena put a schematic of the Thallian city up on the screen. The cloning lab was highlighted. "That's where we're headed. Once the *Veracity* gets down to the city, we'll have to circle it to see where we can dock. The Thallians' hangar was here—" she pointed "—but Eilif leveled it as we left. I don't know where the Templars have been docking, but they must have a plan for getting out of the city. None of the experts seem to think they can swim."

She met each of their eyes and began to lay out her plan.

"I want us to come off the ship hot. That means, Haoun, as soon as we're docked, you start firing the *Veracity*'s guns at anything that moves. Coni, I want you up in the turret. Gisela, you're at the airlock to cover us. I'm out first, then Mykah."

Raena paused long enough to let them absorb all that. "Gisela, if the guards are robots like Outrider, they will be really well shielded. Aim for their guns."

She stepped away from the screen and let it go back to sleep. "If we can't dock, Mykah and I will swim over."

Mykah raised his hand.

"I know," Raena said. "You don't swim. I can pull you, but that means you'll have to cover me."

"Do you want us to hang around?" Haoun asked.

"No. The leviathans will be drawn to the sound of *Veracity*'s engines. Go back up to the surface and wait 'til we call you."

"What if you don't call?" Gisela asked.

"We'll be dead."

Coni took Mykah's hand, but nobody refuted that.

* * *

Raena joined Gisela and Haoun in the cockpit. The last time the *Veracity* came through the asteroid belt inside the Thallians' home system, Coni had teased the codes for safe passage through the minefield out of the *Raptor*'s memory. This time, all the satellites rotated erratically, tumbling blindly through space.

Ahead of them, Drusingyi was a dead gray mass shrouded by turbulent clouds. Raena scanned it for any signs of life. The *Veracity*'s scanners hadn't made Vezali's upgrade list yet, but the crew didn't normally have much use for them. Using the *Veracity*'s outdated technology, Raena couldn't find anything on the planet that passed for life. Whatever lived there, it was hidden under the ocean.

Haoun brought them through the atmosphere at a steep trajectory. The plan was to land long enough to let the hull cool before they dove into the ocean.

"What's that?" he asked.

Raena looked up to see what he was pointing at. A black smudge discolored the snow at the edge of a glacier. Raena focused in as much as she could.

"It was the *Sundog*," she said. "Looks like Kavanaugh got attacked before they could get away."

Haoun slowed enough that they could circle.

Raena ran through the channels, searching for Vezali or Kavanaugh's comms.

"Nice to see you," Kavanaugh said.

Haoun let out a sigh of relief.

"Where are you?" Raena asked.

"Snow cave. Near where you found the *Arbiter* survivors."

"Got you locked," Haoun said. "We'll be right there."

* * *

Kavanaugh waved his arms as Haoun brought the *Veracity* down. The old veteran's face was covered by a scrap of cloth, which he pulled down to reveal the ice crystals in his gingery beard. He waved like a man so relieved to see rescue that he had trouble staying on his feet.

Haoun cut the engines and let the *Veracity* drop the last twenty meters, rather than make the mistake he did the last time: melting the snow, which then refroze around the landing gear and locked them in place, until Mykah and Coni cut them lose. The *Veracity* landed with a good bump. Raena hoped Gisela's hard head didn't knock up against anything. The girl had been warned of the dangers.

A frigid wind rushed suddenly through the *Veracity*. Coni must have opened the hatch to let Kavanaugh onboard.

Raena realized she should have set a test for him. What if he was a replica, like the Revan had been?

She unhooked herself from the crash webbing and raced back to the hatch.

By the time she got there, the Kavanaugh had Coni's throat in the crook of his arm, his gun against her head. Coni's lavender eyes had gone round with shock.

Raena skidded to a halt at the sight of them.

Kavanaugh re-aimed his gun and shot her.

* * *

Raena came to with Jimi Thallian leaning over her, shining a flashlight into her eye. Raena knocked his hands away from her face. Jimi jumped backward like a startled cat.

"They stunned you," he explained quickly. "Gisela said she had a concussion from when she fell. I wanted to make sure you didn't."

Raena sat up. Adrenaline sang through her, casting off the last of the stun's effects. "I'm fine," she snarled. "Don't touch me again."

"Sorry." Jimi switched off the flashlight.

"Where are the others?"

"Everyone is okay. We're down in the city now. The Templar Master wants to speak to you, when you're up to it."

"I'm up to it now."

"They'll probably come for us soon. First, though: the others wouldn't tell me. Is my mother safe?"

Raena made no attempt to soften the news. "Eilif is dead. The Revan android shot her the night they captured you."

The boy closed his eyes against the realization that he'd allowed his mother's killer onto the ship. "I knew it," he said. "They wouldn't tell me, but I knew."

Raena watched him. Jimi looked a startling amount like Jain had when she'd broken him. Like his brother, Jimi faced the loss of the last of everything. The struggle reflected on his face: rage and despair and grief and fear. He was only a boy, twelve or thirteen at most, a sheltered prince whose father had been an abusive tyrant. She couldn't imagine what it had been like, growing up with his wolf pack of brothers, but she had to respect Jimi for surviving more than a decade of life with Thallian when three years had been enough for her.

Jimi didn't cry, though. A resolved mask snapped down over his emotions. He stared at Raena, prepared for the fight to come.

That she could work with.

"Do you know what the Templar Master wants?" she asked.

"No," Jimi said. "He has some kind of mission for us, you and me."

The door slid open. Two Outriders stood there, flanked by a ring of soldiers in gray. Now that the soldiers weren't wearing their mirrored helmets, she could see they weren't all humanoid after all. Maybe, if Raena watched the news, she would recognize the celebrity each of them was supposed to represent.

"Please give us a fight," one of the Outriders invited.

"No," Raena said. "Your boss needs me, so disassembling you wouldn't be much fun."

The pair of them stood back out of the way so she and Jimi could come into the hallway.

The rest of the *Veracity* crew was gathered from the adjoining rooms. Mykah sidled up to her. "What do we do?"

"Wait," Raena said. "I need to know what this has been about."

* * *

Raena wasn't sure what to expect when the gray soldiers marched the *Veracity*'s crew into the cavernous cloning lab. The room was much busier than when she'd visited it before. Then there had been only a handful of Jonan's clones maturing in the vats, chubby young boys almost ready to breathe on their own. There had also been eight clones of Raena, practically full-term infants. Raena had slaughtered them all without remorse.

Now that the Templar Master had taken over, every vat seemed full: maybe a hundred in all. Raena didn't know how the Templars reproduced back before the War. She'd assumed there had been a queen somewhere, busily laying eggs, but she couldn't remember ever seeing an immature Templar. Like so many other things related to nonhumans, she had only concerned herself with how to kill them, not with how they lived.

She marveled that the Templar Master would bring her here. If he knew who Raena really was and whom she'd served, she would have expected him to keep her far from any opportunity to finish what Jonan had started. Had he fallen for Coni's new biography—or was this a test?

As she and the crew of the *Veracity* passed vat after vat of maturing Templars, the Templar Master rose up at the far end of the room. He was taller than the recordings of any other Templars she'd seen before, a towering figure with far too many legs. The flat surface of his face swirled with more colors than Raena could name.

At his side stood Vezali. She flowed forward to greet her crewmates, caressing Mykah's shoulder with one tentacle, offering another to Kavanaugh, training Raena's hair back away from her face with a third.

"Nice to see you all again," she said.

"Have they treated you all right?" Raena asked.

"Yes. They've treated me like an honored guest."

"Welcome, Raena Zacari," the Templar Master said through the translator around Vezali's middle. His voice had a rich genderless tone like a cello. He must be transmitting his thoughts to the translator somehow. He continued, "You have proved yourself to be the warrior that we need."

"To do what?" Raena asked.

"Prevent the spread of what the galaxy calls the Templar plague."

Raena frowned, trying to make sense of that. "Those who conceived of the plague, those who manufactured it, and the one who spread it are all dead."

"Because the plague is no longer a threat, I have returned to the galaxy."

"What do you want me to do?" she asked skeptically.

"You will go back in time. You will stave off the genocide spawned by humanity. You will save my people."

Of course, Templars could travel in time. Gooseflesh shivered up over her. Surviving Sloane's attacks with the Messiah drug had shown her how fragile the past could be. More than anything, she did not want to fool around with time. "Why?" She waved at the rows of clones maturing around them. "Why mess with the past when you have all these to claim the future?"

"These are flawed. The plague contaminated our dead. They cannot be cloned. Only I am pure, because my people locked me away in one of our tombs to wait out the devastation. All of these are cloned from me. Not one of them is a queen. We can no longer reproduce in any way, except by cloning. This makes the Templar too fragile to survive."

Mykah asked, "Why not find an antidote to the plague and send it back to protect your people?"

"Templar cannot journey backward in time."

That shocked Raena. What good was having the technology to travel in time if it only allowed you to move forward? She wondered if any Templars had been able to escape to the future to survive the plague. Maybe if the galaxy progressed far enough, they would find Templars already there, waiting for them. Or maybe the Templars that fled forward had already been infected with the plague and died.

Mykah stepped forward. The gray soldiers trained their guns on him, but he ignored them. "I will go."

"You are nonessential," the Templar Master said. "Jimi Thallian and Raena Zacari will go back in time. They will prevent the plague."

"Why us?"

It didn't answer her. She wasn't sure if it understood the question.

The Templar Master's head turned toward her, but without eyes, a mouth, anything that might hint at facial features, she could only stare at the hypnotic swirl of colors, everything from a rancid white to a bloody crimson shot through with poisonous yellow.

"The last functional temporal manipulation device is hidden on the Templar tombworld. Do you accept this mission, Raena Zacari?"

"What if we don't succeed?" Raena asked.

"All your friends will die. All humans will die. Anyone who shelters humans will die."

It was mad, she realized. The greatest power in the universe had gone insane during its imprisonment. Raena looked at the gray soldiers, who could pass anywhere and destroy anything. Outriders were probably already in place to do the most possible damage to any government that might protect humanity. She faced a creature who really had nothing left to lose and no reason not to destroy the galaxy in its death throes.

She closed her eyes. She could kill the Templar Master here, now—but the gray soldiers standing around would butcher the *Veracity*'s crew in immediate retaliation. And the Outriders ranged around the galaxy wouldn't stand down just because their master was dead. If there were other gray soldiers elsewhere, they'd proven they loved mayhem too much to simply stop killing everything that crossed their paths. She saw no way to prevent the galactic slaughter from here.

Unwillingly, she said, "I need a ship to get to the Templar tombworld."

"You will take *Veracity*. It will go back in time with you."

"Neither Jimi nor I can pilot it," Raena lied. She did not want to be alone with the Thallian boy. She didn't trust him to help her do whatever must be done.

"I will go," Gisela volunteered. "I've been training to pilot the *Veracity*."

"I can fly her," Kavanaugh said. "I will go."

"It's my ship," Mykah reminded them. "You're not going without me."

Raena looked at Mykah, Tarik, and Gisela. Any person she took with her was more likely to survive than those she left behind. She'd given Ariel her word that she would try to protect Gisela. That meant accepting her as part of the crew.

She would have liked to take Haoun and Coni along too, but she suspected the Templar wanted some hostages. It killed her to be so cold, but she couldn't save everyone.

The Templar Master cocked its head at Raena. "Raena Zacari, do you accept this crew?"

"Yes."

The gray soldiers converged on them, pulling the human volunteers away and herding them toward the exit from the cloning lab.

"Wait!" Coni shouted. "Mykah . . ."

"I love you!" he yelled at her.

Raena turned to give Haoun a smile. He nodded at her. They hadn't talked of love. What they had wasn't love. She would come back for him nonetheless.

Vezali flowed through the cloning lab after them. The gray soldiers didn't try to stop her. At the door of the cloning lab, she said, "Just in case," and pressed her translator into Mykah's hand.

CHAPTER 15

The grays herded Raena and her crew into a shuttle that would return them to the *Veracity*, still parked on the planet's surface. On the ride, Raena looked her crewmates over. Kavanaugh looked none the worse for wear, even if he was old enough to be everyone else's father. Mykah was taut with resolve, aware he was about to do the grandest thing he'd ever attempted in his life. Jimi's face was expressionless, but she suspected his thoughts were busy behind the mask. Gisela had gone paler still, practically ill with excitement.

Raena wasn't sure whether this Kavanaugh was the real one or the copy. She wasn't sure if the Templar Master planned to send androids back with them to make sure they got the job done. But if androids could do the job, surely the Templar Master would have already dispatched them. All the same, she decided it wouldn't be a bad idea to test her crew. She'd just have to come up with the right riddles to ask.

On the planet's surface, the grays escorted them back onto the *Veracity*. One of these guards was a copy of Raena herself. "We will escort you to the Templar tombworld," she said. "If the *Veracity* deviates from the course we set for you, one hostage will be executed. If the *Veracity* fires on our ships, one hostage will be executed. If the *Veracity* does not return from the past, all hostages will be executed.

The elimination of the human race will begin in one standard week's time, unless you succeed in erasing the plague."

Raena studied the android. It was hard to see where it differed from her, other than it still bore the scar her mother had given her, the one that bisected her left eyebrow and nearly cost her an eye. Raena supposed that meant that the android had been manufactured before she'd gone to Capitol City and had the scar removed. She wondered what sort of trouble it had stirred up in her likeness. Had it been one of the soldiers she fought outside Mellix's apartment?

"We are ready to go, as soon as we can warm the engines up," Raena said. "Get off our ship."

The Raena android smirked at her, but turned on its high-heeled boot and left.

The real Raena sighed. She hoped she had never flounced out of anywhere like that. It was just embarrassing.

As Kavanaugh and Gisela went forward to warm the *Veracity* up, Raena followed Mykah into his cabin. "Question," she said. "Tell me the ingredients in your nightcap."

"Cinnamon, nutmeg, ground cloves, rice milk, and rum."

"What's the secret to making one?"

He looked at her skeptically. "Pouring the rice milk into the rum from a height, so that the heat of the milk doesn't boil away all the alcohol."

Raena smiled. "You pass. You are not an android."

"You think one of us is a spy?"

"I don't know. Since Kavanaugh shot me the last time I saw him, I thought it would be a good idea to check."

"How do I know you're not an android?" Mykah asked.

"Test me."

"How did we meet?"

"That's too simple, Mykah," she scolded. "You were working in that restaurant on Kai. I climbed up the cliff from the beach and you were my waiter. After I'd had a couple of drinks, I put the lily from the table decoration over my ear."

"What did I tell you about you and Ariel later?"

"You thought I was flirting with my mother."

"You pass. Let's find Jim."

The boy was in the lounge, strapping himself down. He looked up at them. "Am I in trouble?"

"What was the first photo you sent me?" Raena asked.

His answer came immediately. "I sent you a picture of me with the sabershark I'd caught. I was trying to impress you."

"What did I send you in return?"

"A holo of you sitting on a jet bike. You had on gargoyle sunglasses. You only let me see the image for a moment, before it evaporated."

"He passes," she told Mykah.

"Three down," he said.

The vibration of the *Veracity*'s engines began to hum beneath their feet.

"I don't know Gisela well enough to test her," Raena said.

Jimi suggested, "Ask what her favorite game is."

So Raena went up to the cockpit and put the question to the girl. Raena wasn't sure what she expected, but Gisela said, "We call it Kill By Numbers. We play it in the target range."

Raena laughed. "I know it. I used to play with your mom."

"You testing us for robots?" Kavanaugh asked.

"Yeah."

"Go ahead and hit me."

She saw he chose the phrase to tease her. She was pretty sure he was not an android, but she asked, "When we met, we played cards to pass the time. What was weird about how I played?"

Without hesitation, he said, "You cheated to lose. I couldn't figure out how or why, but you lost more than statistically plausible." He looked at her. "So which of us is the android?"

"No one," Raena said. "I don't understand what the Templar is doing."

"You've got time to puzzle it out. Go strap yourself down. We're ready to fly."

Raena went to her bunk and climbed into the crash web, still worrying about the androids. What was the Templar Master using them for? Why had it been important to let her know he had one that looked like her?

For that matter, why was the Templar Master trusting the *Veracity*'s crew to do his bidding back in time? What if instead they decided to kill him in the past? That assumed they could distinguish him from the other Templars of the time, but was there any real reason to let him live?

She rubbed her temples, still hungry and disoriented from being stunned. If they assassinated the Templar Master in the past, who would unleash the gray soldiers in the present time? Would it make any difference to the galaxy if the grays didn't hunt her, if she didn't fight them? She was proud of surviving her encounters with them. She didn't want to give those memories up. And the galaxy had decided she was a hero now, so score one for humanity.

She was too selfish to be a hero, Raena decided. She didn't want to sacrifice who she was to save the galaxy.

* * *

The gray soldiers, in a trio of refurbished Imperial-surplus ships rescued from the wreckage of the Thallians' hangar, kept pace with the *Veracity* and made certain it didn't stray.

Raena put the *Veracity* under a communications blackout, which was rough on Mykah. She let him watch the news coming in, but forbade him to contact Mellix to consult on the upcoming exposé on Kai. She warned him not to draw the gray soldiers' attention to Mellix, even through a series of scramblers.

For similar reasons, she and Gisela didn't speak to Ariel, either. It was better that they do this job quickly and quietly and didn't draw anyone else in.

Mykah cooked to pass the time. Raena worked out with anyone who would join her in the gym. Kavanaugh taught the kids to play poker. Jimi tinkered with the *Veracity*'s weapons systems. Gisela's head finally healed up enough that Raena stopped worrying about her.

* * *

Raena was surprised when Jimi Thallian walked into her gym.

"I never thought I'd miss sparring," he said. "My father used to pit us against each other. Jain won almost every bout. He didn't care who got hurt or how. He just wanted the praise our father heaped on him afterward."

Raena stopped chinning herself up over the bar to listen.

"I thought I hated the fights. I never avoided getting hurt, because I didn't enjoy hurting the others." Jimi pulled off his heavy engineer's boots and lined them up precisely beside the door. "But I miss the camaraderie when we all fought against my father, when he was trying to form us into a team."

Raena dropped to her feet. "How long has it been since you've sparred with anyone?"

"Since before we saw that video of you flying on Kai. After that, Father was too focused on capturing you to declare the games."

"Come at me, then," Raena suggested. "I'll only defend."

For someone out of practice, Jimi was still in pretty good shape. She recognized a kick combination as something his father had taught him. An intensity came into his gray eyes that took her back: a combination of determination and admiration marked him as his father's son.

Raena went easy on him, merely blocking his attacks, but he was fast and lithe and she found herself enjoying the exercise. With her boots on, he was almost exactly her height.

They were both warmed up when Jimi stepped back. He held up a finger—one of his father's gestures—as he caught his breath. Then he said, "Teach me something my father doesn't know."

Raena turned a one-handed cartwheel and came up quickly, punching hard with her other hand. "Nice," Jimi said. "Teach me that."

* * *

Mykah couldn't believe how much he'd missed being in the galley. This was his first opportunity ever to cook for a wholly human crew, so he went for comfort food: breaded pork chops, mashed potatoes, strawberry shortcake. He felt like he was recreating an ancestral meal—one none of the others, with their shattered childhoods, had ever had a chance to eat.

Once they had settled around the table and had a few moments to enjoy the food, Mykah asked, "Do we have a plan?"

When no one else spoke up, Raena said, "No. I can't figure out what game the Templar Master is playing with us. I don't trust him. I don't think the Templars were ever cuddly, fluffy intragalactic friends. I think they were rigid, brutal, and shortsighted. As much as I think it's a tragedy they were wiped out, I'm not convinced the galaxy wants them back in charge. This Templar Master has a goal, but he sent back an assassin and a Thallian to see it met. That's not a peacekeeping team."

"He wants us to stop the plague," Kavanaugh reminded.

"How?" Raena asked.

"We know the Thallian family created and manufactured the plague," Mykah said. "We know Jonan Thallian spread it across the galaxy. Can we stop it at either of those points? Let's make it simple, try to change as little as possible."

"Change as little as possible?" Raena scoffed. "The Templar Master sent us back to *stop the plague*. That will change everything. If there's no plague, does the War ever end? If the Empire doesn't win, do the Templars? Can you imagine them ever making peace with humanity? And on a entirely selfish note, Kavanaugh won't get me out of that tomb, because the Templars will still be guarding the planet."

"You might not be imprisoned," Kavanaugh countered, "if Marchan couldn't get down onto the planet to lock you in."

"If I vanish suddenly, I guess you'll know that the Empire decided on a firing squad for me after all." Raena sawed off a bite of pork and chewed on it meditatively.

Gisela watched them with a puzzled expression, but Jimi and Mykah clearly understood what she was talking about. Raena could not bear the compassion in Mykah's expression, so she turned away from it.

"Marchan got down to the Templar tombworld somehow the first time," Raena said. "The plague hadn't been unleashed when they locked me up. The Templars should have still been guarding the planet. But somehow Marchan got me into the Templar Master's tomb . . ."

"You think the conspiracy goes that far back?" Kavanaugh asked.

They stared at each other. "I don't know what to think," Raena said.

"If we don't stop the plague," Mykah said, "Coni and Haoun will be killed. The human race will be wiped out."

"The Templar threatened that," Kavanaugh pointed out, "but how is he going to accomplish it? The galaxy knows about the Outriders and the Messiah drug now. We don't know how many grays there are, but we haven't seen enough to crew a warship. What kind of weapon do they have to wipe humanity out? We're scattered . . ."

"A plague," Gisela guessed.

"A plague that wipes out humanity," Jimi said. "That would be poetic justice."

"Don't look to me to solve this," Raena said at last. "I'm too para-lyzed by the enormity of it. I don't dare make a move."

* * *

Eventually, they reached the Templar tombworld. "I never thought I'd have any reason to come back here," Kavanaugh said. He flew over the abandoned bunker complex and the Templar Master's tomb, for old times' sake. He pointed them out to Mykah and Jimi, but Raena didn't bother to look. She made certain her knives were sheathed in her boot tops. If anyone got any ideas about imprisoning her here again, she was going to slit her own throat. Everyone else would have to fend for themselves, but she was taking no chances.

The grays sent over landing coordinates. The landing zone turned out to be inside one of the mountains. When they reached it, another crew of androids had already opened the cave's entrance. It was large enough to fly the *Veracity* inside.

An android that Raena did not recognize called over a final message. "The device is prepared for you. It is locked onto a time coordinate in the past and keyed to the *Veracity*'s numerical ID. If the *Veracity* is damaged, you will have to retrieve its ID signature. No other vehicle number will trigger your return."

"What happens when we arrive in the past?" Mykah asked. "The Templars will still be guarding their planet. Will they let us out of here?"

"Yours is not the first Imperial ship we've commandeered," the android told him. "They will assume you are on a mission from the future."

Gooseflesh shivered over Raena's skin. She wondered again how Marchan had succeeded in locking her into the Templar Master's tomb at the height of the Human-Templar War.

"What happens after we succeed in preventing the plague?" Mykah asked. "When we come back here in the past, Templars will still be guarding these tombs. Will they allow us to use the time machine to return?"

"Play them this message," the android said. It sent over a fragment of flashing colors: Templar speech.

"Anything else we need to know?" Mykah asked.

"For the sake of your species, do not fail."

"No pressure, then," Kavanaugh muttered. He rotated the *Veracity* around and backed it into the cavern.

Raena's head pounded as if it would split, so hard and fast that she feared she would have a stroke. Sweat slicked her whole body. Mykah came over to hold her in his arms. Raena scrunched her eyes closed and clung to him. It didn't help. She felt like she was dying.

"This is only a panic attack," he whispered. "I know it feels like it will kill you, but it won't."

"This is the hardest thing I've ever done," she said quietly. "I don't want to be trapped again."

"I know."

"How will we know when it works?" Gisela asked.

"The *Veracity*'s clock will reset," Kavanaugh said. "It's linked to GST."

The *Veracity* gave a horrific moan. Raena echoed it.

The ship's power shut off abruptly. The *Veracity* started to fall out of the air. Kavanaugh fought for control as Gisela slapped blindly at switches, trying to regain some kind of spark. Suddenly, independent of anything they'd done, the ship blazed back to life. The engine reengaged. The repulsors caught them before they bottomed out.

Jimi leaned forward to check the clock. "We've gone back," he said. "The War is on, but the plague hasn't begun yet."

* * *

Raena drew a shaky breath and pushed gently out of Mykah's arms to stand on her own feet again. Her body felt wrung out. She put a hand on the bulkhead, just for stability, and asked, "Mykah, do you have Vezali's translator?"

"It's in my cabin."

"Let's listen to the Templar Master's message before we play it for anyone else."

As he went to retrieve the translator, Kavanaugh asked, "What do you expect it to say?"

"Kill us all," Raena said. "The Templar Master can't let us return to the future, knowing he has a time machine."

"What makes you suspect it?" Gisela asked shakily.

"That we're not supposed to play it until we get back to the planet. If this trip is straightforward and the Templar in the past would support what we're doing, why don't we have a message for them when we come out of the machine now—so they could help us?"

They stood around in tense silence until Mykah returned. "You know how the translator works?" Raena asked.

"Not really. I think it's on all the time, unless you intentionally switch it off, which I don't know how to do." He set the translator on the *Veracity*'s console. Kavanaugh triggered the message to play.

The translator reeled off a bunch of syllables. They didn't make any immediate sense to Raena. "Play it again," she said.

Afterward Kavanaugh asked, "Is that Standard?"

"It's a formula," Jimi realized. He pulled a handheld out of his jacket, poised to take notes. "Let me hear it again."

Kavanaugh played it a third time.

"Yeah, it's a formula. Some of it's chemical, some's genetic."

"Can you decipher it?" Mykah asked.

"I don't know. Maybe. We all had to study genetic code, but it wasn't what I was best at."

"If it's the antidote to the plague, why would the Templar want us to play it to the Templars guarding the tombs after our mission?" Gisela asked.

"It could be the plague to wipe humanity out," Raena said. "The Templar Master probably got hold of the Thallians' notes and made a few tweaks, since our physiologies are supposed to be so similar."

The others stared at her in silence.

"I know how we can decipher it," Jimi said at last. "We just need to get onto Drusingyi and access the family's computers."

* * *

As Kavanaugh eased the *Veracity* forward out of the mountain, the constant wind rocked it. He turned to look over his shoulder at Raena. "While we're here . . ." he started.

She cut him off. "No. She would be insane by now. She would kill us. If not as soon as we opened her tomb, then as soon as she saw this ship. She would recognize it and know where it came from."

"But she would know me," Kavanaugh protested. "She would recognize you . . ."

"No," Raena repeated. "Don't tempt me. If we let her out now, who knows what that would do to the future? I could cease to exist. We could all cease to exist. All the Templar Master would know in the future was that we did not come home. We can't risk the fate of humanity. Let her be. As long as I don't suddenly vanish, we know that she survives her imprisonment."

Templars crawled around in the gritty wind on the tombworld, but none of them paid any attention to the Imperial transport exiting from one of their mountains. A shudder ran through Raena as the *Veracity* headed into space.

"What are we doing then?" Mykah asked.

"Set a course for Drusingyi," Raena suggested. "Jimi needs to access those computers."

He suggested, "My father could get us clearance. And we have the perfect bait for him."

Everyone stared at the boy, but Raena understood what he meant. "Me," she said. "Jonan will come anywhere in the galaxy to get me. It's just a matter of luring Jonan into suggesting he meet us on Drusingyi."

"What if he thinks you've been captured by bounty hunters?" Mykah suggested. "Kavanaugh and I could claim we tracked you down."

Raena looked at them: Kavanaugh with his bristling red beard, Mykah with his headful of braids. They could pose as hunters, if not for the *Veracity*. "I hate to suggest drastic changes in your appearance, gentlemen, but we're aboard an Imperial transport. Do you think you could pass for officers? Mykah, you'd have to captain. Gisela could be your aide. Jimi, you'll have to make certain your father doesn't see your eyes."

"Call me Jim, please," he said quietly. "I don't want to be that other person any more."

Raena nodded. She of all people could appreciate that.

"What would we do for uniforms?" Kavanaugh asked.

"We still have the Thallian soldiers' livery in the ship's stores," Raena said. "We can spin you as some kind of Special Ops."

"What are you going to do to distract them while Jim works?" Mykah asked.

Raena gazed at him and slowly smiled.

"I'll draw up a map of the city," Jim said, "so you'll know where to meet us if you bust out of detention before I can come and get you."

* * *

Raena took apart Eilif's former cabin and reconfigured it to look more like an Imperial detention cell. She removed every comfort that Eilif had added and reinstalled the restraints.

She couldn't restore her long hair or replace the scar across her face, but she was certain Jonan would recognize her despite the superficial changes. Especially if she dressed in such a way to highlight her other scars.

Once she'd gotten the setting arranged to her satisfaction, she checked on the other actors.

Mykah and Kavanaugh had shaved off their beards. Gisela had cut their hair in passable approximations of Imperial style. Jim found uniforms for everyone, along with appropriate sidearms.

"Here's the scenario," Raena said. "Feel free to tweak it. I've escaped from the tomb. You lucky gentlemen found me. If we send the message from the vicinity of Drusingyi, Thallian should suggest that we meet him there. He won't want the *Arbiter*'s officers to know what he's up to. I'll do what I can to provide distraction for the Thallians while you figure out the Templar Master's message and what to do about it. Without that message—or something like it—we can't get back onto the Templar world to get home, so you'll have to figure that out, too."

"With any luck," Mykah said, "we can get the job done and get out of there before the *Arbiter* arrives."

"I particularly like the part where we leave before Thallian arrives," Kavanaugh said.

Raena turned to Jim. "Come to the galley and tell me everything you remember about your family before the plague."

He followed her and joined her at the table over bottles of cider. Mykah and the others came, too.

Jim bit his lips before he began. "Uncle Revan used to tell us stories about the time before the planet was destroyed. The family lived in a city-sized palazzo on the edge of the Shining Lake. The lake was in the middle of a mountain range, which protected them from the monsters that crawled in and out of the ocean."

"How many in the family?"

"Seventy, more or less. There were some left from my grandfather's generation, then twenty or thirty of my father's generation. The rest were Aten's sons. Not all of them would have been at home at once. Some followed my father into Imperial service. Others would be out trading or traveling."

"How many slaves did they keep?"

Jim looked puzzled by her bitterness. "None."

"That's hard to believe."

"It's true. The initial settlers brought slaves, but there was a revolt. After that, the family just cloned enough sons to keep the city running. Well, they used sons and machinery. They didn't allow anyone into the city who wasn't genetically related, other than the alpha's wife. And she couldn't get out without a genetic escort."

"So," Raena said, "Seventy Thallians at the outside."

"You don't think that we could just talk to them?" Mykah asked. "Explain what will happen to the family—and the galaxy—if they decide to manufacture the plague?"

Raena looked at Jim, but he didn't answer. She said, "I don't imagine that they had very much choice in the matter. Whether Jonan was onboard to disseminate the plague or not, the Thallians on Drusingyi were a small out-of-the-way outpost. The Empire only had to threaten. They had no way to defend themselves."

Kavanaugh made a disgusted snort.

Raena only smiled, remembering the old political arguments with Ariel.

"Who was the alpha clone then?" Raena asked.

"Aten. He was injured during the War and had to live in a mechanized chair after that. You might have seen him on Drusingyi."

Raena remembered seeing his corpse. "What about the one who was the head of family security when you ran away?"

"Merin. He served on the *Conciliator* during the War. He won't be on the planet now."

"Was Revan at home in those years?"

"Not often. He was kind of an adventurer. He made supply runs for the family."

"Good. Then we don't have to worry about the brothers who survived the War seeing either of us, as long as we can keep out of Aten's way. Were there boys your age, so that you can get in and out of the palazzo?"

"Yes. Aten's sons."

"Maybe we can capture one and you can pass for him?" Mykah suggested.

When Jim didn't answer immediately, Raena said, "This is where we need you, Jim. You have a better chance of understanding the Templar's formula than any of us and a much better possibility of disrupting the Thallians' design or manufacture of the plague. Can we trust you?"

"This is a lot to process," Jim said slowly. "I've always thought that my family's participation in the Plague was horrific. But now I wonder: were they set up to be scapegoats? Why did the Emperor 'honor' my family? Surely there were other scientists working in genetics that could have created this plague. Why were we chosen?"

Raena answered, "Because of your father. Because Jonan had become a threat to the stability of the Empire. He was an unrestrained serial killer in command of one of the most powerful ships in the Imperial fleet. He wanted to be in line for the throne. But while the Emperor didn't trust Jonan, he couldn't get rid of him either. Your father had allies across the Empire—and your family to back him up. As long as Jonan was obsessed with finding me, he wasn't an organized danger. After I was locked up, the Emperor put Jonan in charge of the plague. It was his last chance to prove he was more useful than Marchan."

Gisela asked quietly, "You were alive during the War?"

Mykah laughed. "I don't know why Coni went to so much trouble for your cover story."

Raena shrugged. "Yes," she admitted. "There's only one of me and I'm it."

Working it out, the girl said, "You were my mother's slave."

"Yes. And Jim's father's girlfriend. And I was imprisoned in a Templar tomb before the plague was spread. And Kavanaugh let me out six months ago. That's my sad and sordid life." Raena sighed. "I just want to move forward. Why does the past insist on dragging me down?"

"Because your former boss exterminated a people who seem to have had more than one way to bend time," Mykah pointed out.

"It needs to stop," Raena said. "I didn't have anything to do with killing the Templars."

"Now you have the chance to rescue them," Kavanaugh said. He changed the subject back. "What are we going to say to Thallian?"

"You two are errand boys who answer directly to the Emperor. That will explain why Thallian doesn't recognize the ship. Mykah is going to be a young upstart, eager to make himself useful and get a boost up the chain of command. The key here, Mykah, is that very few people could lie to Thallian and survive." She nodded at Jim to underscore her point. "So keep your pitch short and get the camera onto me as soon as you can. I will sell the story to him."

* * *

Raena let Mykah set up the camera angles and the lights in the cell she'd made. She coached him through a couple of practice runs of his speech, until she was certain he could hold the character. Then she lay facedown on the bench in her new cell, out of camera range, and listened to him record the first message.

"Lord Thallian," Mykah said. "I am Mykah Chen, in command of *ISS Veracity*. While on a mission on Lautan, we recaptured an Imperial deserter. I understand that you were her commander."

Gisela moved forward with the second camera to focus in on Raena, who swooned on the bench as if under heavy stun. Raena had chosen to wear a breast band over a pair of leggings, which left the scars on her bare back visible.

In voiceover, Mykah continued, "With the rate at which we're having to stun her to keep her docile, I am becoming concerned about the potential for permanent damage. Can you advise?"

Gisela held the shot, then Mykah said, "I'll get that edited and sent off to him. How long do you think it will take him to reply?"

"At a guess?" Raena asked. "Don't take off your uniform."

CHAPTER 16

"**C**aptain," Kavanaugh called from the cockpit. "We have a message coming in on Imperial Priority One."

Mykah met Raena's eyes as he put his coffee cup down on the galley table. "Any last-minute advice?"

"Stand up straight as you can. Meet his eyes momentarily, then look over his shoulder." She smiled, showing teeth. It wasn't comforting. "Don't look nervous."

As Mykah stood up, he tugged his dress jacket down into place. Raena had one more sip of her tea and strode back to her cell.

Mykah went up to the cockpit and nodded at Kavanaugh.

The man whose image filled the screen was familiar from all the research Mykah had done. Jonan Thallian wore a pointed beard to emphasize his cheekbones. Both his hair and beard were blue-black, which made the sheen of his silvery gray eyes that much more striking. Before it could reach his expression, Mykah locked down the stab of recognition he felt.

Thallian snapped, "Explain your message, Captain Chen."

"We were investigating an arms retailer on Lautan for Coalition contamination, when we were attacked by our prisoner. She killed four of my men before my aide took her down. Once we had her onboard the *Veracity*, the genetic trace named her as Raena Zacari."

"Raena Zacari is dead," Thallian said.

"Yes, my lord. So the official record says. However, after we dosed her with RespirAll, she told us an unbelievable story about being imprisoned in a cave on the Templar tombworld."

Gisela walked up to Mykah and reported, "She's awake again, sir."

Mykah nodded crisply and met Thallian's eyes. "My lord, do you have any suggestions for keeping her under control?"

"Let me see her."

Mykah nodded to Kavanaugh, who toggled on the camera in Raena's cell. She was upside down in a handstand, doing press-ups.

Thallian's sigh made the hair stand up on the back of Mykah's neck. Mykah hoped like hell that Raena couldn't hear it. "My lord?"

"Doze gas," Thallian said. "I will send you the dosage." Thallian consulted something offscreen, then said, "Your message indicates you are still amongst the Border Worlds, correct?"

"Yes, sir."

"You will detour to Drusingyi. I will tell my family to expect you."

"What do I tell the Emperor, my lord?"

"Tell him nothing, until I confirm her identity," Thallian barked. "I am three days out from Drusingyi myself. Wait for me there. I'd like to commend you personally, Captain."

"Very good, sir. Thank you."

Kavanaugh shut down the comm system and shuddered. Mykah shuddered himself. "Can we get to Drusingyi and away in three days?" he asked.

"It'll be cutting it close."

"I don't want her to have to face him," Mykah said. "We need to put our plan put together so Jim can get in there and we can head back to the time machine before Thallian arrives."

He looked down at Jim in the copilot's chair. The boy stared rigidly at the controls. Mykah placed a hand on his shoulder. "You all right?"

The boy didn't jump. "How can she toy with him like this?"

Mykah remembered something Raena told him the first time she went to Drusingyi. "She is his greatest weakness."

Jim nodded. "That is true."

"There must be something you can say to inspire her before she faces the rest of them." Mykah realized that was a lot of pressure to put on the kid, but no one knew the Thallians better than the scion who loathed them.

* * *

Jim found Raena in her gym. She'd gone there to work off the adrenaline of her glancing interaction with Thallian. She hadn't expected it would upset her so. "Did you want something?" she asked the boy.

"Can you tell me anything good about my father?"

Raena looked at the boy. Like Jain, Jim seemed to have realized that though she had known his father for a much shorter span of years, her knowledge of him ran much deeper.

Raena laughed at the first good point that occurred to her. "Jonan was gentle after he beat me. Since he didn't want me to go to the infirmary to have my injuries treated . . ."

Jim interrupted, "Why not?"

"Because then there would have been an official record of how he abused me. He might have been reprimanded, even demoted. So he taught himself to care for me. He bound my wounds and changed my bandages and made excuses for me when I had to relax under a bone-mender for days at a time. He fed and cared for me when I couldn't get out of bed. I think it entertained him to have a toy he could break and repair in secret."

Jim shook his head at the thought. "My mother took care of us."

"Where do you think she learned how to do it?"

Rather than answer, Jim changed the subject. "Did you know he had been forbidden to mate?"

"Forbidden by whom?"

"Family doctrine. It dated back to the family's earliest colonization of Drusingyi. Only the alpha clone was allowed to take a wife."

"I wasn't ever Thallian's wife," Raena argued.

Jim raised an eyebrow.

"Concubine, maybe."

It was his turn to laugh. "No one was supposed to have an ongoing relationship with a woman. That was easy for most of them, because they never left the planet. Others dated when they traveled, but I think those were mostly business transactions. What my father had with you could have gotten him exiled or killed on Drusingyi, if Uncle Aten discovered it. It meant Father's first loyalty wasn't to the family. That's why Uncle Revan and Uncle Merin remained bachelors all their lives."

She nodded, wondering if Jim knew about the unrequited passion between Revan and his mother.

Jim continued, "My father killed Aten's wife and sons after Uncle Aten was crippled. Once my father became the alpha, he considered everyone who did not belong to him a threat. So he executed them all, even though we'd already lost so much. Revan protested, but there was precedent for it. Merin supported my father."

Raena hadn't realized Jonan's murderous streak had applied to his nephews as well. She felt a pang of sympathy for his son. How had he survived more than a decade with his father?

She relented and answered Jim's question. "Jonan liked to look at the stars. He taught me to name them. He loved anything that gave him the illusion of flight: zero g, jet packs, free fall, wings. His favorite color, unsurprisingly, was crimson. He loved the flavor of blackberries and the scent of lilies."

Jim nodded, trying to digest all of that. "Did you ever know him when he was sane?"

"Never. He left home to fight for the Empire because his ambition was bigger than to rule one family on one planet. He was willing to do anything to other people because no one else was ever real to him. He lived alone in a universe peopled with ghosts."

"You were real to him," Jim pointed out.

"Only after I ran from him. Then he knew what he'd lost."

The boy considered that. "You think he was cruel to us because we weren't real to him?"

She turned that question around. "Do you know what happened to Jain?"

"Mother said they made him stand on a parapet with a noose around his neck. Jain hung himself."

"That's true," Raena said. "Jain revealed my position to the family. When your brothers attacked me, I killed them all as Jain watched. Jain hung himself afterward. Your father did not face me himself until he'd sent everyone else against me. Everyone but your mother, whom he'd already forgotten. Even after your brothers were dead, he didn't grieve for them. He collected their bodies together to serve as guests for our wedding feast. Alive or dead, his family was all the same to him."

Jim sighed shakily, but did not start to cry. Raena wondered if he had liked any of his brothers, if anyone had ever been kind to him, beyond Revan and Eilif.

His next question was unexpected. "Do you think that Father was crazy because something went wrong in the cloning process? My family meant to create a hyena, but they got a shark instead?"

"I think that's very possible—but I don't want to give Jonan an excuse. I watched him learn to love torture. It saddened me, but didn't surprise me, to discover he'd carried out the genocide. He may have been born broken, but he chose to do evil."

✳ ✳ ✳

Once they reached Drusingyi, the Thallians sent ships to meet the *Veracity* and escort it through their satellite defenses in the asteroid belt. Kavanaugh flew carefully, noting landmarks in case they needed to blast out of there in a hurry. Luckily, it seemed that most of the defenses faced out toward the galaxy instead of in toward the planet. Still, if the *Veracity* made a big enough ruckus when they left, he was sure things could be quickly reconfigured. While the rest of the crew were busy on the planet, Kavanaugh would make it his job to figure out how to escape the satellite net.

Raena was in the galley, eating the huge meal Mykah had prepared especially for her and Jim. Kavanaugh heard Raena laughing, a wonderful sound, full of life. He didn't see how she could survive being a prisoner of Thallian's family, but now that her death was imminent, she seemed to have shed her fear.

"Why didn't anyone tell me who she really was?" Gisela asked quietly from the copilot's chair.

"Because she isn't that person any more," Kavanaugh answered.

The girl thought about that answer, before asking, "Did you know her before the War?"

"No. When I met her, she was already running from Thallian. She wasn't too much older than you are now."

"And her back . . . ?"

"Yeah, Thallian had already scarred her."

"How can she sound so happy?" Emotion choked Gisela's voice, so similar to Ariel that it was hard for Kavanaugh to remember that the two of them weren't actually blood. "Doesn't Raena know what's going to happen to her?"

"She has a better idea than any of us do," Kavanaugh explained. "She's taking all the pleasure she can in the time she has left."

He glanced over at Gisela. Tears sparkled in her deep blue eyes and she looked more like a child than ever. What the hell was she doing here? Anger rushed over him: that there could be such innocence in the galaxy while Thallian was busy plotting genocide in humanity's name. Kavanaugh hoped the crew could protect Gisela from the madman, whether or not they accomplished anything else.

"I'm sorry to have to tell you this," he said, "but Raena needs you to be strong right now. She can't worry about us while she's facing them. I want to say goodbye to her, but if you can't do it, go hide in your cabin until she's gone."

Gisela nodded and wiped her eyes on her sleeve. "I can do it. Give me a minute."

"Good." Kavanaugh gave her some time to calm herself, then pressed the intercom and said, "We should be landing in an hour. Raena, would you come up before then?"

* * *

"I guess I'm wanted." Raena took one last mouthful of the honey wine Mykah had opened for her. It tasted like summer, like the flowers in the sunny garden at Ariel's villa. "Thank you for that meal, Mykah. It was perfect."

He swooped down to grab her up in a hug. Raena clasped her hands behind his neck and pulled herself closer, eyes shut to make the moment last.

"I hugged you for luck the last time you went down to face the Thallians," he reminded.

"And that turned out pretty well," she remembered. "Don't worry about me."

He squeezed her, then leaned over to set her feet on the floor. "I know you can take care of yourself."

"I'll do my best," she promised.

Jim stood at attention beside the table. Raena offered him her hand. The boy looked surprised, but he took it.

"Good luck," she said.

"You, too."

She gave his fingers an extra squeeze, then turned to go forward.

Kavanaugh stood when she entered the cockpit. He opened his arms, so she pressed herself into them and kissed his cheek.

He grinned at her. "Give 'em hell."

"That's my plan."

Gisela climbed awkwardly out of her copilot's chair. Her lower lip trembled.

"Don't cry," Raena said. "You'll ruin my hero moment."

Gisela laughed and blinked hard.

Raena gave the girl a quick hug. "Make your mother proud."

Gisela nodded, unable to speak.

Raena went back to her cell and changed into Jain's jumpsuit. Like a prayer, she buckled on her silver-heeled boots. Then she lay down on the bunk. She had recalculated Thallian's dosage of the Doze gas so that it would knock her out, but not for too long. She didn't want to spend any more time unconscious in the Thallians' detention than was absolutely necessary.

✳ ✳ ✳

Kavanaugh set the *Veracity* down gently on the pad the Thallians had lit up for him. The last hours of night engulfed this part of the Thallian homeworld, which struck him as fitting. Dawn was barely an hour away.

Mykah met Kavanaugh outside Raena's cell. They peeked at her through the window in the door. She was out cold, mouth open and eyes rolled back. Mykah hit the remote in his pocket to release the restraints she'd used as crash protection on the way down. Her limbs sprawled bonelessly.

"Did you vent the cell already?" Kavanaugh asked.

"Yeah. It should be clear now."

"Got the prisoner transfer paperwork?"

"Gisela does. I'm glad Jim dug up that antique datascreen."

They stood there awkwardly, until Gisela commed back to them. "There's a welcoming party forming up outside," she reported. "A heavily armed welcoming party."

"You okay?" Kavanaugh asked her.

"I'm under control," the girl promised.

Mykah looked curious, but he didn't ask. Instead, he tugged his uniform jacket down and asked Kavanaugh, "Ready?"

"Let's do it."

Mykah opened the door and Kavanaugh went in to sling Raena over his shoulder. She weighed little more than a child.

* * *

Jim met them at the hatch with the restraints. He and Gisela pinned Raena's arms behind her back, then hobbled her at knees and ankles.

Mykah tugged the uniform jacket down one last time and nodded to Gisela to open the hatch. He stepped out of the *Veracity* first, followed by his "aide." Kavanaugh came last, with Raena slung over his shoulder. Jim stayed hidden aboard the ship.

Ten Thallians stood on the landing pad. All but one stood at attention. The last, dressed in silver and black brocade, was Aaron Thallian, head of Thallian family security.

Raena had drilled Mykah on how to behave. Any Imperial officer, she said, believed himself superior to any planetary officer. Mykah was to hold himself graciously, managing neither to condescend nor be too familiar. He was better than the Thallians, but the character he was playing still wanted a favor from Jonan and, by extension, his family.

"Thank you for taking her off our hands, Lord Thallian." Mykah reached out to Gisela, who placed the datascreen in his hand.

Aaron seemed in no hurry to take it. "She doesn't look very threatening, Captain Chen."

"Not now," Mykah agreed. "However, I'm sure your brother has apprised you of her criminal record."

A moment ticked past and Mykah understood that Jonan Thallian had done no such thing. He changed the subject. "With your kind permission, we will await the arrival of the *Arbiter* here. We have some necessary repairs to make before we resume orbit."

"Nothing serious, I hope."

"The last time we allowed her to become conscious, Zacari managed to kill two more of my men, Lord Thallian. We have a hastily patched hull breach to attend to."

Aaron Thallian looked back at Raena. Mykah had suggested that she simply pretend to be sedated and attack the Thallians on the landing platform, but Kavanaugh pointed out that they couldn't assume the Thallians would shoot to stun, especially once she started killing them. It was better, Raena agreed, that they underestimate her—even if that would insult Mykah's character's vanity.

Aaron Thallian took the datascreen and signed off on the prisoner transfer. He signaled one of the clones to step forward and take Raena from Kavanaugh's arms.

Mykah kept his face impassive as he accepted the datascreen back. "Do we have your permission to make our repairs?"

"Yes," Aaron said grudgingly. "Let us know if you require assistance."

* * *

As Jim watched the security detail go back into the city, he studied the city's defenses. Not surprisingly, the wall had a genetic lock, which Aaron overrode to take Raena into the city. She would need that same code to get herself out.

The boy had yet to set foot in the city where his family lived before the War. He'd seen its ruins from a distance, of course, but even a decade after the bombing, the rubble had still been too contaminated to explore.

In that future, Uncle Revan had believed that the boys should know their history, so he had taken it upon himself to model the city for them—in hopes that someday the boys would be able to bring it back to life. Jim wasn't alone in believing Uncle Revan was deluded about ever living on the planet's surface again. Even so, family history had interested him. He'd been an attentive student.

After daybreak, when family members started to come and go into the city, Jim combed his hair a final time and checked the shine on his boots. Then he slipped out of the *Veracity*.

His first real test would be the gate in the city wall. Jim approached it casually, aware that Kavanaugh and Gisela were hidden behind him on the mountainside, watching his progress through snipers' rifles. Gisela promised that if anything about Jim triggered the city's defenses or alerted the guards on the wall, she would give him time to run.

No alarms went off. The city recognized him as a Thallian.

Jim turned left inside the gate and walked to the boys' barracks. Luck was with him. He didn't have to wait very long before a boy about his age came back from breakfast alone. Jim waited until he was sure which locker belonged to the boy, then snuck up behind him and slapped the palm needle into the back of his neck. Raena was right. The saxitoxin worked almost immediately.

Jim caught the boy as he collapsed. He dragged him over to an unused locker and tucked him inside. Raena had warned that while the toxin would make his victim docile, it would also make it difficult for him to breathe. He had to be propped up somewhere, or he'd suffocate.

Jim hadn't thought he would care. He had loathed his family members with varying degrees of hatred. This kid was a stranger who merely shared his likeness. But now, facing his doppelgänger, Jim couldn't help identifying with his cousin. The boy shared Jim's gray eyes and jawline, the blue-black hair and the long straight nose. Maybe he was a victim of his elders' abuse, just as Jim had been. Something like pity trembled through Jim. Before he left, he would try to leave the kid where someone could find him and give him the antitoxin.

Then Jim took a deep breath, shut the locker door, and returned to the kid's own locker. He stole the boy's clothing, datascreen, and security passes. Jim hoped that any adults he encountered would be too preoccupied to examine him closely. Despite what the *Veracity* crew believed, the clones were adept at telling each other apart. Jim was glad Gisela had cut his hair to be less distinctive.

Jim left the barracks and entered the library next door. Inside, after roaming a bit, he found a quartet of isolated study carrels. Because his family's tech never progressed after the War isolated them, Jim knew what to expect from the city's computer systems. He'd come prepared. After a few minutes, he had his anachronistic handheld connected to a terminal. Opening his translation of the Templar Master's formula, he called on the city's databanks to begin analyzing it, taking pains to keep the data flowing into his handheld, not the other way around.

The handheld lit up with an initial screenful of information. He'd been right: it indicated a foundation of human genetics plus viral manipulation. Unfortunately, it was at a much higher level than he could comprehend. He asked the computer to begin a deeper analysis and attached the handheld to the underside of the desk to let it process without interruption.

Jim moved to the carrel adjacent and cabled another handheld—Mykah's—to the terminal there. This handheld contained nothing but a modification of Coni's kill-switch program. He readied it to run as soon as he finished his analysis of the Templar formula. Once started, the program would begin to multiply itself, overwriting the city databanks with random bytes and destroying all of the family's research.

Jim settled into the next carrel and turned on its terminal. He poked through the research reports in his family's files. Some of what he found was familiar: projects that had been built upon while he was living at home. Other things, especially the art and musical experiments, had been abandoned after the War.

Something strange caught his attention. There were references to his father's last visit home and the "animals" he'd brought along.

Jim hadn't known that the family ever kept a menagerie beyond the beasts they bred for food.

He suspected the handheld decoding the Templar's message would be working a while longer. He had time to take a walk and see what had captured his father's interest.

* * *

When Raena woke, she lay on a smooth white block of stone. Assaultively bright light filled the cell. In place of its fourth wall hung a forcefield so steady and seamless as to be invisible. Outside it stood a gray-eyed man with strict military posture.

Raena looked up into the Thallian clone's face. This one looked much more like Raena's memories of Jonan than the man she'd set on fire in his bed. This clone wore a short black beard, cut close to emphasize his jawline, but his eyes glowed the same hard silver as she remembered Jonan's did.

"Tell me why my brother wants you kept alive," the clone said.

Raena smiled. "I used to work for him aboard the *Arbiter*. I served as his aide."

"Past tense?" he asked.

"I objected to his treatment of a Coalition prisoner," Raena said. "Your younger brother put a bounty on me when I left his service."

"Not a reason for your continued survival, then."

"This is: as far as Jonan knew, I was still imprisoned in the Master's tomb on the Templar tombworld. He will want to know how I escaped. I consent to be your prisoner until he comes to reclaim me."

"You consent?" the clone scoffed.

"Yes."

That fazed him enough that he left without a response.

* * *

Jim stopped inside the building's doors to let his eyes adjust. At the heart of the darkened bunker, several clones of his father's generation had gathered inside a plastic-sheathed room. Beneath hyper-bright lights, they were garbed in surgical robes and wore breathing masks.

Jim tried to look like he had a purpose as he drew nearer. He traced the pipes running into the surgical tent. One was labeled as cyanogen, a hot-burning gas he had used for dismantling ships. Jim glanced around, seeing stalls instead of machinery. He stared at the surgical suite, trying to figure out what they were doing here.

Inside the tent, something spasmed, something deep brown and covered with wiry whiskers. It took Jim a moment to identify it as the hind leg of a Templar.

"Lock that down," snarled one of the clones. Jim shivered at the familiar tone of command.

Another clone restrained the flailing limb.

A third clone sparked a cutting torch. Jim could smell it, poisonous and hot, before they cut into the Templar. The scent abruptly went putrid.

"That's lighting it up good," the first clone said. "Keep on with that."

Swallowing hard against the bile that burned his throat, Jim walked with measured steps out of the bunker.

He marched over to the vehicle depot. Using his stolen ID, Jim checked out a jet bike. He'd concocted a story about where he was going, but the bored clone manning the garage didn't care. It was a beautiful sunny day. That was excuse enough.

Jim went over what he was going to tell Captain Chen, but he couldn't think of anything that kept him from feeling ashamed.

* * *

After the girl had been given her breakfast—which she refused to eat—Aaron Thallian returned to stand outside the forcefield. This time he brought an armed guard, in case he needed to interrogate the girl. "You were correct," he told her. "Jonan wants you alive. He is coming home with all speed."

The girl nodded calmly. "Did he tell you also that he's bringing a message from the Emperor?"

Aaron stared at her. "How could you know that?"

"Who do you think let me out of the Templar Master's tomb?"

"Why didn't Jonan do it?"

"He has a mission to fulfill. Has he given you any indication what that might be?"

Aaron did not like the way the girl played with him. Granted, his interaction with females had been limited, since family doctrine forbade him to mate. Be that as it may, she appeared too much in control for someone ostensibly his prisoner.

He touched the lock outside her cell, then passed through the forcefield. She merely sat on her bunk and watched him.

"Who are you really?" he insisted.

"Your brother told you who I am."

"The Empire executed Raena Zacari for treason."

"You haven't found any recording of my execution, have you?"

Rather than answer, he said, "The wanted poster shows that Zacari had a scar across her face."

"I had it removed," Raena said.

"Jonan said your back would be scarred."

Zacari stood languidly. She grabbed hold of the zipper of her jumpsuit and opened it to the waist. She let the sleeves drop from her shoulders, then turned to display the ridges of scar tissue that striped diagonally across her back. "Did he tell you how he marked me like this?"

Aaron's mouth went dry. He wanted to touch her scars so badly that he quivered.

She did not turn to gauge his reaction. Instead, she stood at attention, proud of what she'd survived. She might have been a Thallian herself, Aaron thought, before he shook the thought away.

"He striped me with accelerant and set me on fire," she said, "in his stateroom aboard the *Arbiter*. He was furious that I'd dared to distract him from torturing a Coalition smuggler. He couldn't forgive me for being jealous."

She turned to face Aaron again, naked to the hips except for a tight black band across her small breasts. She pointed to the scar just beneath her ribs. "While protecting your brother, I was shot in the conference room aboard the *Arbiter*. Your brother licked my blood from his gloved fingers."

When she didn't say anything more, Aaron dragged his gaze back up to her face.

"Shall I tell you the stories of the rest of my scars?" she asked. He would have said she was flirting with him. "Or have you seen enough?"

"Enough." Aaron tore himself away, retreating out of the cell.

Raena Zacari shrugged back into her clothing and sat down again.

✱ ✱ ✱

"Vivisection?" Kavanaugh echoed, disgust thick in his voice. "Why would they need to do that to make the plague?"

"They're not making the plague yet," Mykah corrected. "Thallian hasn't brought them the order. They're just learning to torture the 'bugs.'"

Jim nodded. "They could harvest whatever DNA they need to sequence without hurting the Templars. This is cruelty for evil's sake."

"I didn't know any Templars were ever captured alive," Mykah said.

"Does it surprise you they kept it quiet?" Kavanaugh asked bitterly.

Gisela cut across Mykah's response. "How many Templars are there?"

"Four," Jim answered, "including the one I saw tortured."

"Can we fit them onto the *Veracity*?"

The others looked at her.

"Look, we are *not* leaving them here." Gisela's voice quivered with anger, daring them to argue. "If we can take them forward in time, then the Templar Master will have other Templars to clone from, right? So that would add to the genetic diversity."

"If we succeed in ending the plague, it won't matter," Mykah pointed out. "But you're right: it's still the right thing to do."

"I'll see what I can do about clearing out the hold," Kavanaugh volunteered. "I don't have any idea how to make it comfortable for them."

"What do they eat?" Mykah asked, but no one had an answer. "All right, it doesn't matter. Whatever we can offer them, it will be better than what they have now."

"You're fixating on the wrong details," Gisela scolded. "The question is: how can we get them out of the city?"

Kavanaugh shook his head. "You're not thinking like an Imperial officer," he told Mykah. "Tell the Thallians you already know the Templars are here. Say that the Emperor asked you to interrogate them. Don't allow them to say no."

★ ★ ★

Some fair amount of time passed. Unlike her cell on Kai, where she could see the sky, this cell was either deep inside a building or else underground. As in her tomb, Raena had no way to measure time here.

She had already had enough of being imprisoned. She jumped up enough to hook her fingers over her shoulders into the ventilation grate. Then she slowly pulled her feet up over her head, toes pointed, legs extended, straining her muscles and perfecting her form. She repeated the exercise until her fingers cramped, until her arms trembled with fatigue.

Some of the younger clones came to watch her. None of them spoke to her. She hoped that fear of Jonan would provide her a measure of protection, but it no longer really mattered. She was committed to buying Jim and the others time to figure out how to prevent the Templar from wiping out humanity. She would do whatever she had to, to keep the Thallians distracted.

She wondered if she would sense it when Jonan returned home. Would the tension in the air change? Would the clones all bustle around, attempting to look busy? She knew that he had been the alpha clone after the demolition of his homeworld. She was curious how they'd felt about him while the planet still lived.

* * *

"Uncle Aaron," Avan said, "there's a private message from Captain Chen."

Aaron stepped over to his nephew's station to look down at the boy's screen. The message bore an Imperial code number, one Aaron didn't recognize. "Put it through to my office."

He didn't hurry to pick it up. The *Veracity's* continued presence on Drusingyi was a mystery. Why had Jonan sent them here, rather than having them report directly to the *Arbiter*? Captain Chen's aide, the pretty blue-eyed girl, seemed little more than a child. He wasn't sure why that disturbed him. And their captive, Raena Zacari, was certainly more than she claimed. As a rule, Aaron didn't care for mystery.

He pressed a key on his desk and said, "Captain Chen."

"Lord Thallian, I've received a message coded Priority One directing me to interrogate the Templars in your custody."

Whatever Aaron might have expected to hear, that wasn't it. "I'm sorry," he said icily, "I don't understand."

Chen's smile went a touch smug. "Your brother reported to the Emperor that he had delivered several Templars to you. We captured a device that we believe will translate the bugs' color language into

Standard. His Imperial Majesty has given me leave to test the device on your captives."

Aaron took a moment to phrase his response. "Captain Chen, we do not allow off-worlders into our city."

Chen's expression crossed the line into condescension. "Of course, I am willing to wait until the *Arbiter* arrives," he said. "Unfortunately, the Emperor is not. I have been authorized to remind you that His Majesty has been content to allow Drusingyi its autonomy as a favor to your brother for all his diligent service."

He didn't go on to speak the threat, but Aaron heard it nonetheless.

＊　＊　＊

Aaron returned when the monitors showed that Zacari was asleep. He stood in the darkened corridor outside the cell and watched her.

As if she could sense him there, she opened her eyes.

Neither of them spoke.

Eventually, she smiled. With a shudder, Aaron walked away.

CHAPTER 17

As a condition of interrogating the Templars, the Thallians insisted that the *Veracity*'s crew leave their weapons outside the city. Mykah let himself into Raena's cabin and opened the panel above her bunk. Inside hung the pair of chipped stone knives. He slipped one into the top of his boot, the way she did.

Kavanaugh and Gisela met him at the hatch. Jim had contrived a case for Vezali's translator that made it look rare and special. It was cutting-edge tech from twenty years in the future: guaranteed the Thallians had never seen anything like it. Kavanaugh would carry the translator, while Jim stayed with the ship and got its engines primed for takeoff.

Gisela was armed with Vezali's little zip gun. She had also broken down a Stinger and split the pieces between the three of them. Its power pack was tucked into the box with the translator. Other than that, they didn't want to push the Thallians' restrictions. Getting thrown into detention wouldn't help anyone.

The three of them presented themselves at the city gate. One of Aaron's lieutenants passed them through the energy scanner and let them inside the city. The Thallian clones were very interested in the translator, but of course none of the *Veracity*'s crew admitted to speaking anything but Imperial Standard, so they had no way to test it.

A six-man honor guard escorted Mykah and the others into a bunker built down into the surface of the ground. Mykah noted the weird smells Jim had mentioned.

"We believe this is a queen," one of the Thallian clones said. He halted in front of one of the darkened stalls.

Mykah peered into the shadows inside. "Is it restrained?"

"Yes."

"Open the door."

"Captain, these things are deadly."

"The creature from whom we took the translator was wearing it," Mykah said, sparing a fond thought for Vezali. "We believe it needs to make bodily contact with the subject to work."

"It's your funeral." The Thallian reached forward and placed his hand on the lock screen.

Mykah pulled the translator over his head and stepped into the shadowy stall. He wasn't at all sure this would work. The Templars spoke in colors and the translator worked in sound, but somehow the apparatus had been able to translate for Raena and the Templar Master on Drusingyi.

"I'm called Mykah," he thought to the bulk in front of him. "Can you understand me?"

The creature crawled around to face him. Primary colors, shot through with vivid green, swirled across its face.

"Yes," it said. "Welcome, Mykah Chen. We have been awaiting you." He could hear the Templar's words inside his head, like a thunderstorm. He clenched his eyes shut and wondered if there was a way to turn the translator down.

Aloud, Mykah asked, "Do you know why we're here?"

"Yes." The Templar's voice was genderless and low, a musical hum that made the air quiver.

The Thallians gathered close to the door of the stall, startled to hear the Templar speaking aloud.

"How many of you are there here?"

"Four."

"Are you a breeding queen?"

"Yes."

The Thallians suddenly rustled behind him, all of them snapping to attention at once, their hands to their earpieces. Mykah had a sinking feeling.

"Captain Chen," the lieutenant said, "the *Arbiter* is entering the system."

"Excellent," Mykah said aloud, forcing enthusiasm to cover his dread. "I look forward to reporting to your brother at the first opportunity."

To the Templar queen, he thought, "We need to get out of here now."

It rushed toward him, snatching him up in its forelegs. He shouted in surprise. Gisela took the distraction to shoot the two Thallians closest to her. Kavanaugh snatched up one of their guns as everyone dodged in separate directions, looking for cover. Gisela ducked inside the Templar Queen's cell, reloading her zip gun.

Mykah stared at her. The girl seemed scarily calm, even though he could see two bodies sprawled outside the cell. Somehow, he hadn't believed she was a killer like Raena.

He bent to saw at the ropes pinioning the Queen with Raena's stone knife. It was surprisingly sharp.

* * *

Three clones stood outside Raena's cell. They had not turned on the hallway lights, or the lights in her cell. They stood in the twilight, watching her pretend to sleep. They were young men, Jonan's younger brothers. She wondered if they had ever been off the planet before, if they'd seen a girl. Spoken to one. Touched one.

Raena smiled at them, but didn't get up. "Did you want something?" She pitched the tone of her voice to make them shiver.

"Why are you here?" one of the clones asked.

"I've seen the error of my ways. I want to return to serving your brother."

"But why did you come *here?*" he repeated. "Why didn't you go directly back to the *Arbiter?*"

"Jonan directed Captain Chen to bring me here."

Another clone hissed at her.

She laughed. "Does it trouble you that I am intimate enough with your brother to use his given name?"

"Just how intimate were you?" the clone wanted to know. His voice was lower pitched than his brother's.

Raena met his eyes. "Very."

As if that was the permission they wanted, they let themselves into her cell. They stood over her in a pack, gloating to have her in their power. One of them let her in on their joke: "You'll be glad to know that the *Arbiter* has entered the system."

So they knew they had to make use of her quickly, before Jonan took her away.

Raena shoved herself upward. She remembered what Jim told her about the boys being trained to work as a team. She hadn't seen that amongst the younger ones on her first trip to Drusingyi, but these were adult, more practiced. Raena kicked the first in the crotch hard enough to lift him from the floor. The other two charged her.

The fight had to be over with fast, she realized. The attackers hadn't turned the lights up, but unless they'd turned off the cameras, she had to assume someone was monitoring the show. Reinforcements, when they came, would be better armed.

The leader flung himself atop her, trying to pin her to the bunk. He grabbed both of her hands in one of his, wrenched them over his head. She went limp, as if she'd lost the will to fight. All she needed was for his attention to wander. When he reached for the zipper of her jumpsuit, Raena twisted one hand free. He jerked his head away, so she missed her target, but her nails sunk deep into his eye socket instead. Now he knew she was serious.

He scrambled backward, fear overpowering his hormones, Raena launched herself off the bunk. She slammed into him, hands around his wrists so he couldn't slow his fall as he toppled. His head whacked the floor good enough that he went limp.

The third one grabbed her foot to haul her backward. He'd underestimated how sharp her boot heels were and how motivated Raena was to use them. They only wanted to rape her. They wanted her awake and aware enough to know what was happening to her. She had no such restrictions. She slashed open the lad's femoral artery. He collapsed, cursing, trying to stanch the blood.

She rolled back to her feet and spun toward the first clone. His face had gone a sour green color, but he'd managed to get himself to his knees.

"All I want is out," Raena said. "Let me go and you can still save your brother's life."

"There are guards in the hall," he panted as he struggled to his feet.

"Will they give me as much trouble as you three have?" She advanced on him again, slowly, to give him time to think. He hadn't called for assistance, even though it was close at hand. He hadn't wanted the others to see how badly she'd beaten them.

He dragged himself to his full height, got his hands up into the semblance of a defensive position.

Raena skipped toward him. When she brought her knee up fast, he dropped his hands. She answered him with a punch in the throat. Now he couldn't change his mind and call for aid.

She slipped behind him and forced his left arm up between his shoulder blades. If he didn't twist just the right way, he'd dislocate his own shoulder.

She marched him over to the lock, nodded down to it. She didn't need to apply much pressure to his wrist to make unlocking the cell seem like a good idea.

As soon as the forcefield started to shimmer, Raena knocked his head into the wall. Holding him up, she searched his pockets. The back of his collar hid a knife sheath. She stole the blade and let him drop over the threshold of the cell.

He was correct. Two guards stood at the end of the hall. They carried handguns, both sheathed. One had a bandolier of sleep grenades.

She weighed the knife in her hand, then flung it. The clone on the left slumped.

She leaned into a run as the second guard drew his gun. If he'd had a Stinger, she might have worried. They powered up fast. The quick start cost power in the bolt, but the gun reacted quickly enough to draw and fire while hunting. This gun was some kind of clunky Imperial firearm, designed for continuous fire. A brute weapon, not anything that required skill.

She made it halfway down the hall before he fired his first shot. It went past her, wide enough that she didn't even feel the heat.

He kept his finger on the trigger, sweeping toward her. Raena flung herself into a roll.

Something behind her sparked, caught fire. The fire suppression system kicked in, filling the hallway with mist.

The guard let up on the trigger, unsure if he'd hit her. He'd just realized he should have sounded the alarm. As soon as he glanced toward it, Raena flung herself forward. She barreled into him, mashing him against the wall as she pulled the pin of one of the sleep grenades. The gas whooshed up into his face.

With her free hand, she snatched the breather from his belt, switched it on, held it over her face, and danced back to watch the show.

He fumbled weakly at the grenades, trying to figure out which was leaking, unable to see them on his chest. He hadn't thought to drop the gun, so he only had one free hand. Before long it didn't matter. She pulled the hissing grenade from the bandolier and pitched it back down the hall toward her cell.

Raena searched the guards quickly. She stole their gun belts, the bandolier of grenades, and retrieved the knife from the dead man's eye. She wiped it off on his uniform. Then she jammed the blade between the doors of the elevator and ran it down the slot, searching for the emergency release.

She could hear the elevator car coming down. Reinforcements were on their way.

* * *

The Templar Queen set Mykah carefully back on the floor. "Thank you," he told her. He triggered his comm bracelet.

"On my way," Jim said.

"The *Arbiter* has entered the system."

"I know." Fear constricted the boy's voice. "Are you safe?"

"For the moment."

"I have a quick detour to make. It's going to cost you your handheld."

"Do it," Mykah said.

"See you soon."

Mykah came out of the Templar Queen's stall to find Gisela arming herself with the fallen Thallians' guns. Kavanaugh was examining the lock on the second stall.

"Can you shoot it open?" Mykah asked.

"It'll be faster to slice it off." Kavanaugh picked up one of the cyanogen cutting torches.

Mykah turned back to the queen. "Do you have food or other provisions you need from here?"

"The food is contaminated," she said. She brushed gently past him and went to stand in front of one of the stalls. "This one of us is badly wounded. He will not survive the trip."

Mykah put his hand on her carapace. "We can't leave him here for the Thallians."

"You will have to kill him," she said. "Do you know how?"

"No." Mykah wanted to tell her that he'd never killed anything. He wanted to ask one of the others to do it, but Gisela was just a kid—even though she'd just gunned down half a dozen Thallians—and Kavanaugh was busy cutting open the other stalls.

The Templar Queen twisted her head toward Mykah. Her face was a swirl of shades of brown and black.

"Tell me what I need to do," Mykah said.

* * *

Jim armed the incendiary bomb as he got the *Veracity* into the air. He'd never done this before, but he'd had to run through the bombing simulators with his brothers. He knew the sequence. He prayed his aim was up to the job. This strike needed to be surgical.

The *Veracity* hovered above the Thallians' library. It tore at him to damage the city. He reminded himself that, by his time, everything was already gone. Either he destroyed the library now or the galaxy would do it when they murdered the planet. One way or another, all its knowledge was ash—and there was no time to go retrieve the Templar's message and Mykah's handheld from the study carrels. He couldn't allow those things to fall into his family's hands.

He released the bomb and pulled the *Veracity* away toward the bunker where the Templars had been imprisoned.

* * *

Raena launched herself across the elevator shaft. Her fingers caught the cage around the access ladder. She scrambled through the entry gap, one eye on the elevator car plunging down at her. It stopped at the floor she'd just left.

The bandolier of sleep grenades got hung up on the cage as she climbed. She stopped to untangle it. In her hurry, she fumbled it. It dropped out of reach.

No time to worry about it now, she told herself. She made herself climb. It wouldn't take them long to secure the detention floor and figure out where she'd gone. As far as she knew, there was only one way in or out.

If the *Arbiter* had entered the system, it would take a while for Jonan's shuttle to bring him to the planet's surface. The *Veracity* was going to have to get up and off the planet quickly and quietly. She had to get the hell out of this building fast if she wanted to go with them.

An enormous explosion sounded over her head. Around her, the elevator shaft flexed. Raena clung to ladder rungs, waiting for debris to rain down. When it didn't, she pushed herself to climb.

The target had not been the building she was in, but it must have been next door or very nearby. Sounded like an incendiary bomb. It didn't make sense for the *Arbiter* to bomb Jonan's home world— and they should have been too far away. The bomb must have been dropped by the *Veracity*—and only Jim would know how to load the bomb or drop it.

She doubled her pace up the ladder. Was Jim simply sending her a message that it was time to go? If the *Veracity* was airborne enough to drop incendiaries and not get caught in the heatwave, she wasn't going to catch up to it. It was out of here.

Maybe they were telling her goodbye.

✳   ✳   ✳

Jim dropped a concussion bomb that was small enough to level a building—the cloning lab, he was pretty sure. He set the *Veracity* down in the wreckage.

Small arms fire pinged off the ship's hull. Jim popped open the controls for the ship's guns. He fired blindly, trying to chase his attackers back under cover. The handguns didn't pose any danger to the *Veracity*, but they would slow the others down from escaping.

Once things had settled momentarily, Mykah raced with the Templars for the *Veracity*. Kavanaugh and Gisela ran interference for them.

As soon as Kavanaugh hurried into the cockpit, Jim relinquished the controls. He rushed past Mykah, who was herding the Templars into the hold.

"Where are you going?" Mykah asked.

"To get Raena. She's out of her cell."

"How do you know?"

"There was a security alert."

"I'm going with you," Gisela said.

"No." Jim's tone was commanding enough to rock her back. "I can pass. They'll be too panicked by all the damage to look too closely at me, but they'll kill you on sight. They'll know you're not family."

Gisela unbuckled the stolen gun belt slung around her hips and held it out.

"Thanks." Jim took all the weapons she offered. "Tell Mr. Kavanaugh to bomb the ship depot as soon as he's in the air. I marked it on the schematic. The bomb is already loaded. That'll keep them from following you."

"See you at the rendezvous site," Mykah told him. "Good luck."

"You, too."

The boy jumped out the hatch and started to run. Gisela fired over his head, clearing him a path, as Kavanaugh got them back into the air.

* * *

Raena's legs trembled with strain as she crawled out of the elevator shaft at last. All these weeks of imprisonment had been hell on her conditioning.

The maintenance hallway in which she found herself was featureless, no indication which way she should run. She chose right and ran flat out. No need to conserve energy now. Either she could find the *Veracity* and get to it, or she'd have to get to the ship depot and steal something—any of the Thallians' War-era craft were well within her outdated skill set, she realized with a grin—and get herself off the planet. Better to die alone in space than to be taken back aboard the *Arbiter*.

Something else exploded, a series of booms, one setting off the next. So much for the ship depot. Apparently, Jim had decided to leave his family no way off the planet.

The lights in the corridor flickered out. Raena skidded to a halt and pressed herself flat against a wall, waiting for the fuel silo to go.

Nothing more exploded as she caught her breath. The emergency lighting kicked in. In the dimness, Raena ran some more. She took the next left. Ahead of her stood a door with a lock screen. That was a problem. Raena ran at it anyway. She was covered with enough Thallian blood that she hoped she could pass. She licked her hand, rubbed it against the blood flaking from her jumpsuit, and slapped her palm down on the lock.

The computer considered, then slid the door open for her.

She found herself in a city on fire. Smoke smeared the night sky. The air smelled toxic and her recently suctioned lungs were sensitive. She pulled the stolen breather back on, hoping its filter would get her safely out of the city.

An enormous explosion slammed her back against the building. Her head hit hard enough that she saw stars. The Thallians had lost the battle with the fire on their fuel silo.

All right. She couldn't get off the planet. She still had to get out of the city before Jonan came. She loped toward the hangar that held the jet bikes.

* * *

Raena drained the stolen handguns on her way through the city. She didn't wait for the Thallians to fire on her; she merely took them out wherever she saw them. As far as she was concerned, only four of the clones had to survive into the future—and three of those were off the planet. As long as she didn't kill Aten by mistake, she'd done no irreparable damage.

One of the Thallian clones waited for her at the vehicle depot. He looked remarkably like Jonan—the same obsessively muscled body, the same sharpened teeth. More than just brothers, these two could have been twins. They must have been clones from the same batch.

Raena stopped running, breathing hard, her body on fire with adrenaline. Exhaustion lingered not far off. "You must be Aten."

"You've heard of me."

She nodded. "I didn't hear about many of Jonan's brothers by name, but I know about you and Revan." What was the alpha clone doing here alone? Were other clones hiding nearby, ready to shoot her down? Or had Aten sent the others to fight the fires and save the city? If any of the Thallian brothers had been sane, their behavior would have been easier to predict.

"I've heard about you, too," he warned. "The Empire didn't exaggerate when they called you dangerous. Why didn't they kill you like they said they would?"

She caught herself about to tell him the truth. Aten survived the War. She would kill him twenty-some years in the future. She could do nothing that would change how he reacted to her name then. "They did kill her," Raena lied. "Raena Zacari was buried alive in a Templar tomb as a way to control your brother."

"What was her relationship with my brother?"

"She served as his aide."

"Is that all?"

"She did anything he required her to."

He snarled, "Did she fuck him?"

Raena looked at him, uncertain how to answer. She knew Jonan supplanted Aten as the alpha clone. She just didn't know when. If she admitted her relationship with Jonan, would she destroy his chance to advance in the family? It was tempting to get some payback, however petty it might be.

Was this where the future disintegrated for her? If she said too much, would Aten have Jonan killed? Plague or no, she still stood a chance of being rescued from her tomb by Kavanaugh and Sloane. She might still go to Kai and see Ariel again. But if Jonan didn't become the alpha clone, his men would not hunt her on Kai. She wouldn't steal the *Veracity*. She wouldn't run away with Mykah and Coni and the others. She'd never go back to Drusingyi to rescue Jimi and she'd never stop the Messiah drug and she'd never take up with Haoun on Lautan. If she killed Aten Thallian now, she would break the future. The last year of her life would be rewritten.

It was a sacrifice she didn't want to make.

Luckily, Aten backtracked in the conversation. "Who are you?"

"My name is also Raena Zacari," she said, letting him hear the truth in her voice.

"Who cloned you?"

Raena didn't know how to answer that.

"I saw the genetic analysis," he said. "I saw markers from Jonan's DNA."

She remembered bleeding out on Drusingyi, after Jonan had shot her. She remembered the family's medical robot preparing to operate on her. Had they transfused her with Thallian's blood while she was out? Was his blood replicating inside her still? Raena shuddered at the thought.

"I need to get out of here," she told him.

"Not until I get some answers." Aten settled himself in her path, ready for a fight. "Whom do you serve?"

"That's a complicated question." During the War, there had been three sides: the Empire, the Templars—and the Coalition, trying to rescue what they could from the collision between the other two. "I serve humanity."

Aten's next question surprised her. "What mission has the Emperor given my brother?"

Raena allowed herself a little smile. "Are you testing me?"

"Yes."

"Your brothers are commanded to create a plague genetically keyed to the Templar. Jonan is meant to use the *Arbiter* to sue for peace as a cover for spreading this plague."

"And you're here to stop the plague?"

"Yes."

"What makes you think we can deny the will of the Empire?"

"I don't."

"Then why are you doing this to us?"

When she didn't answer, he pounced at her, gloved hand raised to strike. Raena watched his eyes, not his hand. As the blow fell, she flung herself to the opposite side, grabbed his left arm and pulled him off balance, danced away. This was the fight she had trained for all her life: when a Thallian was still young and fit enough to test her, but she was old and wily and strong enough to match him.

Aten attacked, trying to shove her against the wall of the vehicle depot. She blocked him and stood her ground. He was startled when her fist slipped past his guard and landed hard enough on his jaw that he bit his tongue with his sharpened teeth. Blood trickled from the corner of his mouth.

Raena darted around him enough that he never knew which direction her next attack would come from. He grimaced, surprised to find her his equal. Blood streaked his teeth.

She hit him again in the jaw and barely got away when he grabbed for her. She raised her fist to lick his blood from her knuckles.

He watched her, seemingly captivated. Then, without warning, he swept her feet out from beneath her. She landed on the stone floor.

He kicked her hard as he could in the thigh. Raena rolled with the blow, managed to get to her hands and knees before he kicked her again. And again. And again.

She forced her eyes open, locking the pain away somewhere else. She had to think.

Next time he kicked her, she sat up fast. Grabbed his calf and held on. Forced his foot up higher. Kicked his standing shin hard with her sharpened heel.

When he lost his balance, she pounced on him.

As she tightened her hands around his throat, Raena smiled into Aten's eyes. She knew where to put her fingers to cut off his oxygen, to slow the blood to his brain, to give him the most pain without allowing him to lose consciousness.

She thought he would struggle more. She thought he would argue or try to tempt her. Instead, as it had when she killed his twin in the future, masochism got the better of him. Aten surrendered to the sensation of death tightening around his throat.

Clarity chilled her. She wanted to kill Aten as much as she'd ever wanted anything in her life. But why? As a way to hurt Jonan? To punish Aten for his part in developing the plague? She didn't know this man. She had no way or right to judge him. Her crew had already set his city on fire, bombed his family's only route of escape, and killed uncounted numbers of his uncles, brothers, and sons.

The Thallians had lost. She didn't need to do this. She couldn't do this. The future might still come . . .

Of their own accord, Raena's hands unlocked on Aten's throat.

Aten opened eyes gone bloodshot to peer at her. Raena sat back on his chest, staring at him, shocked at herself.

He punched her in the head. Luckily, from this angle, the blow didn't have much speed behind it. She let him overbalance her.

Something crashed down atop Aten and he collapsed over her. Past his shoulder, Raena saw the face of one of the boy clones. Something in his expression told her it was Jim.

He rolled Aten's body off of her. "Did my uncle hurt you?"

"No more than your father ever did," Raena said.

"Can you walk?"

Raena allowed him to help her to her feet. "Yes." The deep bruise made her right thigh quiver, but the leg held her weight.

"They moved the *Veracity* to the rendezvous site," Jim warned her. He led her to a jet bike and jumped on.

Raena clambered up behind him. She wondered if Haoun still existed in the future, if he would remember her. If he still liked human girls. If the Empire fell, or if it made peace with the Templars. If there was anything familiar worth going back to or if they had destroyed it all.

* * *

At some point, they passed out of the city. Raena didn't notice. They rode until the jet bike ran out of fuel. Then they ran. The next thing that caught her attention was Mykah standing guard near a spire of rock. Dawn was breaking over the mountains.

Mykah hissed when he saw her. Raena wanted to tell him that the damage looked worse than it was, but really, she was worse than she looked, so she kept silent. He put his arm around her waist and took some of her weight off her injured leg.

She forced herself to jog across a wide grassy field. She had disjointed impressions: purple wildflowers spangling the grass; the air alive with birdsong. Yellow sunlight poured warmth over her skin. She'd had no idea how beautiful Drusingyi had been, before the galaxy murdered it. This must be breaking Jim's heart.

Gisela stood in the doorway of the *Veracity*, covering their approach. She had the sniper rifle upraised, staring through the scope over Raena's head. Raena didn't look back to see if she was being followed. She no longer had the strength to care. The people in the past had ceased to be her problem.

Mykah glanced over her shoulder and put on a burst of speed. "We've got to go," he urged.

"Go," Raena said. "Go back to her."

"Run!" he ordered.

She didn't want to. She felt all her years now in the aches in her body, in the heaviness of her heart. She could just lie down here, in the glorious sunshine, and be one with the grasses and flowers. She was done. Let Mykah go home and face down the Templar Master, beg for the survival of humanity.

Mykah kept pulling her forward, increasing the length of his stride. And she ran beside him, calling on the dregs of her strength. The *Veracity* was the only home she had ever loved. She ran for it.

Jim dashed ahead of them. In the ship's hatchway, he reached back to drag Raena inside. Mykah leapt in after her, pounded his fist down on the lock.

Raena sprawled on the deck, certain that her heart would tear itself apart. Jagged breath cut the inside of her throat.

She lay there, gasping, as the others made the ship ready to leave. She felt the engines powering up.

"Raena, strap down," Mykah ordered over the comm.

She shook her head, unable to push herself up off the deck.

Something soft brushed her cheek. It was insistent. She opened her eyes to see a Templar leaning over her, stroking an antenna across her face.

The Templar picked her up in its many legs, gently cradling her against its chitinous underside. At this point, she didn't care if it planned to eat her. She closed her eyes and let herself swoon, but the deep unconsciousness she craved remained out of reach.

The Templar moved to brace itself. It was too big to fit into any of the crash webbing aboard the *Veracity*, but it could wedge itself into the main passageway.

The ship shot upward at a steep angle. That probably meant Kavanaugh was flying. He had been doing it for decades now, maybe longer than Haoun had been alive. As he forced the old ship through a series of punishing evasive maneuvers, adrenaline surged into Raena's blood despite herself.

"What's going on?" she shouted forward, but either they were concentrating or they didn't hear her.

"Fighters from the *Arbiter* are pursuing us," a voice said. It sounded like a stringed instrument, its voice so low that Raena felt it in her chest.

"Are you speaking to me, Templar?" she asked softly.

"Yes. We have the translation apparatus now."

The running wasn't over yet. She had to get up, get into the turret, and man the guns. She had to protect the others.

"Can you help me get aft?"

"Yes."

The Templar pulled itself through the *Veracity*, carrying Raena along with it. When they reached the turret guns, Raena said, "Let me go now. I will try to convince them to leave us alone."

She crawled up into the bubble, switching on the comm inside. "Route some power to the guns."

"We're going to jump as soon as I can get clear of the asteroids," Kavanaugh said.

"If you lose me, so be it. I'll give you a chance to run."

* * *

Jim crept up into the turret with her. He didn't say anything, just powered up the other gun and climbed in.

He was, unsurprisingly, a good shot. Raena felt better for his company, since the black eye left her completely reliant on the computer targeting. She laid down covering fire and let Jim pick off the fighters coming alongside them. The two of them made a good team.

She wondered if he had any regrets killing these strangers. She couldn't see the boy's face, but she imagined he was smiling.

Finally the *Veracity* got out beyond the asteroid belt. Kavanaugh gave the ship her head, letting her run flat out as he calculated the jump back to the Templars' tombworld.

Mykah came to the base of the turret guns. "Come down," he said. "We're clear."

Raena let Jim go down first. Once he'd gotten out of her way, she called down to Mykah, "Will you catch me? My leg's frozen up. I can't manage the climb."

"I've got you," he assured.

* * *

Raena shut herself in her cabin and did not come out to eat. Kavanaugh let her get away with that for one day, then he overrode the lock on her door and let himself in.

She sat in the darkness. One eye had swollen shut. The other glittered in the red power light of her screen.

She'd showered. Some of her fingers were taped together. She'd gotten her cuts and burns bandaged. She sat wound up in the coverlet, but hadn't bothered to dress. Even in the dimness, he could see the black shadow of an enormous bruise on her thigh. It must go down to the femur.

"Is it broken?" he asked.

"Just bruised."

Kavanaugh set the tray on her desk, then handed her the cup of tea, double sweet and full of rice milk, the way Mykah said she liked it. Kavanaugh sat beside her on the bed, with his back against the bulkhead.

"You should see the other guy," she joked quietly.

"Jim said you were fighting the alpha clone."

She nodded.

"Did you kill him?"

"No." She sipped her tea. "I had a realization in the middle of the fight. I was going to kill Aten because he looked like Jonan. Because Jonan was evil. Because I couldn't kill Jonan again."

"When I was a kid, it was easy to tell the bad guys," Kavanaugh said. "The Empire was evil. The Coalition said they would protect us. The Templars said they would accept us into the galaxy. And the Thallians stripped away those promises because they killed the Templars and turned the galaxy against us. It must have been difficult to let any of the Thallians live."

"I told myself I'd changed, but twice now, I've gone to Drusingyi and killed nearly everyone I came across, man and boy." Raena asked despairingly, "How am I different from the monsters?"

"You've been trained to be a monster," Kavanaugh told her, just as quietly. "You've loved and been loved by monsters. But the galaxy is just the galaxy. Most of us are only people. We will forgive you for being a monster, as long as you only show us part of who you are. Humanity needs someone to protect it. We need you to fight for us, even if you feel like a monster."

She shook her head. "I knew if I killed Aten, I was destroying the future. Jonan wouldn't become the alpha clone. He wouldn't hunt me down after you got me got out of the tomb. I wouldn't steal the *Veracity*. Jim probably wouldn't even have been cloned. Everything that's happened to me in the last six months would cease to exist." She sipped her tea. "I held the future in my hands. I wanted so very badly to break it."

"But you didn't," Kavanaugh pointed out. "Jim is still with us. We rescued a Templar Queen and two young females. We can save the Templars after all. We can make things right in the galaxy."

Raena set the teacup aside and turned to kiss him. Kavanaugh submitted to her. Even injured, she was still strong enough to hurt him, and he didn't want to be hurt. He wanted the same thing he had always wanted: to fix her. To rescue her. So he let her use him, to prove something to herself.

He had to close his eyes, so he couldn't see how badly she'd been beaten.

In all the years he'd imagined saving her, it had never been exactly like this. She was gentler than he expected, more invested in the sensation of it than the consummation. He tried to relax into it, let her take what she needed, but it was difficult to separate himself from all the years of fantasies and dreams.

In the end, she was entirely quiet. Afterward, he only held her and asked nothing more. He knew that this would only happen once. Both of them had exorcised their demons. When he saw Ariel again and asked her to marry him, Raena would give them both her blessing. He hoped she would find some peace with Haoun, if only for a while.

Raena curled her head against Kavanaugh's shoulder, closed her good eye, and went to sleep. His heart broke for her just a little bit more. He kissed her forehead, on the side that wasn't swollen and bruised.

CHAPTER 18

When Kavanaugh woke, Raena was sitting up at her desk, eating the meal Mykah sent in for her earlier. She had gotten herself dressed. Her color seemed normal now. Her blackened eye had faded toward green and come open a slit.

"Feeling better?" he asked.

"You're the best doctor I've ever had." The return of her sense of humor let him know that the crisis had passed.

"Maybe the most hands-on," he teased.

"Mykah commed back about ten minutes ago," she said. "We're coming up on the Templar tombworld."

"Should I hustle?" Kavanaugh asked.

"You've got time," she told him.

"Come out with me," he suggested. "The Templars would like to get to know their savior."

"I didn't save them," Raena pointed out. "You and Mykah and Gisela did. Jim did."

"You bought us the time," he answered. "They were prisoners, too, facing vivisection so the Thallians could create the plague. They understand that you sacrificed yourself so we could rescue them."

She put her fork down and twisted to face him. "I'm not a hero, Tarik. I don't want anyone to treat me like one."

"Understood. But Mykah and the kids will worry about you, if you don't come out." He grinned at her. "You don't want everyone else busting in here the way I did."

"You're right about that." She gave him a smile in return before concentrating on her cold food.

He got up to dress.

* * *

Raena limped out as far as the lounge. Mykah helped her get strapped into the crash webbing. His eyes wouldn't meet hers.

"It's okay," she promised. "I'm healing."

Jim strapped himself in beside her. Once he was settled, Raena gave him the photo of Eilif that she'd found in Revan's coat. "This was in her cabin," Raena said, "when I took it apart to build the cell. Revan treasured it. I like it because she looks so happy. I thought you would want it."

"Thank you."

Mykah strapped himself in on the other side of her. Once he was settled, he reached out to take her hand. "We're ready," he called up to the cockpit.

"Okay," Gisela said. "We're broadcasting the new message from the queen. Here's hoping it will get us through their security net."

* * *

Whatever the Queen said to them, the Templars guarding the tombs let the *Veracity* land on the tombworld. One of the queen's female attendants was a time engineer. She crawled out of the *Veracity* to examine the time machine, to make certain it really would allow the *Veracity* to go home.

While she was busy, Raena went to speak with the queen.

The Templar Queen bent forward to caress Raena's bruised face with her antennae. Raena stood straight and still, enduring it. The Templar had no eyes that she could see, only the hypnotic swirl of colors that was its face.

Over Vezali's translator, the Queen said, "Mykah Chen told us that you distracted the Thallians' security while the crew of *Veracity* rescued us."

"We are a team," Raena said.

"And we will be forever grateful to you. But one thing confuses us."

"Tell me."

"The one who calls himself the Templar Master? How did he survive the plague that killed everyone else?"

"He said his people shut him in one of the Templar tombs to wait until the Thallians were gone."

"This is what confuses us. Jimi Thallian survives."

"Jimi Thallian is a hero."

The queen did not deny it. "Jimi Thallian says this plague was keyed to the Templar."

"Yes."

"He says that the plague died out when the Templar died out."

"Jim would understand that better than I do," Raena admitted.

"But the Templar Master did not die out. And it is not our way to imprison our own people," the queen said. Raena waited for the translator to catch up with the maelstrom of colors flashing and flaring across her face. "We think this Templar is a coward who fled from the past and, when he found himself alone, plotted revenge."

Raena nodded. "He could have sent us to rescue Templars from the past, but he didn't. He sent us to unleash a plague to destroy humanity."

"We have seen the message that he wanted you to transmit. If he was not a criminal before, he is a criminal now," the queen said. "The answer to insanity is not more madness. The answer to genocide is not more genocide."

"What do your people do to their criminals?" Raena asked.

"Kill them."

She had expected that. "How?"

"No," the queen said. "The answer is when."

* * *

Once the Templars' time machine was ready, Kavanaugh backed the *Veracity* into the mountain. This time he set down before the ship lost power. Everything went black momentarily, before chugging to life once more.

When Kavanaugh pulled them out of the mountain into the gritty wind, the *Veracity's* scanners showed no other life on the planet. The ships full of androids orbited overhead. The Queen hailed them before they could communicate with their master.

Raena watched the energy signatures coming off the ships, waiting to see if their guns heated up. They didn't.

"What does that mean?" Mykah asked.

"She must know what to say to them," Raena said. "Call Coni. See if the Templar Master will let you talk to her."

* * *

The Templar Queen and the Master kept in constant communication as the *Veracity* returned to Drusingyi. Raena didn't know what they were saying to each other—Vezali's translator couldn't keep up—but she suspected at least one of them spoke of love.

Mykah did connect with Coni—and was able to confirm that she wasn't an android. She said the grays had started a countdown when the *Veracity* went into the time machine, but almost no time had passed before it came back out. For the time being, the hostages were being treated like guests.

The galaxy did not seem to have been ruined. Jim pointed out that he'd known the city had been attacked during the War. He just hadn't known when. He didn't discount Raena's theory that the *Veracity's* attack had pushed the Thallians into making the plague, but his answer echoed what she'd said to him about Jonan: "They may have been broken, but they chose to do evil."

This time, when they returned to the Thallian homeworld, they took the *Veracity* into Drusingyi's ocean. The android-crewed ships served as an honor guard, fighting off the leviathans who took interest in them. When they parked in the newly built hangar outside the cloning lab, the Templar Master came to meet them.

Inside the *Veracity*'s hatch, the queen called, "Mykah Chen."

Mykah stepped up to her and put his hand on her carapace. She touched his face with her antenna.

"Please take back your translation device. I do not want it to be damaged."

Mykah gently unwound it from her. While he was holding it, her voice sounded in his head. "Thank you for all your assistance."

"My pleasure."

Gisela keyed open the hatch and the *Veracity*'s crew went out first. They walked down the ramp and moved aside, so the Templars could follow. The Queen came last. Her face was aglow with shades of yellow and pale green.

The Templar Master rushed toward her, trundling over his androids, knocking them aside like broken toys.

Vezali glided over to join the rest of the crew. She took the translator from Mykah, said, "You'll thank me for this," and shut the device off.

Raena grinned. "Good. We did not want to hear whatever they're going to say to each other."

The Queen reared up on her hindmost legs. The Templar Master rose up to meet her, but she easily knocked him onto his back and began to take her pleasure from him.

"Um," Mykah said.

"What did you think was going to happen?" Raena asked.

"There are kids present."

She laughed. "It's all natural, right? This is how the Templars return to the universe."

"Do we have to watch?" Kavanaugh asked, wincing.

"You don't," Raena told them. "She wanted me to stay."

So Mykah and the others went off to find Coni and Haoun. All throughout the cloning dome, androids were frozen in strange postures. Something about their master's distraction had disrupted their autonomy.

"We should deactivate them now, while they can't fight back," Jim suggested.

"I'll help," Gisela said.

Mykah left the others to it. The present was not going to feel saved to him until he held Coni in his arms.

* * *

Once the Queen finished with the Templar Master, each of her attendants had a go at him. Raena used the time to behead the androids in the hangar. She took special pleasure in taking the Raena decoy apart.

She stacked the android heads in the airlock and let them get washed out into the ocean. She wasn't sure if the water would corrode them, but at least some of the heads were eaten by the leviathans swimming outside the dome. That made her smile.

Finally, the Templars finished breeding. Raena came to look at the Master, lying on his back, his legs moving lazily in the air. He paid no attention to her as she moved up behind his head. She placed her Stinger against his face and fired.

The colors on his face flared angry orange and painful red. Raena carved across them and closed her eyes. Killing a Templar was just as awful as Mykah warned her it would be.

When at last the job was done, the female Templars fell upon his body and began to feast.

* * *

Haoun met her when she walked alone out of the hangar. He didn't say anything, simply gathered her close in his arms and held her. Raena had never been so relieved to be held before.

When at last he let her go, he handed her a green and gold scarf folded in the shape of a bird. "Welcome home."

"Thank you, Haoun." She unwrapped the scarf, then held it against his scales to admire the color. She wound it around her throat. "But I'm not home yet," she said. "We need to take Kavanaugh and the kids back to Ariel. I expect we've got a wedding to attend. Once the *Veracity* is in space after that, I'll feel I've come home."

"That may be a while yet," Haoun warned. "Mykah has plans to announce the return of the Templars to the galaxy."

Raena heaved a mock sigh. "I suppose we'll have to be media heroes again."

Haoun laughed at her and took her hand. "We've got some time to kill before that happens."

ACKNOWLEDGMENTS

Thanks one last time to Martha Allard and Mason Jones, who kept my head above water as this book expanded from a rough outline to the novel you hold in your hands. Their encouragement and careful eyes kept me plowing forward. I've never written so hard or so fast and I couldn't have done it without their help.

Thanks to Brian, Kelly, and Paul, fellow members of The Chowder Society, who have stoked my love for science fiction ever since I met them decades ago.

Thanks to Dana Fredsti for the marvelous blurb and being such an inspiration. Thanks to Borderlands Bookstore for their support throughout my writing career. Thanks to Emerian Rich, Anya Martin, SL Schmitz, Kate Jonez, John Palisano, and all my other fellow writers who helped me spread the word about this trilogy.

Thanks to Cody Tilson for the spectacular cover image.

A special shout-out to Nick and the crew of San Francisco's Mercury Cafe, where I've spent many, many hours reading, writing, and editing. The title of this book comes from a song Nick was playing one morning while I was writing.

Thanks also to Jason Katzman and Cory Allyn for being patient as I wrestled this book into submission and to Martin Cahill, who encouraged all my crazy promotional ideas.

Finally, thanks to my champion, editor Jeremy Lassen. This book would not have been written without his encouragement, inspiration, and tough love.

Photo courtesy of Ken Goudey

ABOUT THE AUTHOR

Loren Rhoads is the co-author (with Brian Thomas) of *As Above, So Below*. She's the author of a book of essays called *Wish You Were Here: Adventures in Cemetery Travel* and editor of *The Haunted Mansion Project: Year Two* and *Morbid Curiosity Cures the Blues*. Her science fiction short stories were collected into the chapbook *Ashes & Rust*. She remembers the Christmas there were men on the moon and looks forward to the New Year's Day there will be women on Mars.